A Novel

Garden of Eve

from the author of the best-selling TIME IN A GARDEN

Mary A. Agria

LIFE IN THE GARDEN Series - 2

To John for his love and tireless efforts
in making this garden—the *LIFE IN THE GARDEN Series*—grow.
Deepest gratitude also to Helice Agria, Joyce Giguere, Julie Lane,
Ellen McGill, Sandi Meyer, Carol McDonnell and Bill Thompson for
their wise advice, skilled and faithful editing.
Warmest thanks to Jean Long for designing Eve's garden
and the Bay View Memorial Garden team for its precious inspiration.
To Fred Lee of Sang Lee Farms for his insights
into the operation of a nursery.
To Sheila Kromas for her advice in shaping the cover design.
To my daughters and grandchildren for their loving
lessons in what it means to be 'family'.
To my mother, Lydia Metzig, for her wisdom and encouragement
—the strongest woman I know.

**visit Mary Agria online at www.maryagria.com
for excerpts from her work and to arrange
for live author chats or signings**

Copyright ©2011 by Mary A. Agria
ISBN: 978-1-4583-6799-0
All rights reserved.

...What reviewers say of Mary Agria's novels

TIME in a Garden,
"**must-read for the contemplative gardener...**"
Suffolk Times, 2006

VOX HUMANA: The Human Voice
"**A reflective portrayal of the ascent of goodness, reconciliation and love.**"
American Guild of Organists Magazine, 2007

IN TRANSIT
"**Wisdom, the kind that only a lifetime of experience can wield,**"
Dan's Hamptons, 2008.

COMMUNITY OF SCHOLARS
"**Five Stars, highly recommended. . .a riveting thriller of academe.**" *Midwest Book Review, 2009*

"Richly drawn characters who continue to be haunted by ultimate questions of mortality and spirituality. . . pure wisdom."
5-Stars, Amazon.com

". . . one of my top ten best reads. The characters are beautiful. I loved this book. It garnered positive reviews from our book club." Barnes & Noble, 5-Star Review

"From the very first paragraph until the very last, I was hooked." 5-Star Review, Amazon.com

"A unique voice; excellent, intelligent, witty writing; simply wonderful. Engaging, interesting, believable writing; pure magic." Gather.com

"One of the most thought-provoking, profound yet beautifully, simply written books I have ever read," Naples, FL

GARDEN
OF EVE

We are not alone as long as we find
a poppy beautiful, the English painter
John Berger once said. It proves we
are more wedded to existence than
our solitary lives would lead
us to believe.

From Eve Brennerman's Journal

One
February

Grief changes everything. My time in the garden has become a perpetual winter. All around me I sense a colorless wasteland, glacial and dark. By the calendar, life goes on and the seasons pursue their course. Suns rise early, set late. Ground thaws. The earth's magnificent garden stirs and buds and bursts into exuberant bloom. And still the heart remains locked in that frozen world, powerless to grow, much less to flower.

By force of habit, I have learned to rise with the day again, breathe in and out, eat and sleep when my eyes could no longer take in what I saw around me. Always the gardener, I weed out the irrelevant and unbearable. I deadhead anything that drains energy I cannot afford to squander. Spurred on by a weekly deadline, I sift through the chaff of my existence in my modest little essays on gardeners and gardening for the Xenaphon, Michigan, *Gazette*.

It was February. This week's column was long overdue. I keystroked my byline, *Eve Brennerman*. Though my heart wasn't in it, I willed myself to keep going. At first halting words, then whole lines began to spring up on the screen of my laptop.

Once again Ground Hog Day has come and gone in northern Michigan. And still winter holds on.

In far-off Pennsylvania, Phil saw his shadow. New Jersey's Essex Ed didn't. On Staten Island, Charles G. Hogg bit the mayor. Glean from those folksy prophets what you will.

Meanwhile, winter can be a bleak and lonely time for a gardener in our corner of the world. Gray flannel days descend into bone-chilling nights that seem to go on forever.

We gardeners tend to grasp at advice and wisdom, any

promise of spring, whenever and wherever we find it. Calendars, almanacs, zodiacs and horoscopes, books and blogs and weather channels—even furry rodents.

As a gardener, I too long to sense life teeming in the frozen world around me. I yearn to make sense of the forces I battle and simply cannot hope to change. Weather, the rhythm of the seasons and the length of days defy my intervention.

Like a band of winter-weary Punxatawney Phils, all of my loyal gardening buddies try to raise my flagging spirits. They share tall tales of braving the snowbanks en route to their sheds and garages.

Time to hone and sharpen, they tell me. *Another growing season looms ahead.*

I wish I could share their sense of certainty. Right now I will settle for spring—whenever and however it happens to come.

Too much edginess in my humor?

I speculated how much that showed to anyone unfamiliar with my story. But then anonymity is impossible, collective memory also very long in my tiny northern Michigan town. In Xenaphon, an ambulance run and the heartbreak that goes with it are front page news.

Suddenly and without warning as Adam Groft came into my life, he was gone—lost to a heart attack fifteen months ago. Son of a prominent local family, he had risen to the top of a major Chicago ad firm. In retirement, he inherited and ran the largest nursery and greenhouse operation in the county. His death came as a blow to the whole community.

True, all of it. Except some of the most significant things in life never make it to an obituary. Adam Groft was the love of my life. Joy for me proved to be a gift meted out with teaspoons not trowels. Without him, the calendar of my days stretched ahead like a barren, snow-swept field toward the horizon.

My expectations had been so simple, even mundane, when I moved to northern Michigan. As a widow and recent retiree, a quiet inner voice had persuaded me it was time to reclaim my roots. I had raised two daughters in Chicago, virtually alone in a loveless marriage. My modestly successful career no longer held me there. The plan was to set up housekeeping in the Xenaphon homestead that had been in my mother's family for generations. I would freelance for the *Gazette*. Saturdays volunteering in the community garden would become the high point of my social life, such as it was.

Two survivors, Xenaphon and me. The town barely holds on as our county seat, despite the optimistic pioneer habit of naming communities after the ancient Classical world. Greek and Roman from Leonidas to Pompeii, Athens to Ithaca, Michigan has its share. Like Xenaphon, many of them languish as mere shadows of their former selves.

It was there in the April mud of the community garden that Adam and I found each other, Adam Groft and Eve Brennerman. *Adam and Eve in the garden.* We laughed a lot about that. Heedless of the long shadows and waning of the day that are bound to follow, we dared to flower like the perennials we tended. We forgot that all growing seasons have an end.

And so I find that I have become a cliche. I am a woman of a certain age and alone. I know what my life could have been. Living with what remains comes hard. If there was a rock bottom, I had yet to find it.

"Dear God . . . a meltdown over Groundhog Day."

By any other name, my words were a prayer. I had no idea where the crazy column—or I—was going.

On an impatient gesture, I point-and-clicked my way to Off. For a good while I stared at the darkening screen of my laptop. It seemed pointless to sit there taking potshots at rodents and folksy crystal-ball gazing. The *real* target of my anger was revelation of a different sort entirely.

"Make sense of the forces we battle," I had written.

Which explains why on that first Sunday in February I found myself slipping into a pew near the back of the town's lone surviving Protestant church, tousle-haired and feeling very much out of place. Historic Peace Episcopal was the congregation of Adam's childhood, not mine. The nearby Methodist church where my grandparents were married and from which they were buried had closed its doors a decade ago. Just one more victim of consolidation.

I showed up late by a good ten minutes. Vicar Ben Gaskill had begun the lessons for the day. Mid-thirties and fresh out of seminary, Father Gaskill was assigned Xenaphon last summer as his first solo congregation. It had fallen to me to write a feature article for the *Gazette* about the new priest's appointment. *A nice enough guy*, I had concluded at the time. There was a lean, earthy-crunchy look about the man that fit right in with the younger locals struggling to eke out a living in the resort communities to the north of us.

But then no one ever said that blooming where we are planted is easy. The young priest's voice had taken on the world-weary certitude of someone whose tiny parish had no chance at all of paying his salary.

"Job. Chapter seven, verse 7," he read, "*I shall never know happiness again.*"

With a shock, I knew I had met this Job of the Old Testament before. Grief-wracked and broken, the man had lost everything that mattered to him. If this was meant to inspire, it was tough stuff for our fragile little community. For years, unemployment in our isolated rural county had hung on with the tenacity of our double-digit wind chills. The population was dwindling and aging, both at an alarming pace.

Tough stuff for me, to sit there in the sanctuary and confront the reality of where I found myself. *I shall never see happiness again.*

"There are times when we all cry out for answers in our darkness," I half-heard Father Gaskill say through the dull thudding in my ears. "Life doesn't always work that way. Our faith runs aground on the eternal *Why?* Sometimes our only hope is to believe that someone is out there listening, while we rage against the storm."

Whatever else our young priest shared about Job's outpouring of cosmic anguish was largely lost to me. Most of the sermon was spent apologizing that he pirated the text from the Roman Catholic calendar of readings for the week, not strictly kosher. He claimed to be inspired by his weekly lunch with the battle-worn veteran Father Brannen from St. Mary's across the road from the library. In fact, I suspect the sub-zero temperatures and shoveling yet another layer of lake-effect snow off the sidewalk in front of the rectory also had a great deal to do with it.

I didn't wait for the rumbling of the organ to send me out into the world with anything resembling peace. I needed something—a gesture of defiance, *anything*—rather than wed my fate to Job sitting on that ash heap. So, I cut out before the last hymn. Unlike their Roman Catholic brethren, apparently Episcopalians don't make a habit of that either.

Fortunately I was seated on the aisle. Heads turned in the sparsely populated sanctuary all the same. These were my friends, my neighbors around me. I was bound to hear about my premature exodus before the week was out.

Outside the church, the air felt raw. The sky matched my mood. It was a sullen gunmetal, promising nothing good. Still, as I stood on the sand-strewn steps something deep in me stirred, all but cried out to return to the berm overlooking the interstate off-ramp where our story had begun.

"Desperation," I told myself.

This time of year, the access road to the berm was impassible. Our garden lay shrouded under an ice-glazed sheet of white. The memories smacked too much of another journey my boss, George Herberg, and I had made through snow–choked streets, only to find the man I was about to marry lying pale and still on an emergency room gurney.

I reached out to adjust the rearview mirror and caught my own reflection. Tears welled up, hot and stinging, at what I read in those eyes staring back at me. I clenched the wheel all the tighter, refused to let them fall. As if with a will of its own, the Taurus struck off on the road north out of town toward the nursery. The miles crept past.

Gang Green. That's the name locals affectionately pinned on our senior citizen gardening crew. Our mission was and remained to beautify the off-ramp and maybe entice a stray tourist into town. Unfortunately, time has not been kind to our numbers. Within a half-year of each other, we lost Adam and his elderly mentor, Dutch. Our frail World War II vet, Howard, lost a battle with pneumonia. Margot, his feisty slip of a wife, wound up in a nursing home downstate.

I visited her once and found a mere shadow of the tough 90-plus-year-old who had braved the merciless sun of our hillside garden. Margot gave no sign that she knew me as I cradled her pale-veined hands in mine. I talked on about the berm, the perennials and how much her life story had changed my own. When I left, her eyes followed me to the door. I could have sworn for a split-second, she knew who I was.

"Take care of yourself, Dearie," she smiled.

Several years my junior, the head of the garden crew, Bea Duiksma, survived recent rounds of forced-retirements at Social Services. She wasn't so optimistic about the status of our lovely little patch of perennials on the berm. Semi-retired trucker Artie and former school counselor Vivian were so much an item now that their names came out in one breath. The two picked up the slack as best they could. For though I, too, continued to show up faithfully at Saturday morning work sessions with the ragged band of survivors, my heart was elsewhere, sequestered in some dark, deep cavern of pain.

Impatient now, I switched on the windshield wipers. Up ahead through the salt-streaked windshield, I strained to catch a flash of blue from the nursery signboard. An art student from the high school had volunteered to repaint it end of last season. At my suggestion, a faint watermark of a daisy now flowered on a pale blue-green ground. A darker vine-like script spelled out the letters, *G-r-o-f-t'-s*.

This pilgrimage too made no sense on so many levels. Below the large signboard, a smaller white one swung precariously in the wind. *Closed for the Season.* With no heirs to lay claim to it, the nursery was Groft's in name only since Adam's death.

I told myself that maybe something of Adam and his dream was still there in that garden center he had left for me to run. And just maybe, in spite of all the wintery desolation in and around me, I needed to cling to a tattered shred of faith, more a hope really. Like the February thaw forecasters kept predicting for next week, spring might eventually come, even for me.

The Taurus slid to a stop on the shoulder. I had company. Someone was sitting in a battered boat of a vehicle half in and half out of the Groft's parking lot. From the look of it, the driver apparently ran aground on the towering banks thrown up by county plows.

I crossed the highway, picking my way flat-footed over the patches of black ice. The vehicle's motor wasn't running. Its driver-side door was cracked open. I could hear the car door alarm protesting, aggrieved and relentless. The sound set my teeth on edge.

"Someone could freeze to death out here in no time flat," I told myself. I quickened my pace.

From a distance, even the driver's gender wasn't a given. The bulky down coat, garish neon green wool hat and ski gloves obscured my view. Closer-up, the luminous eyes and delicate features resolved the question marks. I would have guessed the woman to be early-thirties though something in the set of her mouth testified to a pain beyond the power of a birth certificate or calendars to measure.

"We're closed," I said. "Is there some way I can help you?"

The woman just looked at me from those troubled gray depths, blinked. "*Groft's.* That's you?"

"Not exactly. But, yes."

"I'm out of gas," she said.

"I can drive you into—"

"And money. And I think the alternator just quit."

"I have a cell phone, if you would like to make a call."

She didn't dignify that with a response. I looked again, harder.

10

Through a cracked and partially ice-fogged rear passenger window, I saw the back seat was crammed with collapsing cardboard boxes. Spilling out from the whimsical heap of clothes and household goods were a pair of flip-flops, snow boots and a toaster oven. For everything, a season.

The question was half on the tip of my tongue. *What was she going to do?* Obviously, that wasn't the point. Our encounter had a hapless feel like coming across a boat sinking fifty yards off shore in Lake Michigan. I stood there without a life ring on the gravelly sand, watching it sink.

"I live a few miles from here in Xenaphon," I said, plunging ahead before I could change my mind. "There isn't a gas station or garage any closer. Do you drink coffee? Or tea, I have that, too. It'll buy you some time to figure things out. You can't stay here."

She took her time reacting. I couldn't read her expression.

"I'm not some charity case," she said.

"I didn't think you were. I just figured something hot might be good right now. It's colder than blue blazes out here."

My daughters told me nobody says 'blue blazes' anymore. The woman's eyes narrowed. "You're not some kind of Fundy-nut-case, are you?"

I had forgotten where I had just been. My sleek black go-to-church quilted coat and mid-calf tweed skirt were dead giveaways. As we spoke, the wind was lashing my bare head. The heels of my high leather boots had begun to embed themselves in the rutted ice-pack at my feet.

"Not hardly." I laughed, but there was no humor in it. "God and I aren't exactly on the best of speaking terms right now."

"All right, then."

Grabbing a denim bag from the passenger seat, the woman got out and shut the door behind her. She didn't bother to lock it. The key was still in the ignition.

"If I'm lucky, maybe somebody will steal the thing. Save me the dump fee."

That last was laced with a couple of F-Bombs, the casual intensity of which shocked me momentarily into silence. I flashed what I hoped was a reassuring smile. This woman was in trouble beyond a cup of hot tea and respite from the biting cold.

"You aren't from around here?" I assumed out loud.

Not many could claim that distinction. Those who could, like me, were a dying breed. Like so many other rural villages in Michigan,

Xenaphon's population too had shrunk in our most recent economic catastrophe.

"Detroit by way of East Lansing," the woman said. "A cousin of mine who worked in a ski resort north of here said they were hiring. But by the time I made it this far, they weren't and she was on her way to Denver."

"A waitress." Something told me as guesses went, this shot wide of the mark.

"That was the plan. Though my degrees are in English and journalism. For what it's worth, the diplomas are in that mess in the back seat somewhere. I assume there isn't a newspaper or a print shop around here."

I winced. "Sort of. I work for Xenaphon's weekly *Gazette*."

The woman chewed on that while she settled down into the passenger seat of my Taurus. Her cranky shoulder belt snapped into place. "Not a whole lot of newspapers in small towns any more."

"Ours is on life support," I chuckled. "The publisher-editor is supposedly retired. I'm the only staffer. My so-called salary nets me enough to buy grass seed. That's about it."

She didn't seem surprised. "So, how *do* people make a living around here?"

"They don't, mostly. The median age is seventy. Our county government employs some. The local restaurant is family owned and run. We've settled in to something of a barter economy up here. A summer's worth of veggies might swap for ground venison, wrapped and frozen. Fix a leaky faucet next door and the neighbor's kid comes over with a mower."

We were passing a boarded up gas station. The place was relatively new but fell victim to the latest Mid-East oil fracas. My passenger had turned and was staring out the window.

"I'm Eve, by the way," I told her. "Eve Brennerman."

"You're a native?"

I shrugged. "Depends on how you define 'native'. My people started out here. I spent most of my career in Chicago."

"Journalism."

"Advertising. When I retired, I moved back into my family's homestead."

"Quite a change."

"Easier than you might think," I said. "Good people here."

12

After a conspicuous silence, the woman shot a glance my way. "Gruin," she said. "My name's Gruin—rhymes with ruin. Most people call me Ann. I wrote and designed an in-house magazine for an auto parts chain based in Detroit."

I caught the past tense. "You need a job."

"Among other things."

"I can't promise you much more than a roof over your head until you get that car fixed."

"You don't know me from Adam."

I winced at the unfortunate metaphor. Since Adam's death, the book of Genesis had become off-limits. And yet so much of our language revolves around Eden, from talk of snakes in the grass and forbidden fruit to the Addam's family.

"No, I don't," I told her, "but then you don't know me either."

"Then, why?"

"Call it a hunch."

The soles of her threadbare cross-trainers were creating a muddy lagoon on the floor mat. Under other circumstances I could have found myself in those self-same shoes easily enough. For starters, if I had chosen to divorce my faithless husband and had taken off with my two daughters on my own.

"For all you know, I could steal you blind."

I laughed. "Lots of luck. The only things of any value around my place are a few antiques. All of them are too big to get in someone's trunk. And right now yours seems pretty full."

It was the first time I saw her smile. Guarded, I thought, but nice.

"Actually, my first name is really Ann-ees," she said. "Spelled like the flavoring, anise. Accent on the last syllable. My parents were German but owned a Greek bakery. Go figure. At the very least I could offer to cook for room and board."

"A deal . . . *Anise*," I said. "It isn't an awful lot of fun cooking just for one. And peanut butter out of the jar gets monotonous after a while."

"Everything I own is in that damn car."

"I have a friend, Artie, who has a truck and a winch. We can stash your car in my driveway until you figure out what to do with it."

We were pulling up to the homestead as we spoke. I had spent a lot of time here as a girl and knew every inch of that gray and white farmhouse gothic facade. Gardening with my grandmother meant twice daily rounds of the flower beds tucked in alongside the fieldstone

13

foundation. In the mid-day heat we took refuge on the wraparound porch while we sipped at our lemonade. The sights and sounds and smells of those golden summers permeated every board and bit of mortar, even after all those years.

Unusual for Xenaphon, the rectangular house stood sideways on a double-lot, slightly wider than it was deep. But then at one time the farmhouse and its numerous add-ons had been surrounded by acres of field crops instead of the mail-order catalog homes crowded tight against their lot lines up and down the block. As a child, I thought the wraparound porch left over from the early 1900s made the gable above it look like a ship thrusting its bow above the foam-crested waters.

With the help of paint chips I had salvaged, my plan eventually was to restore the homestead's original five-color scheme. Meanwhile here sat Anise—gaze fixed on the peeling trim boards near the peak of the roof.

"This isn't the Bates motel, if that's what's worrying you," I said.

Anise laughed, but I could hear the tension in her voice. She, too, was uneasy about this whole business. Somehow my sensing that did a great deal to relieve my own anxiety about where we found ourselves.

"I remember they have a name for those teeth-carvings under the eaves," she said.

"Dentil molding. Somewhere along the line my ancestors pulled down some of the gingerbread and went for ancient Greek. The lacy supports on the porch columns are still the originals though."

At that, I clicked off my shoulder belt, opened the door and got out. By the time I had maneuvered around the front of the car, Anise had exited as well. Her bag was clutched in front of her like a blue denim life-vest.

"After you," she said.

A substantial distance between us, we struggled through the snowbanks toward the sidewalk. The walk itself was slick, treacherous. I had already sprung for a record supply of salt and sand. An ugly gray trail of grit had begun to scour away at the paint job on my front porch.

There was no need to fumble around in my purse for keys. The heavy oak and glass-fronted door wasn't locked.

Anise's eyebrow arched. "Not much of a crime rate around here?"

"Worse than it used to be. But then I have a very attentive neighbor. Better than a security service."

I looked up in time to see the filmy curtains at the side window of the house next door slipping back into place. Addie and Lucille had a special place in my memory banks. The two reclusive sisters bore precious witness to my awkward leave-taking from Adam on the front lawn in the weeks before my daughter surprised us together *in flagrante delicto* in Grandma Eva's bedroom There was no point in discretion after that, no point in so many things.

By now I had fled into the warmth of my living room and had begun to shed coat and boots. Anise had stopped dead just inside the door frame, the faceted glass still cracked open behind her. A half-smile twisted at the corner of my mouth as I passed the hall mirror. I found myself trying to see myself as she must be doing. No botox here, just Grandma Eva's strong cheekbones. The vestiges of my gardener's tan made up a little for the lack of makeup. Older by miles, true, but then no *Hush, Hush Sweet Charlotte* either.

"I'll warn you, I set the thermostat at sixty-nine," I told her.

"Sorry." She eased the door shut behind her, her gaze darting from the heaps of computer paper stacked on the sofa to the ragged stacks of gardening books on my dining room table.

"The place is a mess," I said. "I've been writing nonstop."

"Long, from the look of it."

"Close to a year now." Starting several months after Adam's death.

"I meant, whatever you've been writing seems definitely bigger than a breadbox."

"A memoir of sorts. Way too many typos, but apart from that, it's as done as it's going to be."

Thankfully, Anise didn't pursue why—as a random older woman living out in the boonies of northern Michigan—I would feel anyone would want to read my story. My boss, George, had been urging me to go public with the manuscript ever since I offered to let him read it. Meanwhile there it lay, my *TIME in a Garden*. Draft after draft covered most of the available surfaces in my living and dining room.

I could remember almost nothing of the time it had taken to write that anguished outpouring of love and memory. The experience had left me drained and empty. Eventually the flame that had fueled those pages burned to a graying ash. I sank into a depression beyond even my capacity to ask, what next.

Job's story this morning blind-sided me. It seemed at once a mirror and a reproof. I had told myself those manuscript pages represented closure. Truth was, on some level I sensed my journey through the valley of the shadow had only begun.

"You can hang your coat in that closet there to your right," I said.

Anise slowly took my suggestion. That incredibly hideous psychedelic ski hat hid a close-cropped thatch of spiky auburn hair, most definitely the real deal. It made her skin glow with a porcelain fragility, totally out of synch with those strikingly confident features. She was a Renaissance portrait come to life, one of the most unusually beautiful women I ever met. Everything about her said, enigma wrapped in a riddle in a mystery—though even the bulky sweater couldn't conceal the rest.

"When is the baby due?" I said.

Something I couldn't read flickered in her otherwise expressive eyes. "Late June."

"Boy? Girl?"

"Ultrasounds are a little out of my price range."

All that was said as if she could have been talking about the weather. For better or worse, I had let this woman tentatively into my life, not just into my living room. There was no going back now.

"Find a place to sit, wander around, whatever turns you on," I told her. "I'm going to the kitchen and make us some tea. And then we're going to talk."

Anise evaded my gaze. For a split-second her face crumpled. Her breathing heavy and ragged, she won the battle to regain her composure, more or less. Except for those eyes.

"Fair enough. I can live with that," she nodded.

I already had the distinct impression that Anise Gruin, rhymes with ruin, had been living with a heck of a lot worse than sub-zero wind chills and a cranky alternator. When I returned from the kitchen with a tray loaded with a plate of store-bought cookies, two mugs and a pot of steaming green tea, I found my young visitor back-turned, standing at the fireplace. She seemed intent on making sense of the array of photos on the mantle.

"You were married," Anise said.

In her hand was a photo of Adam and me in front of some random Chicago brownstone doorway carved with flowing marble vines and filagree. His arm was around my shoulder drawing me close. The love in our eyes didn't need an explanation, but I decided to offer one anyway.

"Engaged. I had just bought my wedding dress when Adam died."

Anise took one long last look at the photo, carefully set it back in its place, front and center among the ones of my daughters, Leslie and Gina, and their families, including one taken with their father, Joel. I saw no point in dragging out my disastrous first marriage in front of this stranger, left him out of the picture entirely.

"I'm sorry," Anise said.

"It's been over a year now."

My gaze kept returning to that photo as Adam's face swam in and out of focus. Time seemed to be compressing like a video on fast forward with an audible murmur of voices and memories that left me feeling light-headed, disoriented. That photo was taken the month before Adam died. We were on a shopping expedition to Chicago. I had just found my wedding dress and with it the basic black intended for the rehearsal dinner. Instead, I would wear it to his memorial service.

It seemed hard to catch my breath. I could have sworn that captured in those grainy pixels, lingering there behind Adam's brilliant smile, was something I hadn't noticed before. A wistful awareness of how much we had. How fragile it all was.

Had he known he was living on borrowed time? The thought surfaced, ugly and untenable. I beat back the possibility, knowing as I did that some things, once imagined, never totally leave us.

Anise was looking at me strangely. "Life has a way of socking it to us sometimes," she said softly.

"Nobody tells us about the wreckage love can leave behind."

"True enough," her laugh was brittle, ended as quickly as it began. "Only in my case the guy was already married—unfortunately, not to me. *My bad* . . . I should have known better."

"I suspect you're being too hard on yourself."

Anise shrugged. "Terrible timing, anyway. With the apocalypse in the auto industry, our employer took the opportunity to downsize my department out of existence."

"You worked with him then, the baby's father. Does he . . . I assume he knows that you're—"

"No." By what appeared to be force of habit, she rested a hand gingerly on the barely perceptible curve of her belly. The weave of the sweater was pilling.

"Gutsy, doing this on your own."

"Or stupid," she shrugged off her tale of woe. "Like everyone else, I was overextended. The bank foreclosed, so I figured I had to do something radical—raise some start-up capital. *Buy American,* my job description at the magazine insisted. Okay, except when I tried to trade my hot new domestic wheels for that junker of an '85 Impala, I practically had to give the darn thing away. *Come north,* my cousin said . . . with that early snow in November, the ski season was booming. Meantime, *she* decided to head west with some jock to try her luck on the Colorado resort circuit."

"Leaving you here, out of gas."

"Pretty much."

"And your family?"

"Phoenix, in one of those assisted living, seniors only communities. They left Michigan for Arizona the minute the new owner bought out the bakery ten years ago. Both of them are frailer now—Alzheimer's and cancer. They certainly don't need this."

"Brothers or sisters?"

Anise shrugged. "Scattered over the years. I was adopted, odd man out in the family. The closest to me in age and other-wise got religion a couple of years back. Not the most hospitable place to go *sans* ring and job and sporting a baby bump."

The familial geography she was describing could have fit any one of the folks my age or older in Xenaphon. "My daughters are based north of Chicago, and would you believe it, Tucson," I told her. "We get together when we can."

"You were married before."

"Widowed. Before I could file for divorce."

My ex-husband Joel and our failed relationship seemed now like another lifetime entirely. The pain of it was blunted like an old wound that only twinges when it rains. How much of both joy and sorrow we human beings take for granted in the great scheme of things.

"And three grandkids," Anise said. "They're cute. Freckles."

A good journalist, that woman, I decided. *Observant in a low-key way.* But then a lot of my life—more than I perhaps had intended—was on display on that fireplace mantle. Adam had come to many of the same conclusions on that same spot, without any prompting from me.

"Emma's six now, spent ten days with me last summer," I told her, "Baby brother Harry will be two. My Tucson grandson is Emma's age and quite the little man."

"So, what's with you and that nursery? Groft's?"

I took a deep breath. "It was in Adam's family for three generations. He left it and some incredible lake-front property to me and one of his former employees. Sadly, my co-owner, Dutch, died last May."

It had been a long, hard year of goodbyes. Six months to the week after Adam's fatal heart attack, my dear old friend had gone quietly to sleep and never woke up. A teenage crush for his boss' wife had kept him working for the Groft family all those years. To him, Adam was the son he never had. Loyal to the last, I knew Dutch had hung on only long enough after Adam's death to help me get started in the nursery business. As I made the burial arrangements, I kept telling myself that Dutch finally was at peace. His grave site lay in the Episcopal churchyard, a stone's throw from where they had buried Adam's grandmother.

Tough stuff. I sipped cautiously at my tea and let the memories play themselves out. Dutch was a man of big hands and even bigger heart. The first time we met he had shepherded pot after pot of donated perennials from the nursery into my hatchback for the community garden. And all that while behind him in the greenhouse doorway Adam Groft had stood watching us, his face inscrutable.

These were the faces of love in my life. Even then.

"You miss him," Anise said.

I drew in a deep breath. "I had to shut the nursery for the winter," I told her. "Oil prices what they are, there's no way to afford heat for those greenhouses. Plan is to open again if and when this snow ever melts."

Anise thought about it. "You sound like you need help."

True, actually. Our greenhouse manager was in grad school, wouldn't come back on staff until June. The high school student Adam relied on to cover the counter left for college as well. Since then her family moved south looking for milder weather and a lower cost of living. There was no reason for the young woman to return. I couldn't keep imposing on my friends, Viv and Artie, or even my daughters and their spouses when they showed up in town.

"Know anything about plants?" I said.

"No. But I can run a cash register. How tough is it to learn the rest?"

"Depends on how much you like getting your hands dirty."

"Try working in a bakery. Even with the hair nets and gloves, there's an awful lot of flour dust. Then there are the burn scars from the ovens. Nasty. I've got my share, trust me."

Anise could have been describing how the past year had gone for me. Scars and all. I had the irrational feeling that in another lifetime, she and I could have been siblings or best of friends or both.

"Welcome to Xenaphon," I told her. "That friend with the truck who is going to help us, Artie—he took to watching the squirrels last fall. If he's right, it's going to be a very late growing season."

19

T<small>wo</small>

February Thaw

Didn't you know yet how it works, insect that you are in the great scheme of things? We have just planted, have hardly cast the seed into the ground and our roots have barely taken hold in the ground when the storm carries us off as easily as stalks drying out in the wind. A<small>DAPTED FROM</small> I<small>SAIAH</small> 40

I woke mid-dream. My granddaughter Emma had been pulling weeds alongside me in the garden. The white-gold halo of her hair caught the rising sun. Her bare feet left tiny toe-marks in the muddy hillocks. She stopped long enough to tug at my sleeve. Eyes wide, she pointed to the rows of ankle-high plants glistening from the morning dew.

"Bugs, Grandma. We've got 'em on the pole beans," came my granddaughter's anxious whisper. "New since yesterday. What are we going to do?"

Before I could respond, Emma's image scattered like the white cloud of my breath trailing out into chill air of the bedroom. I sat up, wide awake.

It had to be well past midnight. The bank of windows facing the street shuddered with a rhythmic tattoo that marked the arrival of the warm front. By tomorrow it would be in the fifties, unheard of for northern Michigan in February. Just as bizarre, a few feet down the hall from me, a total stranger had taken up residence in my house.

I drew in my breath, waiting for my pulse to sound an alarm as

Emma had in my dream. Instead, I felt a strange sense of calm. *Anise Gruin rhymes with ruin.* From what little I knew of her story, it seemed that unlike Job with his solitary anguish, I was no longer quite so alone with mine.

Coincidence at work? I turned to the laptop lying on the coverlet alongside me, trying to catch up on my online journal while I waited for my head to clear:

> I'll admit that when it came to organized religion or spirituality, I've maintained a cautious distance since my girls were grown. Since Adam's memorial service at Peace, I hadn't darkened the door of a church again. I'm not at all certain what led me to rediscover it now.
>
> *Timing is all.* If Shakespeare didn't write it, he should have. The loose and fraying ends of our stories connect when and how they will. Whether a blessing or something we will come to regret? Only time will tell.
>
> That woman's wreck of an Impala could have quit anywhere along the icy stretch of roadway. And yet, circumstances, coincidence, fate mysteriously intervene. Call it what we will, but I have to believe something drew Anise Gruin to that snowbank and me to that sanctuary.
>
> Like a lot of my gardening friends, I cling to my almanacs and climate zone maps to structure my world. But in the shuddering fury of a midnight storm or the ambivalence of a February warm spell, we all sooner or later come face to face with how little we truly understand, much less control.
>
> *Time beyond our knowing,* the prophetic books describe it. I don't pretend to have a better explanation than that.

The green battery light on my laptop stared out at me, unblinking. *Daring me,* I thought, to reach out to that vast nameless, faceless network pouring out its collective soul into the ether. An hourglass on the computer screen marked the frustration of time passing.

On a whim I had googled the keyword *lectionary,* the official term for the calendar of readings in the Christian tradition. With a few more clicks of the mouse, the Biblical texts for the first Sunday in February swam into focus. There it was for the Roman Catholic calendar, dated Year B in a three-year cycle of readings. *Job. Chapter seven.*

I checked out a Protestant site for the same month and hit instead on a series of bleak Old Testament readings from Isaiah. Our young priest was right about making the switch. I didn't need the prophet's talk of bugs and aggressive weeding to tell me how vulnerable and finite I felt. Compared to that, even Job was an improvement. At least humankind stood with a fist thrust in defiance of the pain that living can inflict.

On that thought, my eyes closed. The cursor shifted under my fingertips, clicked randomly on an entry and connected with the Psalm that had been read on Sunday. I realized I must have blocked out hearing the lush poetry and its images of meadows warmed by the sun and gentle, life-giving rain.

How can you keep from singing, when the One who made you covers the heavens with clouds, prepares for the rain to fall upon the earth and causes the grass to grow on the hillsides? Brokenhearted one, healing comes without your asking. ADAPTED FROM PSALM 147

The ancient text couldn't help but strike at the gardener in my soul. Plants grow and flower. They return to the earth from which they spring—a journey as subtle as the course of the dunes along Little Traverse Bay or the ebb and flow of the waves against the Michigan shoreline where Dutch and I had laid Adam's ashes to rest.

Above the wind outside the homestead windows, I sensed the whispers of my childhood faith sighing to me in the darkness. "For everything there is a season," the voice said, "a time for every purpose."

Try as I might, the landscape of those hope-filled verses couldn't be farther from where I found myself. In the emptiness of my grandmother's high-backed bed, I could only imagine what the rest of the month had to offer. If I remembered correctly, Lent was coming.

A faint rustling at my bedroom door startled me. Quickly I shut the case, then slid the laptop onto the heavy quilt alongside me.

"I'm awake," I said.

My new boarder stood in the doorway, silhouetted by the night light in the hall. She was wearing a flannel nightgown I had loaned her. It had a field of daisies and buttercups on a sky-blue ground. Granddaughter Emma gave it to me for Christmas. The other choices in the drawer were shapeless, way too worn for public consumption.

"When it's cold, you can wear your garden," my granddaughter had said. "See, there are even tiny suns." Emma had half-frowned as she pointed out the shapes on the fabric. I saw that same look when she was weeding alongside me in my veggie garden. Forehead knit in concentration, her tiny fingers worked around the feathery carrot tops.

"I guess you must have heard it, too," Anise said. "The whole house is shaking with that gosh-awful wind. Should we be heading toward the basement or something?"

A smile tugged at the corner of my mouth. Her voice sounded high-pitched and thin. Like an anxious child.

"The homestead survived a tornado, if that's what's bothering you," I said. "And it isn't the season. This front should be through by morning. After that, it's supposed to be warming up. Fifties and sixties will be a real heat wave. The old timers say they haven't seen anything like it since 1925."

Anise didn't sound convinced. "I'm a big city girl, remember. And definitely not used to all this *nature*, raw and uncensored."

"It grows on you."

"I suppose," she yawned. "Right now it seems pretty darn cold. Sorry if I woke you."

"No problem. The wind woke me, too. And I'm used to it. You can find more blankets in the chest at the foot of the bed if you need them."

I wasn't being totally honest. I hadn't had a decent night's sleep since Adam was gone.

"Thanks," Anise said. "See you in the morning."

The door closed. I heard her padding along the hall to her room. When I finally retrieved my laptop, I stuck to foraging through a Farmers Almanac online. It seemed obsessed with countdowns to the solstice.

Spring comes to us when winter starts to get unbearable. It is tough to tell anymore whether the patina on the fenders in line at the carwash is snow or road salt. After all that antiseptic white, we hunger for a thousand greens, springing from earth and branch and stem. THE ONLINE GARDENERS COMPANION

We hunger for a thousand greens, the phrase kept replaying in my head.

My bedside clock read 2 A.M. and even I finally had enough. I stashed the computer on the floor and picked my way cautiously across the smooth-worn pine boards toward the bedroom window. Anise didn't need any more ominous noises down the hall to convince her the place must be haunted.

Except for a porch light across the street that cast its cold halo on the snow, the neighborhood looked deserted. More and more snowbirds in Xenaphon were winging south every year. Barren branches of the trees along the wide frontage of the homestead reached heavenward in mute appeal. Ice crystals glistened like unshed tears on the delicate branches.

Grandmother Eva had planted three of those small-leaf lindens on the boulevard the year she died. "The Czech national tree," she had told me. "In Berlin where my people came from, a whole avenue of lindens stretches straight through the heart of the city. A picture in the family album of the trees is faded now. But if you look hard, Evella, you could recognize the shape of that tree anywhere."

For all the years between us, her precious testaments to my heritage stood defiant in the February night. The wind was howling. My feet were bare, freezing.

"So much for spring," I muttered through chattering teeth.

The thick floral comforter on the bed was as close as I was going to get. Lush sprays of poppies and narcissus blossomed on the blue-green jungle of polished chintz, the spring garden in its prime. I had helped to 'tie' that quilt when I was in my teens. We clamped the fabric taut on a crude wooden frame over Grandmother Eva's dining room table. With lengths of wool secured on thick needles, the trick was to find a consistent spot in the fabric's pattern and pull the threads through. After tying a simple knot, we clipped the ends. I didn't know it then, but our hands were creating a garden meant to flower across the generations.

I finally drifted off. Before I did, I also must have shut off the alarm. The next thing I knew, sunlight danced golden-haired through the room. In the depths of the homestead's cobbled Michigan basement, the stolid old furnace had begun to do its job.

My watch read nine-thirty. I got dressed in a sleep-drugged fog, tucked the laptop under my arm and headed for the kitchen. Half-way down the stairs I caught the unmistakable smell of something baking, cinnamon-laced and yeasty.

"Breakfast buns," Anise informed me with a shy flash of a smile. "After all our prowling around last night, I figured we could both use some comfort food. Hope you don't mind . . . "

I grinned. "Did I tell you, you're hired?"

As I watched, a tin of perfectly done baked goods emerged from the oven. That took real skill. My oven baked consistently hot.

"Guten Appetit!"

Anise slid a freshly frosted bun on to a plate and set it before me. My eyes closed as I savored the subtle hint of vanilla. Anybody who could bake like that had a future in Xenaphon.

"Nothing against the baked goods counter at the local grocery," I told her, "but I haven't tasted anything like that since I moved here. Ever."

"I like to bake—always did—even at the height of my adolescent rebellion."

"It shows. Wow!"

"Thanks," she smiled. "By the way, teal looks good on you."

It was the same thing Adam always told me. Truth was, I just grabbed the first thing in my closet.

"You're going to want your own things out of the car, too, I'm sure," I said.

"I can wait . . ."

I already had picked up the phone, but caught my friend Artie's machine. "Give me a call when you get home, will you?" I said. "If you're not busy, I've got a tow-job for you."

I remembered now. Artie was on the road and wouldn't be back until the end of the week. I knew if I dialed our mutual friend Vivian, I could probably pin down his estimated time of arrival. But Viv would have blushed like a stand of Monarda if someone assumed she was the keeper of Artie's calendar.

"I really ought to start job hunting," Anise said. "But I can't—not looking like this. It's tough anyway, without a car."

"No problem. You can use mine."

Anise frowned. "You need it yourself. To drive to the print shop."

"Walk. Unless it's too icy. I've got no problem with your using it."

"Well, you won't find me gone and the car abandoned somewhere along the interstate," she said. "No money for gas."

I flushed. "As in *steal* the thing—that never occurred to me," I said.

"I wouldn't blame you, if it had."

It was going to be one of those mornings. I had just finished the last of my cinnamon bun when Artie called. He was still on the road but would be back as planned. I told him about Anise. We made arrangements to move her car.

The phone rang a second time. Ever since Adam was gone, my

oldest daughter had taken to calling me every morning just to make sure I was still kicking.

"Not necessary," I insisted.

"It's either that," Leslie said, "or I'm going to sign you up with one of those Life-Line gadgets."

Like clockwork, she continued to call. Something in my voice on this particular morning must have caught her attention.

"You've got company," she said. "I'm sorry."

"Actually, I've taken in a boarder."

Silence. Anise turned toward the sink and began to sort noisily through the accumulated dishes and silverware stashed there. The front of the dishwasher was yawning open, waiting to be fed.

"Boarder. Anyone I know?"

"No. In fact, we just met yesterday."

Again dead silence from the other end of the line. Anise had moved on to rinsing out our coffee cups.

"Are you going to tell me?" Leslie said.

"Anise is a writer. Her car broke down in the lot at Groft's."

"Mom, you don't even know her."

"Her family owned a Greek bakery in East Lansing. She just whipped me up a batch of cinnamon buns."

Even to me, the credentials sounded sketchy. "Are you sure you know what you're doing, Mom?"

"No," I said slowly. "But if I'm going to have the time to figure out how to make a go of the nursery, I need the time to get on with it. Anise has offered to cook for her room and board, run the counter at Groft's and help out with the plants. One more year like last one and I'm going to have to nail the doors shut permanently. I don't want that on my watch."

Long distance, my daughter's husband, Dan, had advised me as best he could and had cobbled together my tax statements. I wasn't exaggerating the precariousness of the situation and Leslie knew it. Her Dan had been out of work since just before Christmas. I hadn't had the heart to burden either one of them with my troubles.

"Adam couldn't have anticipated the downturn or how much worse the economy up there was going to get," my daughter said. "He would be the first to tell you that the biggest problems at the nursery are beyond your or anyone's control. The fuel costs, rising costs of—"

"I know that. But eventually even passive-aggressive Job took responsibility for himself and crawled off that ash heap."

Leslie must have been wondering what on earth I was talking about. I tried to picture her at her office, cell-phone in one hand and the other already calling up her day's accumulation of emails. She had inherited my unruly hair, that no-nonsense set to her brows and germanic profile—her mother's daughter in so many ways. A good heart, this daughter of mine. I had to love her for it.

A conspicuous pause was followed by an audible out-rush of breath from the other end of the line. "Well, let us know what you need," she said. "We were thinking about coming up for Easter or Mother's Day or both."

I felt the tears threatening and heavy behind my eyes. "That would be great, honey. Better than great. And yes, I will keep you in the loop."

All that while Anise had been standing there, forced to eavesdrop. I laid the portable phone down on the table, made eye contact in time to read the awareness in her eyes.

"My daughter," I said. "We've got this mid-morning check-in thing going."

Anise nodded. "I guessed as much. That's great."

Her face had taken on a shuttered look. Whatever else she thought of my end of the conversation with my daughter, she chose not to share it. Including the obvious discussion of her role in all this.

"Unfortunately, I've got to drag myself down to the printshop." My chair made a scraping sound as I stood up, plate and empty coffee mug in hand. "That garden column of mine is due and I've been procrastinating."

"Not exactly gardening weather."

"The weather channel said by week's end, it'll be in the fifties."

Evading my gaze, she relieved me of my breakfast utensils. I was free to go, but didn't.

"With the snow cover gone, plants like daisies are even more exposed and vulnerable to hard freezes, ice and wind," I said. "When in doubt, I can write a column on that, I suppose."

"Depressing stuff."

"Perhaps."

"Can't gardeners plan ahead . . . *do* something about it?"

"Some try snow fences," I told her, "or mulch. Others say it only makes things worse."

Anise drew herself erect. "I know you mean well, Ms. Brennerman," her voice crackled with resolve. "But I don't think I can do this. I can't just sit around and do nothing. And I certainly can't take

27

advantage of you like this."

I tried to make eye contact. Anise was looking beyond me and where she found herself, toward a reality only she could see.

"The name is Eve," I told her quietly. "Keep cooking like this and we're good. I'll expect to see you when I get home. Say around one?"

Anise started to say something, began again. "I found some root veggies when I rummaged in the bottom of the fridge," she said. "If it's okay, I thought I might whip us up some comfort food for dinner—some good old Yooper *pasties.* You have nutmeg, I assume. Though I think you're running out of flour."

At the rate she was going, I would pack on five pounds by the end of the week. "I haven't exactly been stocking the old larder lately. I have a line of credit at the grocery. The owner's a friend of mine. Just sign your name and you can get whatever you think we need."

"Small town living," Anise shook her head. "I thought that sort of stuff only went on in the movies . . . ?!"

I laughed. She sounded like a tourist exposed to our local spring delicacy, *morels,* for the first time. More expensive than filet mignon, the mushrooms look as alien as a moonscape staring up from a plate—though one bite was enough to make a convert of anyone.

Two cups of coffee and another cinnamon-bun later, I decided a trip down to the print shop was a bad idea. My gloomy column-in-progress on the philosophical significance of groundhogs would have to do. I tinkered around on it for a while, then finally reshaped the piece as a commentary on the unpredictability of life in general.

Sun or no sun is no guarantee how plants are going to survive. Gardeners get anxious when the gale starts howling and the wind-chill hovers in the minus-teens. It is such a relief to see the sun again. And so we underestimate the one-two punch of the mid-winter thaw or the sub-zero blast that is bound to follow.

Change can be benign or devastating. Nothing is certain, especially the weather. And our storm channels, almanacs and even ground hogs can only do so much to steer a safe course for us through the seasons ahead. The garden survives as best it can.

My advice to Phil and all his furry colleagues? Forget pretending to predict the future. Go back to bed and enjoy that long winter's nap if you can With or without you, in its own good time, spring will come.

Eventually the word count settled at 350. When the spell-checker came up empty, I fired the column to George at the print shop.

Tomorrow, I said in the cover email to my boss. I would definitely check in tomorrow.

Monday passed, then Tuesday. I talked Anise into supplementing her wardrobe with some now woefully undersized blouses of mine stashed at the back of my closet. They were a perfect fit. While she filled the freezer with mountains of leftovers and baked goods, I escaped into endless googling and games of spider solitaire.

Outside our four walls, the warm front hovered over Illinois and stuck. But then, I was a fine one to pass judgment. Mid-week came before I finally made myself step foot out of the house.

My boss must have heard rather than seen me blow in, wind-scoured and my breath icicle-hard in my throat. I caught him fixating on the sales counter with the *Gazette*'s upcoming Classified Section splayed out in front of him. He never even looked up. If anything, his cork-shaped frame bent even tauter over the counter top.

"You're still with us," he grunted.

Something was wrong. George Herberg may have been borderline obsessive when it came to the survival of the county's tiny weekly, but he wasn't a grouch. His patience with me, especially over the past year since Adam's death, had been legendary. It took a lot to phase the man. The proof-ink smudges on the sleeves of his turtleneck gave me the first clue.

The classifieds. It had become my forte to tweak the weekly accumulation of ads into some semblance of order. Except I had been MIA while all this stuff was piling up.

"Oh, m' gosh, the Valentine's Day specials. George, *I am so sorry*—"

At the moment the classified section looked like one of those gigantic borderless puzzles. It seemed nothing but odd and random rectangles without definable shape or plan. *My life, writ large.* On any other morning, George would have laughed me out of my malaise if I said that. His uni-brow of a scowl warned he was not amused.

"We'll live. Finish your column."

"Done. Sent it Monday."

"Haven't checked."

Whatever was bothering him went well beyond piecing together a bunch of odd-sized ads aimed at love and lovers. George wasn't disclosing the source. I sucked in a breath, then slowly let it out again.

"For what it's worth, it's been a zoo at my place. I've taken in a boarder." I wasn't trying for defensive, it just came out that way.

"Anybody I know?"

"A young journalist from Detroit. Her car broke down in front of Groft's on the weekend. She's out of work. It was either take her in or let her freeze out there."

George's frown deepened. "There isn't much call for staff writers—"

"Her name's Anise Gruin. She also turns out to be one heck of a baker."

"As in bread."

"Bread, cake, pastries, pies. Right now we're trading rent for home-cooked meals. Nice after a steady diet of TV dinners."

I could still taste those flaky as a cloud pasties of hers, smelling of cloves and nutmeg—wickedly caloric, carb-laden and utterly delicious. My boss hadn't moved a muscle. His coffee stood untouched on the counter. Whatever was bothering him, he showed no signs of sharing it.

"You'll feel better if you let me fool with that layout," I probed gently.

My boss glanced in disgust at the ink-smeared ads on the counter in front of him. "All yours," he said. He slid off the stool inviting me to take his place. "These aren't going to fit. No way, no how."

"No problem. Give me ten minutes, max. But you know and I know that's not what has you harumphing like a walrus."

I saw his jaw tighten. "I'm expecting company of my own," George said. "He's due in next week."

"*He*," I said finally.

"My son. Mark."

"Your . . . say again. You were married."

"A month. Jocelyn was pregnant. I was a freshman in college at Pitt and in denial, big time. As deep in the closet as a good Jewish kid can get."

My instincts had been dead-on. George could be a terrible flirt. Still, I always suspected his heart wasn't in it.

I tried to picture him as a young man. Balding yarmulka fashion now with a trim-kept fringe of silvery hair, no one would describe him as handsome. But there was something about those intense dark eyes and olive-tinged features, the quick wit and intelligence that went with them, that made him loom larger in life than his stature.

"Oh, George, I'm so—"

"Don't be." He flashed a wan smile. "It's amazing how ugly things can get in one short month. Funny thing, her family officially figured it out before I did. I haven't seen Jocelyn since and she tried her darndest to reciprocate—for starters, made sure I saw as little of our son as possible. Last time I heard, the kid hated my guts. Only he isn't a kid anymore and the consulting firm he works for is taking a tough look at the outstanding loans at the bank.

"You're talking as in, shut folks down. Foreclose."

George winced. "It's the way things usually work, isn't it?"

When the market went south, I knew my boss had taken out a second mortgage on the shop. Dangerous for someone on a pension. And without straining too hard, I could have come up with a similar list of at least a dozen more enterprises in Xenaphon operating in similar fashion.

"The *Gazette* could be in trouble."

My boss chuckled softly. "That had occurred to me."

"So, he . . . your son called you, then?"

"The CEO down at the bank, Glen Dornbush, stopped me yesterday and shared a memo. The Board has called in a hired gun from a firm in Pittsburgh. Of course I recognized the name. *Blandis.* He seems to have become quite the fiscal hatchet man, my son. One tough, tough hombre."

George tossed a printout on the counter in front of me. *Mark Blandis*, it read.

My boss' name was Herberg, so I never would have made the connection. The resemblance to George was subtle, if at all. Even in the grainy black and white digital photograph, those eyes riveted on mine seemed driven, unflinching. That tight slash of a smile did little to soften the harsh planes of his features, revealed none of the warmth I so often saw in my boss' open face.

"Jocelyn came from old money," my boss said. "Second time around her family got into the act and hooked her up with some local Pittsburgh magnate's son. I was out of the picture, had joined the Navy. Eventually got my degree in night school. Meanwhile my son wound up on the A-list."

31

At that last we made eye contact. The pain I read in that look was enough to make me forget my fretting over the mess of manuscripts in my living room, the state of the community garden and even my heartache over Groft's shaky finances.

"Your son knows you're here?"

"I doubt that he misses much."

"So, what are you going to do?"

"Sit tight. Try to talk you into slapping 'A Novel' on the cover of that so-called 'memoir' of yours, tweak it a bit so your daughters don't sue and then get it out there, pronto."

I just looked at him. "I would stand a better chance of striking paydirt on the Biggest Loser than finding an agent."

"Me."

"It takes a publisher."

"Also me."

My eyebrows shot through the roof. "And sell the thing, where?"

"Locally, for starters. The tourists love regional Americana."

"All six of them."

"Okay, then, with the attention the book is bound to generate, you just might help promote the nursery, scare up recruits for the community garden—"

"And then I'll sign up to pilot the space shuttle."

George chuckled softly to himself, shook his head. "Nice try, Evie," he said. "You said the same thing when I suggested you write a garden column in the first place. Those gardening buddies of yours were all fired up at one time about running tours and educational programs out at the berm. So, use your book to inspire folks to go green. Teach them how to mulch. With the economy in the tank, families are looking for cheap entertainment close to home. *Stay-cations.* Why not in our own back yard?"

"Not much of a business plan."

"I've heard of worse. Just look around the place," George shrugged over his shoulder toward the presses. "We've got all this equipment, Evie-Girl, collecting cobwebs. If the circulation and ad revenue keep dropping, something better happen soon in a positive direction. And if the trade rags are to be believed, the Boomer generation is standing in line to share its story. That book of yours would give us an excuse to experiment with our own little regional on-demand press."

"*TIME in a Garden* as a best-seller. Somehow I doubt it."

"What have either one of us got to lose at this point?"

"You're delusional."

"Try, desperate," he said. "Failing that, we can try compiling all those weekly inches about gardens you've been generating and put out a collection of your columns. I'm open to suggestions."

I could read one unspoken agenda in his eyes. Apart from the personal loss for both of us if the *Gazette* were to go under, our fragile weekly was one of the precious few institutions still holding our little community together. Just imagining the possibility was enough to get my dander up and my creative juices flowing.

"*Done . . . !*"

"You'll go with the plan, then."

"Dream on, dream on," I laughed, rotated the taped-together Classified Section in his direction. "I just meant these ads were a perfect fit."

"Way too easy," he said.

"You really ought to join the millennium and do this on the computer."

George shot me one of those aggrieved looks that told me he knew exactly what he was doing. "When I have you around, Evie? But then, designing the typography for that manuscript of yours—now that I *can* manage."

I took that as my cue to head back to my laptop. When in doubt, write. In quick bold strokes, I began to sketch out a column in advance for the following week. All the while I kept picturing that tight, unflinching look on Mark Blandis' face.

Plants have their own personalities. Some are aggressive, others get lost in the crowd.

Perennials don't need much encouragement. Those brash alpha dogs rush to fill any space allotted to them. And it's tempting to let them do it. Self-starters are a good thing, right?

But then one morning I wake up and wonder what happened to my bleeding heart and lungwort! The Siberian iris roots and some daisy-like invader are so entangled, that to separate them takes an axe.

A gardener's job is to nurture a healthy community. The task requires juggling the executive, legislative and judicial all in one. It's a balancing act that I cannot seem to master.

The problem starts back at the nursery. Pots come labeled with subtle warnings (or at least hints) about plants that might be invasive. To me that is code for "that one's a survivor."

Once a bed is established, I also find it hard to whack away at otherwise healthy plants simply because they get a little uppity. But then, most plants left on their own just keep on testing the limits, crowding out their more timid neighbors.

Play nice, our Moms taught us—in the sandbox, the garden and life. Looking around at the neighborhood, there hasn't been a lot of that lately. And nobody seems to want to step up and referee.

It isn't smart to live in denial forever. Face it, there comes a time when somebody needs to break out the shovels.

"HERE'S YOUR CHANCE," I slipped in a tag at the end, along with the paper's email address. "Share your favorite story of garden entrepreneurs that have gotten out of hand."

While I worked, I sensed a non-stop coming and going around me. Phones rang. Doors slammed. And still I wrote. Finally with an audible sigh, I looked up to see George taking dictation. From the sound of it yet another ad was coming in over our phone line. Meanwhile a live walk-in stood fidgeting with a flyer clutched in his hand.

I shoved the laptop aside and ambled toward the counter. "How can I help you?"

The guy thrust the faded promotional piece in my hand. "Gotta update this darn thing and I've still got a box of these old *broh*-schures sitting in the basement." I forced a smile and went to work translating the man's grumbling into a to-do list of changes. Across the street, the weathervane on the courthouse annex had swung to a balmy south-southwest. Tired and cranky, I told George I was heading home for lunch.

"Happy Valentine's Day, Evie," he said. "I couldn't have done it without you."

The cosmic sadness in his eyes momentarily stopped me in my tracks. "You too, George."

Love and caring take many guises. I wasn't the only one with ghosts. There are times when our separate pain and loss may be the most powerful bond between us.

Three
Hearts and Flowers

Winter was on the defensive. The heat wave had arrived. Xenaphon was pushing sixty degrees, a near-record for February. Rusty pickups with their windows cracked and woofers thumping plied the muddy waters of Main Street, looking all the world like a Lake Michigan boat parade. When Glen Dornbush, the CEO at the bank, picked his way through the melting ice in front of Marty's Log Cabin Inn, one of the junkers doused him in its muddy wake. The poor man was wearing a suit, a rarity in itself. His face looked like a thundercloud.

"February's calendar *had* to be the invention of some bored gardener waiting around for the planting season," I told my boss. "Who else would have come up with holidays dependent on over-sized rodents, a celebration for lovers and a patriotic homage to dead presidents—all within days of each other!"

All along my route between work and home, storefronts and house windows had bloomed with crinkly red and pink crepe paper dianthus and carnations. A couple were still draped in faded bunting from Labor Day last fall. The Irish were getting a head-start on St. Paddy's Day with vitriolic green cardstock shamrocks.

"Any or every excuse to celebrate," my boss laughed. "Lord knows the town needs it. Valentine's the closest. But green beer at Marty's also has a certain appeal. Take your pick."

I did when I put my column together for the week. Shamrocks would keep until March.

Agonizing over what kind of flowers to give that special 'Someone' for Valentine's Day? The Internet can help crack the lovers' code for everything from roses to the lowly carnation.

Victorians especially were obsessed by the language of flowers. The 19th century writer Henry Ward Beecher wasn't nearly as particular. His essay, "Discourse on Flowers", claims that how we react to the gift of flowers is not just a matter of personal taste. Flowers elevate the material to a spiritual plane. Through them we connect with the sacred, from Creation to the Creator.

It's tough to go wrong with cosmic faith in the power of a mixed bouquet. My advice is a lot simpler. Just go for it!

My column went on to list some of the most common cut flowers and what they represent in courtships past and present. Handy research, I told myself. Certainly not a waste if I decided to stock some cut floral arrangements at the nursery this season. The choice of all-occasion bouquets down at the grocery were nonexistent.

On a personal note, I enjoyed an early valentine in the form of the snowdrops flowering in the rapidly melting banks on the sunny side of the courthouse. I had lost track of the date. My trucker friend Artie was back from the road, early. As I got within sight of the homestead, I saw him standing with Anise on the front sidewalk.

A rock, that man. Their conversation appeared so animated, they didn't even see me coming. In my driveway sat my new tenant's wreck of an Impala. Anise was laughing, head thrown back and giving herself to the moment. It never occurred to me before, how similar from a distance my shaggy salt-and-pepper hairstyle appeared to hers—apart from that unmistakable blaze of coppery red.

"I see you two have met," I said.

My friend Artie grinned, then pulled me into an awkward hug. I felt the burly strength I had come to depend on, the rasp of his black and red woodsman's jacket against my hands.

"Good for you, girl!" his broad, open face smiled down at me. "You finally got yourself some company rattling around in this old barn of a house of yours."

With Artie, what you saw, you got. Before I could react myself, he went to the rescue of Anise, who had her arms wrapped around an unwieldy black garbage bag doubling for a suitcase.

"Moving in," she apologized, anxiously scanning my face. "Your

36

friend Artie just dug out my pitiful excuse for a ride and dragged it over here."

"Nothin' to it," he grinned. "A hundred-fifty-thousand miles is nothing for a car like that—can't kill 'em if you whack 'em with a stick. Just say the word and I'll try to get that bucket of bolts up and running again. Can't have you skating around on icy sidewalks. A bad idea with your little one on the way."

Anise flushed and dropped her gaze. "Nice, but I'm fine, Artie. Really, I can manage."

"No 'buts' about it," he told her. "In a family way and all, you shouldn't be hauling all that stuff."

Shivering in her jeans and the blouse I had loaned her, whatever Anise thought of his gruff and outspoken attempt at nurturing, she gave up and went. I had half a mind to join her. My shoes weren't taking kindly to the rising tide of slush in the front yard. Artie's bulldog frown stopped me.

"It'll be like Florida around here before the day is out," he said, "then another bout of freezing rain blowing through. Sounds like we should be worried about the berm."

I remembered our leader Bea's grim prognosis for our daisies, even the hardier Arctic varieties. "We dug in snow fencing to hold the drifts around the more vulnerable plantings," I said. "Other than that, Bea said there isn't much we can do."

Artie listened, his jowled and beefy face stern and anxious. "And the peonies?"

I could have hugged the man. *Artie the Teamster*, Adam and I had affectionately called him. I couldn't imagine what I would have done the past year without him. It amused the Gang Green no end that the gaudiest, most extravagant blooms in the garden had become the trucker's personal favorite, ants and all.

"Peonies are tougher than they look once they get going," I said.

"But still, I would hate to see us lose 'em," he shifted from foot to foot as if suddenly impatient to get on the road.

"We can always replace them from the stock at the nursery if we have to. Not ideal, of course."

"I've been thinking about that. If those snowbanks keep shrinking, the customer lot at Groft's should be a heck of a lot clearer by the weekend. Maybe it'd be a good time for us to reconnoiter out there. We've got a truck chock full of bulbs and lilies headed our way one of these days. Seems to me we better have a plan."

37

The Easter shipment. I had been suppressing it. When the spring wholesale order forms had hit us late fall, the priority was how to shut down the nursery for the season. In desperation, I simply rubber-stamped a repeat of Adam's plant orders from the previous year. Given where the economy was headed, that was probably a big mistake.

"No point in turning on the gas until we have to," I speculated out loud. "We don't want to be heating the whole neighborhood out there."

"Best, though, to make sure it's working. Viv's been checking online about sprout times. If the shipment of lilies is late, we still gotta think about setting out those annuals and veggies in their starter pots. Green as all of us are at this, it just might take a while . . . "

The lilies weren't the only things that had slipped my mind. "Oh m' gosh, Artie, I forgot to tell you—at least reinforcements are on the way. Dave Fetters called, ready and willing to sign on for another season as greenhouse manager once the semester ends."

For the first time this year, staffing the place fell square on my shoulders. Last year our seasoned greenhouse manager Dave Fetters had finally picked up on Adam's prodding and had started a degree program in horticulture downstate. The good news was that in June he would be back at Groft's fulltime. But that was then and this was now. Apart from Dave's occasional weekend trips to check out how things were going, it would be up to me or the crew to organize most of the planting this season.

The numbers were staggering. Filling the now barren main propagation house with healthy seedlings—some hundred-twenty-thousand herbs, annuals and perennials—would stretch our pieced-together team to the limits.

"Oh, and when Dave asked about where things stood, I said that from the road I think I spotted a few missing windows in the retail house."

Artie had the look of a man mentally rolling up his sleeves. "Not to worry, kiddo. Dutch always said we might get some breakage even in the best of years. Easy enough for me to fix."

Dutch. For the first time since his passing, I heard my old friend's name without a dull ache of sorrow building inside me. There was something funny, impossible and wonderful about Artie trying to step in to those worn and faithful work boots.

"So if we can get in there and take a look by the weekend," I said, "would Viv want to join us?"

"Dunno," Artie shook his head. "Her sciatica really kicked up again when I was on the road. I keep telling her to let the snow sit—just wait for me to get back with the plow. But you know Viv. Sitting around waiting for spring isn't her style. You should see the grow lights she's got set up all over the cellar rooting those herbs of hers."

It never occurred to me my friends might be facing struggles with their own mortality. "Give her my best," I said quickly. "I'll try to get over to see her this afternoon. That is, if George and I ever put the blasted Valentine issue to bed."

"She'd like that," Artie called out over his shoulder as he half-skated, half-sprinted his way to his truck.

The walkway felt so slick, I picked my way a lot more cautiously toward the front porch. *Not good with my new boarder's center of gravity changing by the day*, I thought, *a lawsuit waiting to happen*. At the risk of trashing my entryway floor even more than I already had, it was time to break out more sand.

For a split-second after the heavy leaded-glass and oak door swung shut behind me, I thought I had blundered into the wrong house. The smell of lemon polish was overpowering. A vacuum cleaner I didn't even remember owning had appeared mysteriously in the living room, plugged in at the ready. On my dining room table sat a gigantic box, stuffed to bulging with file folders that most definitely hadn't been there before. A second one slightly less obese stood alongside it, identified in inch-high letters, Final Drafts.

"You've been cleaning," I said.

Anise looked very pleased with herself. "Sorry about the mess. . ."

"I thought about grabbing my cell to report a home invasion."

"Mostly filing, so far. But I have plans."

Quickly shedding my coat, I helped her maneuver the awkward storage containers over to the window seat. Close up, I could see that the tight-packed documents were labeled boldly with black permanent marker in that same assertive hand. *Under the End Table. Dining Room Left-Front Corner.*

"Interesting filing system," I said.

"Those empty banker's boxes were in the attic. It was tough going without dates, but at least I was able to keep the drafts separate, I think."

"Wow!"

"Not yet. Give me another hour."

"Well, the place sure doesn't looks like a recycling center any more. I've got to hand it to you."

Right then and there, I vowed it was time to clean house, metaphorically speaking, on other fronts as well. On the way home from the print shop late afternoon, I stopped by Vivian's as promised. Artie was hunched out in the side-yard, using a feudal-looking chopper to excavate a stubborn patch of ice that had built up under one of the down-spouts.

"You *could* just let it melt," I called out to him as I shut the car door behind me. "It's supposed to get up in the high forties again tomorrow."

"Viv was worried the melt 'n freeze would smother this bed of herbs. And she shouldn't be out here. Told her so, flat out."

"She's in bed, then?"

"Kitchen."

I found my friend ensconced at the table in an oversized beige and burgundy bathrobe stamped with a vintage fifties print, from the look of it, Artie's. A heating pad cord snaked upward from her chair to an outlet positioned mid-wall. This wasn't the meticulous Viv I knew, whose wardrobe consisted of nothing but pleated slacks, iron-only blouses and cardigans for every conceivable climate condition. A wisp of hair had strayed from her otherwise tidy up-do. Her delicate features had taken on an ashen pallor. *Hurting*, that much was certain.

Despite my protests, she insisted on limping from stove to cupboard organizing steaming hot cups of homemade rose hip tea from her garden. She spread her whole grain muffins thick with butter and her incredible lemon balm jelly.

Herbs were Vivian's passion, a carryover from her days as a school counselor when she had lined her windowsills with pot after pot of fragrant tarragon, basil and parsley. *Therapeutic*, she said, *in more ways than one.* Slips and roots from her carefully tended beds even had begun to take up residence in what had once been my grandmother's veggie garden. Hers was a living gift and consummate mark of friendship, something only another gardener would understand and treasure.

Outside the kitchen window we could hear Artie patiently chipping away at the ice, mindful of the vulnerable greenery slumbering below. I still found it difficult to imagine the two of them together, the outspoken union trucker and the reserved former school counselor. But then I could only rejoice in the genuine affection I saw springing up between them.

"He's hard at it out there," I said.

Vivian flushed. "That man wants to treat me like I'm made of glass. I'll admit sciatica is no picnic, but—"

"I should have come over, Viv . . . should have asked if you needed help. Something."

"All of us on the garden crew have been holing up like marmots since New Year's. Bea called a while back, asking if I'd seen you. But then she dropped off the radar herself. And you certainly have had every excuse, with that new tenant and all. If anybody should be apologizing it's me, parked here cooking my backside."

The teakettle had begun to groan softly, a shuddering protest. When Vivian stood up to deal with it, I noticed her face twist momentarily with the effort. Head bowed and her two hands braced against the edge of the counter, she went through a cautious series of stretches before she rejoined me at the table.

"You okay?" I said.

"Comes and goes. But if I don't stand up once in a while, stretch out those muscles, I'm going to turn into a human pretzel."

"Well, I'm not sure what *my* excuse for hiding out has been. Even my long-suffering boss is starting to get disgusted."

Vivian studied my face, her own an open book. "It takes time to grieve," she said softly.

More than time, I thought. As a young woman Vivian had lost a fiancé in some distant conflict, its purpose and outcome obscured by the decades. Close as she and Artie had become, something in her still remembered as though it were yesterday.

"I honestly thought when I got all those feelings out on paper last year, the worst would be over," I said. "And then I finished *Time* . . . at least as good as it was going to get. There they sat, all those manuscript pages. Only instead of relief, I felt like someone had pulled an electric cord out of the wall. Some days even getting out of bed seemed more than I could—"

"Post-partum blues, Eve. It happens. When I was still working for the district down-state, I used to get that way every June after the school year ended."

I felt an eyebrow arch. "Time off from all those over-medicated adolescents? I probably would have run for the exits."

"You would certainly think so. But badly as I needed a break, those kids and all their angst left a hole in my life that no amount of peace and quiet could fill. . ."

Her voice quavered and fell still. Viv rarely expressed regrets on the subject of marriage or motherhood. It never occurred to me that her relationship with Artie might be causing her to rethink the choices that brought her to this point.

"Right now, just getting a good night's sleep would help," I told her. "The parade of horribles is endless. What's going to happen with Groft's . . . when do I open out there for the season, if ever? I have no idea at all what to do about Adam's cottage. And don't even get me started about our garden at the berm. We've lost so many of us. How are we ever going to keep *that* going"

"I was worried about that myself," Vivian said. "Every time I haul out the heating pad it hits home. None of us are getting any younger."

Vivian and my ages were only a year apart and our birthdays fell within weeks of each other's. I realized with a shock that though I had been looking, I hadn't been truly seeing. Sometime in the past few months my friend, too, had begun to let her hair go natural. Her usual sandy blond was streaked with shades of silvery gray.

Time was passing. Like that teakettle my friend left too long on the boil, a thought had begun to simmer away in my skull. Without claiming a great deal of credit for it, the cast of characters in my story appeared to have been growing.

"You're right," I said slowly. "Okay, so we've got to work smarter not harder. We need to put some fresh blood to work."

"In *Xenaphon*?"

"For starters. There's my boarder, Anise—you're going to like her, by the way. She's having a baby in June, but after that she's fair game. From the look of it, the new priest at Peace Episcopal could stand some sun. Or take George, my boss . . . he's no spring chicken, but he's down on his knees every day with a camera in hand. Why not hand him a trowel on the berm? "

"I suppose there's always my neighbor's boy, " she sighed, "around fifteen and working off his community service. He's had a tough road, that kid. Since he landed on Bea's caseload, she's been ready to throw up her hands. Somebody has to be pretty desperate to haul off that huge concrete chicken sitting in the side yard of the ag co-op and plant it on the courthouse lawn."

"Sounds resourceful to me. It's gotta weigh—what?—five hundred pounds."

"At least," Viv chuckled, shook her head. "I've had to restrain Artie from intervening, even taking the kid under his wing. Though I imagine he doesn't know a weed from a hydrangea."

I half-smiled, remembering Adam's first day on the berm with his Rolex and out-of-the-box work boots. "You never know," I said. "If Artie's right and that truckload of daffs and lilies shows up anytime soon, beggars can't be choosers. After carting off a dinosaur of a chicken, schlepping those heavy flats sounds right up the kid's alley—better than leaving it to either one of us."

"Don't count me out. I can always plant myself on the front stoop in a lawn chair at Groft's and play traffic control."

"You just worry about getting better."

Vivian shifted in her chair, felt a twinge but straightened anyway. "And you need to *stop*—worrying, that is. You aren't alone in all of this. Give us our marching orders and somehow the bunch of us will help haul in all that greenery when it shows up. *The moving it out again* . . . sorry, that *is* your department."

My nonexistent marketing plan. Procrastination only carries a guy so far in this world.

"Slavedriver," my frown was pure theater and Viv knew it. "You want tough, you got it! Groft's. Friday. Nine sharp."

"Now that sounds like the Eve Brennerman I know and love," she said.

It was my turn to wince. "Ouch. Has it really been that long?"

My friend just smiled. "Nobody's counting."

At least chronic insomnia was good for something. I spent the next couple of nights drawing up a tentative marketing strategy through Mother's Day, complete with drafts of a fair number of space ads, radio spots and flyers to post around town where gardeners were likely to congregate.

On Friday, the crew showed up at Groft's ready for a weekend of housecleaning. While Artie messed around outside reconnecting the water and plumbing he had drained in fall to keep them from freezing, Vivian and I straightened up in the office, dusted and restocked the tight-crammed shelves in the sales room. Anise insisted on joining us, though I balked at assigning her to the cleaning crew in her condition.

"Fumes," I told her, "chemicals that would peel the paint off a barn. All of it toxic and none of it good for man or beast."

My tone left no room for argument. Instead, baby bump and all, she maneuvered her way through the narrow greenhouse aisles with a clipboard and checklist, on the lookout for broken glass, rusted out pipe and wood rot on the potting benches.

43

"I must look like the QE-III trying to navigate in a bathtub," she grumbled as she turned in her legal pad full of notes.

"A navy man myself," Artie winked. "We'll have this place shipshape in no time."

The to-do list was not as bad as I had feared. For watering we still relied on simple manual nozzles hooked to hoses suspended overhead the full length of the greenhouses. From Artie's test run, there seemed to be few leaks or problems there. Outside of several missing windows in one of the propagation houses, the three vintage Dutch-roofed greenhouses survived the winter intact—each of them twenty-two by ninety-six feet, sheltered only by fragile white-washed panes overhead.

Before Adam died, he had installed safety glass and converted the manual ventilation mechanism for the main propagation house to an automatic thermal-sensitive system. At least that took some of the guesswork and risk out of managing consistent heat levels, as long as the sensors were functioning. A heating system installed under the propagation tables made it still easier to hold a steady sixty-five to seventy degrees in the beds.

Groft's second propagation house was and had been moth-balled for several seasons even before Adam took over the nursery operation. That left the third hothouse—the one we used for bulbs, annuals and perennials purchased from other growers. Like the unused propagation house, it still depended on a chain-and-pulley manual venting system to keep temperatures from shooting up to dangerous levels.

"Cheap enough to operate," Adam told me once, "if the staff does its job and opens those vents."

There wasn't much room for error. Temperatures could spike under all that glass in less than fifteen minutes and fry the entire inventory before we even knew what hit us. *Every nursery operator's worst nightmare*, Adam always said. With the retail space and office attached to the second operational greenhouse, temperature regulation was job number one for the sales staff every morning.

Before I knew he was gone, Artie drove into town the minute high school classes let out for the day. He came back with our latest recruit, Vivian's neighbor. When I learned the teen was on probation, my instinct was to suspend judgment. That was before I found myself face to face with a gangly adolescent with a buzz cut, nose ring and a tattoo of a chain link fence running around the base of his skull. *What on earth was Artie thinking?*

"C.C.," I guessed, forced a smile. "As in CC-Rider?"

Our young felon stared sullenly at his shoes. "Never heard of the dude," he mumbled. "Ya grow any weed out here?"

Artie shot him a look. "I heard the bailiff over at the courthouse call out Christopher Charles Demort loud and clear," he said. "And if you're hell bent on pursuing this sorry excuse for a crime spree of yours, you're likely to wind up 'deh mort' for real, as in D-E-A-D."

That finally drew a protest. "You *ratted me out.* She knows about the bird!"

I did, but it was important to hear it from him. The kid seemed genuinely embarrassed. I took that as grounds for hope.

"Impressive, making off with a ten-foot mascot on Main Street in broad daylight," I said. "That rooster in front of the co-op must weigh a ton."

"You're right there. So I borrowed . . . "

Silence. CC caught Artie's raised eyebrow, revised his choice of vocabulary. "So, when I took . . . *stole* Artie's . . . Mr. Wilker's truck, I made sure it had a winch."

The felonies were compounding as we spoke. "Not the smartest thing in the world."

"What can I say? The kid sure has more guts than brains,"Artie shrugged. "Bea got social services into the act, talked me into telling that to the judge. So our bandito here drew two years of probation instead of—"

"That Nazi of a judge says I gotta finish high school."

"Talk sense, kid," Artie growled. "A diploma sure as hell beats hanging out at the mini-mart with those other low-life bobble-heads. Or running down alleys with spray cans and words on the wall you can't even spell. Going nowhere . . . !"

CC just looked at him. His jaw dropped, clamped tight again.

"So, *Chris,*" I said, "what do you know about plants?"

Not much as it turns out, but until closing time I set him to filling environmentally friendly peat cell packs with pearlite-laced peat, seeds and an infusion of starter fertilizer. Progress was painfully slow, mainly the parsleys and a few of the other seed-based herbs. I had hopes that after a Saturday on the job, the kid would start to get the hang of it and work his way to the annuals.

Plans change. I had barely opened up the nursery office Saturday morning when I heard an ominous rumbling coming from the direction of the parking lot. Incredulous, I looked out the front window to see this monster of a truck inching its way around the potholes. On the run, Artie popped into the office long enough to shout the alarm.

"Bulbs!" he said. The rest was unprintable.

Greenhouse profits are calculated by income per square foot. *When in doubt*, Adam once told me, *we need to think flowers.* Blooming things are a luxury, veggies a necessity. Anything edible always commands less of a price than annuals and perennials in the retail market. By the time we finished unloading our share of stock on that semi, not a single square inch of bench space in the seasonal greenhouse would go to waste.

I grabbed my cell and put out a 'Mayday' to Viv and Anise. While Artie and young Chris helped the driver unload, Viv and I blitzed potting the herbs in the propagation house. With the same efficient enthusiasm she showed sorting through the mountains of manuscripts in my living and dining rooms, Anise orchestrated placement of the incoming flats of bulbs.

Born gardeners, I smiled. *The lot of them.*

The whole business went a lot quicker than I thought. To celebrate, Artie hauled out the ladder and took down the Closed for the Season sign. A scant half-hour later a half-dozen customers showed up. They were just local moms with toddlers in tow, out trolling for a field trip. The cash outlay was nonexistent, but the visitors made up for it with oooh's and aah's at all those bulbs budding and blooming out there in Greenhouse A.

I sprang for pizza for the crew. Let whatever winter lay ahead do its worst, within that glass-domed sanctuary we basked in the subtle colors of spring. Vivid pinks nestled alongside pristine whites, buttercup yellows and regal purples. Groft's was ready for another season.

"No shit," Chris said. "We did it."

I couldn't have expressed it better myself. In bed by eight o'clock, for once I didn't have to worry about insomnia. I nodded off working on my electronic journal and didn't stir again until sunlight woke me. Still lying on the bedspread alongside me where I had left it, the computer was hibernating, but sprang to life with a simple touch.

My words still spoke to me as I had written them:

How miraculous are the random acts of kindness a garden can inspire. Plants were sitting out in the cold at the nursery. Viv's sciatica was acting up. Anise was green in the face from morning sickness. Artie was the lone man

46

in the crew. I wouldn't have believed it, but even our Bad Boy Chris sensed how vulnerable the tiny seedlings were and got into the spirit of things. He may have been muttering under his breath, but he did what had to be done, hauling flat after flat to safety on the pallets in the greenhouses.

I was witnessing stealth charity as impulsive as breathing. Together we saw a need. We met it.

Chris and his Cheshire-grin when we were finished pretty much said it all. It was the same feeling I got when I passed my neighbor's weed-choked beds that summer she had a hip replacement. It felt good in almost a wicked sort of way to reach down and blitz a couple of square feet of neglected earth for her, then move on again. To be there when it counted.

At the bed in front of the public library, something always needs deadheading. A guy can stand there and fuss that somebody isn't doing their job. It creates far less frown lines and only takes a split-second to stoop down and pinch back the worst offenders.

The more I've turned inward since Adam has been gone, the less I seem to have recognized those ah-ha moments around me. It is so tempting with our personal pain so real and close to wait for the grand gesture to turn our lives around. Still, those precious inches, feet and hands of unsung generosity add up. Everybody wins.

Life appears to be flowing back into my world with precious little help from me except for the sense to acknowledge it when I see it. There stands Anise in my kitchen, baking out her loneliness one tray of muffins at a time. Vivian aches with every step, but insists on brewing up friendship in the form of her home-grown rose hip tea.

When I reread Job last week, I couldn't get beyond my sense of anger at the Hollywood ending. The reward for the man's hard-headed faithfulness was to magically replicate everything he had lost. Hebraic scholars claim it apparently was intended as a metaphor. But in real-time, love is not interchangeable. Loss leaves holes in our hearts that sometimes nothing short of heaven can fill. Try as I will, mine aches at the thought.

February doesn't help. The world is turning on its axis. A formless breath of change is in the air— blowing me with it, ready or not.

Xenaphon's winter was by no means over, still the air felt different somehow—no longer that brittle chill like breathing in broken glass. Slowly but surely, something had begun to melt and thaw inside me as well.

Spring fever. Just an early case of spring fever.

Whatever it was, it seemed contagious. Artie showed up at the nursery next morning all restless determination. He was toting an odd assortment of lumber, pipe, metal track and a couple of over-sized crank handles.

"An invention," he enthused, "just in time for planting. Gonna convert that middle section of the propagation house into a rolling bench."

"Rolling. Exactly where . . . and *why?"*

Artie's voice took on the weary patience of a math teacher explaining multiplication tables to a particularly dense fourth grader. "More room for flats," he said. "Right now we got two aisles eating up space. A waste, when we only need one aisle at a time to get at the plants. If we can shift the center potting bench from side to side, I could make the whole darn bench two-foot wider. Two-foot by a hundred-foot long equals one heck of a lot more pots as I see it."

Made sense, I had to admit. By 10 A.M., Bea had weighed in over the phone with ideas of her own. She and Viv had talked about a clean-up at the berm for late March or early April. It seems Viv already had filled her in about Artie's plans for Groft's potting benches.

"If Artie's right, Groft's could have quite a few seedlings left over," Bea speculated. "Handy for filling in whatever froze out over the winter on the berm."

Lost dollar signs flashed through my head. Still, it was a relief to know all our work wouldn't be wasted, one way or the other.

I didn't have long to dwell on it. Shortly before noon, my boss, George, tracked me down at the nursery. The man seemed more upbeat than I had seen him in months. Camera around his neck, he had supplemented his usual turtleneck with a heavy, hunter-red fleece jacket. Over both he had buttoned an army-green photographer's vest. Its pockets bulged alarmingly with strange widgets, filters and extra memory sticks.

"Going somewhere?" I said.

"Cabin fever. I locked up the shop and left a sign on the door. There's a publishers' conference downstate. I hadn't planned on going, but what the heck. I leave the place in your very capable hands."

"A lot of paparazzis plan to cover the events down there—or just you?"

"Very funny. If the weather holds on the way back, I thought I might spend a couple of hours chasing lighthouses along the Michigan shore."

"Just don't slide off any of those break walls, George. Remember what happened to Bill Deutscher when he joined the Polar Bear club. . . "

The *Gazette* ran a two-inch story—front page—after their New Year plunge. Although most of them now were in their fifties or sixties, it was their newest and youngest member by a good two decades who had wound up in the hospital with pneumonia. Darn near died, from all reports.

My boss just grinned. "Nice try. But you can't get rid of me that easily, Evie girl!"

The historic St. Joseph Harbor and Pier lights were located in that general vicinity, both a must-see for lighthouse fans. Every calendar in the state boasted at least one shot of the St. Joseph break wall thrusting the length of three football fields into Lake Michigan. If a photographer caught the narrow cement walkway just right mid-winter, thick curtains of icicles shrouded the ironwork and arching antique light fixtures. Wave after wave breaking overhead doused the entire structure in half-frozen foam.

I never experienced the sight myself. But ever since a reader's spectacular grab shot had taken first prize in the *Gazette*'s annual Northern Michigan Resort Country Photo Contest, George had been vowing to try to duplicate it. I wished him luck, asked Artie to cover for me at Groft's and headed downtown.

Life, it seems, still had the power to surprise. Valentine's Day I was on desk duty at the print shop. George hadn't come back from his junket south. Mid-afternoon I heard a sizeable truck maneuvering out front. We weren't expecting a delivery.

I looked up to see a burly UPS driver headed our way. In his arms he balanced a huge carton. He was breathing hard by the time he came back frowning over the inventory screen on his mini-computer.

"You have to sign here," he said.

"I assume this is for George—"

"Eve. Eve Brennerman."

"You got me." I took the pen, signed off on the screen. "Though how you caught me here, I can't imagine."

The driver shook his head. "You are one very interesting lady to find. The GPS misplaced Gratiot Street. Some guy at the mini-mart said most likely you'd be here anyway."

A couple of deft maneuvers with the box cutter took care of the carton. Inside, I found a gigantic tower-style food basket. Three staggered-size wicker boxes spilled over with an orgy of foil wrapped truffles, rum-flavored hot cocoa in a tin, espresso beans dipped in dark chocolate, white chocolate biscotti and a package of chocolate-crunch swizzle sticks. The entire pyramid was swaddled in wide, gauzy lilac ribbon.

"*Holy smokes*," I breathed. "How am I supposed to eat all that?"

"Not my problem, lady. I just deliver 'em."

I offered to share one of the truffles. The delivery man politely declined.

"Trust me. If I were you, I'd leave the thing in one piece until you get home," he said.

The card read, "Indulge yourself, Mom. You deserve it!"

It bore the names of both my girls and their families. The afterthought had to be Emma or Justin's doing. "Be our Valentine, G-ma."

My two oldest grandchildren were now a worldly-wise six, born within months of each other. Their loving postscript conjured up memories of generations of shoe boxes decked out with sheets of red construction paper and strewn with lacy snowflake doilies and pink paper hearts. Had I ever been so young?

My throat felt tight. Here stood a chance to pack on more calories than I could hope to tally without a calculator. Even in my prime I wouldn't have indulged in this kind of wanton hedonism.

I shut the shop early, left the answering machine in charge. The only foot traffic on Main Street consisted of desperation shoppers headed for the drug store. I suspect they were checking out the Valentine cards and the depleted display of impulse gifts. With some difficulty, I managed to schlep the Chocolate Decadence Tower home on foot.

It was five before Anise got home from her shift at Groft's. The

Chocolate Decadence Tower still sat unopened where I had left it, on the kitchen table.

"*Zowza*," she said with a low whistle.

"I thought so, too."

"A secret admirer? Or just George's idea of penance for working you to death!"

"My daughters, go figure. What say we indulge ourselves?"

"Trust me, the calorie count sitting on that table is way beyond indulge. I'd say it qualifies as 'orgy'. Is this a fluke or some regular thing that they—?"

"Actually, I was expecting something more along the lines of a derma-braiser or a book on Zen gardens."

"A hint then," Anise laughed. "As in c'mon, Mom. Live it up a little."

"Now that *would* be a first. What say we go hog wild—rent us some incredibly schlocky chick-flix from the mini-mart. After dinner, we can work ourselves into a major sugar high. That baby of yours will love it."

Anise winced. "Would you believe, Marty's is booked *solid* for their three-course *Hearts and Flowers* special. The bar, the restaurant and everything in between. Nobody *ever* makes a reservation down there. I dropped off a resume on the way home from the nursery. The second one in as many weeks. The owner handed me an apron and order pad on the spot."

"You start tonight? You already put in a full shift."

"A job's a job. Gotta take it when it comes. One of the wait-staff is out sick, but maybe with any kind of luck, Marty's will decide they can't do without me . . . "

She was holding the apron and Marty's punk-logo tee in one hand. With the other, she snagged a truffle from the top tier of the tower. The bright red foil crackled as she unwrapped it.

"M-M-Mhhhm . . . ," her eyes closed as her taste buds made contact with the mousse-like center.

"You're going to be dead on your feet."

Anise shrugged. "C'est la vie."

"At least put your feet up and—"

"I've got twenty minutes. It's going to take that long to squeeze into that goofy X-X-L shirt. I'm going to look like a graffiti-covered water-tower!"

51

I laughed. "You can thank one of the owner's teenage grandkids for that spray-can art. I've been watching the lettering that shows up on walls and road signs around here. So far, no match."

"Just so I see a signature on a paycheck every week—I'm good!"

It doesn't take long for someone to make the rounds of the employers in Xenaphon with a stack of resumes. Still, this had to be some kind of a record on Anise's part.

"Are you sure hauling heavy trays and crockery is a good idea?"

"In my condition, you mean. I'm preggers, not *dead*. Dead tired maybe, but still breathing. Right now I'm more worried about what could happen smelling all that carb-laden home-cooking twenty-four-seven. As is, I'll be thinking *biscotti* all night."

"So much for a Girls' Night In."

"I won't guarantee I can keep my eyes open for a whole flick. But you have yourself a date."

I did. And it was for Valentine's Day, no less.

In the interim, I had some serious thanking to do. Juggling the limits on phone plans with the reality of families scattered across the time zones makes it impossible to call anybody any more. I dialed my oldest. On the far side of Lake Michigan, she's on Central Standard. I caught Leslie in the car on the way home to her suburb north of Chicago.

"Gotta talk fast," she said. "I ran over my minutes last month. Hope something isn't—"

"I'm fine. Just wanted to tell you I got the Valentine and—"

"You hated it."

"How can somebody hate anything that sinful. Ridiculous, given what my scale tells me. But wonderful."

"Thank goodness. I had my doubts. But Gina prevailed."

"She's next on my to-call list. Anyway, say Hi to Emma. Are you and Dan doing anything special?"

"Poor guy hasn't had an interview in two weeks. It's been pretty grim around our place—but yeah, he says Valentine's Day is non-negotiable. If worse comes to worst, we'll hang out at Mickey-D's."

"You shouldn't have splurged on me like—"

"Yes. We should and did. I'm really glad you like it."

Her minutes, I had forgotten. The clock was ticking. "I better let you go."

"I'll call again soon . . . really, I will. We love you, Mom."

"Me, too," I said. "Very much."

Arizona is the only state in the union that chooses in its entirety not to go on Daylight Savings Time. Regardless of the season, I forget whether the difference is two or three hours from my own Eastern Standard. But then I have no idea either whether it's Pacific or Mountain time, though I've googled the online map repeatedly. From the speed at which Gina picked up, I guessed I caught her at work.

"Mom, just got out of a meeting. What's up?"

"Senile, obviously," I said. "What time *is* it out there anyway? I just wanted to thank you for the goodies."

"Glad you liked 'em. I know half the world is on a diet. What a bummer to cross chocolate permanently off our lists."

"My thought exactly."

"Planning anything special, Mom?"

"Besides a total pig-out, you mean?" I shared what Anise and I had on the burner for the evening.

The pause was subtle but I caught it. "How's that working out for you—having somebody in the house all the time?"

"Good. Great, actually."

"She, Anise, is still unemployed, I gather. Tough in this economy."

"She's working on it, waiting tables for now. Actually the woman has great skills. I keep telling her to go into business for herself. She has baked so much for me, I may have to invest in a new freezer."

"Didn't you . . . I thought Leslie told me she's a writer or something like that."

Gina's not-so-subtle poking around the edges of my new living arrangements wasn't lost on me. Clearly my girls had been talking.

"Anise was an in-house publication editor for an auto-parts distributor."

"The same kind of thing you used to do in Chicago?"

"I hadn't thought about it that way, but yeah." I hesitated, drew a deep breath. "You're concerned."

"Yes . . . no . . . not really. It's just that you didn't know her at all when she moved in. It's natural to worry somebody might—"

"Bludgeon me to death in my sleep."

"I was going to say, *take advantage*." Gina sounded hurt.

"I know you and your sister only want the best for me. What can I say except, *I'm fine*. Really. You would like her. Trust me, it's good not to be rattling around by myself in this huge place for a change."

"You know we would come more often if we could."

"I understand completely. You have your jobs and the kids. It's as it should be. Plus, air fare has been astronomical."

Gina hesitated. "You could fly down here, too, you know. Spend a couple of weeks, longer even. Justin would love someone to trounce at video games. I can't seem to get anything done after work. Will has been on the road a lot lately."

"I'm still working, too," I reminded her gently. "My boss is worried about losing the paper. Now is not a good time to go anywhere."

"Well, we miss you," my daughter said. "I hope you know that. And that you'll let us know if—"

"Anise makes off with the family silver," I laughed. "Trust me, I'm good. Missing you, too, of course. But otherwise, surviving."

I heard noises in the background and the sound of muffled voices. "Mom, sorry, I gotta go. We've got a major meltdown going here."

"No problem. I just wanted to thank you, let you know that you made my day."

"I'm glad. Leslie wasn't so sure."

"Well, you were right. Thank you. And please, don't worry. Call when you can."

"Will do."

My laptop was parked on the dining room table in Hibernation mode. I roused it and summoned up the entries for 'Time Zones'. A good half hour later, I key-stroked my gleanings into my journal:

> Time creeps toward the last syllable recorded about it and there's certainly a lot. I'm also vaguely alarmed that mouse-clicks in cyberspace are becoming my equivalent of J. Alfred Prufrock's coffee spoons. The measure of my days.
>
> Little did I know, but my googling enlightened me. There are a whopping twenty-five Time Zones worldwide. Russia has so many—eleven—that when the sun rises in one it sets in the other. What bizarre lengths we go to in order to keep our lives more or less in synch.
>
> And so while Xenaphon sleeps, the worldwide web becomes my portal to a twilight land of insomniacs and bored workers at their laptops somewhere on the far side of the globe, kids texting under their desks, people I don't know and will never meet. Two billion pairs of hands like mine reach out into the ether every day. A good 700

million live in Asia, another 400 million in Europe and half that number in North America.

Unusual, perhaps, for a grandmother to be obsessed with communication driven by bits and bytes, zeroes and ones. The average age for a computer junkie is twenty-eight, give or take a month.

I can understand why they call it 'the web'. The darn thing is addictive, lures you in before you know it. It occurs to me to wonder what would happen if the whole network came crashing down one night—like the hypothetical tree falling in the forest. The world of high finance might implode. Commerce could cease. X-rays would go unread. As the last leaf and branch would settle to earth, the silence would be profound. And here in Grandma Eva's bedroom, I would find myself left with only the neighbor's halogen porch light for company. Alone.

But not this particular Valentine's eve. And for that, I gave quiet thanks.

Anise got home at ten. Though she was limping, she was still determined to party. When I offered to rub her swollen ankles, with a grateful sigh, she accepted.

"I missed doing that for my daughters when they were pregnant," I told her, "except toward the end."

"Nice," she said as she picked out a truffle. The mugs of hot cocoa I served up were still too steamy to tackle.

"Did you finally get in touch with your girls?" she wondered.

"Yes. They're both fine."

In a matter of speaking. It both touched and bothered me to know that from afar my daughters were worried that I might be losing it. Hand-held devices with keypads can be sadly devoid of humanity—*hand-holding* a rare and priceless commodity. If Anise sensed how conflicted I was about my family's absence, she was too polite to say.

Aristotle, Plato or one of the other Greeks once said that all children are our children, all parents are our parents—and vice versa. I was beginning to understand what that meant. Anise was here. Through no fault of their own or mine, my children were half a continent away. We may have to struggle to get beyond DNA and love where and how we can, but sometimes in life that has to be enough. Hard, but enough.

Our rental movie was one of those British costume epics. Forget the love story. The cinematographer spent half the time indulging a personal love affair with flowering landscapes, not surprising coming from a nation of gardeners. I found myself shamelessly ogling rose arbors and cottage gardens. Eventually, I lost track of the plot altogether.

Delphinium shot upward like fireworks from the backs of the beds. Velvet-clad roses preened in rosy pastels among the greenery. I could almost feel the bare earth steaming under my feet. During the special features at the end, it came as a genuine shock to discover that nature in all its cinematic finery had a lot of help. For one of the most sensual and romantic scenes, shot in the mist and rain, the tech-crew had to spray paint the grass to cover up the sea of mud churned up by all the cameras and lighting equipment.

"Botox," Anise shrugged. "It's everywhere."

"How I would love to try that in my front yard! Spray cans of paint instead of fertilizer and weed killer. It'd be greener *and* cheaper."

"Wears off fast, though, I'll bet. I think I would hold out for laying sod."

"At what that stuff costs a square foot? I vote for green tinted cement."

Anise just shook her head. "Admit it, you'd go stir crazy without all that digging around in the dirt, watching stuff grow. You should see your face light up when you talk about gardening. Even from the little time I've spent at Groft's, I'm beginning to understand why it's so addictive. That green-woodsy smell in the greenhouse is something else. Positively primal."

I fought a smile. She, too, had caught the bug. Who would have thought it?

After we called it a night, I was far too wound up to sleep. My circuits on overload from all that sugar, I decided to feed the insatiable maw of my file on garden column ideas.

If you're like me these days—borderline desperate to get out in the garden—think inside the box. The computer, that is. At least 54 million "gardening" entries await you.

Best place to start is with the National Gardening Association. Their inspiration-packed website touts everything from edible landscapes to video clips about transplanting perennials. It is all good stuff that reassures us spring is coming.

The NGA reminds us that even our dark and moldy cellars can satisfy our urge to grow. With the simplest of layouts, it is possible to harvest mushrooms two to three times a month. Their seven to ten-day incubation period is as close to instant gratification as it gets.

The less direct sunlight the better. Just be careful how close the mushroom garden is placed to the furnace. To create humidity, try using garbage bags as a cover and a simple spray mister.

Anticipation can be another great cure for the winter blahs—as in, forcing forsythia in a pot on your dining room table. Now's also the time to start seedlings indoors. A modest investment in seeds, dirt matrix, peat pots and grow lights works quicker on the psyche than a supply of anti-depressants.

Just surfing the web itself taps into a whole world of winter-weary souls longing for the kind of earthy fellowship only a garden can give. Gardeners of the world, unite!

I had to chuckle, knew exactly what I was doing. It felt vaguely wicked to set some other cabin-fever-plagued gardener in Xenaphon on a wild hunt googling 'fungus'.

Before I packed it in for the night, I picked out an animated freebie E-card and sent it off to both my girls. Across the canvas of the computer screen and its simple Thank You, wherever the cursor clicked, flowers sprang into bloom. The sun rose and birds swooped across a rainbow sky. Whoever designed the card had used catchy sing-song children's tune for a sound track. It stayed in my head for days and it took me fully that long to resurrect the lyrics from among my childhood memories.

" . . . *how does your garden grow?* The answer was right there in front of me in the bleak Michigan mid-winter. Loneliness had become a choice to make. And it was mine and mine alone. Quietly and unbidden, their patience boundless, the faces of family and friends and community had been gathering to fill my emptiness.

Their expectations were simple. *Nothing in my hands I bring.* I just needed to show up, to be present for myself as well as them—simply *to let myself be loved* for healing to come. That wasn't a great deal to ask in the great scheme of things. Not much at all.

Four

Ashes of Roses

March is the stuff of manic-depression. What other month spends the entire time allotted to it fussing over lions and lambs? For Xenaphon, the month dawned gray and sullen. Lent was upon us.

Not quite sure how I got there, I found myself waiting in the aisle of the sanctuary at Peace Episcopal to receive the traditional Ash Wednesday blessing. Before and behind me waited a handful of my elderly neighbors—no strangers to life, any of us. Still, I wasn't prepared for the potent images roiling in my head.

Anger, guilt and regret. *Ashes of roses*. Roses and once again, roses.

Light years removed from the Biblical Job and his ash heap, but there it was, stuck in my memory. The epiphany comes early-on in Colleen McCullough's saga of lost love, *The Thornbirds*. Her heroine Maggie loves a duty-bound and ambitious young priest. Vulnerable and barely out of adolescence, she goes to meet him in a garden—radiant in a dress of pale and dusky pink, the color whimsically described as *ashes of roses*. At the sight of her in that dress, Father Ralph makes a fateful choice. He crushes his feelings for her underfoot like fragile petals ground into the hard-caked earth. The anger, guilt and regret begin, for both of them.

I too knew that unholy trinity well. More often than not, it revealed itself among my memories of Adam and our last days together.

"The warning signs were there," a persistent Greek chorus in my head kept telling me. *"You should have seen that heart attack coming."*

But then had Adam himself suspected and ignored it? It was futile to speculate. The results were always the same. He was gone without a word, in a heartbeat, leaving me to walk the garden alone as best I could.

"Dust you are," young Vicar Gaskill said.

And to dust you shall return. His gesture of absolution felt cool against my fevered forehead. Disoriented, as I turned to go, I came face to face with Adam and Eve in the Garden in luminous stained glass on the sidewall of the sanctuary.

I read somewhere that in Hebrew, Eden translates as "delight". And Grandmother Groft had caught those ephemeral moments in her sketches. Some unknown craftsman's hands translated them into glowing shards of glass. Oblivious to their naked vulnerability, the couple's radiant faces were young and beautiful, in love with life and each other. Their bare feet moved over a carpet of violets and primroses.

Like those first gardeners, our biblical namesakes, Adam and I too believed that it would never end. *But then dust you are and to dust you shall return.*

The artist of the Eden window in the sanctuary at Peace doesn't show the rest of the story, how at the gate to that Paradise, a flaming sword bars any hope of return. None of us goes living from this life. *No one.* But directly opposite from that glorious window in the sanctuary loomed another—of a grieving Mary seated at the empty tomb. We who survive are meant to live another day, to rise above the ruins of our lives. Forget how.

Unwittingly, I had embarked on a perilous spiritual journey in the slush and sleet of Lent. "Bloom," my wounded heart whispered in the silence. "I dare you to bloom."

The weather didn't help. March roared in tight-coiled like a predator at the height of its charge. No mercy here.

Unlike mushrooms, we need light to grow and Xenaphon's thick overcast had been dumping snow for days now, no end in sight. We were assailed by flakes, pellets, icy mix and hard-driving sheets of gritty, face-scouring white. The town and every access to it lay buried once again. Warnings of hazardous driving conditions dominated the weather channel.

Business was so slow at the print shop that George and I minded the store on alternate days. We turned the thermostat down to 62 to save on the heat bills. I layered a bulky wool ski sweater over thermal underwear to fend off the bone-numbing chill as I took my turn at the desk. The shop's phone had just rung, someone complaining about our pay-as-you-go obituary policy, when I heard the bell over the door-frame jangle.

A man in his forties strode toward the counter, tall and European-slender in his cashmere overcoat, well-cut dark pin-stripe suit and burgundy power tie. His salon haircut had 'outsider' stamped all over it. Except I knew that face. From the press release George shared about his son, those angular cheekbone and the pewter at the temples were unmistakable.

My mouth felt dry. I finished with the caller and hung up the phone. Visibly impatient, the man was looking through and around me. I tried to see the place through his critical eyes—shabby office furniture, stained and crumbling tile on the floor. Surplus stacks of bond and cardstock piled up on the shelving along the walls.

"George Herberg. I understand he works here."

I decided to go for it, forced a cheery smile. "You must be his son. Mark, right? George told me you might be stopping by."

"The name is Blandis," his tone was all business. "And you would be . . . ?"

"I answer to Eve. Eve Brennerman. I write the garden column, lay out the Classifieds and—"

"You're telling me, George is out."

"Publishers' conference. He won't be back in until tomorrow. But I'll be happy to tell him you—"

I found myself staring at the man's retreating back. A tub-ring of road salt marred the otherwise perfect shine of his black dress shoes.

"I'm sure he'll be happy to see you," I called out.

As lies went, mine was brazen, though forgivable. Mark Blandis paused, a leather-gloved hand on the antique brass door knob. He could have ignored me. Instead, he turned and made eye-contact.

"I sincerely doubt that, Ms. Brennerman."

Suddenly our local banker's business suit and ill humor of late made a great deal more sense. The community had been crackling with rumors of a new guy in town, guns at the ready and spoiling for a fight. Not in the mood to dodge questions on the subject at Marty's, I went home for lunch.

As it turns out, George got back early. Unexpectedly he stopped by the shop just before closing time. He listened without visible reaction to my tale of the encounter with his son.

"Brace yourself," he said.

60

"I suspect you'll be needing this."

Without fanfare I held out a flash drive containing the latest draft of my manuscript. On impulse I had picked the thing up on my lunch break. My boss just stared at the fragile USB stick, finally took it. I didn't have to tell him the contents or that I was giving him a year out of my life in electronic form.

"Eve, you can't imagine how much . . . you won't regret this."

I struggled to reserve judgment. "I took your advice. You'll notice how I tried to soften the edges in spots since your last read," I told him quickly. "But I need your help to take it the rest of the way. Feel free to chop and change . . . whatever works, do it. Main thing is, I don't want my daughters or friends to wake up and see themselves cannibalized for posterity."

"Understood. Have your girls read it?"

I shook my head. "Not yet."

"You'll want to do that . . . soon. I would never in a million years want this to drive a wedge between—"

"I know that, George. And it won't come to that, I can promise you. If you catch me metaphorically going over the edge, I trust you to pull me back."

A hint of a smile flickered at the corner of his mouth. "Evie, I appreciate the kind of courage it takes to share your journey. Given what could be coming, I can't say the same—haven't found it in myself to advertise the fact that Mark is my son."

"You have no reason to apologize for him or anything else. People know how much you have done for this town. Keeping a newspaper going these days is no easy business."

At that, I saw the emotions wash over his face, raw and out there for all to see. Shared deadlines were becoming our salvation when the ground underfoot was anything but steady. We kept going, pure and simple, because to stand still was no longer an option.

My boarder Anise wasn't letting any grass grow under her feet either. Her one-night Valentine's stint at Marty's quickly turned into a regular gig on their wait-staff.

"Starting right now," she announced. "I'm paying you rent. I also told Marty's if you need me at the nursery, Groft's comes first."

"I wasn't expecting that."

"Well, I was and am. You've already done so much. Payback time."

I didn't need the money, but for both our sakes I accepted. Anise needed—deserved—her pride. The news also was bound to reassure my girls. Whatever had motivated me to take in a boarder, Anise Gruin wasn't taking that hospitality for granted. But then she wasn't the only one entitled to ultimatums.

"They're giving you bennies?"

Anise shook her head. "Part-time and six months probation. My baby bump is pretty obvious and they've gotten cautious about turnover. I guess I can understand that."

"Well, insured or not, you are going to let me drag you and that 'baby bump' down to the walk-in clinic, *today*. It's long past time."

A giant in all but stature, Doc Wieland restored my faith in humanity. With one stroke of a pen while Anise was clambering up on the examining table, he discreetly scrawled Pro Bono on a sticky-pad affixed to the top of her patient chart.

"Portrait time," he announced after the usual poking and prodding. He was already hauling over the ultrasound equipment. "You're going to want to get yourself a baby book for these."

"Too expensive," she started to sit up, awkward on that narrow examining table. "I can't . . . won't let you do all this for nothing."

"Ah-h-h," he smiled, "but you see, your reputation precedes you, young lady. Who said anything about a 'freebie' here?"

Clicking his pen couple of times, he scrawled out an IOU on a prescription pad, and pressed into her hand before she could object. *Standing Order*, it read. *Elephant Ears. Streusel. Sticky Buns.*

"Sign it," he said.

Word travels fast. Although Anise hadn't graced the doors of the sanctuary at Peace with me once since her arrival, she had been baking like a fiend for coffee hours. Attendance blossomed and even the most curmudgeonly of the old timers who never stuck around after the service admitted they hadn't seen a spread like that at coffee hour in years. With the clinic the only game in town medically speaking, Doc Wieland would have been among the first to know who was responsible and why.

Anise clutched his scrip as if it were a winning lottery ticket. "You've got it," she said firmly, "fresh—every other morning."

"You want to give an old man hardening of the arteries?" he shook his head. "I'm on clinic duty Mondays and Fridays. Once a week is just fine, although by the time that baby of yours is knocking on the door, I'll be in Florida. For good this time. After that you'll be dealing with Doc

Jaidev. He's a youngster but top-notch. You'll like him. Plan is to live local, not a circuit-rider like me. I've noticed he has a major addiction to chocolate."

"I'll start him off with brownies then," she said. "Stuffed with cream cheese and dark cherry jelly."

With a twinkle in his eye, Doc pried his scrip out of her hand long enough to write, *Stuffed Brownies*. When his assistant wandered in to finish the ultrasound, Doc had her make a copy of the note and tacked it in Anise's patient file.

"We haven't had a population surge like this in ages," I said. "A new live-in doctor on the clinic staff. The guy must be a skier."

"Just learning, I'm told," Doc chuckled. "Good for the economy, his being here."

And meanwhile there *he* was—the newest addition to Xenaphon's population, baby male Gruin—in glorious black and white. As near as I could tell from the grainy image on the ultrasound monitor, he was doing cartwheels. I could have sworn the baby was smiling.

"Heartbeat loud and clear," the assistant said. Then she pointed out the identifiable body parts.

My eyes misted over watching Anise. Her face was transfixed by the fuzzy images. Doc's assistant printed a couple of the grainy photos for her to take home.

"So, now we don't have to keep talking about 'it' any more," Anise said. "He's Caleb."

"Biblical."

"Yeah, well," she flashed an embarrassed little smile. "I swiped a baby book from the church library last time I delivered the baked goods. Caleb is Hebrew for dog of all things—*Bulldog*, With what's out here waiting for the kid, I've got to hope it's on target. *Fearlessness in the face of impossible odds.* I like the sound of that. Caleb."

"So do I," I said.

If she had anything to do with what her son became, the name was bound to fit. Within days of hiring on at Marty's, Anise also had talked them into adding her homemade cinnamon rolls to their breakfast menu. The *Gazette* was running ads for her fresh-made desserts on weekends.

In her own quiet, chin-squared way, Anise Gruin was making her presence in Xenaphon felt. She was becoming one of us.

Except for the blizzards. My heart went out to her, lying wide awake in her room down the hall as a whole series of fronts came through.

63

The homestead creaked and groaned and shook in the gusting wind. One last four-inch blanket of white stuff settled heavily over the landscape.

When morning showed no signs of a respite, I got up, scraped off the windshield and drove out to Groft's. There was no sign of storm damage, except to our cash flow. Nobody was going out who didn't have to. The roads and our sales counter were deserted.

In a Nor'easter of a mood myself, I checked in at the print shop over the noon hour to mess with the Classifieds, all the while wishing I were in Arizona. My boss came back from lunch blowing on his ungloved hands.

"You never told me Anise is working down at Marty's," he frowned.

"Since Valentine's Day. But then you've been out of the loop, clambering over every frozen breakwall between Ludington and Grand Rapids with that camera of yours. The whole town is talking about the additions to Marty's dessert menu. I hope you tried something."

"No, but I slipped her a heck of a tip . . . not enough, considering."

"What's this all about, George?"

"I just met my son for lunch. Stick to public places if you're expecting a scene. No bloodshed. Except, unfortunately, Mark's Big City expectations about service don't exactly cut it in Xenaphon."

"Anise is tough. If she was on the receiving end, I doubt much fazes her."

"I have to hand it to the woman, she certainly gave as good as she got. *It may seem like we're still living in the trees around here*, her exact words, *but then I'm sure with 'bottom lines' your business and all, you can appreciate we don't exactly get a lot of call for lattes with a double shot of espresso. If you plan on staying a while, I'm sure the boss might rethink his business plan.*"

"Okay-y-y . . . !"

George drew in a thoughtful breath. "I thought I actually saw the man blush."

"Glad I wasn't in the line of fire. Though I'm not sure you can say the same."

"Could have been worse," he shrugged. "I spent way too much of the time dodging my son's attempts to grill me about who is who around here. But at least we're speaking. Anise sure gave him both barrels about what the locals think of his presence a heck of a lot better than I could."

"Do you . . . did Mark talk about what he's planning to—?"

"Not hardly. But reading between the lines, I think he has started to draw up a hit list."

Fathers and sons, I thought, as I stared into the deep well of sadness in George's eyes. My own experience in parenting had been limited to daughters. For most of their younger years they assumed that their mother was more or less too dumb to live. Just *when* that had begun to change, I couldn't remember. Having children of their own certainly helped. Sadly, some of the closeness I came to feel with my daughters I owed to Adam's death and the vulnerability on my part that came after.

A tight knot had begun to form in my throat. George was a good boss and a good friend. He didn't deserve this.

"What are you going to do, George?"

"Keep him talking, as long as he agrees." My boss' jaw hardened as he thought about it. "But guaranteed . . . I will not let him take whatever demons are driving him out on these good neighbors of ours. Money isn't personal, he says. Strictly business. What happened over at Marty's at lunch . . . that was uncalled for and next time our paths cross, I can't let him think I leave it to Anise Gruin to fight that one for me."

George wasn't the only one in Xenaphon with promises to keep. Anise was churning out baked goods and trucking the results over to the clinic, partly for immediate consumption, some for Doc while on the road. The rest she left for him in neatly packaged ready-to-freeze portions. She had begun to buy ingredients in bulk.

"The word is 'wholesale'," she said when I asked her about the bulging overflow in the freezer. "I can save a lot of oven-time by handling the orders at Marty's, the clinic and Peace as a single job."

I laughed, shook my head. "You really ought to go into business, you know."

"After what my parents went through?" She shot me a stricken look. "No way . . . no how . . . !"

I started to use her blatant over-scheduling technique to keep myself from sinking into the depression I knew still lay so alarmingly close to the surface. It seemed to be working. Even tripling my caffeine intake to keep myself going, I had begun sleeping through the night for the first time since Adam was gone.

"Insomniacs have much better options than popping pills," I cheekily advised in my weekly column. "They can garden. Fresh air, physical labor. It works every time."

But before you begin to garden for the season—like any contact sport—I highly recommend good warmups and stretches before you start.

And never stay in one spot for too long. First day out last season, I was so caught up in weeding and deadheading, I lost track of the time. An hour-plus later, when I finally tried to stand up, I dropped to my knees with a bout of sciatica. Not pretty.

Scouring the Internet, I came across all sorts of tips for gardeners to loosen up those rusty and creaking joints for the season. Pay special attention to ones for the knees, lower back and hamstrings.

But then not all pre-garden exercises are physical. Just last week, three more garden catalogs showed up in my mailbox. Before I knew it, I had begun to turn down pages to mark perennials I had always wanted to try to cultivate.

Funny thing about wish lists, they test our capacity to change. My grandmother knew she was pushing her luck to cultivate magnolias in our unforgiving climate. That didn't stop her from trying.

Gardens don't hold a grudge. At season's end, our painful disasters and miscalculations quietly lose themselves in the same soil from which our new dreams will blossom in the spring to follow. There is something comforting in that thought.

Subtly but surely, I had begun to take my own advice. I was no longer going through the motions. As a habit, life could improve with practice.

These days my work was better than on time. It was early. And with the minimum of yelling and screaming, my boss and I had negotiated our way through the revisions for the first quarter of my novel.

"Enough already!" I told him. "Let's not push our luck. It's your call now . . . I've had it. Don't want to see those darn pages again until they're in print."

"We're on a roll."

I shot him a look. "Whatever. Right now, I'm thinking 'fresh air'. Head home to pick up some yogurt and a thermos of green tea with ginseng. Get in the car and drive out to the berm. Watch the snow melt."

Plans are meant for changing. As I rounded the corner of my street, I stopped mid-stride. Parked at the curb in front of the homestead, its motor running, was a spanking-new Mercedes with rental plates. None of my friends drove a high-end vehicle like that, certainly nothing manufactured post-2000.

On the front porch, back turned my way, stood a guy in designer jeans and shirt-sleeves. With the one hand he was trying to rouse my non-functioning doorbell. In the other, he clutched a cone of pale mauve tissue paper filled with what looked suspiciously like Groft's high-end all-occasion cut-flower mix.

"You're looking for someone?"

By the way he turned—visibly startled, half-embarrassed—I knew he hadn't heard me coming. It took me a split-second to put that Miami Vice stubble along his jaw together with the Wall Street power-look when he showed up for the first time in the print shop. *George's son.*

"Brennerman," he half-scowled before he pulled the name from his memory banks. "I was beginning to wonder if I had the wrong house. This *is* where . . . I've heard Ms. Gruin is staying here . . ."

"The bell doesn't work."

"I thought maybe she didn't hear—"

"You must have caught her between jobs. She's working swing shifts at Marty's, helping out at the nursery."

"That place north of town . . ."

"Groft's."

He glanced down at the flowers, as if only now putting them in some kind of context. "I owe Ms. Gruin an apology . . ."

"So, I've heard."

He hesitated, his jaw tight. "Anyway Groft's doesn't seem to deliver. It's too early in the season or the delivery guy only works weekends, some such thing. I was on my way up to Traverse City for the day—thought I would drop them off . . ."

The guy was learning. I fought a smile.

"I'll see she gets these," I said.

"I appreciate that."

George's son thrust the unwieldy floral offering in my direction. As I got a closer look, I decided Chris must have been out at the nursery learning basic cut-flower etiquette. These must have escaped Artie's quality control. There were way too many yellow roses.

"What do you . . . do you want me to tell her anything in particular?"

He shrugged. "You could say I behaved like an arrogant jerk."

"I'll tell her. Mark, isn't it . . . Mark Blandis?"

"Right." His gaze was still fixed on the peace-offering in my hands. "I guess it doesn't make a whole lot of sense giving flowers to someone who works for a florist."

Just that fast, he was down the steps. I stood there with the bouquet in hand, watching him pick his way through the muddy patches on the lawn as if he were traversing a mine field.

Now I had seen everything. I thought about sharing the visit with my boss, decided against it. Without any evidence to support it, I had the distinct feeling the two men must have had words—harsh ones, at that. Whatever had passed between them, the result was this self-conscious display of guilt and expiation.

Anise didn't seem surprised. She accepted the apology with an amused quirk of an eyebrow.

"I heard the guy has been eating down there regularly," she said. "He hasn't happened to hit one of my shifts lately."

"You've made quite a fan."

She laughed. "Or something. My friends say he's actually a good tipper."

"Let's hope some of your civilizing influence carries over to his negotiations down at the bank."

I wasn't confident enough to bet on it—only to admit that no one is ever as heartless or insensitive as they might appear. This was his Dad's home turf Mark was invading. The cook pot of community was forcing him to confront more than the ethics of putting your father out of business. Mark Blandis was a smart man. It must occur to him to wonder what kind of parent George would have made. *Or could still be*, I realized, if his son chose to let him.

But then the anger of abandonment can be all-consuming. I had been walking in those very shoes every day since Adam's death. After half a lifetime to think about it, Mark had plenty of time for a quiet rage to build over the hand he had been dealt. I couldn't even pretend to know how either father or son could or would cope with something like that. There are some things even gestures like Groft's best all-occasion floral mix cannot easily salve or atone.

68

None of that philosophizing about familial love and betrayal prepared me for the phone call that came twenty-four hours later. My bedside alarm read 2 A.M. The gruff, unfamiliar voice on the line didn't bother with Hello.

"Sheriff Mingal. We got a kid down here . . . name'a Demort. Claims you can make bail . . . you and a list of character references a mile long. Though right now, if ya ask me, the little punk don't deserve a one of 'em . . ."

"How on earth . . . can you tell me what—?"

"Threw a goddamn rock through one a' those historic windows over at the Episcopal church. Don't wanna be in the kid's shoes when Father Ben gets down here."

I couldn't bring myself to ask which historic window he was talking about. It had to be bad, whatever it was. Pulling on the first things at hand in my bedroom closet and driving downtown didn't leave a lot of time to dwell on the possibilities. Once inside the jail with its scarred black woodwork and crumbling gray plaster, I encountered a visibly very scared Chris Demort in cuffs and shackles, sitting alongside a hulking sheriff's deputy. A split lip and black eye stood out like angry welts against the teen's ashen skin.

"Hello, Chris," I said.

He didn't make eye contact. I took whatever he muttered under his breath as an attempt at some kind of acknowledgment of my presence. Looking as bleary-eyed as I felt, Artie and Father Gaskill had arrived ahead of me. Under the green-tinged glare from the economy bulbs overhead, the tableaux of the three of us facing Xenaphon's Finest had the frozen-in-time aura of a Roden sculpture—good burghers dragged from a sound sleep into the painful quest for justice. What little I knew about the night's events conjured up charges of 'malicious' or 'felony' mischief, maybe even worse.

"Got us a serious problem here," Artie said.

"I heard."

In jeans and a scruffy Michigan-State sweat shirt, Ben Gaskill could have passed for a kid himself. His usual clerical collar was nowhere in sight. "Fortunately the leading in the window was old enough," he said, "it gave out before most of the glass itself had a chance to shatter."

"Which—?"

"Angel of the Empty Tomb. It'll take some work to piece the glass back together, but I suspect it can be done."

69

My mouth felt stiff. "The newspaper has photos, if that will help. George did a spread for Easter a couple of years back. The closeups were in color."

"Good," Father Gaskill gave a curt nod. "Piecing it together, I saw a shadow moving out in the graveyard so I dialed 9-1-1 to ask for a drive-by. Sheriff here was on patrol in the neighborhood. He stopped things before they got really out of hand."

"Chris . . . I gather he was alone then?"

"Not some gang vandalism, if that's what you mean. The young man took quite a beating earlier at the hands of his mother's latest boy friend—was hurt badly enough, the sheriff insisted they stop by the emergency room on the way to the courthouse to check things out. One angry kid. I guess God seemed as likely a target as any."

"That bastard of a boyfriend is the one you *ought* to be rounding up here, Sheriff . . . lock up the drunken SOB and throw away the key!" Artie whipped off his Green Bay Packers ballcap and ground it into a wad in his hand. "And what kind of a mother would—"

He blinked and stopped himself cold before he could give voice to what we all were thinking. The boy had reacted as if struck, his body curled tight against the massive bulk of the deputy sitting alongside him. In life there are some blows as bad or worse than the ones that fists can inflict.

"We're on the lookout," Sheriff Mingal said in a gravelly undertone. "Not to worry. I'd say we'd have 'im before the night is over."

Lightheaded, I took a deep breath. "*So* . . . what next?"

"Up to Father Gaskill here," the Sheriff's eyes narrowed as he scanned our faces for a response. "Said he won't press charges. When I saw that mess of glass hangin' and half-splayed out over the carpet, it wasn't my take on things. Tonight's work has gone way beyond stealing concrete chickens—"

"Item one, the kid's gotta get out of that house, away from guys who use him for a punching bag," Artie growled. "Jail's no place for him either, that's for sure. I got room over my way. More than enough. And trust me, I'll keep a close eye on him. Guarantee it!"

The sheriff chewed on the inside of his cheek. *Torn*, I thought. Fearing the odds and yet half-knowing that Artie might be right.

"Gotta write this up," the Sheriff said. "Who knows what the county attorney will make of it."

"If we're facing an arraignment, I would be willing to talk to the judge in court or in chambers," Ben Gaskill said. "Who knows what any one of us would do pushed to the limits as this young man has been."

Chris sat drawn in on himself, staring at his knees through all of this. A lost soul, if ever I saw one.

"Bea from social services needs to get involved," I said. "I believe Chris has a real talent at growing things. Breaking them, too, I grant you. But Father Gaskill is right. It seems there have been extraordinary circumstances at work."

Sheriff Mingal sighed and gestured toward the deputy. "We're releasing him in Artie's custody. I'll expect the both of 'em in the county attorney's office by start of business tomorrow. That's as far as I'm willing to go."

By nine next morning the word was out. Not just the members of Peace but the community itself was shocked and grieving. It was hard to go anywhere in town without talk of twisted rods of fragile metal and shards of glass lying on a sanctuary floor. And the perpetrator was one of our own, still almost a boy. God only knew what misery had brought him to this point.

Grim timing—the whole squalid business. Ahead lay seven long weeks of Lenten wilderness. *Advent on steroids. No star light or angel choirs here,* only memories that rose up to haunt of things done and left undone. At the end of it, palms and hosannas would give way to stories of betrayal, unspeakable loss and suffering. Whatever their differences, churches in a town like Xenaphon shared more in troubled times than an official liturgical calendar. Father Brannen from St. Mary's called the paper about setting up a community fund. The guys down at the firehouse pledged to bring their 'collection boots' curbside for the next several weekends.

I forced myself to wait until Sunday to survey the wreckage in the sanctuary. George wandered over to Peace with a camera before press deadline and came back shaking his head. I didn't let myself dwell on the photo that ran top of page three in the *Gazette.*

"Word is, it'll be back by Easter," my boss said. A glassworks north of here is working on it. I'm not holding my breath."

My usual pew near the back of the sanctuary offered distance of sorts. On the right wall toward the front where sun-washed glass of a grieving woman in a garden should have been, I encountered only a rough sheet of plywood. At least someone had the wisdom to paint it black so that the gaping hole didn't call quite as much attention to itself. The hollow feeling it left in my heart was painful enough.

There was no doubt what was expected of us. The organist had just started her shaky prelude when Artie headed up the center aisle with a scrubbed and polished looking Chris in tow. I hadn't seen Artie in a suit since Adam's memorial service. *A tough Roman Catholic Teamster*, I found myself thinking, *trying to live out his faith as best he could.*

The gesture wasn't lost on the parishioners. For once heads didn't swivel at the prospect of newcomers as the two took a seat in the front row. During the announcements, Artie leaned over and said something to the teen sitting alongside him. Guided by Father Gaskill, Chris got up and stood alone at the lectern while he mumbled a halting apology. He had written out the stiff and awkward text on two sides of a single notecard. I thought I caught a couple of Artie-isms in the wording.

Man and boy stayed on for the coffee hour. At first the tight circles of friends and families stood off to the side with their donuts and coffee cake. I chalked up the congregation's reserve to embarrassment. But Father Gaskill didn't hesitate when he saw what was going on. He drew Chris and his mentor personally with him from group to group—the unmistakable body language of acceptance and forgiveness.

I was pouring punch and dispensing coffee at the time, a silent witness to grace in action. Part of my own emotional and spiritual anchor had been wrenched from me with that window in the most violent and senseless of ways. I could understand fully where my neighbors were coming from. Monday after school Chris and I were scheduled for duty together at Groft's. Whatever I felt about him or the window, I was going to have to deal with it.

"I'll pick the kid up after school," Artie took me aside on the way out the door. "He'll be at work by three-fifteen."

My smile felt tight. "See you then, Chris."

All that Monday morning and long afternoon within the nursery's glass-clad garden, fields of lilies bloomed. The light filtered gently through the paint-washed panes. I was forewarned that with Father Gaskill unwilling to press charges and the prosecutor reluctant to class what the boy had done to the window as a hate crime, the previous probation conditions of the court for Chris—supervised community service at the nursery—prevailed. Though I had agreed readily enough to the arrangement, I quickly sensed as we tap-danced around one another in the propagation house after school that Chris felt uneasy in my presence.

Artie had left us alone as we began to prepare and tend the endless

72

trays of seed pots. All around us on the potting benches, life went on oblivious to the human drama in which the tiny plants found themselves. Some few of them planted earlier had begun to stir and stretch toward each other and the skylight overhead. Each solitary plant was living out its unique history, drop by drop, as the water descended toward the thirsty roots.

Peace truly must feel like this. Eyes closed, I savored the slow rise and fall of my breath, the steadying of the pulse, as I filled my lungs with the moist and heavy greenhouse air.

I opened my eyes to catch Chris looking at me from across the dense-packed expanse of growth matrix. He had a peat pot in hand. Even from that distance, the contents seemed far too green to be all seeds and no weeds. It took a while for him to ask the question I read in his eyes.

"You ain't a Groft," he said.

"No. I'm not."

"The window . . . it has their name on it."

"Yes."

Time warped and folded back on itself as I shared the saga of the Groft family as I knew and lived it. I told about the long-ago love of a young man named Dutch for plants and for his boss' wife, the woman who came to design the windows—a sacrificial, life-changing love that shaped Adam, the man who in time came to love me. I speculated out loud what the windows meant to all of them. I said for certain what they meant to me.

"Time and stories, Chris. In the end they are all we have. Both can be tough at times, I grant you. But too important to waste or squander, that's for sure."

Chris listened without comment. "I shouldna done it," he said. "I know that."

"We all have moments of anger or pain—moments when we would love to lash out at everything around us."

"Afterward, it doesn't feel any better."

"No. It doesn't."

The young man's eye was still an angry purple. Around the edges it had begun to fade to a citron yellow. "This ain't a bad job here," he said. "You said that I'm good at growing things."

"Yes. I've noticed that."

"It's easy to care about plants." Chris dropped his gaze. "I mean, even fish go after each other . . . right? We had some in a tank in biology class. But plants don't hurt anybody or anything. They just . . . *hang out, quiet like . . . "*

I smiled. "Most of the time. But they can crowd each other, too. Fight for space in their own way, I suppose."

"But that's our job . . . what we . . . what garden people do," he said.

"Garden people."

"Artie, you, Vivian and Anise. I've been watching you. You try to make it *safe*, so things can grow."

Making it safe to grow. Tears rose up thick behind my eyes and I had to look away. I had never thought of my role as a gardener that way before. Chris had started out adding himself to that list, but decided against it. My heart went out to him in that moment.

"And you," I said. "It's your job, too, now."

Chris turned and settled the peat pot carefully into the spot from which he had taken it. Through all that had happened, columns began shaping themselves in my head as they hadn't in months.

Among the most breath-taking moments for a gardener is the sight of those first green shoots appearing in a bed. The blade-like tips of the monocots (like the daffodils) stand at attention.

Soon the dicots we planted in our indoor peat pots will pop up as well. But it will take their second growth—the second budding of their 'true' leaves—to reveal their real identities. A mystery wrapped in an enigma.

Life can be like that. Just when we think we have nothing more to learn, life surprises us. If we are truly lucky, as we grow older we will embrace that truth with both hands and heart.

"You're retired, right?" folks ask when they spot my gray hair bent over the flower bed. My answer is simple. *There is no retirement from life.*

A lot of people turn to gardening in their senior years, even though their physical stamina isn't always up to it. I like to think it's because gardening is one way we remind ourselves that a new generation is coming. And as gardeners, our job becomes to make it safe for those upcoming sprouts and seedlings to grow.

Making it safe to grow. Not bad if we're looking around for something to do—at any age. The future depends on it.

In life and death hard as we try, we hurt one another, whether we will it or not. Adam was gone through no fault of his own or mine. But then and there I quietly vowed I would not allow myself to wither and shrink and

74

diminish my life until the dreams we shared became nothing more than a distant memory.

Ashes of roses. Adam would not have wanted our story to end like that. To bury our history or cast it as a gleaming marble monument—even as a way of coping with his loss—wouldn't bring him back. Everything we experienced, all those precious living memories, certainly deserved better.

We are the protagonists of our own lives. Maybe we cannot write the ending, at least not in the ultimate sense, any more than we controlled our beginnings. But we can shape a great deal of what lies in between.

Those stories deserved to be told. George wanted to publish the manuscript of *TIME in a Garden* by mid-summer. This was one deadline I intended to meet.

Five
Beware the Ides

Beware the Ides. When Shakespeare's Brutus passed along the warning to Julius Caesar, he was talking about the days of the full moon that fall roughly mid-month in January, March, May, July and October of our modern calendars. To the early Romans—a superstitious lot—the Ides of March were especially notorious, as inauspicious as black cats and walking under ladders. Someone should have shared their misgivings with Xenaphon's weather forecasters that had been puzzling over northern Michigan's mild winter.

By mid-March temperatures in Xenaphon sizzled in the seventies. Our remaining snow-cover morphed like quicksilver into morning fogs that shrouded the town until noon. Ski resort owners were desperate. Come-to-blows arguments raged down at Marty's over global warming and climate change. What that might mean for the coming season in our community garden, I shuddered to think. Our fearless leader Bea wasn't very encouraging.

"I know our growing zone has been gerrymandered south. But all this freeze and thaw is deadly," she told me on a frustrated sigh.

I decided to put out an alert in my column for the week:

To plant or not to plant—and what to plant when you do it? The calendar doesn't always give us a clue. Ditto for almanacs and long-range weather forecasts. Plenty of folks out there are eager enough to share their supposed wisdom or mutual ignorance.

Legend has it, the

original Roman lunar calendar was created in 753 BC by the empire's founder Romulus himself. His 'Year' consisted of ten equal months and 61 free-floating days in winter, for a total of 364. Problem was to square up with the lunar cycle, the total should be 365.25.

Rome fiddled around for 700 years about how to fix the system. Even the Roman Senate got into the act. Changes in the calendar—like adding a so-called *Mensis interclarus* or 'leap month' every year or two—threatened to impact term limits.

Finally in 45 BC Julius Caesar took charge. His astronomer Alexander of Sosigenes came up with a plan to divide the year into 12 months, but then to slip in an extra day or two once in a while in order to deal with the leftovers.

For the next fifteen-hundred years, that Julian calendar was law throughout the empire. And it stayed that way until the Gregorian calendar with its own version of Leap Year took over in the mid-1500s. Even our word for "calendar" stems from the Latin for the first day of the month, *kalendae.*

Every school kid learns what that kind of hubris got poor Julius Caesar. The electorate or *populi Romani* weren't buying it. An obsessive compulsive lot like the rest of us, they thought uneven months were unlucky. Bottom line: what happened to poor Julius on the way to the Forum was anything but funny.

And if all that leaves you still wondering when to plant with all this crazy weather of ours, don't look at me! Next week, stay tuned for the latest insider info on climate zones.

We human beings find it hard to live without certitude and structure. Deadlines are a classic case in point. Except mine miraculously no longer had the power to intimidate or alarm.

Creating the illusion of certainty—*disambiguation,* the philosophers call it. We consult horoscopes, demand closure. The inventors of day planners and Palm Pilots make a mint pandering to that basic human instinct.

To the human psyche, *time* smacks of the sacred. Almost every civilization, from the ancient Middle East to the native peoples of the New World, infused the structure and accounting of time with religious significance. Their priests and sages tracked the movement of the sun and moon and planets—created calendar after calendar as they struggled to cope with the unknown. Even in our secular modern world, time has been called the most priceless 'currency' of the age. Amid our finite lives, we obsess over its passing.

How disoriented and confused poor Punxatawney Phil must feel every spring. Chasing shadows on chill February mornings wasn't his idea. *So learn to number your days.* Words of wisdom, indeed. And it is certainly no easier thing to track the rhythms and movements of the human heart.

I find these days my internal clock has begun to align itself toward intangibles, not just red letter days typeset within tiny calendar squares. The ground around me showed the first signs of thaw. I needed no sundial to sense that warmth and light had begun streaming into my solitary burrow of grief and loneliness. Without quite understanding how, my life seemed to be coming unstuck.

Cynics online persist with their dire warnings of March blizzards of yore. I grew up with north woods tales of thunder rumbling in the middle of the night and snow and ice churning the great lakes around us into a deadly frenzy. Instead, I found myself choosing to side with Xenaphon's aging Polar Bear Club running around on Main Street in sandals and shirt sleeves.

Nature eventually proved the pessimists right. Undaunted, I showed up in the rising blizzard minus head gear and wearing my strappy sandals.

"Not you, too?!" my boss shook his head. "Reality check . . . we've had some of the worst storms on record around the spring solstice."

"G-g-good for the soul, George!" I said through chattering teeth. "Ask the Blue Men Club."

"Those crazy Lake Michigan skinny-dippers hanging out at Marty's? I have. Think double pneumonia. We ran a front page story on the last case."

Still muttering to himself, George watched me settle down with the computer. To his credit, he didn't rub it in when I kept my coat on for the better part of the morning. For his part, he had rolled his turtleneck sleeves over his elbows.

Time was, I would have complained along with everyone else while late winter fought its inevitable passing—no longer. Painful as they were, the pins and needles in toes and fingertips were proof positive I was still alive. I found something oddly healing in the raw winds that sent me racing for warmth toward hearth and home. Let it snow.

If I felt myself backsliding, there was always Groft's. Oblivious to time's passing, sacred and profane, I could lose myself in the greenhouse and its virtual spring. Sequestered there I all but missed what proved to be our last four-inch snowfall. It vanished almost as quick as it came in the course of a disrupted business day—but not before extending the ski season one more weekend.

The days were growing longer. Crocuses started to flower in the beds closest to the office door of the nursery. Their delicate-veined gold and white petals ballooned out helium fashion among the more somber Lenten purples.

I wasn't the only one to catch the fever. Much to my surprise and relief, the stock of potted bulbs in flower had begun to dwindle significantly. Even in our tight economic times, my neighbors seemed to find something uplifting in the notion of green things growing.

Our go-to guy out at Groft's these days was none other than our reluctant apprentice gardener Chris, the wannabe felon formerly known as CC Demort. *Enough to make a guy believe in miracles.* With Anise increasingly pregnant and unable to navigate the aisles, Chris swaggered through rounds of the greenhouses after school and on weekends in her place. And like his tough-talking mentor Artie, the young man's knot-browed determination to master the secret world of plants was downright touching.

I had raised only daughters. Chris and his brash, over-the-top young masculinity was an education I would not have missed for the world.

"I keep thinking of the baby whenever Chris comes strolling through the office," I told Anise. "I can't wait to meet that fierce little Caleb of yours."

"You and me both," she winced as her hand traced the ample fabric of her thrift shop tie-die maternity top. "He kicked so hard last night, I think he cracked a rib.

I hadn't gone with her to her last clinic appointment. "That new doctor, has he shown up yet over there?"

"Jaidev. His name is Jaidev. From India originally. He seems very nice. Single though . . . tough in a town like this for someone with his level of education."

"For you, too, I suspect."

Anise chuckled softly. "Yes . . . and no. My job at Marty's is pretty much like taking out a Personals ad in the *Gazette—single, pregnant and old enough to know better*—but do guys hit on me? Rarely. Unless they've spent way too much time at the bar on the way to the dining room."

Motherhood was a touchy subject in Xenaphon, headline news. The paper had run a feature a month ago on teen pregnancy in the county, a downward age trend that had a lot of parents and educators spooked. Sexting, texting and furtive encounters in Dad's pickup—it's astonishing how rural kids manage to occupy themselves without recourse to a multiplex.

"Regrets?" I said.

"Caleb, *never*. His father . . . ?" Anise shrugged. "Not one of my brighter moments. He was charming, intelligent, knew all the right things to say . . . I was predisposed to believe him. When I look back over the year-and-change we were together, I don't think I really knew him at all. And vice versa."

"His loss. You're going to make a wonderful mother, Anise."

"Thanks for that." Her smile didn't reach her eyes. "I just hope Caleb will agree with you."

"You've . . . I assume you've finally told your parents, then?"

"I've called," the tight, careful edge to her voice was subtle but I caught it. "I told Dad that I'm here. That I'm safe. That I'm working."

"I have to believe they would want to know."

Anise dropped her gaze. "Ruthless, how Alzheimer's works . . . even on a good day, the nursing staff says, Mom doesn't know my father any more. Add to that world of hurt, he's back on chemo. Telling him about the baby under the circumstances . . . mine, as well as his? I'm not sure what that would accomplish . . . "

Her voice shook, fell still. *Time to back off.*

"You'll figure it out," I said. "I'll just say that for most of my sorry excuse for a marriage, those girls of mine were my only sanity factor. Loving them and sharing their lives were the best things that ever happened to me."

"When we met, you said something . . . I believe your husband died? Your girls must have taken that hard."

It was my turn to flinch. "It happened before I moved to Xenaphon. DWI. He and a woman were in the car when it hit an abutment—not the first of Joel's affairs, but the last. I never thought death would have the final word on the subject."

"Rough."

I managed a rueful smile. "A classic no-win. One daughter blamed me for staying, the other for driving him away. I owe Adam a great deal for getting beyond that, for tackling the baggage head-on. For all our geographic distance, the girls and I have never been closer."

Anise was looking at me strangely. "I've noticed you . . . maybe it's none of my business, but you rarely talk about him. Adam, I mean."

Stunned into silence, I found myself weighing the truth of what she was saying. "Not intentional. Everyone in town knew us. Maybe I just couldn't face explaining twice a day every day what I was thinking and feeling. A laptop doesn't offer pity or knowing looks, it just takes in whatever you choose to share. I started writing instead."

"Distance, a fast track to closure. Got that down pat myself—but then you already knew that. Trouble is, wherever I thought I was going, I wound up out of gas in the Groft's parking lot."

"Closure's an interesting word," I turned it over in my head. "If we're trading true confessions, I'm beginning to think all I've managed to do in my hot pursuit of it, is to shut out the good along with the painful. In the end, that doesn't leave much."

A ghost of a smile flickered at the corner of her mouth. "I'd say you're talking about him now."

"The situation, not Adam. Not his smile, not his laugh that lit up a room. Not the way he had of making me feel as if I were the only woman in the world . . . "

"For what it's worth, I'm here," she said after a while. "If and when you need someone to listen."

My mouth didn't want to seem to work. Anise wasn't the only one capable of listening. I gave quiet thanks for chance encounters—two shipwrecked fugitives from life cast up on the same desolate shore.

"By the way," Anise said, "his name was David."

"Caleb's father?"

She nodded. "Head of marketing."

"So was Adam, a VP with this blue-label firm in Chicago. After his Dad became ill, he found himself back here, hooked into bailing out the family business."

I would have been willing to bet that job title is where the resemblance between the two men, and where our respective stories, began and ended. But in what little she chose to share, Anise had left me with something far more meaningful than the painful details—*an opening to unload*. I had a long and mostly sleepless night to think about it, my first in a while.

Ancient storytellers hadn't been exposed to modern grief therapy. But they certainly understood the power of the spoken word. From *Gilgamesh* and the saga of Beowulf to Paul Bunyan, nameless bards repeated and distilled the human experience, transmitting the wisdom gleaned from lives lived to another generation, out loud for all to hear. Without them, literature as we know it would not exist.

It was time to take a page from their book. Morning came. I slipped into my jeans, black long-sleeved blouse and a sweater Adam had intended to give me for what would have been our first Christmas as husband and wife. Anise beat me downstairs, already had oatmeal steaming on the burner.

"Great sweater," she said.

I took a deep breath. "Adam gave it to me. I found it gift wrapped with my name on it under the tree after he was gone. I've never worn it."

Anise stopped mid-stir. It was a deja vu moment for both of us. "Teal is definitely your color."

"Funny, Adam always said the same thing."

Ducking my head, I sipped at the coffee she had poured for me. When the painful knot in my throat started to ease, I began to tell her about how Adam and I met out on the berm.

"A disaster," I said. "I had no idea who he was until I wound up having to hit up Groft's for perennials for our sorry little excuse of a community garden."

"What is it folks say about life being what happens when we're planning something else?" she said.

Her hand was resting on the curve of her belly as she said it. On her face was the look of a new mother when the baby begins to stir inside her, a quiet awe at the gift life bestows when and where we least expect it.

She also looked exhausted. Anise didn't ask, but I gave her the morning off at Groft's. Truth was, I welcomed the time on my own out there. Anise didn't protest.

The greenhouse felt different somehow. More of the plants were showing signs of peaking, could be bloomed out by Easter. *Handle it,* I felt Adam's reassuring response. *You have it in you.*

When my young assistant showed up at the nursery after school,

I put him right to work. Adam always told me the trick to inventory management was a healthy sense of when to hold and when to fold.

"Time to start dumping the lilies," I told Chris. "I'll run an ad in the *Gazette* next week. Starting Monday you can drag that sidewalk sign-board out to the road. I don't want Anise trying to do it. Keep things simple: SALE, DAFFS & LILIES 50% OFF. And be sure to haul the sign back at night to save it from getting whacked by ice chunks from the county plows if it snows."

Brow knotted, he silently mouthed the text. "SALE. DAFFS . . . "

"You got it. Only please, don't misspell 'lilies'."

Chris was notorious for emails that even the spell-checker on the office computer couldn't correct. God bless him, in the face of my mothering and fussing, for once he forgot to grumble.

Though I felt twinges as I did so, I had been avoiding that empty window frame at Peace. With Easter two weeks away, I had run out of excuses. The church was fuller than usual, several strangers among them—distant family members, I guessed, arriving for the holiday. Father Gaskill managed to maneuver the gospel of Matthew into an excuse to talk about hospitality and tourism. Two rows ahead of me, I saw the Chamber of Commerce director nodding her head enthusiastically.

On a more personal note, I could have sworn our priest had been eavesdropping on my life. "Forget the national obsession with finding yourself," Father Gaskill said. "It is when we take a chance—lose ourselves by opening our hearts to the stranger, to the unfamiliar—that life becomes what it was meant to be."

He wasn't finished. "A symptom of our broken-ness is that we obsess about control and discipline. We minimize grace. We trivialize the healing power of Lent into a give-up dessert moment when maybe what we ought to be doing instead is celebrating—enjoying life and each other. There's enough pain and guilt in this world already without looking for more."

All that came out straight-faced but with a knot of tension between the brows. Not the most spontaneous guy in the world, but sure a heck of a preacher.

Our young priest was also becoming big on visual aids. Winding things up, he challenged us not just to pass the peace but share the wheat—tall, dried stalks that had been stashed in earthy-looking stoneware crocks on the chancel steps. A symbol, he said, of the basic things that sustain us.

Clever. A theological pun of sorts.

Trouble was, our hands were already busy with bulletins, hymn and prayer books without adding bunches of dried plant material to the collection. Unnerved by the whole business, I lost it. Along with my purse, everything I was juggling cascaded noisily to the floor. Whatever else the priest was intending to say quickly went lost in a confused rustling and turning of heads from the pews in front of me. I stared down, incredulous, at the mess.

"Dear God!"

"Just so I know, prayer or swear?"

The whisper was coming from an unfamiliar, gray-haired parishioner sitting in the pew alongside me. Before I could react, with a low rumble of laughter, he eased himself down between bench and kneeler and began to help scoop up the debris.

"Sorry," I muttered, "not the best way to end a sermon."

"He'll live. I've known that kid up there when he was still in diapers. And I was changing 'em!"

That got my attention. If there was a resemblance, I certainly hadn't picked up on it. No tortured introspection here. The guy's crackling blue eyes, broad smile and hail-fellow aura had *Extrovert* written all over them.

"I guess . . . you must be—"

"His father. And technically vice versa, right?" he flashed a conspiratorial smile. "Although at the moment, my son doesn't seem too pleased about the connection . . . "

The silence from the chancel steps was ominous. I looked up to see our red-faced young priest staring out at the two of us, jaw tight and decidedly unamused. Tough with all the commotion, the rest of the parishioners had muddled their way through the prayers and were rummaging in pockets and purses for the offering.

The elder Mr. Gaskill just grinned. "I'm gonna hear about this one later," he said.

I decided not to stick around and find out. Fascinating as it would have been to watch the interaction between the senior and junior Gaskills at the coffee hour, somehow I felt it wasn't quite fair to either one. The major seismic episode that started it all had been my doing. Better leave well enough alone.

Instead, as fate would have it, on Monday morning I ran into the young priest himself limping down Main Street on the way to the Drug Store, *sans* parent. He gingerly broke mid-step, ground to a halt to shake my hand.

"Snow shoveling can be hazardous to your health," I said with a sympathetic arching of an eyebrow.

"Cleaning the ice out of the gutters over the garage. It's still like the Ice Age up there. Dad found a small lake forming under the shingles."

"Tiger Balm. It works wonders."

"Dad said the same thing."

"I met him yesterday."

"I noticed."

"Bad timing—unintentional, that's for sure. Sorry for disrupting your sermon like that."

Father Gaskill forced a smile. "That wheat business sounded great on the Internet. Less so in practice."

Another closet googler. I changed the subject. "So, I guess your Dad is here for a visit?"

"Since Christmas. Lately he's talked about looking for real estate in the area."

"Nice . . . having family close."

The young priest exhaled sharply. "He and Mom spent their entire married life in the Minneapolis area. I can understand it's difficult there without her. Unfortunately, Mother Church could send me elsewhere any time. I keep telling him, but none of that seems to faze him."

"Who knows why we wind up where we do."

"True enough." By now the vicar had the look of a man casting about for the exits. "So, I guess I'll see you on Sunday . . . "

I didn't commit, one way or the other. "Your list of donors for memorial Easter flowers in the bulletin on Sunday looked pretty anemic. If you like, I can haul over some of the leftovers at Groft's. Mainly daffs, but still . . . "

"Consider yourself a committee of one," he said. "Whatever you come up with should be just fine."

Something about that awkward encounter suddenly got me thinking about Mark Blandis showing up on my front porch with those flowers for Anise. There had to be a column in there somewhere—flowers as a white flag of truce. I tucked the possibility away and kept on going. My hike to work had never gone faster, even counting that time-out on the sidewalk with the good vicar.

"You look very pleased with yourself," my boss said as a I slipped into my office chair, clicked on my laptop.

"Why is it," I said, "we assume everybody *but* us has it all together?"

"Dunno. And it isn't getting any truer. Unemployment rates just rose again in all of Michigan's major labor markets this month. North of us in Mackinac County, they're twenty-eight percent."

My eyebrow arched. "You've heard something about the paper."

"Ninety days to make major progress on the loan or we're done."

"Dear God!"

"My thought, exactly."

"And your son?"

"Sat there listening to Glen Dornbush and me go at it. Unreadable. Not a single word. Dornbush looked like a man on the edge."

"I can't even imagine . . . George, I'm so sorry."

"Stay tuned," my boss shrugged. "I was barely out the door when my cell phone rang. It was Mark. He wants to meet for dinner."

"Dinner?"

"Tonight. So he says."

"This can't be easy for either one of you. It's none of my business, but did his mother . . . does he know why she—"

"That I'm gay?" It came out a question, as if George still was trying the word on for size publicly when it came to himself. "Surprisingly, I don't believe he does. Reading between the lines, the official party line about my character was worse on some level. It was that I had been a cold, indifferent bastard."

"Oh, George."

He shrugged. "Tonight's as good a time as any. I figured I might as well be up front, tell him like it is."

"Those were different times, George. He's bound to understand."

George chuckled softly. "I'm not so sure that I do."

Turns out, the father and son bonding experience didn't turn out anything like George expected. He wandered in next morning looking shell-shocked, headed straight for the coffee pot.

"I've lived long enough to see just about everything," he shook his head.

"Good, bad or—?"

"Different, that's for sure. When I played the gay card, Mark just looked at me and nodded as if to say, *Okay, that makes sense. Next?* What does a guy say after that?"

"All good," I said.

George shrugged. "I was too stunned to say much of anything, just let him talk. He tap-danced around his Pittsburgh childhood, seemed more than willing to revisit college and grad school."

"And you and what you're doing here?"

"Did he care? He certainly did his homework—seemed vastly amused why I would tie my future to a weekly in the only town in Michigan that starts with an "X", pronounced like a *Zee.* For that matter, there are actually *nine* with a Zee."

"Zeeland, Zilwaukee . . . "

"Zeba, Zenith Heights, Zion, Zutpen, Zwemer Beach. He got me curious, so I looked."

I fought a smile. "And how *did* you wind up back in Xenaphon?"

George had known Adam in high school, that much I remembered. Somehow I also learned my boss had chosen upscale Pitt as an undergrad before globe-trotting with the Navy. *Mark was right*, I decided. The bits and pieces I knew of his father's history were not the profile of someone likely to retire to a place like land-locked Xenaphon. Out of the mainstream, that's for sure.

"I interned on the *Gazette* as a kid, more like running out for coffee at the time. But I always remembered. At the point I was looking to relocate up north, the paper was up for grabs, the price too good to be true," George chuckled, stretched his shoulders against the taut fabric of his turtleneck. "Should have been suspicious right there, but I wanted to keep working into retirement. When I made an insanely low offer, they took it. All downhill from there. The prospects of selling out were nil. I had to make a go of it."

"You were always a journalist, then?"

A smile flickered at the corner of George's mouth. "Does the daily gossip rag on board ship count? After I landed my discharge, I finished college with a degree in philosophy."

"Pitt?"

"Night school in Ohio. A daily needed a sports writer. I stayed with the paper until I retired."

Something in that saga both amused and surprised me. Sports news is always a staple of tiny weeklies like ours. Soccer moms seeing their kids' name in print sells papers. George reminded me of the fact often enough whenever I aired my weary tolerance of page after page of box scores, athletes of the week and bar leagues. I had worked for this man for years and on some level, I didn't know him at all.

"You hate sports."

George laughed. "True, but they served me well. Won a couple of regional awards back in the day, even a state-level kudo or two for my feature work. The personal front—now that's another matter entirely. All those years of self-deception came with a price. I can't argue with that."

"How did Mark react to all that soul-bearing?"

"He may be one tough cookie but not vindictive. It seems life was not all wine and roses in Pittsburgh for the Blandis family. That blue-blood stepfather of his was a serial womanizer. Young Mark started out on much the same foot—was engaged twice, broke it off once and got dumped two weeks shy of the altar before he figured out the lifestyle wasn't working for him."

"Opening up after all these years can't be easy for him. It has to mean something."

George shook his head. "I can hope. Sometimes the whole scene smacked less of a burning desire to make up for lost time than a bizarre sense of relief on his part. Like meeting a stranger on a bus and needing to unpack it all."

"Listening is never a given. And light-years from just *hearing*."

"You know the Fourth Estate," George shrugged, "we supposedly specialize in objectivity and detachment—except the pursuit of the truth may still be an art, not a science."

"You have a book in you somewhere, George."

My boss laughed. "Don't we all? I may have kept stats for a living, but like most of us in the trade, I had my own manuscript stashed in the desk drawer. You wrote a column on it a month or so back. The hunger to make sense of our stories is something with which we all can identify."

"Fiction . . . *you*? I had no idea."

"Murder on the fifty yard line . . . the only openly gay quarterback in the NFL. Plot heavy. I never got beyond chapter three, unlike you. Better for both of us."

"The thought of strangers out there reading the thing still makes me catatonic."

George laughed. "Too late to back out now."

"Yeah, right."

"I've been meaning to tell you for a while now," a thoughtful frown settled in between his shaggy salt-and-pepper brows. "I believe Adam would be proud of you, proud of what you did with his story. And your own."

My chest felt tight. I never let myself think in those terms. "I have to hope so."

"We are always our own worst enemies. Who would have thought that cornered in a booth in the back of the bar at Marty's, over a couple of pitchers of Moose Drool lager, I would find out my son's as unsure of the course of his life as I was."

"Do you truly believe that Mark would stand by and watch the *Gazette* go down the tubes?"

George shrugged. "Who knows? From what he says, his little field trip to Xenaphon is strictly business—my little rag's future is only potential collateral damage. I may not totally believe it, but I believe that *he* does. I'm trying to suspend judgment. All I can hope is that he is doing the same."

I had commitments of my own to reconsider—never volunteer. That off-handed promise of mine to Father Gaskill about supplying daffodils for an "Easter Garden" in the sanctuary at Peace seemed as empty as the barn-wood Lenten cross standing at the foot of the chancel steps. The Monday of Holy Week I finally set aside a stash of plants in the back greenhouse at Groft's. It was as far as I got on the project when I picked up the phone and called the rectory.

"I've been meaning to google suggestions on the web," I told Father Gaskill by way of apology for not keeping him in the loop.

"I should warn you," he said, "on Good Friday our altar guild drapes its Lenten cross in purple fabric. That will have to go before

Sunday. We had white netting for the Easter season. But unfortunately, the rectory's sorry excuse of a Michigan basement pretty much trashed it. You may have to make do."

The homestead cellar had those same crude field-stone walls. *Never leave anything down there you care about*, my grandmother Eva always said.   "If it's white fabric you need," I speculated out loud, "Groft's carries a small selection of wedding runners. They're only gauzy paper, a bit stiff for draping, but still . . . "

"You think so?"

"I could try stapling pleats into the runner before trying to drape it. Maybe that would give the material some shape."

"Photos online might give you some ideas," Father Gaskill began warming to the idea. "Easter Gardens and Veneration of the True Cross are ancient as traditions go. *One and only noble tree! None in foliage, none in blossom, None in fruit thy peer may be.* Venantius Honorius Fortunatus, sixth century AD."

"Poetry. I'm impressed."

"Blame it on my Dad. He has this habit of reciting the stuff. There's more, if you're interested. Legend has it, the wood itself sprang from the Tree of Life in the Garden of Eden."

I shivered. "Adam and Eve?"

"Paradise lost, paradise regained. If we look at it that way, Easter Gardens celebrate the human journey from Creation to Holy Week."

My mouth felt stiff. "A lot of pressure for a couple dozen pots of daffodils. . ."

Father Gaskill laughed. "You'll figure something out. Actually, maybe the mold in the basement did us all a favor. In my book, the simpler the better."

The young priest certainly succeeded in tweaking my curiosity. Still wide awake after midnight, I found myself back on my laptop. Ben Gaskill hadn't exaggerated the quantity of sites out there on the subject of Easter and gardens. I took copious notes.

"Keep it simple," the man says. How wonderfully optimistic the young can be, when in fact, nothing in life fits that description.

Freshman year my art history prof spun out a whole theory of Western aesthetics around that principle. When we're young, the good professor argued, we see things in black and white. It is our idealism that draws us to the austere sculpture of the Classical Greek and Romanesque periods—art scoured clean by the centuries of all its vivid color and embellishments. In middle age the more intricate and dramatic images of the Baroque begin to speak to us. Life, we begin to understand, is a complicated business. Not until much later are we ready to appreciate the Rococo's calculated playfulness and laughter—even joy. If we cannot uncomplicate our world, at least we can celebrate it.

The Easter Garden experienced a similar transformation. By the tenth century, what began as a simple display of cross and flowers had evolved into lavish Sepulcher gardens representing the one at Gethsemane. Pilgrims watched at these floral shrines from Holy Friday until the midnight Vigil of Easter, when a joyous procession through the church celebrated the miracle of the empty tomb.

Not surprising with their love of gardening, by the sixteenth century the British had begun to create over-the-top floral display in niches of the church or set up elaborate gardens around portable chests that symbolized the empty tomb. On the Continent—in France and later in Germany—the custom became to stage Easter dramas complete with soldiers and mourners on the chancel steps.

"*Quem queritas*," the angel chants, revealing the empty tomb and abandoned burial cloth. *Whom or what are you seeking?* The angel's challenge tugged at my heart. *Quem queritas*? Far too many things to answer in a single word.

"Understanding," a voice cried out inside me. Wisdom. Peace. Hope. No matter what my art history prof said about the Rococo, I still could not dare to admit the possibility of *Joy*.

I learned as much about myself as the garden in the process. Certainly far more than I needed to carry out my promise to Father Gaskill.

The Thursday before Easter was slow at Groft's. I was on counter duty, a last ditch chance to put something together before the Vigil at Peace. Picking through a storeroom, I found that one of the cheaper wedding runners was thin enough to drape. Some unsold terra cotta pot

91

holders, their pots themselves long since gone or broken, also showed some promise.

"A great craft project for the Sunday School at Peace," I told Chris when he came on shift after school, "You're in charge. How about you start separating out some of the peat pots you planted with veggies and annuals? Once you've stacked them in a couple of black plastic flats, we can haul them over to the church."

His face got that pinched look it always did when the talk got around to the church or its sanctuary. "I don't get it."

"It's so the kids can create Easter gardens in these old terra cotta pot bases," I told him as I prepared to leave him to the task. "I'm told the kids made manger scenes with live plants at Christmas. Nice if they can make the connection. Christmas and Easter—the stories fit. In the end, love leads to sacrifice and hope, if you think about it."

"I'll take your word for it."

With a puzzled frown, he watched me put together a sample. I inserted tiny root balls at random intervals into one of the shallow terra cotta containers. Slowly miniature thickets began to appear.

"When plants are that small," he said, " I guess they *do* look a little like trees and bushes."

"Exactly. A garden. Next on the agenda, you can scoop up a good-sized bucket of pebbles from the pile out back."

"Rocks?"

"Pick from the tiny ones we use for pot drainage. The kids can use the stones to make paths through their gardens. You could even round up some twigs off the brush pile out back for fences . . . get creative."

"Don't we need some angels or stuff like that?"

I could tell by the stricken look on his face that he realized what he had said. In so many words, he was picturing the scene on that damaged window in the sanctuary. The *Gazette* had run a front page story last week with a color photo of the window in the process of reconstruction. If all went well, it was scheduled to be rededicated on Easter Sunday.

Out of the mouth of babes, I thought. *We long for things unseen.* But in the end, we only have each other and the good black earth under our feet to ground us. A definition of Faith if I ever heard one.

"I guess the kids will just have to see those angels in their hearts and imaginations," I said. Amen to that, I thought. In every tiny stalk and blade and bud.

Six

April Showers

The times were out of joint. Trillium should have been blooming. Instead the woods around Xenaphon slumbered fitfully under a blanket of tinder-dry and matted leaves that crumbled to dust underfoot. Morel hunters had taken to writing despondent Letters to the Editor. Good Friday dawned a dismal overcast, but with only a fifty-fifty chance of showers. We needed rain, needed it badly.

The poet T.S. Eliot calls April "the cruelest month". Even as blossoms spring from the barren wasteland world in his poetry, memories rise up to blight that promise of new beginnings. Once again, it seems, I would be spending Easter alone. The talk of a great Brennerman family Easter get-together at the homestead turned out to be just that—*talk*, plus a great deal of denial and wishful thinking on all sides. I had known for weeks a visit from my girls was becoming unlikely. Still, that didn't blunt my disappointment.

I decided to close Groft's on Friday from twelve to three, a tradition that still hung on in Xenaphon. Viv and Artie were covering the morning and truncated afternoon shifts. Anise was on duty at Marty's. The homestead had that claustrophobic feel of early spring—stifling indoors, yet too cold outside to open the windows for the season. I finally gave up on editing my manuscript and wandered over to the print shop, partly for the fresh air. What I really sought was some semblance of human contact.

Passover or not, my boss was hard into spring cleaning. Before I knew it, he put me to work sorting through and tossing a small mountain of outdated catalogs for specialty paper, ink and all the staples of our trade. By the time I finished, it was raining—sheets of gray, icy water streaming down from the sky.

"*Great* . . . wouldn't you know it. I walked over here," I said.

George looked up from his laptop. "C'mon. I'll buy you lunch. Then I'll drive you home."

I blinked—momentarily stunned by my boss' gesture. The offer was a first. I was hungry and cranky, wasn't about to argue with the man. Right inside the shop door we had an odd collection of umbrellas left by customers past. I grabbed one with several spokes bent at an alarming angle. George had his own. Fortunately, his car was parked at the curb right out front, close enough to make a dash for it.

Everybody in town seemed to be as restless and stir-crazy as I felt. The street on either side of Marty's was parked full. I refused to let George martyr himself and drop me at the door.

"Try me in another five years," I said. "Meantime, I won't melt."

He just laughed. Turns out, the only free spot was at the far end of the public lot down the street. We both looked like a couple of drowned rats by the time we picked our way around the puddles to the front door of the restaurant.

I had forgotten Anise was on duty until she met us in the entryway, menus in hand. "Bar or dining room," she said.

Both were beginning to fill up despite the monsoons. I could have sworn I spotted George's son at a booth toward the back of the smoky, dimly lit bar.

"Dining room," I said, "corner table if you have it."

"Back to the wall," Anise smiled. "Not you, too? It's the classic Wild Bill Hickock syndrome."

George's eyebrow arched. "Enlighten me."

I was surprised my boss hadn't heard about the phobia. But then he had quirks of his own. Among them was the unfortunate habit of leaving teeth marks on every No. 2 pencil in the office, unsettling for anyone working with him.

"Some guy—probably with way too much time on his hands—did an informal study of how people behave in restaurants," Anise told him. "An amazing number of folks need to sit so they can see who's out there . . . either that, or they can't eat. The name comes from the gunslinger Wild Bill of Deadwood fame. He sat with his back to the door during a

94

poker game and somebody took the chance to bump him off. Legend has it he was playing a hand of aces and eights, the Dead Man's Hand."

"You're kidding," George frowned.

"True, absolutely," I chimed in. "I googled it once. Among other things, the incident spawned expressions like, 'I've got your back'."

Anise shot a conspiratorial grin our direction. "I heard that, too. You would be surprised how many otherwise totally sane Marty regulars belong to that back-to-the-wall club, without even thinking about it."

"Makes sense," my boss said. "Xenaphon may not be the Wild Wild West, but some might argue it's on the marginally-civilized list. Until recently, Marty's bar still sported those signs about checking shotguns at the door during hunting season."

"*Anyway,* Anise, you're in trouble now," I teased. "With that obvious mastery of obscure factoids, you'd be a perfect victim to rope into playing Trivial Pursuit. It's the one board game I both enjoy and am good at.'"

"Too good," George grumbled. "What she *didn't* tell you is the rest of us have long since stopped volunteering."

"I'll take my chances," Anise said as she ushered us to a quiet spot in the back. "And you lucked out—there's still one corner spot free. I can't imagine why *anybody* would venture out in this monsoon if they didn't have to. Miserable."

Dark as the bar was, Marty's over-the-top decor in the tiny dining room seemed calculated to brighten the mood. Red and white check cloths covered the tables and what light there was outside filtered in through filmy café curtains with those old-fashioned nubby dots woven into the sheer fabric. The owner also made a point of sprinkling around clay pots full of plastic flowers that changed with the seasons. Right now mock crocuses were in bloom.

"In a week or two, expect daffs," Anise shook her head. "Then tulips in season. Plastic fantastic."

I laughed. Marty's had a new head cook—the owner's nephew who just finished culinary school downstate. My boss seemed baffled at how to master the sprawling lunch menu.

"Whatever the culinary merits of this place," he said, "nobody can complain there isn't plenty of variety."

I chose discretion and ordered a portobello wrap under the Light and Tasty Fare. George went for a jumbo burger with coleslaw and beer fries.

"Comin' up!" Anise said.

It was fun to watch her in action. She obviously had won a loyal set of customers, seemed equally at ease with the confused and befuddled tables of us oldsters as she was the testosterone-driven male service club crowd.

"Inveterate flirts, the bunch of them," she sighed. By miles she was the most attractive server in the place.

"Well, you certainly coaxed George and me toward the high-end regional brews on tap," I grumbled. "And how on earth you up-sold me on tapioca pudding for dessert, I'll never know."

Anise smiled. "Comfort food. You're not about to find that on your average trendy resort menu. But Marty's persists."

"Looks like a plate of fish eye-balls," George said.

I laughed. "No weirder than your lox and bagels or the desk drawer you keep full of those orange cheese curls."

By now my boss was settling up the bill. He refused to let me contribute the tip.

"Your family's coming out for Easter," he said.

I shook my head. "Change in plans. Son-in-law Dan is still out of work so Leslie decided to postpone their trek north from Chicago. Maybe in another month the weather and their situation will be a bit more stable. Down in Tucson, Gina's been obsessing about the flu season. They'd have to fly . . . a nightmare for germaphobes. Her Justin is six but she's got this thing about epidemics—which we in the media aren't helping any, by the way."

"Mother's Day is only a month away, Mom," Gina had blurted out after a rambling *mea culpa* about cancelling their flights. "We'll come, I *promise*."

"I understand. No problem," I told both the girls.

And I meant it. But that didn't change the fact I would be on my own.

"I can't blame the girls," I told my boss. "It wasn't that long ago that I struggled to make the same trek north to Xenaphon from Chicago for some holiday or other with the two of them and the sound of pocket video games blaring in the back seat. With families scattered even farther now to the four winds, togetherness is no easy business."

"I'd have to agree with you there."

96

"And you? Have any plans?"

Although George was Jewish, over the years, I had no sense of if or how he was practicing. He rarely talked about it.

"Mark was raised Presbyterian—awkward, huh?" he winced, "and here I am, the lone Semite. Besides there isn't a synagogue in the county. I still don't know quite how to handle that one."

Families, I thought as George and I said our goodbyes. *God love 'em, they're never simple.*

I thanked George for the perk, said I was taking off for the day and let my boss drop me off at home. "Gotta keep slogging away on the manuscript, George. And it's sure a great day to stay out of the wet."

Wind was driving the rain sideways now, creating white caps on the puddles. A fire in the grate began to take the chill off the living room. I found the latest draft of *TIME in a Garden* lying on the wing chair and began to thumb through the pages, searching for where I left off earlier in the day. No matter how hard I tried to concentrate on the text in front of me, I never seemed to get beyond page one.

We all experience our share of dry spells over the years, root out our share of quack grass. My words. Yet despite the six months it had taken to write and rewrite them, they seemed strangely alien and unfamiliar.

On impulse, I wrapped a hand around the cell phone lying on the couch alongside me and began punching in numbers. In no particular order, I ticked off the names. Vivian and Artie, Bea, Anise, Chris Demort and finally my boss George.

"I'm throwing a party," I said. "Strictly potluck on Sunday after the nursery closes for the day. I'll spring for turkey. You guys can bring the trimmings."

To my surprise, I wasn't the only one who was spending the holiday on my own. Except for Bea who was driving South to Ohio to visit her kids, everybody said, Yes.

"And bring your son," I suggested to my boss.

George exhaled sharply. "You're kidding."

"Or not," I shrugged. "But if you're okay with it, so am I. Just thought you should know."

As an afterthought, I told him about his son's visit on my front porch doing penance for his cavalier treatment of Anise. For once, I think I caught my boss by surprise.

"Interesting," he said.

"I thought so. Anyway Marty's is the only restaurant in town and it's going to be closed for the holiday. You can tell him Xenaphon potlucks are legendary."

The impromptu get-together was quickly turning into an orgy. Anise didn't need any excuse to bake up a storm. Vivian and Artie were preparing to kick in an assortment of vegetable sides, including her one-of-a-kind scalloped root vegetable casserole. George offered to bring the vino and some non-alcoholic bubbly.

I was going to have precious little time to think about any of it. When it rains, it pours—flood warnings for everything north of Gaylord. George had to schedule an emergency sit-down with his accountant, leaving me to run the print shop on Saturday. Artie and Viv stepped in to bail me out in what turned out to be the busiest day so far out at the nursery. With the last of the spring inventory all but flying off the shelves at Groft's, our wholesaler chose that moment to show up with the backup installment of plugs and flats of vegetables we had ordered.

Time for Plan B. I closed the print shop. By mid-day we had the whole crew—including Chris—sweating away at Groft's unloading and reorganizing. It took the better part of Holy Saturday afternoon to find a home for tray after tray of plants. As the sun began its descent toward evening, a fairyland forest of the deceptively fragile-looking seedlings in their high-tech growth matrix had taken root in Greenhouse A.

I sent everybody else home and lingered behind myself to lock up. Only then it occurred to me. I had volunteered to decorate the church for Easter. At least Chris and I already had transported the Sunday School pot gardens in that direction earlier in the week. Aching all over and grumbling under my breath, I loaded up my car with the daffodils I had set aside and yawned my way over to Peace.

The place looked deserted—no cars in the lot. But the smells wafting their way through the sanctuary as I worked amounted to intolerable cruelty. Obviously something was cooking down in the undercroft. I had skipped lunch, but it seemed like way too much effort to investigate.

On my final trip from the parking lot with the cart weighed down with daffs, I finally heard a distant "hallooo!" headed in my direction. I assumed it was probably Father Ben. *Wrong Gaskill.*

"They've put you to work, too, I see," I said, brushing a smudge of potting soil from the knees of my new black work slacks.

Shirt sleeves rolled up and with a faded bridge tablecloth tied around his waist as a makeshift apron, the senior Gaskill let himself gingerly down on the chancel steps. In what free space there was, that is. I hadn't quite realized what a sizeable congregation of upturned yellow and gold faces I had been assembling, shoulder-to-shoulder in front of the gleaming wood altar. The tide of color flowed around a barnwood Cross anchored on a small but heavy wooden platform at the base of the chancel steps.

"Not nearly as ambitious as what you've been concocting up here in the sanctuary."

"Your son's idea . . . an Easter garden," I told him. "The Internet is big on the subject. And you? Complicated—all the garlic and lemons simmering downstairs."

"Also my son's doing . . . though that wreck of a stove down there hasn't made it easy," the vicar's Dad chuckled. "He thought folks might enjoy some Greek Easter soup after the Vigil tonight—an old family tradition."

Gaskill. Something of my confusion must have showed in my face.

"My wife's family," he added quickly, "though apparently nobody around here is Greek. I should have guessed when ground lamb at the local market for the meatballs was sadly in short supply—"

"Still . . . I'll bet you've got a hit on your hands."

"Ditto."

"These stairs certainly look very *yellow.*"

His voice had taken on a faraway tone. "Christmas and Easter can be toughies. Most everyone could stand a dose of holiday cheer."

Deja vu, I thought. Not the kind of reaction I was expecting.

"I've always loved that whole family of bulbs," I told him. "There's something so . . . *human* about daffs and narcissus. All those bright nodding little faces. Not as elegant as lilies—"

"Or as tough on allergies. That many Easter lilies on one spot and I would be running for cover."

Faster than I could say 'vermiculite', his hand shot out to steady a heavy stand of foliage and blossoms on the top step that had begun to teeter dangerously. It hadn't occurred to me how unstable the light-weight black nursery pots might be. The entire arrangement looked on the verge of cascading onto the freshly vacuumed carpet.

"I just hope these pots decide to stay put tonight during the Vigil. Those liturgical get-ups your son wears cut a wide swath . . . "

"An easy fix," the senior Gaskill shrugged. "Just set the plants on either end of the steps in cast-iron kettles. I spotted quite a collection in the cupboards downstairs. Wrap those ugly suckers in foil and they should look just fine."

"Mr. Gaskill, you're a man of many talents."

"Tell that to my son," he flashed a grin. "And the name's Matt, by the way."

"Eve. Eve Brennerman. Just point me to those kettles you spotted downstairs. I'm sure by now that cauldron of yours is—"

"Safe. On simmer."

He was already on his feet, a hand stretched in my direction inviting me to join him. "This sure beats hanging out over in the parsonage, listening to Ben hyperventilating over his sermon for the Vigil tonight. To tell you the truth, he makes me nervous—just watching him."

It was hard to imagine this outgoing, fullback-of-a-guy fathering anyone as fiercely ascetic as the new shepherd of the flock at Peace. I could count on the fingers of two hands the times I had ever heard the young man laugh.

"He . . . your son seems to think you might be settling down in the neighborhood," I said, grasping around for small talk.

"The market's right, that's for sure. Everything I've looked at so far is close to half the going rate in the Twin Cities"

"Which is where you—?"

"Born and bred, lived there all my life. But after . . . when my wife passed on three years ago . . . let's say, the heart went out of the place."

He went silent, but then we also had reached the kitchen. Matt made short work of rummaging in one of the bottom cupboards for containers.

"You're retired then," I said.

"Five years. I've thought about moving for a while now. But when it comes down to it, I'm not the type for alligator swamps or sage and dust storms."

"Family?"

"Ben is here and our daughter's in Florida—both of 'em mobile, though, so I shouldn't really count on that. Still, there are a lot worse places to live on a fixed income than Xenaphon, Michigan. If a guy doesn't mind the snow."

"Makes sense to me. It's partly why I left Chicago when I retired."

An eyebrow arched as he piled a stack of mismatched pots and pans into my outstretched hands. "Partly?" he said.

"My family had property here, the old homestead over on Gratiot. After hunting down the lamb, I guess you know first-hand the limitations on cultural diversity. But if you need a plumber or electrician, the price is right."

"Essentially what the Chamber of Commerce director told me at the coffee hour on Sunday. I gather you two have been comparing notes?"

I laughed. "Not lately. Though she was a huge help when I took over the management of Groft's—"

"That greenhouse operation out on the state road."

"Uh-hmmm."

"Also in the family."

"Not exactly."

Thankfully, we were headed up the undercroft stairs—convenient for me to duck the question. Once back in the sanctuary, we made short work of settling the more vulnerable plants into the heavy kitchenware. Matt had tucked a roll of tinfoil under his arm last minute, perfect for concealing the bizarre arrangement.

"Looking good," I said. "Thanks."

"No problem."

I took a swipe at a strand of hair that felt like it was glued to my forehead after a day of shuffling pots and flats around. "That greenhouse you mentioned . . . Groft's," I said. "My fiancé left it to me when he died."

Something raw had crept into my tone. The elder Gaskill picked up on it immediately.

"I'm sorry," he said slowly. "How long has it—?"

"Fifteen months."

Closer to nineteen, I redid the math. The discrepancy was more disturbing than I felt prepared to share. Instead, I reached down and began to fuss with the foliage on one of the daffs that was sprawling onto the tight burgundy plush of the carpet.

"I am not going to hit you with all these platitudes about things getting easier with time," he said finally. "Still, I suspect surrounding yourself with all this beautiful plant stock has got to help. Green things growing, new life. . .spring."

"You garden, then?"

"On and off. At least enough to keep my wife's projects going. The work is tough, physical. I like that. Good for body and soul, she always said."

The words shot out of my mouth before I had time to reconsider. "We've got this community garden project going out at the interstate off-ramp—"

"Xenaphon the Beautiful?" he chuckled. "As I recall, Charlevoix has a lock on that one."

"Technically the berm is in Aurelius, the whistle-stop next door," I said, "but yeah, something like that. The garden is really quite nice. We've got a good Master Gardener cracking the whip—always need help out there."

"I'll keep that in mind."

As we spoke, a shaft of late afternoon sun on the chancel steps was turning the pots of daffs into a sea of burnished gold. My breath caught in my throat. As if from some faraway place, I heard the words speaking to me in the dark and silent sanctuary.

" . . . when all at once I saw a crowd . . . of golden daffodils . . . "

I knew that text. Caught off guard, my gray cells began ruminating over bits and snippets from Brit Lit 101.

"The Romantics," I said. "Poetry. Keats—?"

"Wordsworth . . . all that melancholy about wandering lonely as a cloud," Matt stood up, brusquely unkinking his solid frame in the process. "Sorry. You're dealing with a former English teacher here. Not standard fare for a football coach, but my teams caught the general drift after a losing season—"

"You around, Dad?" a voice called out, muffled. It appeared to be coming from the basement.

Matt winced. "Duty calls . . . "

I laughed. "Happy Easter!"

"And you."

I found myself staring at his retreating back. Interesting folk, the Gaskills—junior and senior. But then I couldn't even pretend to understand the dynamic between two alpha males sharing the same genetic history. Daughters and moms were scary enough.

It didn't take long to dispose of the shreds of foliage and other

102

debris that accumulated on the carpet. That done, I grabbed purse and car keys and slipped out the side door.

I had finished just in time. While I sat in the Taurus with the turn signal clicking away, the head of the vestry was turning in to the church lot in his pickup. He had a well-used charcoal grill bungeed precariously on the truck bed. The Holy Fire had arrived.

They say that smell is our most basic sense. It is the first to register and last to go. I had never associated the homestead with yeast and vanilla, but Anise was changing all that. She greeted me in the kitchen with a pan of what she identified as cheese-stuffed Russian Easter bread clutched in her oversize mitts.

"You look exhausted," she said.

"And starving."

"You never got lunch."

"No. And the whole time I was shuffling daffs around at Peace, I had to smell this fabulous Easter soup cooking in the undercroft."

"Greek. Darn, I should have made baklava. All these goodies are supposed to be over at the church in less than two hours . . . "

She tore me off a chunk from a second smaller loaf she had set aside for our personal consumption. Weak in the knees, I bit into the raisin-laced concoction, closed my eyes as my taste buds sat up and took notice. Anise had spread it with enough butter to clog my arteries for a month.

"This will tide you over."

"Ummm," I wiped a crumb from my lower lip and took another bite. "Who ever took carbs out of our diets ought to be flogged."

Anise laughed as she ran her palm over her sweat-drenched hair. Her face was still flushed from peering into the oven.

"We're quite a pair, you and I," she said.

"Workaholics all."

"So, who gets the shower first?"

"Go ahead, you first," I told her. "So, you really want to go to the Vigil . . . ?"

"A shock, I know," she chuckled. "Especially after the way I lit into you when you plucked me out of that snowbank."

"'Fundy nutcase' . . . how could I forget? I'm about as erratic a 'Faithful' as it gets. Tell you one thing, though—coffee hour sure has ratcheted up a notch since you came on the scene."

"I guess 'making an Easter' is a hangover from childhood," she shrugged. "So, I thought sure, why not? Time to put a name and a face to all the product I've been sending over there."

"To be honest, with that bird thawing in the sink and a boatload of friends coming to dinner tomorrow, I had been half-thinking of skipping tonight myself. Most folks prefer to go on Sunday. The service is a lot shorter . . . "

"I thought the plan was to open Groft's from noon until two."

"Don't remind me," I groaned, polishing off another bit of Easter bread. "It shouldn't be as crazy as Mother's Day, but close enough. When in doubt, gift a plant."

"Well, I'm not going to let you alone out there tomorrow. Not on a holiday!"

And so we headed for Peace together. Candles in hand, we kept Vigil along with a handful of other parishioners. When the lights flashed on in the dimly lit sanctuary symbolizing the Resurrection, my throat felt tight and I felt the sting of tears behind my eyes.

Without fanfare, the Easter window was back. Even with minimal backlighting from the halogens in the yard outside, I could trace the familiar curve and flow of the leading. My eye seemed drawn to the shadowed faces of the angel and the grieving woman at the tomb. With a shock of recognition, I realized they were straight out of the pages of the Groft family album. A young Adam in the face of the angel. What had to be his estranged sister in the features of the young woman seated alone alongside the yawning grave.

The pain of life and death and hope reflected in the images of a rural family. I wondered what Grandmother Groft's good neighbors thought of her artistic vision. But then all that was a long time ago. I hadn't noticed it. I was willing to bet even our young priest had no idea what or who it was he was seeing.

Like everything else in Xenaphon, the parish was aging. Father Gaskill had given up scheduling the Easter Vigil at the traditional midnight. Apparently howls of protest had followed. Still, even at 8 P.M. the new vicar managed to keep the ancient ritual solemn and festive. Sermonizing proved short and sweet. And after smelling that fragrant Greek soup wafting through the place for the entire service, our tiny congregation tore into the feast in the undercroft afterward with the abandon of a high school football team coming off a championship game.

"You've started something with that soup of yours," I told Matt as I dug into my second cup. Anise had ambled up alongside me, so I took the opportunity to introduce the two of them.

"While we're taking a poll, your Russian Easter bread . . . a slam dunk!" he told her. "If that son of mine has a brain in his head, he is *not* going to let you get away, young lady . . . !"

I'm certain Matt meant it benignly enough, but it sure didn't come out that way. Both Anise and our good priest, ten feet away but privy to the whole conversation, blushed a fiery red.

"We're not taking attendance around here," Father Gaskill muttered. "Ms. Gruin is free to come and go as she—"

"I'm just saying—"

"Point taken, Dad."

"In fact, if the two of you don't have plans tomorrow, Eve," the senior Gaskill persisted, "I've got a lamb roast going in the oven, enough to feed half the town."

"*Dad . . . !*"

"Counter duty at the nursery until two," I found myself saying. "And around six a bunch of us are getting together at my place for an Easter potluck. A turkey is ready to go, but you're welcome to bring the lamb—"

"You're on," Matt said.

Around us folks had begun to drift toward the exits. A few of the more energetic souls had begun the cleanup.

Anise stifled a yawn. "I suppose we ought to—"

"You need to get off your feet and pronto, kiddo!"

She didn't argue with me. The two of us collected our stuff and slunk out into the night—clearing now, all velvet black under the crystal veil of stars. Anise sat silent alongside me in the passenger seat, her hand levering space between seat belt and her baby bump.

She walks in beauty, I thought, this contradiction of a young woman sitting alongside me. As gifted with a mixing bowl as she once must have been with her computer keyboard, she slipped quietly through the minefields of life with a grace that was nothing short of astonishing.

"Matt Gaskill seems like a decent guy," she said finally. "Reminds me of my own Dad—a big heart, not afraid to say what's on his mind."

I had been more taken by the stricken look on his son Ben's face. "A character, that's for sure."

"Trust me, I used to react the way his son did," she chuckled softly. "Embarrassed . . . looking around for a hole to crawl in. Funny thing, how a person can miss all that."

"I could conjure up some wince-inducing mother-daughter moments of my own."

It was hard to top the morning Leslie and granddaughter Emma unexpectedly showed up at the homestead to find Adam and I were 'keeping company'. Anise had shifted in her seat and was looking at me strangely.

"A private joke," she said. "Or you want company?"

"TMI, trust me," I winced. "Let's just say, it is a real gift to live long enough to become a source of shock and awe to our children."

"Books on child rearing usually don't venture that far."

I shrugged. "Eventually what goes around, comes around. And how sweet it is—payback time."

The Easter sun rose on a greening world. Cool and dry, it was going to be a beautiful day.

"Instead of driving right out to Groft's," I suggested to Anise, "why don't we leave a little early and go by way of the berm. The garden gang's cleanup to celebrate the March solstice has been on hold two weeks now. Lord knows what's happening out there."

"Threats of high winds and monsoons that never materialized," she nodded. "Go figure."

"Well, next weekend is The Day. Our leader Bea—you probably haven't met her—has been firing off emails at a record clip."

"Bea shows up at Marty's once in a while," Anise said. "A take-charge gal . . . seems like fun. I'd love to see what goes on out there."

The junket proved rough going even for me. As we picked our way down the stubbly meadow, Anise had trouble keeping her footing. I shot out a hand to steady her—finally got tough and insisted she take my arm. Just last week the clinic tentatively had bumped up her due date to early June. Barely two months away.

The winter had been worse than I feared. Even the most tenacious of weeds looked like they were struggling. The garden steamed like a geyser basin punctuated with blade-like shoots of the daffodils stretched heavenward. Buds anywhere near flowering were few and far between.

"You won't be able to manage this soon," I said.

"Not sure I'm managing it all that well now . . . with a cannonball strapped out front. But I'm glad finally to see what you've been raving about all these months. What an amazing view."

With my eyes on the weeds, I hadn't noticed. In redesigning the off-ramp last season, the state's transportation gurus had gotten it right on more than just pragmatic grounds. The wider sweep of the curve on the road and new location of the berm on the hillside gave a whole new perspective on the lush meadows and tree-covered hills stretching off into the distance.

Willows were just beginning to dot the spring landscape with their intense yellow-green. Overhead, a hawk-like silhouette swept silently over the hillside. *Searching*, I thought. A fearful and beautiful thing to behold.

"Almost two years ago to the day, Adam was out here with the crew for the first time," I said after a while. "He had worn fresh-out-of-the box, incredibly dorky work boots. Bea told me to teach him how to deadhead daffs, if you can imagine that."

Anise laughed. "We're not exactly prepared for mud either."

"Spring came a lot earlier that season. The daffs were bloomed out by then."

I had stooped to test the feel of the ground. Ice crystals still felt grainy between my fingers. When I clambered awkwardly to my feet, Anise stood with a hand braced against the small of her back. Thoughtful furrows creased her brow.

"You okay?" I said.

Anise winced, flashed a quick smile. "Caleb must be doing his morning calisthenics, that's all."

"You can see we're going to have problems out here. The wind must have been ferocious. I'm really glad Artie moved Vivian's arbor into storage for the winter."

"I like the way the garden follows the curve and slope of the berm. It must be a traffic stopper mid-summer."

I laughed. "You get used to the sound of brakes grabbing after a while. More effective than a speed limit sign. Once the highway department actually tried to shut us down, a casualty of planned ramp relocation. With a lot of help from Adam and his friends—very powerful ones it turns out— Xenaphon mustered the political will to fight back. It was Adam's parting gift to us. When MDOT rebuilt the off-ramp, they were mandated to help put the garden back the way it was."

"A heck of a model for other places trying to rebuild a sense of community pride."

"That was the plan," I told her. "At the time, folks even threw out all kinds of ideas for gardening classes and eco-tourism. But when Adam died, we lost all that momentum."

Anise smiled. "Spring," she said. "Don't you gardeners consider it a season for resurrections . . . "

With a shock, I realized that I since Adam, I hadn't been letting myself think of it that way. And then from my aimless midnight excursions into cyberspace, I remembered something Martin Luther—tenacious author of the German Reformation—once said. *If the end of the world were to come tomorrow*, he said, *I for one would plant a tree.*

Like Grandmother Eva's lindens, I thought. Anise Gruin seemed half teasing, wasn't expecting a response.

A season for resurrections. "So it is," I said.

Seven
From the Tender Stem

Plants may seem sedentary and root-bound, but in truth they are alive with movement. An English scholar, Terry Mansfield of the University of Lancaster, says plants demonstrate at least four of the senses in order to survive—touch, sight, smell and taste. Even without a central nervous system, they are capable of communicating along the full length of their stems and leaves and roots. They can react to overcrowding and warn of predators. They maintain their balance and shift themselves to draw in sunlight and nutrients. Some can detect even a casual touch as they release their seeds to the four winds. THE ONLINE GARDENERS ALMANAC

We shut up the nursery at three instead of the usual five. It was Easter Sunday, after all. The last customers of the day dawdled over the flats, but eventually walked out with a half dozen pots and one of Chris Demort's rose-heavy table centerpieces. I was beginning to understand his obsession with the flower—beauty among the thorns. It was the story of his young life.

As the day wore on, someone else had been busy. Matt Gaskill tracked me down at Groft's with the news. My cobbled-together Easter dinner had evolved into a full-fledged community to-do in the undercroft at Peace. I wasn't quite sure who suggested the change in venues, but the idea was a good one.

"Of course . . . go for it," I told him. "The more the merrier. My place is open if you want to truck over there and haul the turkey out of the sink, pop it in the oven down at the church."

"You sure?"

"Of course. Feel free to invite my two neighbor ladies, while you're at it. Trust me, they'll know you're there."

He laughed. But when Anise and I arrived at the undercroft, my bird was basking side by side with the Gaskill lamb in the church's oven. Since last night's Vigil, the institutional cement block ambience of the undercroft had been transformed into a spring bower. Three huge pipe-legged banquet tables had been decked out with lacy white cloths, candles and the church's lovely old stoneware and silver. A husband of one of the local Homemakers—an eighty-year-old gentleman who was known for his needlepoint plastic ornaments—had donated a couple dozen neon pastel Easter eggs to adorn the buffet.

I was glad Anise and I had come straight from work. My black slacks and teal sweater were perfect for the occasion. Most of the women had changed from their Easter finery into something more casual. The men had swapped their suits and sport coats for polo shirts or dress shirts minus Sunday ties.

"We're expecting thirty-six by the time the night is out," Matt told me as he handed me a cup of ginger-ale punch. "I hope you didn't mind that my son coopted your evening like this . . . "

"Makes enormous sense. Even Marty's is closed for the day. If folks have no plans, they're stuck alone at home with TV dinners—not exactly festive. I'm glad he thought of it."

Hands down, it also was the most relaxed I had ever seen our young priest. Not quite that bluntly, but I told his father so.

"Punchy, that's all," Matt laughed. "Trust me."

In jeans and a blue button-down collared shirt open at the neck, Ben Gaskill was sporting a Have-you-hugged an Episcopalian apron for the occasion. When the time came, he carved and served the turkey at the makeshift buffet like a pro.

"In the job description," he shrugged when pressed on the subject. "At the seminary, the whole bunch of us would fan out to every food pantry and shelter within a fifty mile radius for the holidays. Thanksgiving, Christmas . . . Cinqo de Mayo. You get pretty good at it after a while."

"Smart move, Father—havin' us all over like this," Artie told him as we mixed and mingled before settling down for the feast. "Now take me— I'm a Catholic. Viv's a Methodist, but they closed a while back. You A-picka-palians kinda wound up the common ground."

Father Gaskill laughed. "Make it just plain Ben, if you like. Nobody's recruiting today, just eating. But thanks."

Which reminded me the hors d'oeuvres tray was starting to look a bit ragged. I took it upon myself to revive it. More revelers were arriving. From the pass-through window in the kitchen, I spotted my boss, George, navigating the steep and narrow basement staircase. He was wearing his yarmulka, a first in my presence. And right behind him on the steps—most definitely a first—was his son. Jewish and mainline Presbyterian, if this didn't qualify as a community, I didn't know what did.

George waded right into a conversation with one of the local farmers who had been advertising his new petting zoo in the *Gazette* on a regular basis in recent weeks. On his own, Mark Blandis drifted off to one side with his cup of punch, like a head of state anticipating an assassination plot. There wasn't a person in that room who didn't know who he was and what mission brought him here to Xenaphon. And he knew it.

Before I could intervene, Anise did. Glowingly pregnant in her rainbow-striped knit sweater and body-hugging jeans, she headed his way, all smiles.

"Just wanted to tell you, I appreciated the flowers," she said.

Her greeting and awkward hug weren't lost on the folks around them. An audible intake of breath in the room was followed by what seemed like a very long seven-second conversational pause. Mark Blandis appeared momentarily as surprised as the rest of them, before he risked a stiff, but credible smile.

"Glad you liked them," Mark said.

I knew the context. So did George. But as chatter slowly resumed around them, it was accompanied by a fair number of lingering glances in their direction.

Good for you, Anise, I thought.

It couldn't have been more than five minutes later that our vicar joined the two of them. Single adults in their thirties and forties were a rarity in our neck of the woods. And here stood three of them, as unlikely a trio as anyone could imagine. Anise and Mark Blandis wound up at my table along with George, Matt Gaskill, Vivian and Artie, as well as several older members of the church choir who were on their own for weekend.

"'*Noli me tangere*,' the risen Christ said to Mary in the Easter Garden," Ben Gaskill said by way of blessing. "*Don't cling to me. Instead, be there for each other.* And so we are—sharing the love. I wish you all a wonderful Easter and Passover."

With that he sat down, claiming the empty chair next to Anise. If it felt intimidating to be caught square between the embodiment of the godly and Mammon, Anise didn't show it. A foil-wrapped pot of daffs had been placed center table—a challenge to any kind of extended conversation.

Mark Blandis must have had the same thought. He had begun toying with the overflowing foliage.

"Daffodils, right?" he said.

"You got it," Anise smiled.

"Thanks to Groft's, it looked like a garden in the sanctuary all day," the vicar told him. "Tonight's table crew took it upon itself to recycle a few."

Anise looked over at me, her eyebrow arched. "You listening to this, Eve . . . ? Hope you brought your sign-up sheet. From the sound of it, you might have a couple of fresh recruits for the berm clean-up next weekend. Bet these two could have the garden looking ship-shape in no time."

"Berm," Mark frowned.

"Our little community development project," I said. "Two years back, we started a perennial garden on the slope above the interstate off-ramp. We thought it might lure tourists downtown or some such thing. Since most of us on the crew are sixty-plus, we can use every bit of younger help we can get."

"And you work at this how often?"

"Every Saturday morning in season."

"All day?"

"A couple hours," I shrugged. "Depends on how hot or cold it gets."

Mark's frown deepened. "Experience necessary, I presume."

"None whatsoever. And no tools required. We have a stash in the shed overlooking the garden. Northern Michigan's growing season is so late this year, we've been postponing the startup. So Eve's right . . . if you have nothing better to do at 9 A.M. on Saturday morning, feel free to join us."

"I just might take you up on that."

All that, coming from taciturn Mark. I don't know who looked more shocked—Anise, my boss . . . or our fiscal watchdog himself.

"You have a green thumb?" Anise said.

"Not unless the stock market counts."

A tentative ripple of laughter spread around the table. He meant it as a bit of self-deprecating humor—awkward, though, considering the context. Mark's jaw clamped tight.

"Well, the drug store carries this great liniment," Ben Gaskill said. "I recommend it highly."

"You've tried it, then?"

Anise stifled a grin behind her linen napkin. "Liniment or gardening," she wondered out loud.

The vicar looked pained. "Wrong season. I made the mistake of trying to chop ice off the garage roof a couple of months ago. Strength training seems to be an unspoken job requirement around here."

At that she laughed out loud. "Good for you! So then, I'm guessing Eve can be expecting both of you out at the berm on Saturday!"

She launched that final zinger without cracking a smile. Neither man responded one way or the other. But the looks on their faces were vintage cave-man.

As for Anise, she had never looked more lovely. Her self-cropped spike of auburn hair made her seem even younger than her years. The hint of vulnerability and steely resolve behind those clear gray eyes of hers conveyed an aura of perpetual mystery. Still from where I sat, I could see what her two dinner companions could not. A high flush had begun to spread across porcelain cheekbones.

"Well, thanks for volunteering." I didn't have the nerve to add, *we'll be counting on you.*

The rest of the evening unfolded without incident. Artie and Viv both chuckled and shared a knowing look when I told them about the night's recruiting efforts I couldn't help but notice that Anise and her two male dinner companions circled each other warily as we all pitched in to clean up and stash the huge banquet tables back against the wall.

Anise and I had driven over together. After a round of "Happy Easters", we headed out. Sunset still came fairly early and several of the older parishioners had chosen to bail some time ago.

113

"Interesting little gathering," I said as I eased the Taurus out of the church parking lot.

"I'd say so. At least you might get some help out of the deal next weekend."

I laughed. "Give 'em a couple of days to think on it. Not very likely."

"Dunno," she said. "Could go either way."

"You certainly didn't let them off the hook."

"Trust me, waiting tables is not for the faint of heart," she said. "Both of those guys have been spending far too much time down at Marty's lately. Something had to be done."

"You're kidding."

Anise chuckled softly. "Desperation on their part, I'm sure. But there it is. Neither one of them seem like bowlers. Not much else to do in Xenaphon."

I was still shaking my head as we turned into the homestead driveway. *Who knew?* I thought.

The street was deserted. While Anise awkwardly extricated herself from the front seat of the Taurus, I stood staring up into the April sky. A ring was forming around the moon and stars glittered behind the filmy veil overhead. Rain was forecast early in the week, though it should clear enough so the mud dried out for the garden clean-up on Saturday.

I opened the door and Anise headed straight up to bed. The subject of Mark Blandis and Ben Gaskill never came up again.

Monday morning started out as an anti-climax. But then one of the more dangerous things about our getting older is the tendency to presume. We have been there. We've done that. Which makes life's little curve balls all the more surprising when they come.

Down at the print shop, George was waxing eloquent over a canned article from one of our feature services for this week's *Gazette*. Out of the blue, the Big Sea Waters of Longfellow and Hemingway were rising—front page news. Only a couple of years ago with the Great Lakes shrinking, we had lived amid threats of water wars with the drought-ravaged West Coast that had roused our Canadian-born governor to warn, *look but don't touch. If you want Michigan's water, then come and visit.*

While my boss figured out what else to squeeze on page one, I was slugging down coffee and quietly agonizing over the decision to have shared my novel with the girls. My boss had run off two proofs of *TIME in a Garden* some time ago, both bound and encased in glossy covers. Two weeks before Easter I finally stuck both copies in priority mail envelopes and mailed them.

The cover note read, "This is our story. You have to live with this as well as I do. Be tough. Be honest," and I signed it, "Love, Mom."

Silence from both Chicago and Tucson was a bad sign, I decided. Leslie and Gina most likely hated what I had written—were collectively afraid to tell me. And then late Monday morning, two packages showed up at the print shop. Hands shaking, I laid the two copies of the novel side-by-side and began to thumb through them. There were occasional pages, sections even, where the red ink accumulated alarmingly.

But the cover notes said it all. *Heartbreaking. Honored to be a part of it.*

"They loved it, George."

My boss looked up from his computer screen, his half-glass perched rakishly mid-nose. "The novel . . . you heard from your girls."

I nodded in the affirmative. "Go figure."

You're surprised," he said.

"Stunned."

"I'd say, I told you so—"

"But you don't want to lose a perfectly good employee."

"My only employee . . . except for the accountant. And technically he's just a temp."

"We underestimate our children, George."

"True," George shook his head. "Apparently mine is a potential gardener."

"Well, you've been telling me to give mine a chance. I guess I just wasn't listening."

At my invitation he began thumbing through their edited proofs, tracking the what and why of the red ink. "I want this out by late July."

"You think?"

"I know."

When George gave me the afternoon off, I decided to indulge in some mothering of a different sort entirely. With her due date coming closer, Anise found it harder to navigate the aisles at Groft's. Standing on her feet all day at Marty's was no picnic either. The restaurant owner had begun to put her to work hosting and handling the cash register. Monday afternoon I stepped in and picked up her stint at Groft's.

I was out back checking on the state of the vents in the propagation house when the office phone rang. The call was automatically forwarded to my cell.

"Eve, it's Gayle. Margot's daughter . . . "

I already suspected the rest. Our eldest surviving gardener on the Gang Green had been failing for some time now. Though I knew from the last visit she would no longer recognize me at all, I had been meaning first chance to drive down to see her.

"She's gone," I said.

"Last night in her sleep. I . . . we've been talking to the funeral home. They're trying to arrange a service in Xenaphon."

An era was passing. "When?"

"Thursday. I was hoping that maybe you and the garden crew could—"

"Of course. Name it."

"I was hoping some on the crew might be pall-bearers. And maybe you could give a eulogy."

"The church would want to hold a luncheon afterward."

"We couldn't expect . . . that would be nice."

"Have you talked to the vicar?"

"Father Gaskill. Yes. He said he would talk to you."

"And I would like to do the flowers."

"Margot would have liked that."

In the end, the tiny church was amazingly full, the organist better than usual and the altar steps a tribute to spring in all its glory. George had used our dry-mount press to put together a photo montage from a piece he had done on Margot and Howard several years back. The vicar wore his best liturgical finery, embroidered with gold ivy and trailing bunches of grapes on an off-white ground. Margot would have laughed out loud.

"A hunk, that guy," she would have winked. "That Anise of yours better watch her step."

Leave it to Margot and her wildly blossoming fantasy life. "I might be older than dirt," she used to remind us. "But I'm sure as heck not dead yet."

116

Folks hung around for almost two hours after the service. The stories that emerged about the garden and Margot and Howard were priceless. A handful of ladies from the Fellowship Committee and the Gaskills lingered behind on cleanup crew. I felt underfoot in the hall and kitchen. There were plenty of hands for putting things right again.

Instead, I headed back upstairs for a final look at the sanctuary where the family had left my floral arrangements behind for Sunday's altar flowers. I couldn't recall whether there were adequate water levels in the containers. With the days growing warmer now, I had better check.

My worries were in vain. The pots were fine, everything happy and blooming. With any kind of luck, the arrangements would still appear fresh on Sunday.

"They're beautiful," a voice said. "I meant to tell you that."

"Matt. Yes . . . thanks. I was pleased with how they came together. Margot was always a great fan of poppies, but I had to settle for something that just looked like Flanders' fields. Wheat stalks, red-orange roses, daisies. I decided that globe artichoke heads look a little like hydrangeas if you squint. "

"Funny, how plants bring that out in us—identifying with one or the other of them. My wife was a big fan of coneflowers. When she died, it was February . . . not the easiest thing to find coneflowers in February."

He had slid into the pew alongside me and his face was like holding up a mirror to my own. There was no mistaking the bittersweet memories hidden behind his eyes. Before I had time to clamp the lid down on my reaction, I felt myself crumple. Shoulders shaking, sobs choking off my breath, the storm raged on—no end in sight.

It was a framed photo of Adam's face I had been remembering in that sanctuary, set on an oaken table and a simple crock of daisies blooming alongside it. His memorial service. The community grieving together, as now, mourning one of its own.

"I know, Eve. Believe me, I know," Matt said.

I believed him. He drew me gently against him the way a parent would soothe a weeping child. Through the numbing grief, I felt his hand tracing awkward circles between my shoulder blades. I had not let myself cry like that since the night Adam died. Not in the long months after, not when I lost Dutch and Howard in quick succession. Not in the loneliness of the homestead before Anise came.

I lost all sense of time in that darkening sanctuary. Gradually it began to dawn on me that it must be late—or about to rain. Either way, I couldn't stay here.

Gaze averted, I turned out of reach and levered enough distance to fish in my pockets for a tissue. "This is . . . I don't know what this was. Certainly didn't mean to drag you—"

"For the record, I'm not a secret stalker," he said quietly. "One look at your face downstairs and I could tell this was coming."

"Am I . . . was I all that . . . ?" I drew in a harsh breath. "Well, I didn't have a clue."

We sat side by side on the bench—silent, not touching. Two strangers, I thought, bound by sorrow beyond words.

"Grief doesn't get us or itself from Point A to B in a straight line," Matt let out his breath in a rush. "Some nights I wake up over there in that parsonage and don't know where I am or how I got there. I came for Christmas, that's it. Trust me . . . moving in with my son was never on my to-do list. But I woke up one morning over there and the thought of going back to the Twin Cities seemed intolerable. Over New Year I had spent an afternoon at the county library. In that big public room downstairs, a recital was going on . . . all these little kids . . . "

He shifted in his seat—made eye contact. My throat felt like it was closing up.

"My wife was an excellent pianist," he said, "gave lessons to an endless parade of urchins on Saturdays. There were times I hated it—breaking up our weekends like that and all those kids traipsing through our living room. What I would give again to have those muddy footprints on her heirloom Persians . . . "

"Your wife's name . . . if you told me, I didn't catch it"

Matt blinked. "I thought for sure I . . . her name was Thalia. Laia for short. One of the three Graces . . . the Greek goddess in charge of blooming, idyllic poetry and comedy. We had a good laugh over it. If anyone fit the poetry and rustic part, it was me. Laia had a PhD in psychology . . . worked as a psychologist for the school district."

"At least you talk about her. I haven't done that with Adam nearly enough. . .not publicly. And I need to. Anise called me on it. She was dead right."

"We all cope in our own way."

"Not always the best ways," I said. "But I'm learning."

Matt Gaskill's smile was sad. "Aren't we all," he said.

Easter had loomed so large, it was easy to forget that April is also National Garden Month, Keep America Beautiful, National Frog Month, National Humor and Stress Awareness Month. Oh yes, and April Fool's Day—already past, but still pertinent.

The morning of the garden clean-up dawned. When I saw the impressive line of cars snaking along the access road, I had to believe my column last week had something to do with it. Somehow for me the whole event had begun to take on a cosmic significance.

Jewish, Christian, Muslim or Hindu—all the world's major religions get excited about green stuff growing. Among my favorites is an Easter hymn set to a 15th century French Christmas carol, NOEL NOUVELET. *Now the green blade rises from the buried grain. Wheat that in the dark earth many years has lain. Love lives again, that with the dead has been. Love is come again, like wheat that springs up green.*

It's how I feel watching the forsythia in full bud outside my kitchen window. John C. Crum, penned that lovely poetry in 1928. A graduate of Oxford, he wrote numerous books on the subject of spirituality. From the titles, he must have been a gardener: "Road Mending on the Sacred Way" and "What Mean Ye by These Stones". He also published "Notes on the Old Glass of the Cathedral of Christ Church Canterbury". I don't think that was a coincidence.

Sometime if you are in downtown Xenaphon, check out the Eden and Resurrection windows at Peace Episcopal. To me, that precious stained glass captures the essence of a garden—each blossom and leaf fusing into a delicate tapestry. The sum of each part is so very much gloriously greater than its whole.

"The same is true of Xenaphon's community gardening team," I finished. "Alone, we would have real trouble keeping up that berm on the off-ramp. I can't think of a better way for folks to celebrate a season of new life than by getting involved."

Considering all that help running around on the berm with sharp objects in hand, we needed a plan. Our fearless leader Bea showed up in walking shorts and toting a kid's chalkboard. On it, she had scrawled out our marching orders in doggerel for maximum effect.

119

Quick and dirty: Chop, lop,
When in doubt, weed and rake.
Save what you can, then spread the wealth
Rest . . . YOURSELF and the plants

Nobody was laughing. Bea's mop of fluff-and-go hair bobbed over a bucket of wicked-looking tools balanced precariously on her rusty Radio Flyer. We looked at the list, at the garden, then each other.

"You're *kidding*!!" Artie let out a despairing groan.

Bea looked downright hurt. "What . . . ? I don't get it."

There were ten of us, counting Bea and a young receptionist from her office at the courthouse. Artie and Viv, Chris our teenage James Dean, George and his son looking uncomfortable in a Hilfiger windbreaker and our vicar in jeans and that ragged-looking Michigan State sweatshirt of his. Matt Gaskill was nowhere in sight. Surprise volunteer of the week was Doc Jaidev from the clinic. He had the foresight to wear gloves and an allergen mask hung at the ready around his neck.

All total, our new recruits represented a lot of muscle and not a great deal of collective expertise. Anise followed a good half-block behind, toting a jug of hot coffee, a lawn chair and what turned out to be some of the most incredible macadamia nut cookies *ever*. Mark and Ben made a beeline to help her down the slope.

It was George who said what out loud what the rest of us were thinking. "If you still want a garden at the end of the day, Bea," he suggested, "some on-the-job-training would be prudent."

Bea drew herself erect, took a couple of audible breaths. She had put on her civil servant game face, sizing up the circle of faces looking to her, clueless. "Fair enough. *Ben* . . . I gather by now your Dad isn't coming?"

"Out of town," he said. "Some business in St. Paul."

"Okay then, you can start clearing the rubble, any remaining stalks and stems. It would be easier if you had help, but Artie will show you the ropes. Viv can take my receptionist Shareen, George Herberg and Mark aside and teach them how and what to weed. Eve, you've got Doc . . . the word is *triage*. Show him how to thin and fill in the holes with the plugs of plant stock you liberate—let Chris do the heavy digging. I'll float."

"And me?" Anise said.

"Every half hour, dole out the liquids and lots of them. After an hour-and-a-half, we'll all blitz whatever is closest to done. We can finish the rest next week, if we have to." Bea scanned her open-mouth crew. "Questions? If not, we're done here . . . let's go!"

We did. Red-faced and sweating in the brisk wind blowing over the crest of the berm, we staked out areas of the garden and went to work. It didn't take long for my team of two to figure out where the trouble spots lay. For starters, the daisies were beyond spotty. Wherever the terrain offered even the slightest protection, shoots huddled together as if fending off imminent hypothermia. But a lot of the area allotted to daisies was simply bald.

"This is a case of trowel work, a surgical strike," I said, handing Dr. Jaidev one of Bea's best thin-blade trowels. "The ground is nice and wet. If we thin out the clumps, we can make a stab at filling in the holes. The plugs we move may not do much this year, but time will tell. At least it's a start."

"What if I damage the roots?"

"Don't," I said. "If we transplant them as quickly as possible, the roots won't dry out. Meanwhile, I'll scout out the rest of the garden for holes and likely replacements."

With a few deft strokes, Dr. Jaidev thinned one end of a clump of the Alaskan daisies. Cradled in his gloved hand, the plug looked so fragile.

"I'd start filling in just outside the fringes of the sturdier plants," I said. "That way if we run short, we can always assign something else to take care of the bare spots."

By mid-morning, progress was being made. No one showed signs of leaving, although tempers were getting short. I suggested to Bea that a time-out might be prudent.

"How about a little perspective around here," I said. "Father Gaskill, if you're willing, it would be nice to lead us in a moment of reflection for Margot. We can't go too wrong if we dedicate our season opening to her . . . "

He did and we did, huddled together in a tight circle mid-garden where Vivian's arbor would ultimately stand again. The wind whipped at our bare heads, kinder than I would have expected for mid-April.

"Amazing how fast folks can feel vested in what we're doing out here," Anise said.

"Gardening is like that," Bea chuckled softly, shook her head. "Even if folks don't always appreciate the distinction between goldenrod shoots and prairie asters, there's something about digging in the dirt. As

121

kids we loved it. As adults we feel we need an excuse."

When work resumed, the tone was different somehow—gentler, more forgiving. I also couldn't help but notice that Mark and our good vicar took more than a few breaks together as the morning went along. Anise handled their attentions with the same genial I'm-in-charge-here-folks strategy she used on the regulars down at Marty's.

It felt good to see all that young blood out there slogging away with us in the mud. Later as I cuddled alone in front of the fire, read and reread my novel on its way to mid-summer publication, my journey through the text was if I was revisiting another world entirely.

By any other name, we were becoming an extended family out there again. We old timers plus Anise, the Gaskills, George and his son, Chris Demort and rarer visits from our new resident physician, Doc Jaidev, I suspected. Bea must have sensed what was happening as well. She was smiling a lot.

But the sad truth was, I hadn't seen my own daughters since Christmas and I missed them. My trips around Chicago to Leslie's suburb on the North Shore and the trip to Tucson over last year's holidays had been hellacious. O'Hare was snowed in for almost a week. It took multiple camp-outs at the airport to finally re-book a flight headed west. In Arizona my allergies went on Red Alert and I wound up with a sinus infection that migrated to my ears on the plane coming back. I was sick for a month. Two rounds of antibiotics later, I vowed never to do that again.

"It's our turn, Mom," they kept reassuring me. "We'll make it up to Xenaphon before spring."

But now Easter had come and gone. I couldn't blame our relationships for drifting. Both girls had troubles of their own. Phone calls can only do so much. It was what it was.

Long-distance, I tried not to overreact about son-in-law Dan's struggles to rebuild his career. Leslie seemed perpetually on edge. If granddaughter Emma grabbed my call first, she talked my ear off about her brother, Harry, and the school terrarium her teacher had entrusted to her care over the Easter break. Meanwhile Gina was working double overtime. Young Justin knocked out a front tooth on the jungle gym—the week before his First Communion. The photos Gina imbedded in her emails revealed a shock of reddish hair, a generous dusting of freckles and a gap-toothed grin that stretched from Tucson to Traverse City.

I was missing all that. My girls' priorities were changing, but then so were mine.

The circle of friends around me had grown beyond recognition. I wasn't alone in the house any longer, hadn't been for months. The column was flowering with a new infusion of ideas, my novel was making progress, Groft's was taking up more and more of my time—the to-do list was getting out of hand. Whenever I looked in the hall mirror these days, I barely recognized the woman staring back at me.

I had no idea where that I-dare-you hint of a smile came from. The thatch of hair was grayer than I remembered, more salt than pepper. Lately, the girl from the salon, Joy, had taken to spiking it aggressively.

"Think young . . . arty," she rotated the chair to let me assess all the angles. "You got good bones. Let 'em show."

"I'm starting to look like Chris Demort."

"That kid with the nose ring, pants always half down around his knees? I don't think so."

I had been getting some sun. All that walking to work even may have whittled off a pound or two. The laugh lines were back with a vengeance. Most unsettling was the self-awareness flickering in those blue-green eyes—only nuanced now, like life itself. Like the Big Lake just before a storm.

Whatever came of my daughters' visit if and when it truly came, I resolved then and there not to let so much water flow randomly over the bedrock of our relationship again. Airfare for me or them wasn't an issue. Groft's was as healthy as I could hope for it to be in our anxious economic times. The community garden was under control.

As for the Groft family lake house, there I drew the line. I wasn't ready to tackle dealing with it. When Artie volunteered to open the place for the season, I said as much.

"We could still have some cold spells," I told him. "No point in jacking up the heat in an empty house. It'll keep."

"You're the boss," he said.

His tone told me otherwise. *Whatcha doin', Evie? Adam wouldn't have wanted the place to sit like some mausoleum out there. You got a good head on your shoulders. Figure it out.*

It wasn't the only thing I had to figure out. But then every one of us has to start somewhere.

123

Eight
Crop Circles

Just when I despaired of spring ever coming, I found it flowering all around me. I half expected to discover a May Pole sprouting in the park across from the courthouse. Instead, I fled to the worldwide web and my nightly journaling to usher in the season.

Who knew? To the ancient Druids, May Day was known as the festival of Beltane—a time for lighting new fire on the hillsides to kindle the springtime sun. Their priests and shamans claimed to possess an elixir to "drink of oblivion" and its fearsome magic made one forget even those things that seemed most beloved to the human heart. Classical Greeks believed that the river of the underworld, Lethe, possessed those self-same powers, a river that the Romans who came after them named the Styx. Passing those dark shores could dull the memory beyond recall of everything loved and left behind.

As for me, I no longer searched for my future along those dark waters. If there was a way to forget the pain of life, without losing its joy, I hadn't found it. *Redeem the memories.* I was thinking of whipping up a magnet on my laptop and posting the mantra on my refrigerator door.

One thing was certain. I had become a case study for why the web was so blasted addictive.

Meanwhile outside my own front door, the sun was shining with no help at all from me. The grass was greening up. Forsythia had begun dropping golden showers of blossoms onto the front sidewalk. Best of all the girls were coming up for Mother's Day in two weeks.

Only one cloud shadowed our reunion. My heart and home were no longer entirely my own and I needed to deal with that.

In her own unassuming way with her baking pans and dust buster, Anise Gruin had carved out a place for herself, not just in the homestead, but in my life. However that might threaten my daughters, I found myself profoundly grateful. In another month, I was about to become an honorary Grandmother. The prospect of another generation growing up in that house filled me with a quiet joy.

I couldn't say the same for the view from my front porch. For weeks now, I had stood watching mange-like patches spreading like a gigantic spider web across the lawn.

Brown patch. Snow mold. A fungus or some other insidious, unidentifiable blight. Whatever the cause, I suspected what was called for. I had to rake up the dying thatch, aerate the ground to improve drainage and reseed in the worst of spots. Last year my attempts landed me a nasty case of tennis elbow that still twinged when it rained, something it was doing a lot lately. Only the dandelions seemed to be popping up everywhere, disgustingly healthy, out of control.

I was running out of time to tackle it before my company showed up. One particular morning, I set my coffee cup on the porch railing, broke out my cell phone. Then I keyed in a familiar number.

"Artie," I said. "What's the state of the roto-tiller?"

"Emphysema, but it's still breathin'."

"If you haul it over here to the house, I'll spring for the gas."

I heard the confusion in his voice. "When?"

"Now."

"Give me fifteen minutes. I'll pick up a can of gas on the way."

I was standing in the yard when Artie showed up with the tiller. He always kept a couple of scraggly wood planks stashed in the truck bed to help him unload the beast. The fumes wafting from caked-on grease on the ancient machine were positively lung-searing, even from that distance.

"Whatcha need?" Artie said.

"Plow it all under," I said. "Every bit of it."

His eyebrow arched. "Ya got me there, Evie."

"The yard, the grass. All of it," I explained.

"That lawn of yours is salvageable," he said. "We had a wet spring. All that rain's bound to be hard on any—"

"Old news, Artie. I've decided I'm not a grass kind of gal. Fertilizer, mowing. They're not me."

"Dunno. Bare dirt out there is gonna look like one of those crop circles, popping up in the middle of the block."

The furrows between Artie's eyes deepened. He was revving up for a fight. I didn't give him time to throw the next punch.

"Yesterday the perennials came in at Groft's," I said. "An awful lot of them. Way too much. I thought I may as well put some of them to good use, start a cottage garden."

Artie sucked in his breath, let it out again. "A cottage garden, huh? Vivian's always talking about 'em. "

"If the tiller runs out of gas, I'll refill it from the can out in my shed," I said. "There's no way, with the economy what it is, that we're going to move all those pots out of the nursery this season. People are planting pole beans not physostegia. I've got a carful of plants stashed on the porch, ready and waiting. We'll still have plenty of overstock left for the berm."

"Wall to wall flowers. Folks aren't used to that around here."

Artie's face had taken on that deliberate patience of someone confronting a recalcitrant child. I fought a smile.

"I realize that," I told him.

From where I stood, I already caught the faint stirring of the curtains next door. Artie took his hands out of his pockets. His huge Teamster hands clenched and unclenched as he thought about it.

"Okay, Evie, I'm in," he shrugged.

I followed close on his heels as he headed for the truck. "Can I help?"

"Just make sure the ramp doesn't shift on me."

"Can do."

Artie hoisted himself into the truck bed and began propping the planks against the opened tailgate. Sweat standing out against his forehead, he maneuvered the huge tiller down the ramp. Once the thing was on terra firma, he went back for the gas can, poured a goodly amount into the tiller's tank. After a few false starts, the machine sputtered to life with an asthmatic growl.

Artie's knuckles stood out like ridges of newly-planted corn as he grasped the tiller's handles and began to break sod. He started with the patchiest grass near the street. From a safe distance, I watched as stripe by stripe the dark earth began to appear where wispy green shoots and occasional stands of quack grass had been.

Dodging the lindens took some doing on his part. From time to time, Artie stopped long enough to mop his brow with an orange farmer's neckerchief. The homestead lot was very wide and shallow out front. It took a while before the tiller began to make a perceptible dent.

"Damn, Evie, I sure hope ya don't change your mind," he hollered over the roar of the machine.

I laughed. "No chance."

No wonder the grass was in extremis. The soil was like concrete. The job took Artie the better part of the morning. I made him stop around 11 o'clock for some iced tea and zucchini bread out of the freezer.

"You can wait on tackling the back yard until later," I told him. "And if you're up to it, I would love to remount this old wrought-iron fence out in the garage. It used to run the full width of the front sidewalk, lot line to lot line. The joints have weakened in spots but—"

"I'll haul out my torch and post-hole digger. Name the day."

"Let me get the plants settled in first. I'll make sure I leave room for us to work around."

"You saying, we're done then?" Artie looked relieved. "By now Vivian's gonna start wondering about the both of us. Gotta say, there's already a heck of a lot of bare dirt lying here lookin' at ya."

"I'll fill it soon enough," I chuckled. "Tell Vivian I said, Hi."

"Will do." Artie didn't waste any time loading up the tiller and tossing the planks into the back of the truck.

I didn't let any grass grow under my feet either. After a lunch of soup cold out of the can, I quickly made a couple more runs to the nursery with the hatchback full of perennials. Anise was hanging out at the counter. Except for raised eyebrows, she didn't ask where all that random plant stock was going.

"Fill you in later," I waved cheerily after my last trip

I couldn't imagine what Artie must have told Vivian when he got back to her place with the tiller in the back of the truck. By two o'clock she showed up herself on foot and in her jogging attire, shovel in hand.

Forehead knit in concentration, I had bent to tuck the fragile roots of a pot of creeping phlox into the hole I had dug for them. I didn't notice Viv standing there.

Open-mouthed, she just leaned on the paint-scuffed handle of her shovel, staring at the sea of black pots dotting my front yard. "I assume you know what you're doing . . . "

I straightened, trying to visualize my predicament through Vivian's eyes. The size of the plants placed hither and yon, still in their pots, across what had been the front yard gave no clue whatsoever to the design plan—if there was any—that guided my little landscape project.

"Vivian . . . I'm fine. You don't have to do this."

"I beg to differ. You're going to be at this for a month."

I shrugged, forced a smiled. "Possibly. Probably. I haven't given it much thought."

Mercifully, Vivian didn't comment. "Where do I start?"

"Hollyhocks. We need to set them in closest to the house. They're starting to look a little droopy. It's hot out here."

"Amen, to that."

Balancing a 12-inch pot with one hand, my friend deftly coaxed out the root ball. The plant sat there on the bare dirt while she planted her sneaker on the shovel blade and began to dig a hole for it. The back rows of the garden butted against the porch supports but still got a fair amount of sun. My plan was to fill the sheltered space with sunflowers, hollyhocks and a stand of midnight blue delphiniums. Along the walks and beside the porch, I tipped in fragrant herbs wherever I could—lavender, mint, lemon balm. Wooly dwarf thyme would fill in once the slate flagstones and wood chips were in place.

All of it spindly looking at the moment, I had to admit. But when I closed my eyes I could imagine the graceful stalks and foliage of the larger plants framing the shorter perennials taking up residence between the house and the sidewalk.

"You could have fixed that lawn of yours," she said. "Wasn't that bad."

"Maybe. Not as interesting as this, though."

"Artie was worried about you," she said.

"Thought I'd lost it, huh?"

Chuckling softly, I began to dig in clump after clump, always with an eye to my plan for the garden to bloom in one way or another during every season of the year. "Can't blame Artie on some level," I told Vivian. "I've been worried about me, too. But if I'm ever going to get on with my life, I decided it was time to try something pretty dramatic."

"This certainly qualifies."

Adam's face smiled down at me from the dusty corners of my memory as I slipped three pots of Shasta daisies into the bed. "I can't help it. I think of him every day, Viv. What would Adam and I be doing? What would he say about the fuel bills . . . what's been going on at Groft's."

Vivian stopped what she doing, leaned on the shovel while she worked the kinks out of her back. "Nobody—not even you—can tell you there's a timetable for grief," she said. "Everyone needs to handle it in their own good time . . . "

Nothing I hadn't heard before, most recently from Matt Gaskill sitting in the half-light of the sanctuary over at Peace. Still, something in the quiet edge to Vivian's voice made me stop and take notice. My friend had losses of her own—among them her fiancé to a military accident. A lifetime ago and still, what I read in Viv's gentle smile spoke volumes. We may cope. But our lives are never the same.

"Maybe. But Groft's doesn't have that kind of time. And it was stupid of me not to rethink the standing orders from the wholesalers last fall. We lucked out with the bulbs . . . though the same is not as likely of the latest shipment. Vegetable gardening is way up this year. I can't imagine what we're going to do with all these perennials—"

"We can always dig some of them in on the berm."

"True. Still, that leaves one awful lot of plants."

"We'll think of something," she said. "You can't get all these plants dug in by nightfall. You're going to kill yourself."

"Just another half-hour . . . then I'm done," I said. "Leslie will be here Friday with Emma and Harry. Her sister is flying in to Traverse City later on that afternoon with Justin—"

"So we'll lose you this weekend at the berm . . . "

"Of course I'll come. The girls can join us while their older kids entertain each other and the baby. Emma loves to dig in the mud."

A thoughtful frown had settled in between Vivian's brows. "I assume you've thought about how you're going to house everybody. You can always count on an extra bed at our place if it comes to that."

"I was planning to put Leslie and her family in the master bedroom. I'll take the couch. Gina can sleep on the pull-out in my office with her son. He's just six. But if he objects to bunking with mom, he might actually like the idea of camping out in the living room with Grama."

A pecking order of sorts—with a wild-card that hadn't been an issue before. Anise was ensconced in the guest bedroom upstairs. It never occurred to me that my grown daughters might find the logistics politically fraught.

It was too late to second-guess myself now. When Vivian finally took her shovel and headed for home, I thanked her profusely for her help and kept on digging. An hour flew past, then two. First thing I knew, Anise had closed up at Groft's and stood watching me from the safety of the curb. I had just finished defining the clump of larkspur closest to the lot line.

Larkspur, delphinium. Grumbling under my breath, I realized that I had included yet another perennial *twice* on my garden plan. Along with *Dianthus* aka carnation and sweet william and probably more I had yet to unearth with all my rooting and digging.

"This probably seems like a ridiculous question," Anise said finally, "but what happened to the lawn?"

"You noticed." I told her about Artie and his tiller. "There are still a lot of holes to fill . . . but you get the general idea."

"I wondered where you were going with all those pots. Cottage garden, huh?"

"That's the plan."

"You certainly have the neighbors guessing."

Lucille and Addie. I straightened in time to catch the sisters next door with their curtains slightly parted, all the better to keep an eye on my progress. "I've pretty much resigned myself to being an endless source of entertainment for my neighbors."

"Jane Austen. *Pride and Prejudice.*"

"I'm impressed."

"Well, I'm confused, to tell you the truth. Between Groft's and the berm I would have guessed you would have had enough of mulch and fertilizer and—"

"Stupid, I suppose," I paused long enough to deal with the rivulets of sweat that were making it hard to see what I was doing. "But then, this garden is about *me* . . . not about community beautification or promises made and kept about the nursery. And I'm going to keep it up come hell

130

or high water . . . !'"

"Eve's Garden," Anise turned the idea over in her head. "Or maybe Garden of Eve. I like that better."

"A little pretentious, don'tcha think?"

"Beats a whole yard full of sun-baked, yellowing grass."

One thing was certain. My daughters wouldn't have to set foot in the house to sense things were different in their mother's life. That cottage garden all but hollered, High Risk.

I dragged out the porch furniture and sat admiring the handiwork. "You're going to be surprised," I warned Leslie on Tuesday morning when she called to check in. "I've been doing some work around the place."

"Sounds drastic . . ."

"I'd say so."

"A hint, then?"

"I want it to be a surprise," I said. But at least my daughter was forewarned.

It takes weeks, sometimes months for potted perennials to recover from transplant shock. These had less than a week. I knew better than to select ones already in bloom, but I wasn't willing to cut back foliage any more than necessary. As is, the new garden had a tentative look about it.

"Maybe it's none of my business, but that squinty-eyed look of yours isn't going to make them grow any faster," Anise said. "Though who am I to talk? Caleb and I have had this ongoing conversation for a month now—about punctuality and filial devotion."

I laughed. "He'll show up when he's good and ready."

"And you're worried about your girls showing up. They're going to find lots of changes around the old homestead."

"The garden."

Anise half-smiled. "And me. Here. Living in *your* house."

"I don't like that word. *Our* sounds much more homey and civilized."

"Semantics. I could skip out while they're here, you know. One of the gals on the wait-staff at Marty's has been bugging me to drive up to Little Traverse some weekend, find a cheap motel and hang out for a day or two. Walk the beach and look for Petoskey stones. After the tourist season starts, *forget it*. Plus by then the baby will be here and—"

"No way. You're staying right here."

"Eve, I get it—your family has a claim on this place. All this was

131

'theirs' once. And here I am, settling in as if I owned the place."

I shrugged. "The girls are adults. They'll handle it."

"Who says age makes change any easier? You're their Mom. Getting stuck in that snowbank was the best thing that happened to me in a long time. But the economy is picking up. I have choices . . . would rather wind back up in my car than causing any kinds of problems between you and your family."

Surely she wasn't thinking of leaving. My chest felt tight at the thought.

"Don't even go there," I said. "You have a place with me as long as you want or need it or both. And selfishly speaking . . . I hope it's a good long while."

We human beings are a strange lot. We pull together and push away. We fear to hold on too tight, to love too little or love too much. We bury those lost to us in gardens of stone, when what we long for most is to keep their precious memories alive and growing.

On Thursday I discovered Peace Episcopal is about to get a *Peace Garden*. Plan is to locate it in the side yard between church and parsonage. Matt Gaskill had just come back from Minneapolis when his son the vicar recruited him to take charge. Still scratching his head over the whole idea, Matt drove out to Groft's for ground cloth. I sold him two rolls of the stuff for the project and threw in an extra compliments of the nursery.

"I guess it'll be low maintenance," Matt said, "in theory, anyway. Rings of field stones should hold down the layers of gardener's cloth to mark the paths. Then I'll mulch the whole thing with wood chips. Personally, if I know weeds, I would go with Agent Orange."

"Sounds like a labyrinth," I said.

"Exactly. Apparently the 'peace' part is more about intent than design. Ben found a photo online of a public garden in Albuquerque. Technically, what he wants is a labyrinth in miniature. Except the darn thing out West has got to be half-a-block across. I have twelve feet—maybe fifteen, tops."

"Sounds like a problem of scale," I said.

"I sure wouldn't let more than one person try walking the thing at a time."

"The sound of one hand clapping," I laughed. "Your Ben seems to be getting into gardening in a big way. He's been showing up faithfully at the berm . . . now this."

Matt winced. "A late bloomer. My wife used to entice Ben to help with her gardens when he was little. At the time he wasn't having any of it. One week under Bea's tutelage and the kid is already eyeing Master Gardener status . . ."

"A dreamer. Can't fault a man for that."

I had a strong suspicion where Ben Gaskill got it. His father's face had taken on a distant, introspective look—one I had seen before when we talked about his life back in the Twin Cities. For all of his blunt-edge coach's style, Matt Gaskill was turning out to be a complicated man.

"My son doesn't know it," he said with an impatient shrug, "or if he does, he isn't saying . . . but he needs a good woman in his life, that's for sure. Someone who will tell him when it's raining. Take the edge off."

"Funny you should mention it. I thought he smiles a lot more lately."

Matt laughed. "Not on my account. If I'm going to stick around here much longer, I really am going to have to find my own digs. The cottage idea came and went . . . I've been thinking somewhere in town. Easy walk to the grocery and health care . . . the usual list. I finally bit the bullet and talked to some realtors back home. All this could take a while, I fear."

"Smart move, deciding to look in town," I said. "We see a lot of tourists around here who spend a lifetime enjoying their woodland retreats. Eventually when they retire and settle full-time, it tends to get ugly. Public transportation in the county can be a real problem."

Matt nodded. "That occurred to me."

"I can't speak for Minnesota, but it's a buyer's market in Xenaphon. I would say one in four houses are up for grabs, one way or the other. Snowbirds get tired of maintaining two places. Unsettled estates can hang on for decade. Lately, we've seen a lot of foreclosures. A good half of the places on the market took down the For Sale sign years ago. No point."

"I'll keep that in mind. Rent to start maybe."

"Easy enough, too."

"Somehow I think Ben won't see it that way . . ."

It wasn't hard to put myself in Matt Gaskill's shoes. I had been dreading that same conversation with my girls after I inherited Adam's lake cottage. Initially anyway, I had toyed with selling the homestead. But then Leslie and Gina hadn't been raised there. Despite warm feelings for the place, they didn't share the same kind of memories I had as a girl.

"It's gorgeous out at the lake," Leslie had told me, "if that's where you want to live. Financially, I know it could be a drain to hang on to both places. No one would blame you if you decided to sell either one."

Even with her imprimatur, a year-and-a-half later I was still nowhere near dealing with the situation. I drifted back to the moment to catch Matt Gaskill looking at me strangely.

"Was it something I said . . . ?"

I managed an embarrassed laugh. "Just wondering where you're going to find the rocks?"

A hint of a smile flickered at the corner of his mouth. "Good question," he said. "Haven't gotten that far yet, but Ben doesn't seem worried. He says the county has agreed to drop off a load of wood chips."

"Good luck."

"With this crazy forced labor program my son schnookered me into, for the house hunt, Lord help me . . .or with the whole father-son thing . . . ?"

"All of the above, I guess."

It was on the tip of my tongue to unload on the subject, but I decided against it. The man had plenty enough on his plate. Though I assumed he hadn't taken a serious look at *my* front yard lately. And he certainly wasn't the only one with issues when it came to adult children.

Thrilled as I was about the girls' visit, I wasn't looking forward to some of the flack that was bound to come with it. Between my relationship with Anise and that impulsive make-over on my front lawn, I knew I was going to have some serious "splaining" to do.

Next time I saw Matt Gaskill, it was in the drug store. I had to fight the impulse to laugh. The guy looked so miserable—had one of those microwave heat pads in hand. He took his time maneuvering in my direction. I noticed he was limping.

"How's it going over there?" I said.

"Rocks. No garden should be without 'em . . . in case you're looking for a column idea, feel free to quote me on that one."

I limited myself to a restrained chuckle. "I try not to cannibalize the lives of friends and neighbors any more than I have to."

"Cannibalize away. I must say that I thoroughly enjoying those google-induced mind trips in your columns—in the solitude and silence of the midnight hour and all that stuff. There's a certain mad poetry in the idea."

"Let me guess . . . William Blake?"

"Probably just some rock band my students tried to pass off as the next Shakespeare. After trying to enlighten tenth graders about poetic exotica for most of my adult life, Beethoven is all well and good, but there are some occasions when only Husker Du will cut it."

"Husker . . . what?"

"Husker Du. I'll have to trot out my original tee shirt one of these days—still wearable, last time I looked."

"Sounds like a Swedish farm co-op."

He laughed. "Try, a bunch of vintage Saint Paul-based punk rockers. Back in the Eighties, they were the first underground group ever to sign on with a major record label."

"You realize now I'm going to have to check them out . . . "

"Google on, Ms. Brennerman! Lord knows, I've been doing enough of it since I started this labyrinth business," Matt shook his head. "Addictive as heck . . . and it's all your fault."

"Why do I think some people don't need much of an excuse!"

Our animated conversation and the laughter that went with it had begun to turn a few heads congregating at the drug store cash register. *Matchmaking*, I winced, *the small town mind at work.*

It never occurred to me to question before how our casual banter might play out in the collective imagination. Vaguely flattering, if it weren't so ridiculously funny. Even if I were looking—which I wasn't—Matt Gaskill wasn't my type.

Paranoia about the situation certainly wasn't helpful. If the guy decided to stay in Xenaphon, it would be all but impossible to avoid one another.

Once safely out on the sidewalk, I turned down Matt's offer of a ride. He headed his way and I mine—the beginning and end of it. But he was right about the column. In my head I was already online, mining for tidbits to add to what I already knew:

Xenaphon is going to have a Peace Garden—ours will be carved in stone. The use of rocks in gardening isn't new.

135

Labyrinths—a common variety of "rock garden"—date back at least to 4000 BC on the island of *Crete.*

Even in ancient times they were considered sacred. Greek myth says that first labyrinth was built by Daedalus. He was an architect so skilled that his structures appeared to come alive and move. By 2000 BC, an image of his labyrinth showed up on a coin minted on Knossos. Christians in Roman Algeria adopted the symbol of the labyrinth as early as 382 AD to express their spiritual walk.

For Daedalus himself, the story ended badly. Exiled by the tyrant Minos, the architect constructed wings of wax to escape with his son Icarus. Only his son flew too close to the sun, fell to earth and drowned. To this day, the shimmering waters of the Icarian Sea bear his name.

Japanese Zen Buddhists actually refer to gardening as the art of "setting upright stones", *shi wo taten koto.* Modern dry landscape gardens in the deserts of the American Southwest draw on that tradition.

But then transforming the ground beneath our feet also has its lighter moments. In the late 1970s, two pranksters began to turn the ripening grain fields of their native England into elaborate crop circles. Conspiracy theorists have had a field day ever since. Could this be the work of Druids—even messengers from outer space? It seems way too simple just to credit a couple of very creative gardeners.

So it seems that Xenaphon is going to get its very own portal to the Eternal Mysteries. Check it out. I'll bet that the construction crew will appreciate some help moving all those rocks.

That last was aimed straight at tweaking Matt Gaskill.

Unless I missed my guess, I would be getting a minor flood of fan mail on the subject. Winds of change were at work in our quiet little backwater. First my cottage garden shows up mid-block on Gratiot Street and now a stone circle in the side yard at Peace Episcopal. I could hear the natives down at the mini mart already.

Nine
Mothers and Daughters

Flowers are a lot like children, George Bernard Shaw once wrote, except we don't mow them down and put them in vases. My girls are coming. I've been looking forward to it since Christmas. So then, why am I expecting the proverbial axe to fall? FROM EVE'S JOURNAL

What is it with the last customers of the day? On Friday I was on the verge of closing the doors at Groft's when the car pulled up out front. There were four of them and apparently they had been reading up on predator control.

As I tried not to shift from foot to foot, ready to bolt out the door, they took their time cleaning out three flats of veggies before moving on to the power sprayers. Someone had told them if you whip an egg, some milk, cooking oil and dish soap into a gallon of water and spread it on the ground around the garden, the concoction will keep the antlered population from eating everything in sight.

Vile stuff. I didn't have the heart to tell them we once tried those egg-based repellents on the berm. No one showed up to weed for a week.

Their sizeable sales tab couldn't change facts—that delay in closing shop couldn't have come at a worse time. I arrived back at the homestead tired and cranky to find Anise already entertaining my daughter Leslie, Emma and her brother Harry on the front porch. From the collective body language when the two women spotted me, I suspected

137

that in my absence daughter Leslie had been carrying out a creditable imitation of the Spanish Inquisition.

My daughter's face, its strong features so like my own, was like a thundercloud. She was wearing sweats and battered running shoes. Odd, how we miss the obvious and zero in on what divides us instead. For a split-second I found myself transported back to that first glimpse of Anise Gruin sitting defiantly in her rusting 'turtle' car—erstwhile symbol of the good life living tenaciously on beyond the production line that had created it.

"Mom," my daughter said. "You're home."

"Sorry I'm late . . . hot, sweaty. I've been repotting seedlings out at Groft's most of the afternoon. And then these fudge-sicles showed up last minute with a list a mile long . . . "

Leslie couldn't suppress a smile. It was an in-joke between us, our own variation on the way locals described long-term cottagers as 'perma-fudgies'. Blocks of fudge in all its manifestations were a staple of the local economy when the tourists descended every summer.

We eased into an awkward hug. Launching herself in our direction, Emma clung to us both while she wished me a happy "Grama's Day". Before anyone else could get a word in edgewise, I found myself fielding her nonstop questions about the colony of perennials that had taken over my front yard since her last visit.

"Cool, Grama," she said finally, "you're gonna have the biggest garden on the block!"

"I'm counting on it."

Meanwhile Anise and the porch swing seemed to have become an unending source of amusement for young Harry. Just as fast the toddler half-crawled up on the webbed seat alongside her, he was down again. Anise had the look of someone casting about for the exits.

"How about I give you guys some alone-time," she said. "I'll go put the burgers on the grill."

Leslie was already on her feet. "Let me, Mom," she said.

I knew sibling rivalry when I saw it. Some stranger seemed to be usurping my daughter's place in my life.

Not the reaction I would have expected of her. Through all the difficult times with her father, my oldest was always the one who took my side. It was her younger sister, Gina, who blamed me for anything and everything, including the wretched state of my marriage—that is, until

138

Adam intervened. Gina had come to Xenaphon determined to dislike the man and Adam knew it. What turned things around was his willingness to sacrifice our relationship if that was what it took to affect a reconciliation, to prove that he knew and respected what my daughters meant in my life.

But that was then. And when it came to the girls, the weather vane had swung one-eighty. It was Leslie, not Gina who seemed bent on taking me to task. There was no Adam to counsel me to keep a level head.

I felt the distance acutely between us as Leslie and I headed for the kitchen. The rush of air from the refrigerator felt cool against my skin. I took my time scrounging the shelves and bins for the ingredients of a cookout.

"By the way, happy Mother's Day yourself," I said. "Your Harry is growing like a weed. And Emma . . . that girl is beautiful. I've really missed them . . . you . . . your sister . . . "

Leslie avoided eye contact. "I know it's been way too long . . . sorry about that. We didn't intend to punk out at Easter. But since the layoff, Dan has had a very rough time of it. He sends his greetings . . . "

"No problem. I understand. It's just so great to see you!"

"But then I can see you've been keeping plenty busy yourself," she hesitated and I could sense she, too, was counting mentally to ten. "Lots of changes."

"A good busy, I think. The novel, of course. And you saw the garden out front. I'm glad you've finally met Anise."

"She's from downstate somewhere . . . "

"Detroit—"

"It must be . . . *different* having someone else underfoot twenty-four seven. Since Adam died, I thought . . . I got the impression you wanted your privacy. To write, for starters."

Want had nothing to do with the situation. Jaw tight, I dropped my gaze. Had our conversation really moved back to square one—to the tense and guarded phone calls months ago when I first announced I was taking in a boarder?

"To be fair, I suspect it was more of a change for Anise than me," I said. "Winters in Xenaphon can be pretty grim for young singles, with nothing but a lot of us oldsters for company."

"Well, she'll sure have enough company this weekend," Leslie's eyebrow arched. "The whole drive up from Chicago, I wondered how on earth you were going to fit the bunch of us in upstairs. The kids and me,

Gina and her Justin . . . and Anise. If it's too crowded, the kids and I can always camp out at the motel."

I struggled hard not to smile, all the while my heart went out to her. *Separation anxiety and the human condition.* For better or worse, it seems that a lost and needy child lurks within us all until the day we die. Trust and sharing are acquired not inherited, two sides of a single coin—a civilizing veneer, though thinner than we realize. Life lessons from the sandbox. What is it Matt Gaskill said about change never coming in straight lines?

It never occurred to me before what a perennial might feel like if and when a gardener chooses to divide it. Gardening out on the berm or almost anywhere certainly depends on the process. Does that calculated act of separating a chunk of roots from the mother plant unleash in both the self-same sense of loss and vulnerability?

Plants bruise. If you crush them, they bleed. Perhaps heartache and loneliness were not humankind's alone to face or conquer.

"No problem," I said briskly. "Got it all figured out. With your Harry so mobile, I thought I would put the three of you in the master bedroom—"

"And Gina?"

"She can bunk in my office. The pull-out is all made up. If Justin doesn't like the idea of sleeping in the same bed as his Mom, I have a sleeping bag."

"Well, I am not going to let you sleep on the floor, Mom."

"Not to worry. I'll take the couch downstairs. Out of the fray."

"It's not right to kick you out of your own bed."

"I'll live. A small price to pay for all of you being here . . . "

Leslie all that while had begun attacking the raw hamburger with two hands. The growing stack of patties on the platter in the middle of my kitchen table had the imprint of her frustration all over them.

"I know we've been preoccupied . . . haven't been as supportive as we should have been in the past six months. Longer . . . "

"You were there for me after Adam died. I appreciate that more than I can say."

"So, what is this all about?"

"*This* . . . ?"

Leslie didn't respond.

"Taking in a boarder," I guessed.

140

"This whole late-life crisis deal. You let a stranger in your house—"

"Not a stranger, Les."

"You rip up the front yard. Chase from Groft's to the print shop every day . . . skip lunch, from the look of it."

This had to be a first. One of my daughters actually considered me too skinny.

"Flattering," I forced a smile, "but I still could stand to lose another ten or so. We may have started out with donuts and pastry, but Anise has me eating way healthier than I have in—"

"It hurts me to watch this!" Leslie said, impatient now. "You're supposed to be retired . . . your time to travel, enjoy life. Gina and I would *love* to have you to stay with us, as long and often as you would like. Surely you know that. The kids are growing up so—"

"And I'm sad not to see them more. But then in this economy, a lot of my friends are still working . . . part-time anyway."

"You're worried about money, is that it?"

"The nursery is still struggling, but no—outside of that, I'm fine."

"So *what*, then?"

"'I'm sure it's hard to believe at your age,'" I said slowly, "but you have no idea what a gift it is finally to be able to work at what you truly love . . . when and how you want to. I hadn't expected that. And I love to write. I love to garden. There are worse ways to spend my retirement. True, like everybody else, I sometimes wish I had more time just to sit and veg-out . . . the existential urge simply to *be*—"

With a shock, I realized I couldn't bring myself to tell my daughter the whole truth. The mere prospect of leaving my comfort zone—Xenaphon, the homestead, even that garden struggling to establish itself where my front lawn had been—was terrifying.

Leslie's brow tightened. "Well, if it's peace and quiet you're after, having a baby underfoot won't be easy, trust me."

"Funny. Anise said the same thing. Almost word for word."

My daughter let out her breath in a tight little rush. "Mom, I just don't get it. You've never been one for the grand gestures . . . unless you count putting up with a dysfunctional marriage all those years. And suddenly, out of nowhere you come up with something like this. Picking someone off the street—"

"Hardly a grand gesture. It was colder than hell. Anise didn't have

141

a place to stay. I had one. I made her a cup of tea. We talked. She baked me cinnamon rolls."

"That was four months ago."

"Three-and-change. And if she left tomorrow, I would miss her."

"So then you go and dig up your front yard, for crying out loud!"

"We overstocked the perennials at Groft's. Our community garden could absorb some, although the master gardener keeps saying, 'Not one more inch under cultivation until we have more volunteers out there.' Plus I've always loved cottage gardens," I finished in a rush. "Most of the bare spots out front should fill in nicely."

"Am I allowed a 'Why?' You've already got Great-Gram's garden out back, the nursery and that berm . . . "

"Because whatever happens beyond my doorstep, this garden is for me. Mine. Right out front . . . impossible to miss. And there's not another one in town remotely like it."

"That I believe . . . "

A wisp of a smile tugged at the corner of my mouth. "Les, sweetheart, you keep trying to make sense of something that—by the frame of my life as you've always known it—is bound to make no sense at all. The whole notion sort of crept up on me, too, for that matter."

"Gina and I, all of us, were devastated for and with you when Adam died. I understand that you've lost something precious . . . can't even imagine the hurt and pain of all that. It's a huge hole to fill."

"*Impossible*," I corrected her. "And you're right . . . *no one knows* until they stand in those shoes . . . "

The silence hung heavily between us. My throat felt as if it were closing tight.

"I tried denial, believe me," I told her, "anger, all of it. For over a year, I tried building a monument to what we had, Adam and I. I thought if I could just lay it all out there, write it all down, then somehow he would still be . . . I wouldn't have to admit that he was truly *gone* . . . "

"You're talking about *TIME in a Garden*."

"Yes."

"I meant every word I said about your manuscript. It's wonderful."

"And that means more to me than I can say. Despite all the tweaking and editing from my boss, it was and is your story, too. That doesn't change the ending . . . where *do* we go the morning after the fairy tale ends? I only know the time is past due for a sequel. And I'm the only

142

one who can write it. Not you or Gina. Not Anise Gruin. Just me."

"*Happily ever after* . . . nice, if we can manage it."

"I'll settle for the inner strength to take life one day at a time. Ultimately, we can't escape where the plot twists in life take us—if we're honest, we all know how things end. But for better or worse, the cast of characters in my world has begun to grow . . . has taken on a life of its own. *We grow or we die.* If you're looking for explanations, that's as good as it's gonna get."

Leslie stared down at the table, her fingers tracing the grain of the wood in ever tighter circles. "And us? Your family . . . your own flesh and blood?"

"Les, if you're honest, you wouldn't *want* me to live vicariously through you and your sister's families. Xenaphon and these people are my home. But even worse than losing Adam, would be to lose you or Gina or those precious grandbabies of mine. I'm your mother. And nothing on earth can fill that void. Ever. Much as I loved him—Adam, of all people, knew that came first."

Leslie's voice was thick with unshed tears. "You could have fooled me."

"Never."

"You think I'm being selfish . . . ridiculous," Leslie said.

I half-smiled—noticed she had left 'jealous" out of the mix. "Aren't we all," I said, "aren't we all likely to . . . overreact. Especially when we wonder if someone we love has totally gone off the end of the board."

"I never said that."

"No. But if you thought it, you wouldn't have been the only one. I am told on good authority, the neighbors are *still* in a tizzy over Artie and his roto-tiller tearing up the sod out there."

"Artie. That teamster guy . . . he actually went along with—?"

"Yup."

Leslie let out an audible breath. "Well, I'm not at all sure what you expect of us, Gina and me."

"Playing catch-up has got to be a big part of it."

"If it's any consolation, what Dan and I have gone through in the past few months has been unprintable."

"A day hasn't gone by without my worrying for both of—"

"And Gina is totally freaked about Justin. Since he started school, the poor kid has been a walking germ factory."

"I would never have pegged your sister as a possessive mom."

"You have no idea. Trust me, a long weekend has no chance of even making a dent on unpacking all of—"

"We can make a stab at it . . . can't we, Les? And while we're figuring it out, I think we have some major fence mending to do on the front porch. By now, I'll bet we've given Anise a real eye-opener about the joys of parenthood . . . !"

Leslie grimaced, awkwardly took the tissue I handed her. "I don't want to be a jerk. I'll admit, she seems less—"

"Less like a serial killer than you feared?" I laughed. "Les, sweetheart, she isn't and you are being far too hard on yourself. You're *human*, both of you. Tough for an oldest sibling like you, I know—admitting that possibility."

"Mothers and daughters."

"We've had some interesting moments over the years."

"When you look back on this one, I hope you won't file it under the heading of Epic Meltdowns . . . "

A howl of protest from the porch cut short any response—all the earmarks of the Terrible Two's at their worst. The siren choked off mid-stream, sputtered back to life on a rising wail

"I'll be right back," Leslie took off at a sprint.

When she didn't immediately return, I took it as a Sign. A good one. By the time we all finished eating supper together, it was dark. The May flies were out, annoying enough that we decided to move indoors. *Quietly under one roof,* the bunch of us.

Gina showed up from the airport in Traverse City with matching luggage and my grandson, Justin, sporting khakis, button-down shirt and a blazer. At least his mother had foregone the rep tie. Still, the contrast to his cousin, Emma, couldn't have been greater. The picture of reserved decorum, Justin gravely reached out and shook my hand before I succeeded in coaxing him into a grandmotherly hug.

"Missed you, Justin," I told him.

It was as if from one day to the next he had grown from toddler into a budding young man. The dusting of freckles across his nose and unruly auburn hair seemed so delightfully out of character, I had to smile.

"He's really grown, hasn't he, Mom?" Gina enthused as we exchanged hugs.

"You've done a great job," I said. "Really, Gina. I'm proud of you."

At first glance, Gina was still so like her father, I found myself thinking, *tall and lanky, a head-turning presence.* I felt almost guilty at how much my preoccupation with her sister Leslie's malaise had distracted me these past months. Somehow while my back was turned, my tight-wound dynamo of a youngest daughter had turned into a generous, womanly adult—a mother herself. When I told her where to stash their luggage, Gina didn't even blink.

The first installment of grandchildren was still awake though running out of steam. Even Justin, trying hard to play the sophisticated traveler with his cousins, was yawning. While my daughters broke out the bedtime snacks and put the crew down for the night, Anise and I straightened up in the kitchen. By the time peace reigned upstairs, I had a fire going in the grate. Our little circle of women settled in to enjoy it.

"I love it . . . just like the old days upstairs, Mom," Gina smiled. "Kids everywhere, remember? Campin' out at Grandma's we used to call it."

Leslie flashed her sister one of those, Now-I've-Heard-Everything looks. My youngest had never been big on nostalgia. If anything, Gina's grin broadened.

Leslie changed the subject. "I was surprised you made it here so early . . . worried the whole time about you going through O'Hare," she said. "They've been predicting possible weather . . . wind shear, something ominous."

"On time, all the way. Luggage made it through. No problem."

"Only it's dark enough . . . you missed Mom's yard."

"Yard."

"Mom had that Teamster guy over the whole thing with a roto-tiller. She's got a cottage garden going on out there."

"The whole thing?"

"Curb to porch," Leslie nodded.

"Different."

"I hope so," I intervened. "That was the plan."

My youngest chuckled, shook her head. "Well, the grass out there was always thin . . . reminded me of a gigantic comb-over. Remember the time we played croquet out front, Les?"

Her memory, not mine. Apparently not Leslie's either or at least she didn't react one way or the other.

"You weren't any too happy about our little unsanctioned Olympics, Mom," Gina said. "All those divets. You said we turned the yard into a prairie dog town."

The Rapture had come and I seemed to be the only one left standing. For once, even Leslie was taking this all in stride.

"Kids are kids," I said.

Anise had been silent all that while. "I'll admit, the three of you certainly have the jump on me when it comes to country living," she said. "I grew up next door to a bakery. Glass in the alley, potholes in the parking lot out back. It's worse now, I expect . . . "

"I've seen the news footage of Detroit," Gina said. "Sad."

"A New Orleans style levee break . . . only instead of walls of water, chalk it up to a flood-tide of greed and lack of a vision."

"I read somewhere Flint is even worse. Something like 20 percent of the housing stock is abandoned."

"And then there's Xenaphon."

"Actually we're doing a bit better lately," I said. "New Doc in town. Name of Jaidev . . . and he's living here not just riding the circuit. From New Delhi or somewhere via the UM-Medical School. Our new vicar at Peace Episcopal has his dad living with him in the parsonage at the moment but I'm told the senior Gaskill is on the lookout for a house in town now. A transplant from Minneapolis."

"And the paper, Mom?"

"Hanging in. George's son is up from Pittsburgh on some kind of mission to straighten out the bank. All sorts of rumors have been flying about how bad things are or aren't. But my boss has family after all these years—kind of nice for him."

"I never knew George was married," Gina looked puzzled.

"Briefly."

Slowly but surely, the conversation had moved on. As Anise and I made eye contact, I read something behind her smile that I hadn't seen since I got home from work. It seemed suspiciously like relief.

Next morning we all gardened together out at the berm. It was way too much like moving an army to the front, but we made it for the last hour anyway. The crew was younging-up considerably. Along with the bunch from last week, we now had toddler Harry, first-graders Emma and Justin.

Our fearless leader Bea looked shell-shocked. The berm's heap of sandy topsoil had taken on the hyperactive intensity of an ant hill. Though still woefully late, the garden itself was showing small signs of improvement. Personally, I was relieved to notice that the daisy plugs we had transplanted seemed to be taking hold.

My gang didn't contribute much to the morning's efforts. Gardening is tough to childproof. The girls spent most of the time scrambling to keep their broods out of trouble. With all those sharp-honed tools lying within easy reach, losing a toe or other appendage was a distinct possibility. Justin seemed to have gotten most of the ooze on his face and jacket—delightful, considering how impeccably clad the boy had shown up on my doorstep. Emma was the only grandchild capable of more than transferring mud from one furrow to another.

"Sorry if it got kind of tough out there," I said as we piled ourselves back into the cars for the trip back into town.

"Gotta be done," Gina smiled. "Saturdays on the berm . . . it's a tradition around here."

Yes, it was. And my family had become a part of it. I was pleased, too, to see that gardening on the berm had become an inter-generational thing. The rest of the long weekend all but flew past. Peace Episcopal's Mens' Club—median age seventy-nine—put together a creditable Mother's Day breakfast, part homage and part fund-raiser. We all went, including Anise as a mother-to-be.

Ever the couple, Artie and Vivian had volunteered for counter duty at Groft's for the day, aided and abetted by their young charge Chris Demort. Gradually they were unlocking the harsh realities of what the young man had experienced for most of his young life. For starters, every time his mother picked up a new guy, Chris wound up sleeping in the storeroom of the mini-mart. In their own understated fashion, Artie and Viv certainly offered him a very different model of what it meant to be 'dating'.

"You're moving in with me, kid," Artie told him, "so there'll be none of that. We got a curfew around here. You'll water my plants and bunk at Vivian's when I'm on the road. Keep the lawn mowed. Trust me, you'll earn your keep."

Of course, Artie's demands were all bluff and bluster. For starters, the 'plants' were several unassuming pots of herbs Vivian had thinned out from her garden last fall. It occurred to me to wonder how my friends planned to reconcile that teenage company with their personal life. I didn't have the nerve to ask—the comings and goings in the homestead right now were complicated enough.

And then I made the colossal mistake of introducing the girls to Matt Gaskill. Matt came on totally in character, the irrepressible coach, always motivating.

"Your Mom is one go-get-'em lady," he said, "certainly has livened things up around here!"

Before I could protest or clarify, he had launched into a side-splitting account of how we met, down to the last cascading hymnal. My girls laughed at all the right moments, but something in the way they looked at each other told me they were getting the wrong idea. Before it got to that point, some emergency called him in the direction of the kitchen.

"New guy in town, huh?" Leslie said.

I managed a laugh. "Originally from Minnesota. He says he is thinking about relocating, but so far no 'Sold' signs. I'll believe it when I see it."

Other priorities quickly took the front burner. Gina had set her sites on getting Justin and Emma to Xenaphon for the summer—together, if possible.

"Quality time with Grama," Gina said. "A great idea."

Leslie didn't hesitate. "My Emma loved it last summer."

"Okay, Mom, so we were thinking maybe between the second weekend in July and early August," Gina enthused. "That would still leave time for the kids to get ready for school in the fall."

I loved my grandchildren. But after a weekend chasing Emma and Justin and Harry, I was beginning to feel my limits. Anise was due in June. I would be going from an empty nest to two kids and a baby in the homestead at the same time. *For a month*. I hoped my panic didn't show in my face.

"Of course, I wasn't thinking all summer for Justin," Gina said quickly. "A long weekend, maybe a week at the most."

"Emma certainly would enjoy the new baby. She was really good when little Harry came along. Even changed diapers. *Not the yucky ones*, Emma used to say. *Just the floods*."

I laughed. "I can imagine."

Emma had been following me everywhere the entire weekend. If I stopped to pull a few weeds in the front yard, she wanted to know the names of every plant within a six-foot radius. When I whipped up a homemade herbed cheese spread with fresh greens from my tiny indoor kitchen garden, she insisted on helping. Together we hauled blocks and toys from the attic to entertain her brother and cousin—treasures saved from their mothers' childhoods.

Wide-eyed through it all, Emma would look up at me as if to say, "You and me, Grandma. The rest of these guys just don't have a clue!"

So much like my Leslie, I thought. And still for all the quirks and mannerisms in common, very much her own little person. Daughter Leslie handled the dynamic with a quiet amusement that both surprised and touched me. I never consciously had taught parenting skills when the two girls were growing up. For better or worse, they simply had experienced my dogged keep-them-busy style—a decided contrast to their father's boisterous, alcohol-fueled intervention that was quick to morph into impatience or indifference.

"Your garden has m-m-mums," Emma said as we picked our way through the clumps of distinctive leaves. "M-m-good. Mums *do* smell good, Grama."

Emma remembered a great deal more about gardening from last summer's visit than I would have thought. My own grandmother had taught me the names of a lot of plants that way—name association or some tall tale that connected flower to name.

"And you told me we gotta pinch 'um back," she said. "Or they'll get sprawly."

"Soon. Give them another inch."

Emma frowned. "We pinched twice last summer."

"And we'll do that again. Once in June—"

"I won't be here yet."

"You will be in July."

"We gotta write it on the calendar."

I smiled. "No need. The plants will tell us when it's time. Six inches is the right height the first time. If the season is late, maybe we will pinch them back a third time so they won't bud too early."

"Will I still be here?"

"I think so. Your Mom hasn't decided yet."

She was digging with the toe of her sneaker in the dirt. "Can this be my garden, too?"

I smiled. "Of course. I brought home these seed packets when I stopped by the nursery today—just so we can plant them together. There's still a hole for them at the back of the bed."

Emma took the crisp white packets in her two hands, frowned as her mouth shaped the letters. "Love . . . in a . . . Mist," she read. "Love Lies B-l-ee-ding. Funny names for plants."

"They're tall and that's what matters. The Love in a Mist would look nice alongside the delphinium—they both flower blue. Love Lies Bleeding would go well behind the poppies, shades of red and red-orange, the both of them."

"What does that A-word say?" Emma frowned.

"Annual."

"I know that word. It means they won't last."

"Not exactly. Some annuals self-seed and come back a second year. If they don't and if we like them, we'll just have to replant. It's getting late for outdoor planting and these packets weren't selling. Still, it's a shame to waste them."

"The pictures look pretty. I wonder why nobody wanted them."

Love never comes without the pain or the risk. Emma was right, maybe the name could have put people off. I had never thought of that when I had filed them in Groft's metal racks along with the more familiar down-home varieties of annuals.

With the tip of my trowel, I scratched shallow grooves in the dirt in several spots. After I tore open a corner of one of the packets, I tipped the contents into my granddaughter's upturned hand.

Emma looked down at the tiny specks cupped carefully in her palm. "It's weird to think such big plants are going to grow from these teensy seeds."

Anise and my daughters were watching us from the porch as we covered the seeds with a thin layer of soil. *These too are the faces of love,* I found myself thinking. *Resilient. Capable of growing to fill the space we allow for it.*

"Since I've never tried these flowers before," I said, "maybe we better fasten the packets on some stakes so we won't root out the baby plants by mistake."

Emma's sandy brow knit tight as she thought about it. "Don't worry, Grama," she said. "I'll remember."

Monday afternoon came far too fast. Both my daughters were headed home. Within minutes of their cars disappearing in the direction of Chicago and Traverse City, I already sensed a gigantic hole in my heart and day-planner. A phone call from Bea changed all that.

"You have something going for lunch?" she said.

"Just sitting in the living room waxing poetic over my grandkids' handprints all over the furniture. I can't bear to think of getting rid of them."

"Quiet over there, huh?"

"Too quiet. I'll see you at Marty's"

"Noon."

She was already waiting for me when I arrived. Dressed as she was in gray tailored slacks and fluffy blue sweater instead of her usual jeans and a faded old sweatshirt, I had to look twice. I caught her fussing with the fake daisies in the centerpiece, half expected her to try some preemptive deadheading.

"OCD," she laughed. "You got me."

"Sure you don't want to dig in another row or two of perennials out on the berm? I noticed Saturday you're carting string and stakes around again."

"Habit," Bea grimaced. "Even with the new folk out there, I think caution makes sense right now. It's hard to predict staying power when we're dealing with volunteers."

"Some of our new recruits are getting itchy." I told her about Ben Gaskill and the Peace Garden.

"Hilarious."

"I thought so, too."

The waitress took our order. I stuck with my low-carb brew on tap, Bea splurged with her favorite alcoholic cider, a taste she acquired on one of her periodic British garden tours. It wasn't like her to go warming up the ale tracing the intricate logo on the glass.

"Any sense of what's going on with Viv and Artie these days?" she said finally.

"I've never seen them so happy. Why . . . ?"

"I understand that Artie has all but 'adopted' Chris Demort—has him living in his place over on Beaufort."

"Is there a problem?"

"Maybe. I had a nasty run-in with Ms. Demort last week at the courthouse. The boyfriend is still in jail. From the sound of it, the woman must have talked to a lawyer. She would never have come up with 'custodial interference' on her own."

"Unbelievable . . . after the 'custodial interference' her boyfriend inflicted on Chris before the kid lost it and lashed out at that Angel of the Empty Tomb. A black eye and split lip—no cracked ribs but close. Someone ought to remind his mother of that."

Bea winced. "Welcome to my world."

"You're going to have to intervene?"

"Already did . . . not quite how Ms. Demort expected, but I did. I reminded her that Social Services technically is obligated to launch an investigation in cases of suspected child abuse. Her boyfriend already spent time in the county jail for assault. If she chose to stir the pot, she could wind up herself in a whole mess of trouble."

"To which she said . . . ?"

"Some choice expletives. Then stomped out of my office."

"You called her bluff."

"I suspect she'll be back if she smells money could be forthcoming somewhere."

"Awful. Sad. Lannie Demort's grandfather owned one of the oldest Centennial Farms in the county. I doubt if she even knows a weed close-up anymore unless to smoke it. And Chris is such a good kid. . ."

Bea sighed. "Not as rare a scenario as you might think. I just hope Artie—Viv, too, for that matter—have thought through what he's gotten himself into."

"Dunno. Artie tends to shoot from the hip. But he's not naive either. I could poke around the edges if you think that might help."

"I would hate to see Artie and Viv hurt, that's all."

She sounded amazingly like my kids on the subject of Anise Gruin. But then miraculously, the long weekend with all of them together in the pressure cooker of the homestead seemed to have softened the concerns considerably.

"We could use a safe house around here," Bea said, "that's the truth. Someplace for kids or families or both to go when their homes or apartments or lives are yanked out from under them. Set them to gardening

152

in the summer, teach them some skills and self-sufficiency. Nothing like pulling up a bunch of carrots or radishes and realizing there may not be a lot of jobs in rural America, but historically at least we know how to feed ourselves."

"Most folks have been off the farm around here long enough, I'm not sure they even make that 'connect' any more."

"True. So we teach 'em. The garden at the berm models the gardening process. We could do the same with veggies. Not by the off-ramp, of course, but somewhere else."

Just that simple, it came to me. "Reclaim Our Roots."

"Say again?" Bea's eyebrow arched.

"Reclaim Our Roots. Teach rural kids and families to garden, bizarre as that sounds. We've been looking for some kind of grandiose project out at the berm, maybe pull in the Groft cottage for workshops and seminars. Problem was, all of the talk was aimed at tourism—which immediately presumes ad budgets and major logistical problems."

"Going nowhere, last time I heard."

"So, what if we rethink. Go local. Work at building our resources from within, not from the outside. Cultivate community gardening on a grand scale. The tourism could still come . . . folks interested in learning more about our seat-of-the-pants development model."

Bea sipped thoughtfully at her ale. "The partners could be endless," she said slowly. "Homemakers. What's left of Future Farmers. Scouts. Master Gardener and Cooperative Extensive programs."

The silence between us had become charged with the kind of ahha-energy I feel after the first ten minutes deadheading—when I look behind me to see how far I had come. It never failed to amaze how such tiny isolated individual actions could have produced so many visible results in such a short interval of time.

"I have half a mind to share this with my boss, George. See what he thinks. I assume you've heard rumors that his son, Mark Blandis, has been having hard-core discussions with the bank?

Bea nodded in the affirmative. "If foreclosures escalate in our area, we could be talking major population reshuffling. Yet again."

She had never recounted for me her experience as a young social worker tackling the desperate migrations in the state during the 1970s. Over a quarter of all the available housing was either for sale or abandoned. The Michigan trailer industry collapsed for good, along with

153

numerous automotive accessories companies—most of them located in small towns or rural communities. At the height of the crisis, talk was of opening moth-balled state mental institutions as shelters for homeless families.

"Deja vu," she said. "All over again."

"Right now George is up to his ears working on a business plan for starting a demand-press. I suspect what you and I are talking about could fit in with his ideas very nicely. Roots aren't just about our farm legacy, but the whole notion of preserving community identity and heritage—our relationship to the land . . . our stories."

Bea smiled. "Reclaim Our Roots."

I looked down at the crock of steaming soup the waitress had just set on the table in front of me. Salsify—I had ordered it without thinking. Was somebody trying to tell me something? I was willing to bet there wasn't a single restaurant elsewhere in the state that heard of the stuff, much less would list it among the daily specials.

What a strange obsession for early pioneer families in a Midwest backwater—light years removed from any ocean, to come up with a poor man's mock seafood chowder. I can't remember the last time I saw salsify among the root vegetables of a grocery anywhere else. When I was a young girl, my grandmother served the creamy concoction with oyster crackers. I always thought they looked like coral islands floating amid the streams of melted butter and flakes of black pepper. Marty's picked up on the tradition—authentic Xenaphon.

"Coincidence, George?" I speculated out loud to my boss later at the print shop, when I told him about the lunch.

"A wake up call, maybe—about the need to rebrand and reposition how we do tourism around here. Certainly not just the usual cherry products, pasties and fudge that tend to pass for 'local'.

"I'm not sure how or if that fits with your regional demand-press idea."

"There are just over two dozen publishers in Michigan," George said slowly. "Several specialize in state history. But most of the better known Michigan gardening books were published by regional presses on the West Coast. I know of a couple of Wisconsin and Minnesota presses that have published books on Michigan foods. But so far, no single in-state publisher seems to have a corner on any of those markets."

"You're saying, we could be looking at a niche."

"Possible."

"Have you shared your research with your son."

"Some. He didn't dismiss the prospects out of hand. The state development folk are making a push for 'green jobs'. There could be another common thread."

"Go for broke," I said, "literally. A solar install not just at the Groft cottage but the nursery could be a huge factor in making us a year-round venture."

George hesitated. "You haven't opened the lake house for the season yet."

"No. Artie has been after me to do it. There didn't seem to be a whole lot of point to it."

"What say you and Bea and I go out there in the next couple of weeks . . . take a look 'round. I don't want anything to distract us from *TIME in a Garden* at this stage of the game. But a look-see wouldn't hurt. Might get some creative juices flowing."

They already were.

Ten
Memories

Xenaphon's Veterans are polishing their gunmetal and brass, their past a silent bond between them. As for me, I turned to the thought-for-a-day calendar my grandson Justin gave me for Christmas several years ago. Shaped like the lattice arch of a garden gate, the tiny frame bulged with business-sized cards, one for all three hundred sixty-five days of the calendar year. I loved the thing, kept it in the kitchen. After the calendar year passed, I couldn't bear to throw it out. Instead I began to revisit the lovely quotes, scrambling the deck just to mix it up a little.

The random quote at the front of the pack for Memorial Day stopped me in my tracks. I found myself holding the well-worn card in my hand a good while before settling it carefully back into the calendar base. The thought was attributed to the prominent theologian, Charles H. Spurgeon.

The trick is not to chisel our epitaphs on marble, Spurgeon said. *We need to chisel them on the heart.*

Reclaim Our Roots. I continued in my own halting fashion, to reclaim mine. While the rest of the Gang Green took time off for the Memorial Day parade, my act of remembrance was going to be to do some major weeding out at the berm. Adam would have had a good chuckle at the gesture.

Wild mustard was running rampant out there again. The stuff was

156

his nemesis. We had spent an entire Saturday together trying to bring a patch of it under control on the berm—one of the few times I ever saw him impatient to the point of irritated.

"Demonic, this stuff," he had growled.

Sweat glistened on his elegant features. His thick shock of silver-white hair stood out against his tan. The consummate gentleman farmer, I remembered thinking, happy at long last in the legacy bequeathed to him.

I had fought a smile. "And you love every single minute of it."

"Tell yourself that. We turn our backs and the roots we missed are already popping up—in full bloom some of them. I swear the darn weed is laughing at the bunch of us."

Laughing, indeed. Last time I looked for wild mustard, the deceptively fragile and invasive intruder had made a significant come-back. I pulled on a pair or ratty garden jeans, a black tank top and fleece that had begun pilling at the cuffs—was half-way out the door when the phone rang.

"Am I talking to Eve . . . Brennerman, right . . . ?"

I tried to put face to voice, with no luck whatsoever. "Speaking."

"It's Jake Dornoski. Adam's friend . . . the guy with the boat. You joined us once on Little Traverse Bay. The Fourth of July."

Perhaps the last person in the world I would have expected. "Of course. Jake, how are you?"

"In the neighborhood, actually. I was heading up to Petoskey for a long weekend to take a look at that money-pit of mine before the season. I thought . . . hoped you might like to come along."

I hesitated a good while before reacting. "There's this friend of mine . . . she's having a baby any minute. I had planned to stay close, maybe work out at the community garden—"

"A day trip. Take your cell phone, just in case. I can have you back by dark. Earlier if it comes to that."

Silence. "All right. Yes. It's been . . . what? A year-and-a-half now."

"Something like that. I'll need some help with your address. The crazy GPS keeps losing the satellite—"

"Or giving error messages, I know." I sketched out a simple route. "Should take you about ten minutes."

"See you then."

I hung up the phone, suddenly self-conscious in my over-the-hill

157

gardening outfit. Temperatures by the lakeshore would be considerably cooler. If I hurried, I had just enough time to slip a new coral fleece over my ribbed black shell and pull on a pair of decent dress slacks.

The bedroom mirror caught my eye. It took me a split-second to reconcile the inner Eve of the past few months with the anxious older woman I saw reflected back at me from the unforgiving glass. Under the circumstances, a hint of makeup wasn't a bad idea either.

My impressions of Jake were fuzzy and not very favorable. But then Adam had seen something in the man. That alone was recommendation enough. I watched for him at the front window. When he showed up sporting a Chicago-to-Mackinaw Race vanity plate on his Porsche, I felt a momentary stab of regret.

This junket certainly was not the way I envisioned myself spending the Memorial Day weekend. When he started up the front walk, he seemed thinner than I remembered. His helmsman's tan had been replaced by a winter pallor that told me he wasn't a skier—or at least not lately. We hugged. And just that quick we were on our way.

There was no point beating around the bush. "I was surprised to get your call," I said.

"Understandable. I didn't get up north much last summer . . . or I would certainly have looked you up."

"I only made it to Petoskey once myself," I said evenly, "when we scattered Adam's ashes on Little Traverse."

Jake's hands flexed momentarily on the steering wheel. He was staring straight ahead, his expression unreadable.

"He would have liked that," he said finally.

"I'd like to think so."

"He was always . . . Adam and I were friends for a long, long time."

"You miss him."

Jake processed that in silence. "You were good for him, you know," he said finally. "Everyone on my 'ship of fools' on the Bay that day could sense it. He was a lucky man . . . "

Traffic was heavy—reason enough to settle back and let Jake concentrate on the road. Ahead of us, the double lanes of concrete sliced through the landscape like parallel scars, close and yet never touching. This unsolicited trip down memory lane was going to be a heck of a lot tougher than I thought.

"I heard somewhere you were living in the Groft cottage for a while," Jake said after a while.

"A couple of months. Maybe I just wasn't ready for all those memories."

"He was entrusting you with his legacy."

My mouth felt stiff. "I know that."

"A tough business, carrying the flame."

"You didn't come here to tell me that."

Jake exhaled sharply. "I've been diagnosed with pancreatic cancer," he said. "They've given me months."

I felt the impatience drain from me in a heartbeat. "I'm so sorry."

"Yeah, well . . . ," he shrugged. "It is what it is."

The question was on the tip of my tongue. "So why *did* you come?"

He shot a quirk of a smile in my direction. "Dunno," he said. "Something. But then Adam probably told you, I've always been an impulse kind of guy."

"You're not just going up there to check on the boat."

"Time to simplify. I'm putting it on the market."

We were passing a crossroads community, its lone gas station boarded shut and its sign swinging precariously from a rusty frame. A few remaining Victorian farmhouses hid their decaying facades behind thick stands of trees. A block further along, an elderly woman in a bathrobe and garish paisley ski jacket picked her way toward a row of mailboxes strung out along the ditch. They reminded me of the metal Quonset huts rusting out on that deserted military base we passed a couple of miles back.

The woman wore her long, silver gray hair in a thin, tight braid that crept down over the mock-fur hood of her jacket. A farm wife, if I had to guess, who had finally given up on the land. So she landed here in what could be one of the isolated rural communes that dot the countryside. I tucked the images away for safe-keeping—yet another slice of our unique northern Michigan story.

Farther north, a few isolated cherry orchards sprawled along the sandy hillsides in the direction of Traverse City. The popular regional Cherry Capitol couldn't be more than a thirty-minute drive to the west. With the Memorial Day traffic thickening as the day went along, we took a roundabout maze of secondary roads to bypass Charlevoix and its beautiful though traffic-snarling drawbridge over the blue water channel between Round Lake and Lake Michigan. On the last leg now, Jake swung the Porsche back onto the two-lane along the Bay headed east toward Petoskey.

Familiar territory, all of this. Ahead a half-mile or so on the left lay a turnout that once had boasted a tiny campground. Stands of birches led down to the sandy shoreline. As if strewn about by some giant hand, dark chunks of limestone jutted up from the shallow water.

"Would you mind if we stopped," I said. "There's an overlook up ahead."

"Done," he said.

Jake eased the Porsche into a parking stall and cut the engine. For a while we just sat there staring out over the Bay. The breeze was stiff. Lines of foam sliced north and east through the glassy layers of blue and purple water.

"I'll be right back," I said.

With that I exited the car and walked briskly toward the water's edge. Jake followed at a distance, his shoulders hunched against the wind.

"Adam and I stopped here that Fourth of July," I told him. "The water was still cold—freezing, actually—but we went for a swim. It's where Dutch and I scattered his ashes."

Jake seemed intent on the horizon. "I would have half-thought on that berm of yours."

"He teased about it once. But I kept coming back to something he said that day on your boat. 'You could bury me right here and now. I would die a happy man.' Strange what we remember."

A faint chuckle broke the silence. "Vintage Adam."

"Yes."

"I've thought about doing the same thing, you know—the ashes bit over the Great Lake," he said. "Not personally, of course. That would fall to somebody else. Awkward what we leave behind."

"But inevitable."

"True. Though actually, since we sailed together that day on Little Traverse, I haven't seen much of the crew—the professor, his wife Margaret and Angie."

"We change," I said. "Life changes and we go with it, whether we want to or not."

Jake winced. "Well, the C-word is a life changer. Trust me. It's almost as if the diagnosis were catching."

"You've made your peace with this."

"The dying thing? You just caught me on a good day, that's all."

The wind rustled impatiently in the birches overhead—a restless sound. The front was passing. By evening it should be calm. We would have our Million Dollar sunset after all.

Ten minutes ago I would have said coming up here was among the bigger mistakes I've made lately. I was wrong.

"Worst was, when Adam died, I never had a chance to say, Goodbye," I told Jake after a while.

He drew himself erect, a thumb cocked in a belt loop. "As good a reason to come up here as any."

"Regrets?"

"Not many . . . a lot. I envied Adam the peace he seemed to have found," Jake said. "It was a long time coming. The Golden Boy and the disappointment of all those expectations shaped so much of what Adam did and was. You changed that."

"We never change each other. All love does, I believe, is free us up to be the best we can be. Wonderful, when it works."

Jake shrugged. "Anyway, that's what I saw. I was planning on coming for the wedding, you know."

"Adam told me."

"So, you're sure you're up to this?"

"Of course."

When Jake chose the same restaurant in the Gaslight District where Adam and I had eaten, I didn't tell him. I sensed the place had been a favorite hang-out of theirs as well. It felt good simply to be there. After lunch we drove around the head of the Bay to Harbor Springs. The boat yard was busy. Random shoppers scouted the For Sale signs. Even in the worst of economic times, the market for high-end toys had an almost desperate appeal.

Jake had begun to negotiate the fate of his *Bonne Heure* with one of the appraisers, so I took the moment to start off along the shoreline toward the village center. Annuals were spilling out of hanging baskets on the lamp posts—velvety purple trailing petunias, variegated ivy, vivid red begonias. Risky when we were known to have frosts as late as June. A lush pocket garden outside a restaurant adjacent to the pier sheltered some elegant wrought iron chairs and tables. I thought of settling down for a glass of merlot, but thought the better of it.

161

The walk out to the end of the pier was one of those traditions not to be missed. Deepest natural harbor on Lake Michigan, the tourist brochures advertise. The description doesn't do the experience justice. In the crystal depths, seaweed billowed like a mermaid's tresses toward the sun. Here and there, schools of fish darted through the magical underwater garden.

I was always fascinated by the rows of yachts, snugged in alongside the pier itself. Their bright-work gleamed as if new. Coiled on the dock, the ends of their mooring ropes resembled garden snails set out at random intervals. I have seen good-sized apartments with far less living space.

Jake caught up with me on the bench near the public water fountain. "Done," he said. "They're optimistic I can unload her quick enough. She's fast, in good shape and the price is right."

She. I had forgotten that particular maritime custom—that, and the name of his boat. The *Bonne Heure.* Time well spent.

Jake and I sat in silence watching the water, the coming and goings along the pier. In the far distance, the city of Petoskey stretched like a thin vein of limestone along the hills overlooking Little Traverse Bay.

"I brought something for you . . . bizarre perhaps, but I thought you might like it."

I reached into my day pack and pulled out an advance copy of *TIME in a Garden.* Jake took it from my outstretched hand.

"A novel," he said.

"About us, Adam and me. You and the boat are in there, sorry about that. Fictionalized. But still . . . "

Jake stared at the front cover cradled between his two hands, his jaw tight. "I had no idea."

"Neither did I when I wrote it. We're launching in July. My boss has ambitious notions of using the book to jump-start a regional heritage on-demand press."

While Jake listened in silence, I shared in rough outline the premise of the novel—that we garden at our best when we garden in community. To my surprise, I found myself drifting from there into an impassioned description of the Reclaim Our Roots project and the potential it had for reshaping not just the economy of the area, but the self-esteem and identity of the people who called Xenaphon home.

"I believe Adam would have understood immediately what we're trying to do," I said. "As I struggle to make my peace with what happened —to find some way to put the Groft cottage and nursery to good use—this is the first time I ever had a sense that his death wasn't just some tragic, senseless . . . *waste*."

"You need a Foundation," Jake said when I finished.

"Foundation. Aren't we getting ahead of ourselves?"

"Raise funds, build an endowment. Make the concept self-supporting and self-sustaining over time. It pays to do things right from the get-go."

I chuckled softly, shook my head. "Right now, we haven't even organized a formal steering committee. I wouldn't have the guts to suggest someone actually drop major bucks on the idea."

Out in the harbor, a vintage wooden water taxi from one of the restaurants was idly criss-crossing the quiet water—one of the regular private hors d'oeuvres cruises so popular with wedding parties and families. On the nearby tennis courts, a couple of matches were playing themselves out. Shadows were lengthening on the grass. We would need to leave soon if we were going to make it home before dark.

"Done," Jake said.

I hadn't been paying attention, but he had shifted on the seat alongside me and fished what looked like a blank check out of his wallet. His pen moved from line to line, signed off with a tight flourish. When he handed the check my way, the wind momentarily took it but I managed a save. A smile twisted at the corner of his mouth as we made eye contact.

"*The Adam Groft Reclaim Our Roots Foundation*," I read out loud.

I seemed to be having trouble deciphering the Cash line. I chalked it up to a combination of Jake's atrocious scrawl and the zeroes and commas swimming before my eyes. It was like trying to pick my way through one of those crazy on-line security codes with nonsensical numbers and letters staggered and broken across a random gray-on-gray background.

My hands were shaking. "I'm not sure I . . . you're joking . . . !"

"Anything but." His smile never reached his eyes. "Obviously, the bank probably is going to have re-cut this. There could be more down the road. I'll have to talk to my lawyers. But this gives you a talking point with the folks in Xenaphon."

I started to shape the words. *One-point-two million.*

"Jake, I—"

"There's nothing to say. We both know Adam was always the idealist . . . a man in search of his destiny. I used to ride him mercilessly for that"

"This is too much."

Jake chuckled softly, shook his head. "It's not like I can sail off into the sunset on the *Bonne Heure* and take all of it with me. You've captured your legacy between two book covers. Mine is right here. A heck of a lot more impersonal, I realize. But then a guy does what he can with what he has. And time for me right now most definitely has become the enemy . . . "

Our master gardener Bea told me recently that even when a season is late—as now—a garden is hell-bent on flowering no matter what. Given, some plants may never come to bud at all. But more often than not, their growing season compresses to fit the time allotted to it. When that happens, an entire garden's flowering can compact into a short week to two-week period.

The result can be frighteningly intense. Species of perennials that never, ever bloom together suddenly peak at once. The garden becomes awash in color, on sensory overload. Even as the wave of reckless bloom touches the outer fringes of the beds, the early bloomers are beginning to curl at the edges. Like a burst of fireworks over the Bay, the petals scatter to the four winds—gone in the blink of an eye.

Adam and I lived that way our glorious summer. And as I looked back over the months since my Groundhog Day epiphany, the momentum of my life without him had been accelerating with a will of its own. We do what we can with what we have.

My throat felt tight. That familiar scratchy sensation behind my eyes signaled a marathon crying jag. Jake deserved better than my sympathy.

"You love this place," I said.

Jake smiled. "Place. The people. The magnificent waters of our Third Coast, stretching out beyond the curve of the horizon."

"I know why Adam respected you so much."

And why their friendship ran so deep. Jake's casual hedonism was not all it appeared to be. Adam understood that and I was beginning to—the deep-seated shared doubts that life could mean so much more than they had let it be all those years.

164

"Impulsive," he shrugged. "Deep pockets. I'm a Director of Individual Giving's dream,"

"Not my forte."

Jake laughed. "I beg to differ. With or without an official 'ask'."

I felt his gift—the painful magnanimity of it—burning a hole in my duffle of a purse. In my heart.

"Adam called me, did he ever tell you that," Jake said, "just before your wedding. You had just gotten back from Chicago. Change in plan, he said. He needed a Best Man. Dutch was going to do the honors, but you wanted him to give you away. That was the excuse anyway.

My eyebrow arched.

"What he really wanted was one of Those Talks. So we did—two hours. More. Like most soul barings, we skittered around the edges of missed opportunities and time wasted. But then guys aren't big on guilt. No point. Instead, we reminisced about sailing Little Traverse, the joys of planked whitefish, thunderclouds at Juilleret's . . . the most incredible bitter chocolate, marshmallow and homemade ice cream concoction on earth."

"They've closed," I told him. "I was shocked . . . noticed on the way over."

"Another local tradition lost to time."

"Like the old Harbor Inn, ripped down years back to put in condos. The largest artesian spring in Michigan, maybe the Midwest flows through those grounds. The historic marker sign is gone."

Jake shook his head. "Keep it simple, Adam told me after the two of you started dating. We spend way too much of our lives trying to make things as complicated as possible. Just love hard. Dig around in the mud, get some stuff to grow if we can. Be as real as we can in our choices . . . especially in how we love the people in our lives."

"What are you going to do, Jake?"

He shrugged. "Hospice, when it comes to that. I was hoping maybe you might consider letting me spend some time at the cottage . . . before it gets that far. I promise not to die on you. Not then, anyway."

"Jake, you'll have to let me know where you are and—"

"No. It's the last thing in the world I want, that you somehow feel obligated to—"

"This has nothing to do with obligation."

"Maybe not for you. I'm talking about me," he said. "Whatever

165

prompted that gift, it needs to stand on its own . . . no payback. No historic markers or maudlin farewells . . . "

Word of wisdom of Philosophy 101 teased in my memory—if generosity comes from a desire to be praised, it ceases to be true virtue. Less certain was the source. Probably one of the big three, as in Shakespeare, the Bible or Plato.

"*Promise me,*" he said again. "No hunting me down. I'll spend some time at the cottage if I can. We'll trade emails."

My mouth felt stiff. "Done," I said.

He had me home by dark, as promised. This time we took the direct route through Charlevoix, then south, so I didn't know what became of the lone woman at the mailbox. Jake didn't prolong our goodbyes. We hugged and then he was gone. The night air in June can be brutally cold. Even so, I stood shivering alone in the glow from the porch light long after the taillights of the Porsche disappeared at the end of the street.

Something next door was blooming. I tasted as much as sensed the subtle fragrance hanging on the night air. We carry each other's presence with us—like the collective scents and sounds and touch of the eternal garden. I had to believe that.

Jake's gift could accomplish so much, but not without a firm hand to plant and cultivate. Not without a common vision. I had relied on Adam for that kind of leadership when the impersonal bureaucracy was threatening the berm. Now, as then, there was no one else. George had his hands full with the *Gazette*. Bea had her job and the berm. The younger generation was still feeling its way.

To look within was the only answer. *And yet* . . . Jake's check lay untouched in the bottom of my bag for a full week before I gathered the courage to look at it. When I finally did, it was not the astronomical sum but Adam's name that swam into focus.

Love and friendship. Jake's parting hug had imprinted itself on my memory, lingered long after he drove me home. Long after the clock on my nightstand glowed a pale two in the morning. Long after I showed George and Bea the check Jake had so casually extended in my direction.

At my boss' suggestion, I shared the turn of events with my lawyer. Then I put some thoughts down on paper— just enough for me to clarify what Jake's gift meant from my point of view. I wasn't much of a grant writer, but Bea was. With something in hand, she quickly could give it all the bureaucratic buzzwords to get us through the incorporation process.

There's a website online from 2001, "Soul of Agriculture". It talks about the rise of land values, the fall of agricultural profits and the ongoing flight of the American farmer from the land. But as the anonymous author sees it, the true roots of rural decline are not economic, but spiritual.

As a culture, our obsession with cheap stuff has cost us more than a way of life but our faith in a safe food supply. It has cost us our souls. Sustainability of life on the planet is not just about the distant future. It is about the "now". It is no small thing to lose our connection to the earth.

Those words, I believe, were written for Xenaphon. The Heritage farms among us are growing rarer, vanishing—and with them, a lifestyle. Important as tourism is to our region, as a community we diminish ourselves when we define ourselves as primarily someone else's playground. Xenaphon's population may be shrinking, but it remains a living organism with deep roots in the soil and water under our feet, our homes and businesses.

The abandoned windmills and crumbling barns in our county stand as mute witness to where we need to go. We need to honor the lives that brought us to this place. We need to lift up the dreams, some of them long lost, that have kept Xenaphon alive through the generations.

Whatever a Foundation to 'reclaim our roots' might do for our economic base, it first must heal and renew the broken hearts and lives of our community's residents. Call it 'civic pride' or 'community identity', we must look within to find it. Only then can we hope to reach out with the confidence required to draw others into the circle.

After I shared what I had written with Bea, we drew the rest of the original Gang Green into the discussions. Along with Artie and Viv. I also invited George, who insisted I bring Adam's attorney, mine now.

All the while we skirted the magnitude of Jake's gift, I kept having flashbacks to that trip north with him—especially the sight of that woman in nightgown and ski jacket collecting her mail. Something in her vulnerability reminded me of Anise that first night in the homestead, spooked by the wind, standing there in the doorway in the flannel nightgown Granddaughter Emma had given me.

167

"It's summer and we've got the berm on the front burner," Bea said finally. "Then there's the stuff going on down at the bank. I suggest we think on it until fall while we separately lay out our own ideas how a Foundation or community center might work. Then in fall when the tourists head south again, we can dig in and formally set up a non-profit, if that's where our collective thinking takes us."

My attorney had sat silent to this point. "Legally," he said, "that Groft cottage and the nursery belong to you, Eve. As things stand, only you can determine how or if they are going to be used for public purposes."

I nodded. "Understood."

Not entirely the truth. But it was a start. And whether I wanted it or not, my friends would be looking to me for leadership. I had to step up and make this happen.

One thing I knew. Whatever we chose to do with Jake's gift and my inheritance—all of it began and ended with people and their stories. Love and loss were inseparable in that living tapestry, courage in the face of death and an enduring hope.

That night online I ran across a quote that I wish I could have shared at the time. It was from the thirteenth century German philosopher Meister Eckhardt. *The greatest gift we can leave behind,* he said, *is to plant trees, even knowing we will never see the grove.*

When I described the Garden Gang's conversations to Jake in an email, I began with Meister Eckhardt's words of wisdom. I didn't expect a reply. None came. But then I didn't need one to tell me Jake would approve.

Eleven
Solstice

Our late spring does not want to leave us. On chill mornings in my cottage garden, I can sense the relentless coming of the solstice as it ushers in another season—turn, turn, inhale, exhale. Poets dream of never-ending summers but by late June, a true gardener can read the heavens. Summer, so hard in coming, already has peaked and is on the down slope. Our moment in the sun is fleeting. The days will grow shorter again, whether we notice the night's subtle encroachment or not.

Curious how perspectives skew our reality. People used to stand in one spot, watch the elliptical comings and goings overhead, and conclude that the earth revolves around the sun. Even the untutored farmer at work in his field sensed how the sun's elevation seemed to rise and retreat in the sky. It was left to the ancient astronomers to track the highpoint of that journey in late June and the low point to December.

The *solstitium. S*ome anonymous star-gazer in the first century BC named that point of change and passage. *The time the sun stands still.*

In Xenaphon the locals were oblivious to all that. Our *solstitium* was marked by the ascendency of the foot traffic on Main Street and the ping of bar-code scanners at the checkout. Bad economy or no, the tourist season had crept up on us. At Groft's, we sensed it when the seasonal cottagers suddenly appeared demanding pots of perennials to repair what winter had done to their flower beds. Counter to the national trend, veggies were moving slower, but I hadn't given up hope. Viv and I had begun to experiment with creating special gift pots that blurred the line between

169

veggie and flower. All were equally edible.

Viv turned out to be a pro at live plant arrangement. Responding to her touch, branches of cherry tomatoes nestled against neon orange and yellow nasturtiums. Miniature pepper plants, curly leaf parsley and trailing Alaskan nasturtium spilled from colorful, sun-drenched hanging planters.

"All of it edible. A feast for the eyes and the palette," Anise said when I brought one of Viv's samples home for her reaction. "Works for me."

Slowly but surely out in front of the homestead, even the residents in my cottage garden were feeling their oats. Purists in the gardening community might object to buying perennials instead of growing them from seed in the bed. But there is something to be said for starting off with well-established plant stock. What had been a mud-hole in my front yard just weeks ago could pass for a much older bed.

Along the sidewalk, the primroses in the border were in spectacular bloom, along with the spotted-leaf pulmonaria and Jacob's Ladder. Behind them towered the spiny buds of the orange-red Oriental Poppy. The iris have always been favorites of mine—not the finicky hybrids, but the tried and true old-fashioned two-tone variety that still crop up along the secondary roadways outside of Xenaphon. Their regal purples and yellows, bronzes and golds stand a living testament to some tired pioneer woman's desperate need for whimsy.

No one would confuse my sprawling little plant community with a show-garden. But I saw it as a giant step up from the mange of a yard that had preceded it. My column for the week all but wrote itself:

A friend was recovering from a nasty divorce. Her counselor told her to go bowling. In her anger and grief, she should imagine anyone who had wronged or disappointed her as a bowling pin. Each time she hurled a ball down that alley, the psychiatrist said, you will feel an enormous sense of relief, even peace.

No counselor's diploma hangs on my wall that entitles me to dole out pithy advice. But instead of knocking down odd-shaped hunks of wood, I recommend gardening.

In the upturned blossoms, I am learning to see the faces of all the people who have brought beauty or love or laughter to my life. It is up to me, as gardener, to nurture and cultivate those precious relationships.

As I weed and deadhead and hoe, I find myself learning constantly from the plants I tend. The growing season may be far too short, especially in our northern climes. But time and adversity become enemies only if we make them so.

Day by day my garden grows, filled with names and faces I never even met a season ago. I came across some wonderful poetry the other day, Psalm 92, that summed up that sense of joy better than I ever could.

Cedars still grow and flourish among the ancient rocks and crags of Lebanon. They are among the slowest growing and oldest of trees. It takes some 40 years before the fertile seeds develop. Symbols of eternity, the cedars are still green and full of life to the end, sheltered among their ancient rocks.

Solomon's temple was built from the dense and beautiful wood. I like that idea—creating a spiritual center for ourselves—better than mowing down bowling pins.

Cultivating relationships takes time and patience, liberally applied doses of forgiveness. Wise words for a culture obsessed with 'Me' and youth and living in the moment. Time is also about the long haul.

I thought especially about Jake and his visit and generous gift as I wrote. He had robbed me of the last of my excuses. It was high time I opened the cottage for the season.

With my Taurus loaded with cleaning supplies, I drove down that narrow dirt road for the first time in six months. Things had not stood still in my absence. A prominent billboard sprouted from the ditch to announce a major public works project. Still others advertised the latest fore-closures. A team of surveyors busied itself on a vacant lot. From the cottages lining the shores of that sandy-bottomed lake, lawn mowers hummed and thrummed like a swarm of beating wings on the June breeze.

Artie too, had been busy. The plywood shutters had been taken down and leaned catty-whumpus against one another alongside the garage. Screens were in place again and the windows of the house peered open and bright-eyed at my arrival.

I took my time ferrying the buckets, mops and an assortment of cleaning supplies from the parking area to the back porch Some things never change. The lock to the back door was as cranky as ever.

Break out the WD-40, I smiled. Even Adam had his problems with that door. I half expected to round the corner into the spacious open living room and find him standing back-turned looking out at the glistening waters of the lake. Instead, I encountered only silence and the pale shafts of light flooding the golden oak beneath my feet.

171

The Great Room with its massive fireplace had the intimacy of a family album left open to the casual beholder. On an end table, a regional throwaway splayed forth some glossy cover story about Michigan lighthouses. An unfamiliar hand had jotted a random phone number across a sticky note—long since curling from humidity and neglect. From somewhere in the house, a clocked chimed the hour. *Late by a scant ten minutes.*

The unspoken expectation was that somehow life would pick up where it had been casually left behind at season's end—a bittersweet testament to lives interrupted. Time lost, I told myself, not squandered.

There was work to do. With a clatter of buckets and running of tap water, I roused myself to take charge. Undetectable except to the touch, a thin and gritty film encased every surface. Even the vertical moldings and bevels of the doors and woodwork had not been spared. Setting things right would take a while. But the sheer physicality of it—the bending and stretching and scrubbing—were just what the doctor ordered.

I took to the therapy with a vengeance. Startled at the jarring ringtone of my cell phone, I found that more than two hours had passed. The connection was fragile, but the caller ID enough to set my heart lurching wildly.

"Anise . . . ?"

I heard harsh, rhythmic breathing. Then through gritted teeth, my name.

"Where . . . are you okay?" I said.

"*Guess*-s-s . . . !"

I drew in a head-clearing breath. "The *baby*?"

Voices in the background drowned out whatever followed. All I caught was a muffled string of expletives.

"I'm on my way." I left everything and ran, stopping only long enough to fiddle with the lock—swearing all the while under my breath. Gravel sprayed noisily across the parking lot. In the rear view mirror, I watched the yellowed cloud of sand retreating behind me. The road crew seemed to be on lunch break. Mercifully, the highway was all but deserted.

The only empty parking spot was in the physicians' lot. Anise sat with bare feet dangling over the edge of a hospital bed. That fiery red hair of hers spiked at odd angles, stiff with sweat. Her skin had taken on the color of the sheets—a bloodless, institutional white. At the sight of me, her expression dissolved into a child's wide-eyed disbelief.

"You never told me it would be like . . . *this* . . . !"

Laughter and tears bubbled geyser-fashion beneath the surface of my smile. "Honey, you can *do* this."

Mentally I already had begun to clock the time between the waves of contractions. Anise grabbed my hand and held on.

"That . . . blasted column of yours on gardens and bowling balls," she managed through gritted teeth, "I never dreamed I was going to have to deliver one."

"You're on the home stretch."

A low groan of a laugh ended in a high-pitched cry. "Stretch. You're kidding, right? We're talking . . . *explode here* . . . "

"Count, Sweetie. Keep counting. We practiced the Lamaze thing, faithfully. Natural childbirth works."

"There's nothing natural about this. Trust me . . . !" A contraction seized her with a fury that sent rivulets of sweat pouring down her temples. "Son of a . . . !"

"Exactly. *Caleb*, your *son*. Just keep thinking, Caleb. And do what you practiced. COUNT!"

Anise did, punctuating each digit with an expletive, while dials and monitors beeped and flashed and measured out the rhythm of new life on its way. *Time* . . . it always came back to that. We kill it, use it, celebrate it. We try our best to ignore its passing.

There was no ignoring *this* moment or the ones that followed. Over the decades, the growing pains of parenting remind us that childbirth is called *labor* for good reason. Anise had begun to tire. As her shoulders slumped momentarily forward in that open-at-the-back hospital gown, I caught a glimpse of the delicate tattoo of a daisy flowering in the region of her bikini line.

Vintage Anise. Tough yet oh so fragile, this child of the garden.

My heart felt too big for my chest. "Hold in there," I whispered. "You're on the home stretch. . . "

Someone else must have heard me. They finally wheeled Anise into the delivery room, my hand still clenched hard in hers. And just that fast, Caleb's head was crowning. I heard Anise give one last quavering primal cry that seemed to go on and on. The video playing itself out around me sped up to a blur of hands and bodies intent on the business of new life. Her baby's high-pitched wail sounded like rising music in the chill of the delivery room.

"Your boy," the doctor grunted.

Anise was shaking as she took the tiny bundle he offered her. "Hello, young Caleb . . . ," she breathed.

"Would you like to cut the cord?"

It took a split-second for me to realize the doctor was extending the shiny medical equivalent of a scissors in my direction. I blinked. Anise and I made eye contact. I could read the smile in those hazel depths.

"Do it," she said.

I did, my own hands trembling now. When it was over, I realized I had been holding my breath.

"He's beautiful," I said.

Dark coarse hair shot up from his tiny head like an unmown lawn, a good three inches of it. His hands and feet seemed huge. He had this funny big toe on either foot that had to be half-again as long as the ones next to them. Prehensile scholars call it—our ancient capacity to grasp. In the human foot, the skill diminishes because our hands and fingers tend to dominate. But the gift is never lost entirely.

Hang on to life, little man, I chuckled. *With hands and feet, however you can.*

"Okay, so are you going to tell me what's so hilarious?" Anise said.

"Adam had toes like that," I told her. "His friend Jake called them sailor's feet. Handy, he said, if you're hiking out over the edge of the rail and you feel like you're about to flip backward into the drink. Just grab at any fixed point on the boat with your toes and hang on, he said. Not the kind of skill that pops up on a guy's resume, but handy all the same."

Anise laughed. "I would never have guessed."

Motherhood became Anise. That Raphael-esque smile as she held her baby came straight out of a Florentine picture gallery. Her intelligent gray eyes glowed with a primal awe, a new-found sense of mystery—the shock when we control freaks discover that some of the most wonderful things in life are unplanned. And no matter how we got to this point, life is good.

"You never told me," I said. "Does Caleb have a middle name?"

"Eugen. My Dad may have run a Greek bakery, but his name was pure German . . . Karl Eugen. Apparently the 'Eugen' is some crazy tradition in the family going back to God—the Germanic equivalent anyway. Just in case the kid ever starts thinking Caleb is too off the wall, he knows the alternative."

"Caleb Eugen Gruin."

I could see Anise turning the sound of it over in her head. "Well born," she said. "It means, well born. Go figure."

And Caleb was all that—well born into a loving family of one and her growing circle of friends. I read the promise of it in Caleb's scrunched and upturned face, squinting hard at the beatific expression on his mother's face staring down at him.

As word spread about the birth, the parade of the Magi began. My boss arrived with a fruit-basket and an alarmingly large teddy bear dressed in overalls, work boots and ball cap. Viv and Artie showed up with a bouquet of mylar balloons and a wooden eighteen wheeler puzzle that had met with an unfortunate accident en route. While Viv cooed over the baby, Artie bent his shaggy head over the table alongside the bed, trying to resurrect the vehicle from its component parts. Matt Gaskill was back in the Twin Cities talking to realtors, but Ben arrived bearing a cradle cross from Peace.

Amid it all, Anise held court with the calm entitlement of European royalty receiving the jewels of the Orient. Alongside her, oblivious to it all, her Caleb snuggled sound asleep in a knit Detroit Lions cap that Chris Demort had brought with him after school.

At that even Anise looked impressed. "Where on earth did you—?"

"Online," he said. "Radical, huh! I wanted a football, too. Only you ever see what they charge for that stuff?"

Anise laughed. But I sensed the tears weren't far behind.

"You're really something," she awkwardly drew him to her and planted a lingering kiss on the young man's cheek.

Chris started to protest, instead flushed a fiery red. "Yeah . . . or somethin'," he muttered.

The nursing staff had their hands full trying to keep any kind of routine going through all that communal bonding. As it stood, Anise and Caleb were in and out of the medical center in twenty-four hours. She already had begun to pack up her meager belongings when her original gynecologist, Doc Wieland, showed up for a visit.

"It's quite a drive over here. I wouldn't have expected it of you, but I'm grateful," she told him. "Sorry, though, no bear claws or sticky buns this time. Seems I've been a little busy."

Doc chuckled softly. "Much better anyway what's been in the

175

oven—this handsome young man of yours."

At her invitation, he reached down and cradled Caleb in his arms. But not before he slipped a small package on the coverlet alongside Anise. She took her time opening it, intent on sparing the wrapping paper. Tiny elephants danced on a pale green ground with cats, fiddles and all sorts of strange and wonderful creatures.

"Doc, you shouldn't have," Anise breathed. Nestled inside the box was a toddler-size spoon—silver with a deep etched heart in a swirl of Celtic foliage at the end of the handle.

Doc's forehead knit in a frown. "Charlotte . . . my wife tells me folks don't use these things anymore. I guess the notion of being born with a silver spoon went out of fashion with our generation. The clinic used to give these to all our new mothers."

"They're all plastic and cartoon characters now anyway," Anise said. "This set is beautiful."

"*Nobody wants to spend time polishing these old silver things anymore*, my wife told me. What I've been saving this one for all these years escapes me." His voice broke off, steadied again. "You take care of yourself and this little guy of yours. But then I know you will."

Hugging Doc proved no easy business with the baby in one arm and the other hand wrapped tight around the box and its precious contents. Anise managed.

"I'll never forget you," she said.

Doc cleared his throat. "Send a photo once in a while . . . after all, little Caleb here was one of my last patients. They sure don't stay small for long."

"What a dear man," Anise said softly after he had gone. "All that over a couple of months' worth of pastry . . . "

Not entirely the truth. I saw Doc's exit hadn't gone unnoticed elsewhere. Through the open doorway to Anise's room, he had stopped to chat up the staff at the nursing station. I saw his shock of silver white-hair disappear in a circle of scrubs-clad staff that rallied to greet him.

Defining moments in our lives, I thought as I settled Anise and Caleb into her room in the homestead. A breath and cry at a time, Anise was learning what it meant to be a mother within these walls. Though nothing could ever replace for me the precious thrill of becoming a grandmother to Emma and Justin and Harry, something in this young woman's unfolding journey touched me deeply.

I had all but suppressed my own path to motherhood. Seven months pregnant—already feeling alone in a marriage I sensed would hold more than its share of heartache—I wandered one afternoon into an art theater near the Chicago apartment I shared with my husband, Joel. On the marquee overhead, in foot-high letters, stood "Disney's masterpiece, *Fantasia.*" The moment was magical. With my daughter Leslie making her presence felt through supportive kicks and nudges, I let the sensory images wash over me in the darkness.

The film had no plot as such—just daring experiments in sight and sound. The whimsical animation of childhood unfolds to some of the most sophisticated orchestral music in Western civilization. Earth gave birth in fire and mist. Seasons unfolded in magical fashion. A demonic Walpurgisnacht on Bald Mountain culminates in the hushed cathedral of the forest. The garden of the imagination bursts into full flower. Mythic images of a Golden Age and our most terrifying nightmares battle and resolve themselves. The garden dances in joy.

The movie struggled for decades before it came into its own. Its release in 1940 nearly buried the Disney studio financially. After repeated cuts and re-releases, one version in the late 1960s finally achieved a measure of commercial success. Its evolution still goes on half-a-century later.

Little did I realize, alone in that nearly empty Chicago art theater, where my own story would lead me. I didn't garden in those days. At most I cobbled together an occasional pot of herbs or annuals on the postage-stamp size balcony of our apartment. But looking back on it, I believe something stirred in me even then—a quiet yearning to ground my life on the pastoral roots of a childhood I had left behind me.

Call it detachment perhaps, but for the first time watching Anise with her baby, I had a conscious sense of generations passing. I know Doc Wieland had felt it, too. In part at least, it was what had brought him to that hospital room.

The Xenaphon we loved was a fragile organism. It had suffered greatly despite the hopeful future its lofty classical name had anticipated for it. New life these days within the town's borders was both rare and precious—a sign of hope and worth the celebrating.

And so, Caleb had his silver spoon—both a legacy and promise from one generation to another. I vowed then and there to add a trowel to that gift. I didn't even know if age appropriate newborn gardening tools

177

existed. But if they did, I was determined to find them.

Meanwhile the community's casserole brigade had anticipated our arrival. When I opened the fridge, determined to take over cooking duties for the duration, I ran head-on into dense-packed shelves of heat-'n-eat goodies.

"Enough for the next six months at least," I told Anise.

"You're kidding . . . people still do that?"

"Easy enough when the door is always open."

At our best, we Americans are a nation of neighbors, I wrote in my journal.

Small town folk have made an art form of creating community over the back fence. The foundation posts are shared need and vulnerability. From cradle to the grave, we rally to nurture and celebrate and comfort. And at this juncture in my life, I am blessed to be a part of that precious circle.

As a gardener, I find a special kinship in the community clustered In front of my own front porch where a whole colony of new perennials stirs and grows in the still hours of the Michigan noonday. *Harebell, bellflower, campanula* will blossom like a carillon before the season is out. I never knew mullein is considered an herb, used for emollients and astringents—always thought it was just an enormous weed growing wild in our sandy meadows.

Miracles happen when we take the time to know each other, wager a second look. Community is not about geography or impersonal census data. It is about touching each other's lives with love and understanding and humor. Smallness of scale may help, but I believe even in the mega-cities of this world, neighborhood is possible.

In 1879 the German scientist de Bary gave that process of community-building a name, *symbiosis.* The name comes from the Greek for the art of 'living together' because it occurs only when all parties benefit.

The popular stereotype of the American character doesn't make community easy. The myth of John Wayne's machismo and the Lone Ranger's solitary ride into the sunset is a powerful force in a land that prizes independence and entrepreneurship.

As for me, I am coming to the conclusion that the

art of 'receiving' is greatly under-rated. It can be tough stuff to admit our neediness and let people love us. But whether we admit it or not, at one time or another in our lives, we are all desperately vulnerable.

It would be easier to live holistically as we are intended if we would truly listen to our gardens. Plants are masterful 'takers' as well as 'givers'. In the very act of drawing sustenance from the soil, they enrich the air around them. Through their life-span they lean on each other for support, a basic principle in any successful garden design. And in the end, they go back to the very earth that gave them life, the ultimate give-back. The process of give and take is the act of living itself.

I spent so much of my life going it alone that I missed the obvious. My life is so full of these hardy givers—whose greatest joy is for me to accept what they freely offer. Learning to honor their gifts may be the hardest thing I have ever done. I have to believe a simple 'thank you' is a great start.

And so I rejoice in little Caleb fast asleep in my arms—Caleb Eugen Gruin, his mother's son. Caleb the fierce and wellborn, Xenaphon's tenacious new citizen swelling the count on the peeling paint of the population sign at the village limits.

So helpless, I tell myself as I gently ease him into the crib waiting for him in the front bedroom of the homestead. In one way or another, we never grow beyond that vulnerability. Time's gift to us seems to be the ability to admit it.

Twelve
Bulbs and Rhizomes and Corms

The June of my childhood had blossomed with whimsical poetry of 'moon and 'spoon', of bridal wreath and orange blossoms. For generations it was *the* month of choice for weddings—until recently, when August unceremoniously bumped June to Number Two. In the innocent Ozzie-and-Harriet world of the Fifties, love and marriage and baby carriages were never far behind. The traditional march down the aisle fell right in line between holidays that honor first Mothers, then Fathers on the calendar.

Families. It doesn't take an elaborate sociological study to recognize they're changing. Even in tiny Xenaphon, the greeting card racks at the drug store have expanded to include an awful lot of variations on the theme of familial love. It is no accident that we gardeners talk about our plants as "families".

In a garden, sharing space is where it's at. *Relationships.* And just to make sure everybody is comfortable with the diverseness of it all, we name everything in the garden at least twice. Lurking in most gardener handbooks are the formal given names in oh-so-correct Latin followed by an endless string of popular nicknames. *Monarda,* one of the few official plant names I actually knew, translates as bee balm or bergamont. *Echinacea purpura* answers to purple coneflower. *A rose by any other name*—whatever works, has become my motto.

Defenders of the 'traditional family' sometimes clamor for emblazoning a *Family Day* in bold print and red letters on the calendar. I have never been one of them. Few of my friends' kids and grandkids fit what could be described as 'traditional' two-parent households. And I had an eloquent case-in-point under my own roof. Whatever her marital status, my young friend Anise had all the makings of a wonderful parent.

I tried not to pontificate too much on the subject of families or parenthood. Caleb was a week old. Anise and I hadn't slept in as many days. At first she protested, but I quietly insisted on taking my turn at midnight diaper detail. Truth was, I felt ancient.

"Are people always this sleep deprived?" Anise wondered out loud.

We had just dug into a perfunctory breakfast of shredded cardboard advertising itself as multi-grain cereal. The sticky bun supply in my freezer had dwindled to a precious few. Baking was not high on anyone's agenda right now. By eight o'clock Anise and I were into our second pot of coffee.

Upstairs and within ear-shot of his baby monitor, Caleb slept on. "I have to believe the routine gets easier, right?" Anise wondered out loud.

"Once a parent . . . ," I chuckled, "always a parent, kiddo. Fifteen years from now, he'll still keep you up. Only then it'll be over tougher stuff than feeding schedules and bowel movements."

I couldn't google my way to Why, but around the world, the biggest fans of Family and Community Days in general are Australia, some Canadian provinces and the state of Arizona. The Aussies made sure that on the calendar theirs coincided with the annual Melbourne Cup in early November. The Arizonians picked the first Sunday in August. None of those annual milestones are to be confused with the American Family Day supposedly in the works—its goal to encourage parents and children to eat together on a regular basis. Ironic to make the rallying point food, when the medical gurus have set a priority of stamping out adult and childhood obesity!

The plant world is ambivalent on the subject of what constitutes a family, I quickly discovered, trying to whack out a column about it:

Gardening and parenthood have a great deal in common. They begin in mystery and end in a lot of work.

In the garden, some plants like strawberries simply arch above-ground to create independent new plants. We call those stems runners or *stolons*.

Geophyte is the technical term for all plants that propagate by means of bulbous structures underground—bulbs, corms, rhizomes and tubers. Though some folks throw the term "bulb" around willy-nilly.

True bulbs are layered like an onion. If you slice them in half, at their center there is a bud which eventually bursts open into leaves and blossoms. Corms are solid—like the fleshy "bulbs" found at the base of crocuses and gladioli stems. Iris grow from what are known as rhizomes, swollen horizontal stems from which flowers and leaves periodically emerge. Potatoes and dahlias—aka tubers—are pretty much in a class by themselves.

Then there all the varieties of seeds and spores. Seeds are so marvelously self-contained. Tiny protective shells hold not just a whole plant embryo, but often the food supply to get the baby plant started. Non-flowering plants get their start as small-cell spores.

TMI, or as my daughters would say, "Way, way too much information!". At the journey of the embryo or zygote on its way toward seedling status, I gave up and closed the laptop—let the whole topic gestate.

My own family dynamics were about to change. Granddaughter Emma's July visit was "on" and I was half afraid that her mother might decide to stay at the homestead with her. Dan still hadn't found a job. Absence on her part, my daughter was hinting, might be a very politic idea. What should have been a laid-back bonding time for Emma with Grandma suddenly had the potential for high-stress family drama.

Anise couldn't help overhearing. "You're going to wind up with a houseful," she said. "Isn't Justin flying out later in the month, too?"

"The Justin visit is on hold—Gina enrolled him in some once-in-a-lifetime junior astronomers' camp. I've been trying to convince Leslie to use her break from Emma to spend quality time with Dan and little Harry."

Anise frowned. "Well, I'm going back to work on the Monday Emma arrives. That should help."

"It's barely been two weeks."

"Caleb knows who I am. I've told Marty's I'll work split-shifts around his schedule. Good for them, good for me."

"Child care?"

"Ben Gaskill recommended this high school girl who is looking for work. With six brothers and sisters, she knows more about babies than I do."

I smiled. Our vicar seems to have graduated to a first-name status.

"By fall the county day care should be a possibility," Anise said. "They take infants . . . have a good reputation."

"You've thought this all through."

Anise shrugged. "I'm lucky. I have a lot of support."

There was more. I could sense it. But Anise clearly wasn't ready to share and it wasn't my place to insist.

"Does your family know about the baby?"

"Not yet. It's on the tip of my tongue. And then something intervenes. They would want to see the baby. I haven't quite figured out how to swing all that."

"If it's the money, I could—"

Anise riveted me with a steady gaze. "I appreciate your generosity, but it's out of the question."

"We've all had help along the way, Anise."

"There are limits,"she said.

Something in her tone told me to let it go. Down at the print shop, George was also on my case.

"In case you haven't noticed, we've got a launch coming up," he snapped, "and you're running on fumes. Is it time for an intervention here—maybe send you off to a day-spa . . . invest in some Ambien?"

I looked up mid-yawn to catch the worry in his eyes. He wasn't kidding.

"I'm fine, George, really . . . "

"For the record, Anise is worried about you, too."

That finally got my dander up. "And my girls, you forgot to add them to the list. *For the record*, I don't like being ganged up on. I can *handle* this!"

"And I just hit the Power Ball. We aren't in our thirties any more, Evie girl. Just thought you might need a friendly little reminder."

"With friends like that—"

"You might live to finish out the decade."

His bulldog scowl was so outrageous, it set me to chuckling. "You remind me of Caleb," I said. "George . . . George . . . what would I do without you!"

"Miss some of the best stuff, apparently. Who ever said the sports page is dull!"

With that he handed me an email from the county's recreation department. I scanned the page once, then a second time. It contained nothing but a series of lists—participants in the summer sports leagues.

"The summer rec program," I said. "Slow-pitch, T-Ball, Little League . . . I don't get it."

"Keep reading."

"T-ball, three-man basketball . . . "

The names jumped out at me—Mark Blandis, Ben Gaskill and filling out the three-some, the male coach of the Xenaphon High School girls' basketball team. My eyebrows arched about the same time my boss started to chuckle.

"*Ok-a-a-ay*," I breathed.

"I gather you didn't know?"

"Those are the guys that play over lunch out back of the elementary school?"

"I've heard the competition isn't half bad. Any idea what this is all about?"

"I don't know the coach. But with the two alpha guys I *do* know, I'd say the competition between them is about something else entirely!"

"You're talking about Anise Gruin."

"Good taste," I felt a smile play at the corner of my mouth. "I'll hand them that."

"What's her take if any on the subject?"

"I'm sure she's noticed all the posturing and jockeying out at the berm. No surprise there. But she's sure not looking, if that's what you mean."

"Who ever said sports reports are boring? It's the last thing in the world I would have expected of either one of them."

"I just work here, boss . . . can't pretend to speculate one way or the other. Your Mark has a mug with his name on it hanging on the wall at Marty's. Ben Gaskill stops at the house from time to time on some pretext or other. I think Anise is planning to have Caleb baptized soon. Marty's already has been talking about throwing a reception afterward."

"Small town life," George shook his head. "Ya gotta love it."

"I gather whatever is happening over at the bank, your son plans to stick around for the summer. Has he talked any more about the print shop?"

"Not a word. We've been meeting mortgage payments . . . barely. Mark is tight-lipped on the subject, but if I were in his shoes, I would take one look at the precarious situation newspapers are in nationwide and insist on seeing a new business plan from us."

"We can't be alone in this. A lot of Must Sell signs have cropped up around town lately. How bad a shape is the bank really in?"

George shrugged. "I can't imagine why our local mortgage and real estate dealings would have been any saner than the rest of the country."

"So, where does that leave the *Gazette* . . . the novel . . . ?"

"I shared with Mark the idea of starting a regional on-demand press."

"And . . . ?"

"He listened—more than listened, really. Either he knows a lot about it or has done some research into publishing. Regional books always have been a niche market, he said, and probably always will be. As coffee table material, if nothing else."

"Not very encouraging."

"At least not *dis*-couraging and a heck of a lot more polite than you were on the subject when I first brought it up. Especially given the state of the industry, I took that as a good sign." With an impatient gesture, George tugged at his tie, succeeded in loosening it a notch. "Bottom line, we keep going. I'll have yet another proof copy of the novel for you, with cover, by day's end."

"Guess I know what I'll be doing this weekend."

George just laughed. "See you out at the berm," he said. "With the way things are going, sounds like your gal Anise needs a chaperone."

If Anise needed a chaperone, I was beginning to think I was in line for a nursing home. I could live with crows' feet and gray hair. The cellulite was safely out of sight. What had begun to send me into a total tizzy were the dozen little losses that plagued my days. Locating my reading glasses had become a perpetual scavenger hunt. Phone numbers, the next to go. And now, most humiliating to date, *my plants.*

When I had dug in the cottage garden in front of the homestead, I had neglected one important little detail. I hadn't labeled a thing. As I watered and weeded and fussed over my growing community of perennials, that decision was coming back to haunt me. I couldn't remember where I put what. Worse, especially when it came to the newcomers in the bunch, I didn't recognize a thing.

After Saturday's work session at the berm, I volunteered to stay behind to help Bea round up the tools and stash them in the shed hidden along the tree-line near the access road. The clean-up took forever in that heat. Somebody had abandoned a trowel in the lavender. Clippers lay discarded among the astilbe. The last straw was the dandelion digger stuck upright like a flag amid the iris.

"I'm glad I'm not the only one who's getting senile," I said. "This has gone *way* beyond misplacing a tool or two."

As I shared my tale of the 'mystery plants' in my own front yard, Bea just laughed. "You certainly aren't the only gardener who ever pulled up the good stuff instead of weeds. We all do it. That's why the gods invented garden stakes with labels."

"Easy for you to say. You're a Master Gardener—can rattle off the Latin names with the best of 'em. I have trouble these days just remembering the common ones. How on earth do you put up with the bunch of us on the crew bumbling along out here, week after week? Clueless, clueless and clueless!"

A dark pool of sweat had formed between the shoulder blades of Bea's Gardeners-know-all-the-best-dirt tee shirt. "For a gang of amateurs, Eve, we're really getting a whole lot better at gardening together . . . *considering.* After all, you and I both had some exposure to weeds and mulch as kids. The rest? Not so much. Gardening isn't just about a single season. It's about the long haul. Even 'Heirloom' seeds don't earn that label overnight! "

Bea had hit on something I never taken into account quite that way before. One underlying measure of my own success as gardener over the years had been an unspoken yardstick, *Can I manage to grow successfully what my Grandma Eva did?* The bottom line always came down to time and people.

Bea had piqued my curiosity and I found myself once again prowling the web for answers. Except for browsing an occasional grower's catalog my friend had passed along to me, the whole world of historic horticulture—Heritage farms, gardens and plant species—lay woefully beyond my area of expertise. The Internet had plenty to say on the subject, all fodder for possible columns down the road.

"The movement to preserve historic plants (and eventually even the family farm itself as an institution) began with the wholesale exodus

186

from the land in our country," I wrote in my computer journal. "In retrospect, a transition I witnessed as a child."

> While the rise of the great industrial cities of the Midwest had been part of my heritage, I was still too young to fully understand what that history meant for places like Xenaphon. By the end of World War II, industrial agriculture on a grand scale had begun to wipe out the family farm. That new thousand-acre dream demanded a very different kind of seed production, the systematic development of weather and pest-resistant hybrids. Too successful, it seems. Wholesale genetic engineering in the 1970s began to call into question the very integrity of the plant stock and our food supply.
>
> The clock was ticking for whole strains of historic plants. Growers joined scientists in a race to track down pioneer plant stock. They surveyed rural areas for historic seeds passed down from generation to generation. Some combed rail beds and roadways. It helped that decades earlier, utopian religious communities like the Amish and Shakers had created thriving businesses preserving and selling some of those historic seed varieties.
>
> Sadly, the fate of Heritage farms was not so encouraging. Between 1979 and 1998 alone, some 300,000 farms ceased operation. Out of two million farms in the U.S., some 98 percent rely on off-farm income for survival. Together, small and family-owned farms account for less than half of our country's agricultural revenue.

Nothing like tough economic times to get folks back to basics, including a new appreciation for the art and science of farming. Since we opened Groft's for the season, the sale of vegetable seeds and plants had been booming. Folks who obviously hadn't tilled or hoed in decades, if ever, had taken to carving out plots for veggies in their backyards.

"If you can grow a plant," Grandmother Eva always told me, "you'll never starve."

Wisdom for our time—although thanks to young Caleb's presence in the homestead, the menu might not include Anise Gruin's fresh-baked pastry. Without even trying, the first two weeks after her little night owl joined us, I had lost six-and-a-half pounds. Bigger, most definitely, is not always better.

Thirteen
Independence Day

Caleb of the thick dark hair and mighty lungs supplied all the fireworks his mother and I needed for the Fourth. The rhythm of our days had been turned upside down and inside out. Where my manuscripts had once dominated the window seat in the dining room, I now saw boxes of wipes and diapers. Bonding with that young man had become my personal declaration of independence. In every hug and touch, I found myself experiencing the precious freedom from despair—the liberating truth that with or without us, life goes on.

Not so for Job. Just when I thought we had seen the last of him, he's back in the lectionary, still crying out to the darkness, a case study of terrible things happening to even the best of people. Finally even the Divinity has enough.

"Get over yourself . . . !" a Voice roars down from the whirlwind. "Gird up your loins like a man."

Overhead, the ancient text says, the stars were laughing. Through the bittersweet lens of memory, so was I. Whenever I wanted to gross-out my daughters over the years, I jokingly referred to them as the "fruit of my loins". Classic TMI—they hated the expression. I couldn't even imagine what the girls would think or say now if they witnessed my vicarious grandparenting and the dark circles accumulating under my eyes.

"You can't keep doing this," Anise said. "You're exhausted."

"Hey, I volunteered . . . am loving every minute of it," I stifled a yawn. "Though I'll admit, these three-hours-at-a-stretch cat-naps every night are a shock to the old system."

Anise seemed to drop the subject. I should have been suspicious when she took my advice for once and postponed going back to work at Marty's for another week. Mid-week she headed out to the grocery, looking cool and collected in a frappe pastel sun-dress. Hours later, she returned frazzled and out of breath, horsing a trunk full of cardboard boxes and strapping tape.

"I've been reading the want ads," she said. "There's a one-bedroom available downtown, the one over Harold & Daughters Hardware. I sign the lease tomorrow. Your granddaughter Emma arrives Sunday. By the end of the week, Caleb and I will have moved out."

I was momentarily shocked speechless. "Say again . . .? "

"It's time," she said. "You've been nothing but gracious, generous—loving. In every way you've given me back my life . . . and Caleb's. I'll never forget that . . . or you. *Ever.* But when your granddaughter Emma shows up next weekend, she's going to need your undivided attention. It's not fair to either one of you to have me and a baby underfoot."

"You know that isn't how I—"

"It's just time, Eve."

"You're starting work again. How on earth are you going to—?"

"I'll manage. Caleb will come with me if I'm working at Groft's. and when I'm on split-shifts at Marty's, I've hired a high school girl, Glen Dornbush's daughter, for the summer. She needs the money for college and the price is right."

"And after school starts?"

"I'll punt."

"You don't have to do this."

"Yes . . . ," her voice shook, steadied again. "Yes, I do. And we both know it."

"Emma is only going to stay for a month. Surely, you can hold off on doing anything so drastic until—"

"It's never going to get any easier. You have a right to a life of your own, Eve . . . not just the prospect of raising yet another generation."

"There are worse ways to spend my retirement. I consider it a privilege to—"

"I know. And I'm more grateful than I can say."

189

But, I was getting nowhere. "Then at least consider another possibility."

She suspended judgement long enough to load the baby into the back seat of my Taurus. Cocooned in skeptical silence, she let me drive us out into the country and down a dirt road lined with pines and cottages set back from the road. I cracked the window, reveling in the familiar rush of green in my nostrils. Eventually the dust kicked up by the tires forced me to close it again.

The first time I ever drove this road, the day had looked like this. In the distance, silver waters of the sandy-bottom lake darted in and out among the trees like bass schooling in the late afternoon sun. The name on the mailbox had weathered badly the last several seasons. Still, with a little effort, it was readable enough.

"Grofts," Anise said.

I brought the car to a stop behind the house and we just sat there, staring out the windshield. Caleb was stirring in his car seat, quieted again.

"What is . . . I don't understand . . . ?"

"Adam's cottage," I said.

I sensed her turning the enormity of it over in her head. "This *mansion* . . . this is what he left you."

And you chose not to live here. Anise didn't ask, but an answer seemed required anyway. If not for her, then for me.

"I tried to move in. Maybe it was just too soon. I couldn't."

Her eyebrows arched. "But somehow you can picture me here. Caleb and me rattling around in this—"

"Yes."

"I've never lived in a place like this in my life."

"There's a first time for everything," I said.

"You're kidding. I couldn't afford the utilities . . . to say nothing of rent. What would a place like this go for? A couple of K a month?"

"The cottage has been moth-balled for almost two years. I pay a caretaker way too much to check on it—moot provided someone's living here. Empty or not, I've kept it heated. That wouldn't change. They plow the road now with more summer people staying on. But if it becomes too difficult to commute, you and Caleb could always spend the worst of the months in town with me. As is, you would be a lot closer here to the nursery than if you lived in town."

"You have it all figured out."

190

"No. But we didn't either when we met. As I see it, we'll just work things out as we go along."

I didn't let her say, No. While she sat there, seatbelt still fastened, I got out of the car, strode around to the rear passenger door and began to unhook Caleb from his car seat. Together we maneuvered him into the front-pack that held him snugged tightly against her. Neither of us spoke as we made our way across the well-manicured lawn toward the back door.

The key didn't want to work in the lock—bittersweet deja vu. The very first night I came here after Adam's death, Dutch had to help me finagle it. This time I persisted.

We had to pass through the kitchen on the way to the living areas. Unplanned, but one look and I could tell Anise was a goner. Sitting in the entryway were those ill-fated cleaning supplies I had been using when I got the call that Caleb was on the way. But the layout itself was a pastry chef's dream—elegant black marble counter space to spare. The cupboards and gleaming stainless steel appliances would have served a small restaurant. A utility island boasted both a double sink and a third bar-sized sink with its own battery of faucets. Over the island hung a collection of pots and pans worthy of the Food Channel.

"That's playing dirty," Anise said.

"True enough. I thought you might like it, though the place certainly could stand a dust-off. When you called me from the hospital, I just dropped everything and ran. I'd be more than happy to finish the job."

She followed through the pantry hall and came to a stop alongside me in the living room. I tried to see the view through her eyes—marveled now as then that the owner of a nursery would have landscaped so simply, with grass and natural outcroppings instead of perennials. Framed by stands of bushes and evergreens, patio and lawn flowed like a meadow toward the lake and graying sky beyond. A family of ducks frolicked at the water's edge, oblivious to our presence.

Somewhere in the house a clock began chiming the hour. The air felt heavy and close from the summer heat streaming in through those massive floor-to-ceiling windows.

"That woman in the painting . . . over the mantle . . . ?" Anise said.

"Adam's grandmother."

"Stunning."

"A wonderful woman, I'm told. I never knew her. She was an

artist, designed that Eden window in the sanctuary at Peace."

Without my prompting now, Anise had begun to make her way farther into the house. I saw her gaze linger on the books and magazines sprawled across the Mission Style coffee table. A jacket was thrown over an antique Morris Chair near the front door—Adam's, but I had taken to wearing it before I closed up last fall. The fabric had felt alive against my skin, that bracing texture of old, dense-woven wool. It was enough to make my bare arms shiver, remembering.

We checked out the upstairs. I couldn't bring myself to follow her into the master suite. Eventually we found ourselves back in the living room. Out on the lake, a lone sailboat was taking advantage of the late afternoon breezes—gentle and laid-back. *Wouldn't send a six-pack sliding across the deck*, Adam said, *sailing at its best.*

"You've decided to leave it as is," Anise said. "Furnished."

"This isn't some kind of shrine or holy-of-holies, if that's what you're wondering," my mouth felt stiff "Feel free to childproof the place, do whatever it takes to make it yours."

"Never in the wildest of parallel universes did I ever picture myself living somewhere like this."

"Neither did I. But here it is. And I can't bring myself to rent it to strangers. It would take a real load off my mind to know the place is lived in, cared for. After all your help at the homestead, I can't imagine anyone better to—

"Some of the antiques around here are priceless. Caleb will be mobile soon enough. If house-sitting is what you want, a toddler isn't exactly—"

"This isn't a museum. Adam grew up in this place. I think he would be pleased to know a family felt at home here again—that someone I cared about could love it the way his family had."

"You really mean this."

"Yes."

Her silence spoke of an awed consent. At least I chose to take it that way. For the moment, I had said enough.

"You don't have to decide now," I told her. "You haven't signed the lease downtown. Just think about it before you do, that's all . . . "

We left it at that. I let her sleep on it. Sleepless myself, I sat propped against the headboard, my laptop snugged against my knees. The words all but wrote themselves:

"Every wall is a door," Ralph Waldo Emerson once said. As a gardener, I have never given a great deal of thought to 'separation anxiety' when it comes to thinning out or dividing my perennials. Timing is all.

Take your cues from the root systems and weather conditions, the Fine Gardening website says. For starters, does the plant in question look good? Healthy helps. Then, too, the process is more successful in cool than warm weather.

Uncertain as the thinning-out process seems, a gardener cannot afford to be timid. When a plant is divided at the top of its game, it is going to expand and grow again by leaps and bounds. A "halved" plant is likely to double in just a growing season—will quickly need thinning again.

Gardeners frequently agonize over the when of it. Some swear by doing the deed in spring. That way a whole new growing season lies ahead for the fragile plants to recoup. Still others prefer fall because the plant root structures are at their strongest.

I am not sure who or what is most vulnerable in that act of parting, plant or gardener. But it has to be done—a great thought to hold on to at that first brutal spade thrust.

For a long time afterward, I stared at the half-empty screen.

Wherever Anise chose to go with Caleb, I was going to lose them. Imagining their laughter and the sound of footsteps warming those empty rooms at the lake house began slowly to ease the ache around my heart. It was only then that I remembered Jake's gift and the memorial to Adam the cottage could become. With a heavy heart I knew that whatever vision I might have for the place, I could not offer Anise sanctuary with one hand and take it away with the other.

Around 3 A.M., baby Caleb began to whimper. I must have dozed off. This once I forced myself not to respond—every nerve ending suddenly alert as I listened to the increasingly impatient cries. After a while I heard movement and the low sound of a voice. Then silence. By the time the drill repeated itself at six, as it always did, I must have been sound asleep.

Anise joined me at the breakfast table. Her eyes were red-rimmed and she seemed on the verge of nodding off. Upstairs in his crib, her son slept on.

"Rough night?"

Anise winced, grasped in her two hands the mug of coffee I

extended her way. "Uhnnn . . . !"

I wasn't up to mindless chatter any more than she. Her expression tight and shuttered, Anise was still sitting at the table when I began to clean up.

"It looks like a warehouse with all those boxes on the front porch," she said finally.

"No problem."

Anise shifted in her chair, drew herself erect. "I've decided to phone the hardware as soon as they open . . . tell them to forget about the lease on the apartment," she said. "If the offer still stands . . . "

"I'm glad, truly *glad*." I hadn't noticed I had been holding my breath. "There's an extra key whenever you're ready—don't let me forget. Though as you could see, that back door is probably going to need some coaxing. In any case, please don't feel like I'm rushing you."

"May as well do it."

Our eye contact said it all. She was having as much trouble with the move as I was.

I had learned a long time ago that short moves are the worst. Packing was a nightmare, but I helped as best I could. We took multiple trips with both Artie's truck, my Taurus and Anise's Impala crammed to overflowing—a great deal of it Caleb's garage sale gear. By Thursday, Anise spent her first night alone with Caleb out at the cottage. Neither one of us could manage to say a proper goodbye.

Keys in hand, she fussed awkwardly with a pack of diapers that threatened to slide down onto Caleb's car seat from the heap in the back seat. Even dog tired as we were, it seemed to be taking her far too long.

"Let me help," I said gently.

"I sure didn't show up with this much stuff."

"True. But then kids change everything."

"What was I thinking? Caleb's not even a month old. How much stuff does a baby need?"

"If it's any consolation, wait until he's ready for college. He'll make that move in a single trip. But trust me, the hole he leaves in your heart will take truckloads of living to fill."

Tears spring up in Anise Gruin's eyes, but she bit them back. "I'm going to miss you," she said.

"You'll do just fine."

It was asking too much to stand there watching them go. She

194

wasn't the only one on the verge of a good crying jag. Anise fiddled with the seatbelt. Her driver side door made a hollow thud as I gently closed it, turned and headed toward the front porch. My cottage garden slept in the dim glow from the porch light. I never looked back.

The living and dining room had never seemed so empty. Months ago the manuscript boxes and now the heaps of freshly-folded onesies on the furniture and window seats were gone. I wandered the hall upstairs for a while, fussing and straightening. Finally I fell asleep on the couch in the living room. The television was blaring and all the lights were on in the house.

I hadn't expected a parting gift, but when I opened the refrigerator Friday morning, one was waiting for me—sticky buns, their gooey icing solid as the pond in the town park in the middle of winter. Anise had left a note.

I know you. Don't even THINK of eating these without nuking them first.   Love, Anise

Alone at my kitchen table waiting for the microwave to ding, I found myself doing what I had wanted to do ever since Anise told me she was going to move. I wept. Then puffy-eyed and with a monster of a headache, I poured myself a steaming mug of coffee. Two of her yeasty concoctions later, I finally roused myself enough to show up at the print shop.

"You look like death," George said.

"I'll take that as a compliment . . . "

When I didn't elaborate, he poured me a cup of coffee. "Cream? Sugar?"

"Black's fine. I feel like I'm running a B-and-B over there. Anise moved out. Emma will be here in a couple of days."

"Moved . . . since when? where? What brought all this on?"

"Yesterday. She's living with Caleb out at the cottage."

George made eye contact. "You're okay with that . . . ?"

I knew what he was thinking—the foundation and our community "Roots" project. "It wasn't my decision for them to move, that's for sure. But at least after all these months, the cottage finally has a tenant."

When it came to the bigger picture, this wasn't a solution. But right now that was all I had.

195

"Who ever said that nothing happens in small towns," George said. " I'm beginning to think somebody spiked the punch at the Fourth of July picnic. Before you walked in that door I got a call from the mayor that—"

Whatever it was would have to keep. I had my back to the door. Something flickered in my boss' face just before the bell warned we were about to get company. I turned to see Mark Blandis, flanked by an entourage—his accountant and attorney, we learned from the hasty introductions.

Time, I decided, to make my excuses and head home to my laptop. I never got the chance to open my mouth.

"This involves you, too, Ms. Brennerman," Mark's tone stopped me in my tracks. "You two and the *Gazette* are more or less the pulse of the community . . . so I wanted you both to hear this first. Though I suspect the rumor may already be out there. Tomorrow it will be official—the Xenaphon Savings' sign is coming down—"

"Our only bank," I heard myself saying.

Mark grimaced. "Tough stuff. Although fortunately, buy-out talks have been in the works for some time now. If the town's lucky, the deal will be final by the end of July."

In fairness, he explained, all the bad debt stemmed less from greed than from too much well-meant charity when it came to the bank's loan policy—compounded, of course, by the desperate economic straits in which the whole region found itself. Former bank CEO Glen Dornbush's house already sported a For-Sale sign.

By now my boss had the look of a man on the edge. "So, you're telling me the new owners . . . I suppose this means they'll be cutting off credit for the shop's—"

"Not likely," Mark shook his head. "An investor has come forward who is willing to float the shop's mortgage—advance the capital to follow through and get the on-demand press off the ground."

"Does that investor have a name," my boss said slowly. "Nobody locally has that kind of cash on—"

Mark didn't blink. "Me."

"You . . . "

"Yes."

"You think the shop. the restructuring is viable?"

Mark seemed careful shaping his words. "A gamble maybe—but yes, I do."

"I can't let you do that."

The 'why' of it hung in the long silence between father and son. But then as a parent, I had been there and knew the laundry list of possibilities by heart—pride, fear, even guilt. To need or take that kind of help from a child is not in the job description. After Adam died, I clung to my girls in much the same way, too vulnerable and beaten to say, No. The assumption is, it's supposed to work the other way around.

George's brows tightened to a single line. "And your family . . . ?"

"Which one . . . ?"

"I will not take a dime from your grandparents' estate or—"

"You won't. And for what it's worth, you won't find me second-guessing you either, once we agree on the terms."

My boss sat down heavily on the counter stool. His jaw was tight. "And after you're back in Pittsburgh," he said, "what then?"

Mark stared his father down. "The shareholders just named me CEO of Northern Michigan Bank Corp.," he said evenly.

"You're . . . that means you'll be staying . . . "

"For six months anyway. I signed a short-term lease on that apartment over the hardware. After that, we'll see."

As if only now remembering I was there, Mark flashed a reassuring glance in my direction. "Of course, your novel is still a *go*," he said. "Dad loaned me an advanced copy and I think you might just have something there. You could have found a niche."

"I appreciate that," I told him. "If it helps the shop, I'm fine with whatever you decide to do."

"You've got a signing coming up in a matter of weeks."

I nodded.

"Let me know how I can help"

I nodded my thanks, speechless. It seemed that Xenaphon and its *Gazette* had found their champion. *An outsider,* no less. *The executioner among us had become an advocate.*

Thoughts on hyperdrive, I tuned out the restrained maneuvering and legalese that followed. If Mark Blandis was right, the shop and maybe even the community could come out of the calamity stronger than before. Our bank might be a chain, but it would stay open. We had seen the alternative in far too many towns around us. Venerable red brick structures with Bank chiseled into the granite lintels had become gift shops—their gilt-lettered, cast iron vaults gaping open to display homemade crafts and

197

local Michigan delicacies. The town of Xenaphon would have never recovered.

After Mark left, silence reigned in the shop. Change in a garden can seem imperceptible, at least until a major blow or the first hard frost hits. If ever there was such a make-or-break point, for either the shop or Xenaphon itself, this was it.

So much about Mark Blandis and his recent conduct suddenly made sense. From the get go, George had gleaned the impression his son felt out of touch with the lifestyle of his Pittsburgh family. In hindsight, it didn't seem so improbable at all that he would find an alternative in Xenaphon. Even our summer rec program's three-man basketball league.

First Adam, then Jake and now Mark Blandis. All three of the men had been accustomed to the fast lane most of their adult lives—all three experienced an epiphany over this special place. What I had pegged initially as arrogant and self-absorbed in all three of them proved nothing but colossal insecurity over where their life choices had brought them.

"Kids," I said finally. "Go figure."

George shook his head. "I'm the wrong one to ask about parenting. For better or worse, I started the whole business later in life than most."

I laughed. "For what it's worth, when stuff like this happens, I've discovered it pays to just take it—breathe a sigh of relief or thanksgiving, whichever comes first."

Next morning on the berm, the hushed whispers and knowing looks from the Gang Green made it plain that news of the bank and Mark's role in its possible survival were all over town. I had to hand it to the guy, he showed up and went straight to work edging the beds with his Dad and Ben Gaskill—an ugly job. Although I caught occasional sidelong glances aimed his way, not one of the gardening crew even brought up the situation or what it could mean for all of us.

Anise also showed up with Caleb in tow. I had to smile watching Ben and Mark scramble to help carry all the baby's paraphernalia on that uneven ground. The whole gang had taken time out to admire the youngest member of Gang Green. Anise had made a point of bringing along the cushy kid-sized tools I had bought for him at the dollar store—had stashed them in the stroller tray.

"Too cute . . . just gotta get that kid a hat to match," Bea laughed. "Straw's too prickly. But the co-op carries those striped denim farmer's hats for kids. A little big maybe, but he'll grow into it."

"Unfortunately, I can't participate for long," Anise said as she gave us both hugs. "I've got to clean up and get over to the restaurant by eleven-thirty. I was hoping maybe I could pop in at the homestead first and use the shower. It's humid as heck out here."

I fought a smile. "Of course. Shower away."

"Emma's not here yet?"

"Early afternoon. She's going to be disappointed not to see Caleb."

Anise looked uncomfortable. "If he's awake at the sitters, I'll stop by after work."

"She'd like that."

In that heat, the garden was making up for lost time. Everything had begun to bud at once—tight little globe-shapes curled in upon themselves that showed every promise of a late but normal bloom. The weeds weren't nearly so reticent. Dandelions were on the attack everywhere. Everyone on the crew not caught up in the heavy spadework around the beds was pressed into service to beat them back.

I went to the task with trepidation. After schlepping boxes all week, every twinge in my back provoked a caution bordering on paranoia.

"Annoying as heck," I said to Bea as I circled the beds yet again with my trowel looking for the tell-tale invaders. "One minute a spot looks fine and next time you pass it, there's a weed. Either it sprouted in less than ten minutes or the darn thing just sat there bold as brass all along, as if it belonged there."

Bea laughed. "Natural selection. Weeds have adaptation down to a science. I have one in my garden at home looks just like phlox. It sits in my bed half the season before I catch on and ferret it out. Never does a thing—no blossoms, nothing. When I finally figure it out, I swear that blasted plant is just sitting there mocking me."

Hope *I'm* that flexible, I told myself. After tool clean-up, I would head home to confront my own new normal—my life without Anise. Turns out, I wasn't alone for long. Emma showed up with her Mom around one.

"You're early!" I had wanted to be waiting for them on the porch with a pitcher of freshly minted lemonade.

Emma appeared to have grown a foot since Mother's Day. She scrambled out the car almost before it stopped. Chin set, she stomped up the front walk dragging a bulging overnight bag in her two hands. A quick hug and then she was off again in the direction of upstairs. I had no time

199

to warn her that the search would come up empty.

She peered down over the staircase rail at me—the picture of confused indignation. "They're gone."

"Not far. You remember Adam's cottage at the lake?"

"That's not fair."

"Think about it, Emma. You're going to spend some time here on your own. Well, Anise and Caleb need a space of their own, too."

Face averted, my granddaughter took her time coming back down. Her glow-light sneakers made thumpity noises with every step.

"Anise is at work. But she and Caleb are probably coming over later," I said.

Emma scowled. "What're we gonna eat for lunch, Grama. Mom wouldn't let us stop."

Just that quick the storm was over—or at least it had moved on. How I envied the young. They make change look so simple. My envy was short-lived. Turns out, my daughter was having separation issues of her own.

"I didn't want to dump Emma and run, but I can only spend two nights," she said. "Hope you don't mind. With a new boss at work, everybody is jockeying for position. Scary, trust me."

"Emma seems to be doing fine . . . . a little grumpy from the trip. But then that was a long time in the car for anyone."

Leslie grimaced. "She's doing better than I am apparently. Why do I feel like the first day I saw her peering back at me out of the school bus window? Ridiculous. She was here last summer."

"True. But not five weeks. Trust me, we'll survive—all three of us. Emma and me *and you*."

"Hope you feel the same a month from now."

Emma's biggest adjustment came at bedtime. After several nights of chin-quivering meltdowns, my granddaughter hit on the solution herself. Once she thought I was asleep, she would slip across the hall and crawl in bed alongside me. I decided not to intervene. If she was going to get all the sleep she needed, I had to get to bed earlier.

And a good thing, too. Sunlight barely began streaming into the bedroom windows when I would sense Emma staring down at me and feel her hand tugging at the sleeve of my nightgown.

Our days began and ended in the garden. The first Saturday, Emma was up crack of dawn, her clippers in hand—ready to head out to the berm. I had scrawled her name on them the day before in permanent marker. A good pair of shears is too precious to lose.

"What're we gonna do today, Grama?"

"Deadheading," I told her.

"Sounds scary."

"Not unless you're careless and pinch a hunk out of your finger instead of the plant. Just think of it as giving the plants a hair cut."

My granddaughter's freckled features shaped themselves into a frown. "Grama, when we garden," she said, "is it work . . . like some kind of job? Or are we doing this just for goodness."

I looked down at her, smiled. My throat felt tight.

"For goodness, Emma-girl," I said. "Goodness."

The days sped past. Several nights a week we drove out to the cottage to see Anise and Caleb. I was trying to spend as little time at the print shop as possible—tough when I was experiencing birth pangs of my own. *TIME in a Garden* had come within days of final printing.

While George and I argued over the last touches on the back matter, including my bio, Emma put together endless collages chopped from over-run issues of the *Gazette*. My boss promised her that by the time her visit was over, he would run off her efforts in multiple-copies on the shop's big press.

"Like a book?" she said shyly.

"Bind the pages, you mean? Of course, so you can show your Mom when you're back home," George smiled.

"Guaranteed both my girls are going to laugh themselves silly when they read those credentials you've cooked up for me," I told him. *"Based on her popular weekly column on gardening*—and you're basing that on what?"

"You get fan mail."

"Once in a blue moon."

Emma looked up from admiring her own handiwork to inspect what my boss and I had been doing. "Your cover is blue, Grama," she said. "'Cept that word 'Time' is bigger than everything else. How come?"

"So people will notice," I smiled. "You did. Besides, time is what I write about. The seasons. Our lives. *Time* pretty much sums up what the book is all about. Some people believe that time is the most precious thing we have."

"More than money?"

"More even than money. No matter how much we have, it's never enough. Some people say that time is so special, that it's holy."

"We're running out of it, that's for darn sure," George muttered.

"You said a naughty word." Emma's vocabulary was growing. "What does 'holy' mean, Grama?"

By way of answer, I took her to Peace on Sunday morning. Fortunately for my credibility on matters of all things spiritual, a few cottagers swelled the thinning ranks of the faithful. Otherwise we could have rolled a bowling ball through the sanctuary and not hit much of anything. Most of the younger regulars would have been on duty at one of the farm stands or shops for the duration of the tourist season.

The sheer spectacle of the experience wasn't lost on Emma. Wide-eyed, she craned over the end of the pew to watch someone's visiting grandson struggling to play crucifer at the head of the opening procession. Father Gaskill followed in his summer chasuble overflowing with boldly embroidered vines and branches.

"He looks like a garden," Emma whispered.

Down the row from us, Matt Gaskill strangled a laugh. Emma shot a puzzled look in his direction.

"Does that man have allergies? Or do you think maybe it's something he ate? I saw them do this Hi-lick thing on TV and the food popped right back out. *E-e-e-ew* . . . !"

Red-faced and shoulders shaking, Matt disappeared behind his hymn book. Any minute I expected a roar of laughter to emerge, but eventually the shaking stopped. Emma had moved on.

"The piece that lady is playing, they call it *Fe-e-er Elise*," she said. "My piano teacher is going to let me learn it, but not 'til I'm bigger. What are they going to do with all that money in the baskets, Grama?"

"The church uses it to help people."

"And pay the man up there in the flower suit?"

"That, too."

Tucked safely beside me at the Communion rail, Emma stared up at Father Gaskill open-mouthed while he blessed her. I braced myself for the stream-of-consciousness dialogue that was bound to follow. But then I could have sworn when the young priest and I made eye contact, he winked.

"I see you have company," Matt said at the coffee hour.

"*Heard* is more like it."

Emma and the young crucifer had installed themselves in front of the brownies at the dessert table. The boy had shed his liturgical garb to reveal cargo pants and tee shirt, but I would have bet my granddaughter was still grilling him about his earlier get-up.

"I was noticing the two of you at the berm yesterday," Matt said. "She really loves to work with you like that."

I chuckled softly. "We have our moments. But then a six to eight-hour shift tomorrow weeding out the peat pots at Groft's could try anybody's patience."

"I've been thinking," Matt said slowly, "if you ever need help out there, just give me a jingle. Or you could email."

It had never occurred to me. "We *are* stretched pretty thin," I said. "Viv, Artie and I are supposedly retired, after all. Anise is doing double-duty down at Marty's and makes more in tips on the dinner shift than a full day at Groft's. Chris will be headed back to high school in fall. We just might take you up on it."

Meanwhile Emma and I prowled the aisles of the propagation house, picking out perennials that most needed digging in. "Time to move them to the shop," I told her.

"I saw an ad on TV once about people who save pets. We could make a 'Dopt-a-Plant sign. Give a P'rennia a Good Home." Emma's face scrunched in a frown. "You never told me, Grama. What's a p'rennia?"

I laughed. "Perenni-a-l. That's a plant that comes back every year. We planted annuals when you were here at Easter, the ones that only last a single season. Remember? I'll show them to you again when we get home, if you like."

"*Perennial.* I think I like that better. Like *me*, Grama—I'm here last summer and this summer . . . and next summer, too!"

She looked so very pleased with herself. I kept thinking of the Psalm we heard read for that Sunday, how our land will yield its increase. The fullness of my world was measured in children's laughter these days. Life was good.

"What say we make like cartoon character explorers," I told my granddaughter when she started to get bored, "on the alert for new adventures. Take a look at that flat over there. It's missing a plant. See, the one in the far corner didn't make it. We're going to have to scour the healthy pots for an extra that's sprouting up where it isn't needed."

Emma located a likely candidate—hesitated. "Maybe the baby plant doesn't wanna move," she said slowly.

My antenna went up. "Sounds like you know how that plant feels," I said.

"Maybe. Dunno. Mom says that if Daddy doesn't find a job soon, maybe we're going to have to go someplace else."

"And you don't like the idea."

Emma shook her head. "No."

"We can learn a lot from plants," I drew in my breath, let it out slowly. "Gardeners call uprooting a plant and moving it, 'transplanting'. Sometimes the plants go into shock for a while if we shuffle them around. But they always seem to come around."

"I always thought that plants and gardens stand still, in one spot."

I chuckled softly, shook my head. "Who knew? Moving is part of their lives, too. And those plants can be a lot tougher than we think."

I told her about transplanting and how plants like strawberry runners move themselves—rummaging through my memory banks for examples from my column a while back. Emma gently began to ease the seedling out of its matrix.

"Maybe they're afraid at first," she said.

"If we watch them closely, we can tell if they need help. We want them to bloom wherever they're planted."

I thought about pursuing the topic further, but my granddaughter had already moved on. She was squinting her way along the black watering hose that stretched overhead the full hundred-feet of the greenhouse, on the prowl for leaks. When she spotted one, I hoisted her up on the potting bench and let her mark the spot with a chalked X. A little father along a cloud of mist sprayed out of one of the seals or patches.

"Like our own private rain forest," she giggled.

"Jungle, too. The weeds will take over if we don't keep after them. Do you think I should get us explorer hats?"

Emma laughed out loud. "Silly," she said. "You would look really funny Grama."

We stopped to shift a few seedlings from pot to pot. *Comfortable together*, I thought. *An old soul, my Emma.*

"Can I write a book about gardens too someday, like yours, Grama?"

That one caught me out of the blue. "A great idea," I smiled. "If you want, tonight we'll set up a computer file on my laptop all your own. You can tell me your story and I'll type in whatever you tell me."

Emma pulled herself erect. Her chin shot forward and her eyes crackled with blue fire. "I can do it myself, Grama."

I believed her. The girl seemed to be shooting up before my eyes. Her face had thinned out over the past few weeks. And when we gardened out at the berm now, her fingers were strong enough to pinch back a lot of bloomed out flower without using a clippers. The little girl in her had not vanished entirely. She accompanied her tenacious deadheading with the sing-song rhythms of childhood. *One o'clock, two o'clock, three o'clock, four.*

Our leader Bea had called it—the growing season was one for the record books. Everything was blooming at once. The flowing pastel seas of astilbe and blue-purple spires of obedience plant and delphinium were slowing traffic on the off-ramp far more effectively than any DOT signage could have hoped to accomplish. Artie the Teamster's beloved peonies flowered the size of hot pink basketballs.

In the front yard of the homestead, the cottage garden had begun to fill in nicely. Emma and I had to tread carefully now as we weeded our way between the plants. In the evening if we sat on the porch together drinking lemonade, we would try to identify the perennials by shape of the plant or its leaves alone.

"When I was growing up, my Grandma Eva and I would play the very same game," I said. "She was an amazing gardener and could name the crops growing along a roadway from a quarter mile away. Grandma Eva told me once that if you listen very hard, especially just after dark, you can even hear the plants growing."

Emma pulled a face. "Plants can't talk!"

But I noticed from the way she cocked her head to the side, she was keeping her ears on high alert—just in case. From all around the neighborhood, the tree frog chorus was in full voice. High-up among the crown of Grandma Eva's lindens, the breeze murmured its secrets to the velvet sky.

"Nope, don't hear 'em," Emma said finally. "But you know what? I can smell them. Not the flowers either. It's the *plants*. And I never, never, ever smelled 'green' before."

"Somebody ought to make a perfume, huh? They would make a fortune."

Emma laughed. "Grama-a-a-!"

Tears glittered in my eyes as she snuggled alongside me on the porch swing. In the warm summer night, I heard quiet whispers of the past and future all around me. Familiar words rose up to comfort and reassure.

On the seventh day, it was time to take stock of all that had been created. And as we looked around us where once only the abyss had been, we saw that everything was good.

Fourteen
TIME in a Garden

Plants don't get hung up about what on earth we call them. I had to keep reminding myself to stave off last-minute anxiety attacks. Yesterday, *TIME in a Garden* hit the shelves at the drug store. My resume had grown. I had become a novelist, an author. It was certainly one of the more surreal job descriptions in my career, with nary an agent or sign of mass distribution in sight. Call my work self-published or 'independently published', I had embarked on a journey to make friends for my work one reader at a time.

But then plants don't get hung up on labels. They quietly go with the flow. *Echinacea purpurea* answers to 'Coneflower'. *Campanula* goes by the common 'bellflower'. As a gardener I briefly toyed with committing all those elegant Latin monikers to memory. No longer. The point is that by any other name, plants are who they are and do what they do. They blossom.

Granddaughter Emma came with me to the launch. She insisted on wearing a garden print dress, white stockings and a straw hat she found in the attic. The hat had a blue grosgrain ribbons trailing down the back.

"It was my mother's," I told her. "Your Greatgrama."

"I like it." And that was that.

It seems Emma's class at school had studied New England ship-building as part of a unit on Pilgrims last Thanksgiving. Their teacher had showed them photos of historic boat launches over the years. One was of a World War II Great Lakes submarine plummeting down the skids toward the water in a typhoon-like sheet of spray. Unlike the East Coast shipyards, the one along the western shore of Lake Michigan in Manitowoc launched its subs sideways.

"You should have seen it, Grama. Awesome!"

Apparently standing on the platform along with the dignitaries had been a little girl in her Forties vintage finery—shiny black Mary Jane's, hat and white gloves with a single button at each wrist. It was my childhood in a microcosm.

"And a lady hit the boat with a bottle," Emma said. "It broke and fizzy stuff was flying all over. Are we going to do that to your book Grandma?"

I laughed. "Plan is to drink the champagne, Emma, not take a bath in it. My boss is throwing me a party afterward. And you're coming, too."

Late July was not the best time in northern Michigan for a regional novel to launch. Tourists had already begun to head back downstate. College students were getting antsy about the fall semester. Near the highway, some of the monoxide-damaged maples had begun to turn. Convenient or not, *TIME in a Garden* was done. And my boss had confidence enough for the both of us.

George had timed the first public signing to coincide with Xenaphon's annual end-of-summer sidewalk sales. The *Gazette* had been running ads for weeks. I was a basket case—the kind of gut-wrenching fear of throwing a party and wondering if anyone would bother to show up.

"Emma wants to douse the book with champagne to make it a real launch," I told him. "I was thinking instead we could burn a copy in the parking lot."

George laughed. "We'll set up a table on the sidewalk. I'll make sure you have at least a dozen pens. They're bound to walk as you go along. And then you are going to smile, greet your friends, neighbors and the idle curious. Sign copies, date 'em. Write something clever if the customer seems to like the idea."

"As in, what?"

"You'll think of something."

A smile twisted at the corners of my mouth. "How about, *Seasons are short. Enjoy yourself while you can.*"

"See? You're getting the idea, already."

"What if nobody shows?"

"They'll show. Read some of the best-seller web sites. Even the Big Guns never know what they might run up against. They might sell six books in an hour or sixty or none. Or somebody asks you to sign a sales receipt from the mini-mart while they tell you they're going to wait and read your book when it shows up in the public library. Worse is when they brag how many people borrowed their copy. Fame is great, but bucks sure help."

"George, you are seriously scaring me here."

"Don't be. If you take this whole author business too seriously, even you won't show up!"

The weather cooperated. It rained, not buckets, but enough to scare the tourists off the beaches and the locals out of their gardens. I hadn't seen crowds downtown like that all summer. To be on the safe side, George had run two hundred copies of the novel. We sold a third of them on the spot.

"Not bad for fiction," he told me. "Not bad at all."

I was so nervous, it was impacting my motor skills. When people told me their names so I could write something personal, I had to ask them to print the letters first on a scrap piece of paper. I was having trouble holding myself together long enough to spell 'Eve'.

Emma was in her element, chattering nonstop. She informed anyone who would listen that her Grama wrote this book. "And everything in it," she said. "She says that maybe someday I can write a book, too."

The two hours allotted for the signing whizzed past. "Broke every sales record," the drug store owner told me. "Except, of course, whenever we got a case of books about that Potter kid."

George had booked the back room at Marty's to celebrate. I was touched to see that Anise had arranged a display of my novel on one of the tables next to an oversized bouquet of daisies that had to be Chris Demort's handiwork. On the wall over the display, the two had hung the lace panel Adam had given me—a fixture ever since in the bank of windows in my dining room. I mentally traced the delicate white on white outline of the fence and hollyhocks, the familiar text in the center of the design. *Time began in a garden.* True for me on so many levels.

Adam would have been the first to propose a toast. Instead, my boss did the honors. "*L'chiam*, Evie," he said, raising his glass. To life.

And so, for the rest of the afternoon my friends and I feasted on appetizer platters from the catering menu and bottles of Cold Duck that Marty's had stocked just for the occasion. "They're billing at cost," George said when I protested the extravagance of it all.

"At a buck a book profit, a kegger in my backyard would have made more sense."

George laughed. "I promised you bubbly and bubbly it is."

Artie and Viv made an executive decision to close early at Groft's so they all could come. Anise brought Caleb. Chris was there, grumbling at his underage status, but sipping dutifully at the carbonated grape juice Marty's had stocked for the occasion. Bea was there, the Gaskills and Doc Jaidev from the clinic. Even some of the restaurant's 'regulars' who were clients at Groft's or the print shop heard the goings-on and stopped by to share the moment. Much to my chagrin, all of them insisted on springing for copies at full sticker price.

"Loyalty way beyond the call of duty," I said.

We toasted to books and friendships. Emma solemnly lifted her Shirley Temple with the adults. Whatever came of the novel, someday she would read it, understand my story and the part she played in it. That alone was worth the bar code price on the cover.

Come Monday morning, George printed two hundred more copies. Mid-week after the press deadline for the *Gazette*, he loaded up the trunk and headed north toward the string of resort communities along Little Traverse Bay.

"Mecca up there," he said. "By my count, a half dozen independent booksellers. While I'm at it, I'll book you for signings through the end of August. If any dates are off-limits, speak now."

"You're the agent," I said. "Do I have a choice?"

"No."

"I didn't think so. Just aim me and I'll be there."

That one signing at the drug store was more than enough to figure out I was in over my depth. It was one thing to write, something else entirely to try to peddle the results. The week-long adrenalin rush was over. Dog-tired and with a killer headache thudding behind my eyes, I babysat the print shop in George's absence. Emma kept me company, far more patient with the whole business than she had any right to be.

"It's our last week coming up," I said. "After I close up shop, how about we do something special."

"Like what, Grama?"

"Go down to Marty's for fish and chips or burgers. Call Anise to see if she would mind if we went swimming at the lake cottage. I'm open to suggestions."

Thunderstorms rolling through the area nixed the trip to the lake. Emma and I grabbed umbrellas and hiked down to Marty's instead. The waitress brought my granddaughter's kiddie menu mac-and-cheese and my lite-fare broiled haddock. In between bites, we played all the paper games printed on our placemats. I had just asked for the bill when I looked up to see Matt Gaskill headed our way. He stood alongside our booth making small talk until I felt compelled to invite him to join us.

"I'll do just that," he said as he slid in alongside Emma in the booth. "I'd been hoping to bump into you ever since the signing last weekend. Quite a read, though I wasn't prepared for the ending."

Are we ever, I thought, but stopped myself before I said as much. Even from the little he told me, if anyone could identify with where my central characters found themselves, it was Matt Gaskill.

"Great timing," I said. "You're my first fan officially weighing in. George would love it—he's up north hustling deals with booksellers. After a whole day hanging out with me at the print shop, Emma deserved a night out. I can't believe she heads home in just over a week."

"So soon, Grama . . . that's not fair."

"There'll be other summers."

Matt smiled. "Another fan, I see."

"My Grama wrote a book."

"Yes, she did."

"You read it?"

"Uh-hmmm. You ought to some day, too, Emma. Says a lot about what's really important in life."

"I already know," Emma said. "People and plants. It's up to us to help things grow."

"Wise gal you've got there, Ms. Brennerman. Wonder where she got that?"

I wasn't touching that one with a ten foot pole. The waitress showed up with the bill and after we retrieved our umbrellas, the three of us headed out. The rain had stopped. Matt offered to walk us home.

"You don't have to, really."

"No problem. It's on my route."

Not exactly, but I let it pass. Once back at the homestead, the two of us talked while Emma shuffled furniture around in her Greatgrama's dollhouse. I had hauled the imposing wooden Victorian structure out of the attic and set it up on a table on the porch in advance of my granddaughter's visit. A faded shoebox full of furnishings had accumulated over the generations. I smiled at the tiny Zuni pots from a gift shop at the Grand Canyon, thick Delft-pattern plates from my junior year in Holland and a slightly oversize Adirondack chair my daughter Leslie made in summer camp. Like I had and her mother before her, Emma could spend hours arranging and rearranging the rooms.

The sun was setting earlier now. Emma didn't fuss when I suggested that she read in bed. I came downstairs from tucking her in—found Matt still ensconced on the porch swing where I had left him. He took the ice tea I offered.

"I sensed a lot of you in those pages," he said.

"Some . . . a lot," I admitted. "Not all."

"Enough. The story rang true from start to finish."

"I only know that sitting there signing books on Main Street, I felt like I had just cobbled together a clothesline in the front yard. And then I went and hung up every bit of underwear I ever owned. The good, the bad and the way over the hill."

Matt chuckled. "I'm trying to picture that."

"So I suspect is half the town," I winced. "I never intended to publish a novel. Writing the thing started out as a desperate attempt at do-it-yourself therapy."

"A literary attempt at getting out of Dodge. In my case, fleeing the Twin Cities was my last-ditch plan to gain some perspective."

"Even 268 pages later, the perspective business is still a work in progress for me." I told him about my wrestling with Job, stalled on the ash heap with his anger.

Matt listened without comment. I was glad I couldn't see his face.

"I don't know about Job," he said finally, "but I flatter myself after teaching all those years that I know something about people. I know I'm gonna sound like Coach Gaskill. But I'd say, you're being too hard on yourself. To know how life works and then get up the courage to act on it as you did are two different things."

"I'm figuring that out. We're not talking about cheap grace here—making lemonade out of lemons. But there has to be a way to live for the 'now' again, take every day as a gift."

"To walk in the valley of the shadow." Something in his voice caught my attention. But from where I was sitting, Matt's face was unreadable. "It's getting late," he said.

"I really appreciate you taking the time to talk about the book," I told him. "If I'm going to keep doing this—the signings and readings and my handwriting scrawled on all those title pages—it helps to know it struck a chord with somebody anyway. You're a great listener."

Matt laughed. "Any time. A guy learns something living with a counselor all those years."

He was on his feet, half-turned to go. I found myself taking a mental snapshot. I caught the genuine warmth in the man's smile and the fullback build that masked a closet poet. Another pilgrim on the road.

Then he was down the stairs and on to the front walk. "Hang in there," he said. "This too shall pass."

For once I was clueless what to write in my journal. Instead, I hauled out a copy of my novel—one with a damaged cover—and started flagging possible passages for a reading or author chat. While Emma and I were out, my boss had left a message on my answering machine. Three bookstores had committed to taking my book. George had scheduled more appearances for me in August. Our venture into the publishing world had begun to take on a life of its own.

Summer with my granddaughter was over. Her mother showed up a day ahead of schedule to collect her. Emma was weeding out front when Leslie's car pulled up at the curb. My granddaughter's shock of recognition was followed by an indignant frown.

"You're early," Emma let her mother hug her.

Leslie winced. "So shoot me."

"Listen to yourselves," I laughed. "Five weeks apart, five seconds together. Let the games begin!"

"You're surprised?!" Leslie's eyebrow arched but she was smiling. "We're talking mothers and daughters here. And you just wrote the book on the subject."

"*Touche*," I chuckled.

Emma was looking at both of us as if we were speaking Chinese.

"I went to Grama's book signing."

"You'll have to tell me all about it," her mother said.

"We got pictures."

Leslie took her time flipping through the press book I was putting together. Emma's hand-printed comments in the margins were hilarious. "Launch" was spelled l-u-n-c-h.

"Good for you, Mom," my daughter said. "I mean it. Wish I could have been there. You had record sales the clipping says. This is *your* time in the garden and you certainly deserve every minute of it"

My time in the garden. I ducked my head so she wouldn't see me blinking back tears. I would have given anything to have rewritten the ending. It wasn't to be.

Emma was full of herself—visibly proud of her new-found independence. She showed off her refrigerator art and the portion of the cottage garden with 'her' flowers. After tuning in to her daughter's half-hour nonstop monolog, Leslie looked wistful, almost disappointed.

"You weren't homesick?" she said.

Emma stopped mid-thought. "Once," she said. "Maybe two times. But I missed you, Mom."

A diplomat that girl, I smiled. Homesickness works both ways. "I'm certainly going to miss Emma," I said. "She's been a real joy."

"I actually thought about asking if she could stay a few more days," my daughter said. "It's been crazy on our end"

"We aren't going to *move*, are we?" Emma demanded.

My daughter flinched and got a stricken look on her face. Out of the mouths of babes, I thought.

"Who said we were going to move?"

"You did. If Daddy didn't get a job, you told him we were going to have to move."

Leslie and I made eye contact. "Sometimes grownups say things out loud but they don't really mean it," she said.

Emma's chin jutted out another notch. "Well, I don't want to move. Only if we move to Grama's."

My laughter sounded forced, even to me. "A nice idea, Emma. But your Mom and Dad have a nice house of their own outside of Chicago. I love it when you come to visit. And when you get home you can call me anytime you want."

We didn't talk about it again. Two hectic hours later, my daughter had hunted down and packed up Emma's belongings. The car was loaded, ready to go.

"I don't remember bringing all this stuff," Leslie said.

"Don't worry," I told her, "if I find anything else, I'll mail it. We'll have a quick lunch and then you can—"

"Thanks, but no," my daughter shook her head. " I don't want to leave Harry with Dan any longer than I have to. Dan's got a big interview coming up on Monday. Emma and I will grab something along the way."

"We didn't stop when we came to Grama's," Emma pouted. "Not once."

"Well, this time we will. I promise."

The tension in my daughter's face spoke volumes. *Talk to me*, I wanted to tell her. *You may think you won't survive, but you will.*

Instead, I gave her a lingering hug. Emma clung to us both before she climbed into the back seat and clicked on the seat belt.

"Be good. Help your Mom," I told her. "I'm going to miss you."

"Me too."

The window alongside Emma was closed. I felt my mouth shape the words and saw my granddaughter lip-synch an 'I love you' in reply. Our high-five on either side of the glass set off a tightness in my throat.

And then they were gone. Just like that, summer was over.

I took my time heading back to the house. A few weeds had cropped up among the border plants and I stooped to pull them. Emma had left her jacket on the porch. I scooped it up, deposited it on the kitchen counter where I wouldn't forget it. When the post office opened tomorrow, I would pop it in the mail.

The phone didn't ring all evening. Around eleven I decided to fool around with a column idea. I didn't allow myself to dwell on the source:

We think of plants as stationery—rooted in one place. In fact, they move a lot. Plant migration is commonly a youngster's game. The parent plant sends out seeds, shoots, roots or tendrils, and a new generation of plants is born.

Nobody claims it is easy. Seventy percent is considered a viable seed germination rate. That leaves three out of ten that never manage to grow.

Transplanting is another common means of plant migration or relocation. But here the gardener takes the initiative and moves already viable seedlings or full-grown plants to a new, more favorable location.

It is not for the faint of heart. If a plant is going to stand a chance and avoid 'transplant shock', the flowers and even foliage need to be pruned and cut back drastically so that all the energy can go to the vulnerable roots.

We Americans could learn from our gardens on that score. Although in recent decades, the moving rate overall has been decreasing compared to the country's vast population shifts during the Great Depression, the current economic conditions could change that.

Like so many other rural communities, Xenaphon's population has shown a steady decline. Jobs have vanished and the fragile employment base continues to shrink.

As we try to reverse that trend, I suggest we , , ,

I broke off mid-thought. A branch was scraping against the bedroom window. SKI-RITCH. SKI-RITCH. As I listened, rain began to drum against the pane.

I shivered. Xenaphon was sleeping even as I wrote—dreaming, I wondered, of its more illustrious past. The former opera house was now storage for the drugstore downstairs. Once the village boasted not one but three grain elevators. And beyond our borders, men and women raised in this place sought to carve out new homes and lives for themselves. Whatever our Roots project did, reviving the old-fashioned 'homecoming' had to be a part of it, I vowed.

As parents I don't think we ever get beyond worrying about our children. Stuff happens—all too often, painful. And like Xenaphon or the parent plant left behind in the bed, we too suffer for a season, a transplant shock of our own.

When out of the blue, Matt Gaskill called the next morning and invited me to lunch, I wasn't expecting it. "I'll bet the house must seem empty with all your company gone," he said.

He wasn't making it easy to say, No. "I really shouldn't. I've got an author chat coming up."

"All the more reason. I thought burgers down at Marty's."

"Dutch," I said. "I'll meet you there."

"Dutch," I heard the faint rumble of laughter from the other end of the line. "Is one too late? By then the rush down there would be over."

"Fine."

He didn't have to say it. No sense in making a production of showing up together.

I arrived at the dot of one, straight from the print shop. No skulking around in the back—Matt already had staked a claim on a booth within eyeshot of the dining room door. His khakis and navy polo shirt had 'man of leisure' written all over them. I noticed that I managed to acquire an ominous looking ink stain on my dress slacks from one of the presses. The damage was invisible under the formica tabletop, but I knew it was there all the same.

"Must have been hectic around your place the last month or so," he said by way of greeting. "Anise is off on her own. Your launch and now your granddaughter's visit. She seems like a pistol, that girl."

"I'll admit, I've had enough of suitcases for a while. But then you've been in and out yourself a lot lately."

"Tell me about it," he winced. "But the end is in sight. I finally found a buyer for the house in Minneapolis and put everything in storage for the time being. Officially, I guess that means I'm homeless."

"A big decision."

Matt shrugged. "Not as big as getting out of my son's hair. I've taken a temporary apartment in that rental a block down from the library. Plan is to have something permanent by Thanksgiving."

"Putting down roots," I said.

He made it sound so simple. Starting in September, he had signed up to referee for the recreation department's flag football league. He was drafting an invitation to the fellowship group at Peace to start a casserole club.

"Nobody knows how tough it is to cook for one until they try it," he said. "This way a guy can cook 'normal' recipes and still wind up with a week's worth of different meals. Beats a freezer full of leftovers."

"Clever."

He shrugged. "Once a month to start. Then we'll see."

I found myself agreeing to give it a try. For now, we stuck to burgers and beer. When the waitress asked whether we wanted one check or two, Matt signaled one before I had a chance to open my mouth.

"I'll take it off my taxes," he said. "Official business. Any job openings in the *Gazette* look promising? Hope you'll give me a call. Part-time, but still . . . "

"You're shameless."

Matt just grinned. "I certainly hope so."

The news of our lunch made it back to the print shop before I did.

"Hear you and Matt Gaskill were chatting down at Marty's," my boss said.

"Low-cal brew on tap. Just had to try it."

My boss looked at me sideways. "Is there something I ought to know here, Evie?"

"Just that with months of TV dinners ahead, eating out for once has a certain charm. Matt's pretty much in the same boat."

"Nothing to it, then?"

My mouth felt stiff. "I had my moment, more than most people ever do."

"Just wondering."

So was I, truth be told. "Why it is that a man and a woman can't do lunch without automatically being classed as an 'item'," I said. "Next thing you know, they'll be saying the same thing about us, George. You *are* my agent after all."

He laughed. "*Touche*—or *touchy*. Not sure which one fits here."

"Seriously, it's none of my business. But I've never seen you with a friend. Steady or otherwise."

"Back on the Sports Desk all those years . . . let's just say, you'd be surprised what happens under the bleachers, so to speak. Farm teams play as long a season on the road as the majors."

I hesitated. "Anything serious?"

"Once. A guy came through the pressroom on the City Beat. Tough in rural Indiana, but a lot of back-slapping and good-ole-boy bravado got us through for a good long while."

"And then he left?"

"Died—years later in San Francisco. Different times, Evie." His voice took on a faraway tone. "Since then, I guess you'd say it's been a long, dry summer."

"I'm sorry."

My boss shrugged. "Don't be. You've been trying on the same shoes. It doesn't always fit. But what's a guy going to do?"

"I'm thinking of getting a cat."

My boss just laughed. "If I see newspapers piling up on your front porch, I'll dial 9-1-1 just in case. Then bring you over a pot of chicken soup."

"You cook, who knew?"

"Grill. Which is about as far as my domesticity carries me. I have a cleaning woman come and shovel out my place twice a month. Civilized, as far as it goes."

I told him about the state of the homestead when Anise showed up in my life. "I've been lucky, since. Whenever the place threatens to get that way again, somebody seems to show up. The kids or grandkids. Anise and Caleb. Can't be too careful—my girls have begun to get that look in their eyes. *Is mom losing it and if so, how fast?* It's a whole lot easier to make sure the dust is off the horizontal surfaces than prove the cobwebs in my head don't spell A-s-s-i-s-t-e-d L-i-v-i-n-g."

"Aging," my boss shook his head. "Gotta love it."

Actually, I decided, I did. Except for an alarming habit of muttering to myself, I found a certain poetry in waking alone and going back to sleep for another half-hour in the morning. The sounds of the homestead whispering all around me—the stories and the memories—had become faithful companions in my day's journey.

I was learning to appreciate human contact in the simplest of things. Handling a wrong number on my cell phone offered an opportunity for graciousness. Holding the door for a package-laden stranger at the post office became an exercise in kindness. The neighbor who loved to bake but never had eggs became an excuse for hospitality. Following my boss' lead, I hired a house cleaner—not twice, but once a month. The smell of lemons and glossy patina of my woodwork when she finished her two-hour shift stayed with me for a full week after she was gone.

Fan mail for my column ceased to be impersonal. Every email became a priceless thread binding my life to another's. I bought tickets for the Volunteer Fire Department fish fries. Like the fragile tendrils of a clematis reaching out for lattice or a porch rail, the act of connecting became the framework upon which my life began to grow again.

I began to take my daughter Leslie's admonition to heart. This was my time in the garden and only I could savor it. Yesterday I walked through my front yard at midnight, clad only in my spaghetti strap nightgown. The neighborhood was asleep. As my bare feet picked their way through the perennials, the earth felt warm and the dew a cooling shower against my skin.

Fall would be coming soon enough. But for now, I swore that I could hear my grandmother's voice beckoning to me in the moonlight. *Listen to the garden growing, Evella. Be still. And listen.*

Fifteen
Dog Days

The seas boiled, wine turned sour, dogs grew mad, and all creatures became languid, causing . . . burning fevers, hysterics and phrensies. FROM BRADY'S CLAVIS CALENDARIUM [1813]

When my grandmother first talked about the "Dog Days", I thought she meant the assorted strays that slept along the steaming asphalt of Xenaphon's Main Street every August. Kipped on their sides, they looked all the world like sailing vessels beached by the sweltering calm.

Once I got up the courage to ask her. Grandma Eva laughed and laughed.

"Dog Days come in late-summer," she said. "You'll know them when your shirt sticks to your backbone just walking out into the yard. The hair at the back of your neck feels wet and sticky. And just when summer is about to end, you start to wish the homestead had air conditioning."

Nothing had changed. Waves of heat still rippled over the asphalt. Drivers swore and swerved around the odd collection of mutts on the roadway—tough survivors bred of past decades of Xenaphon street dogs. The McCulley family owned the hardware for three generations. A day or two before my granddaughter went back to Chicago, we were passing their window en route to the print shop. I caught Emma furtively eyeballing the display for Compact Window Cooling Units, just as I had done as a girl.

220

"No point," I told her. "The homestead's wiring won't take it."

And then just about the time I too decided that I couldn't take those sweltering, sleepless nights any longer, the season showed signs of passing. And my sweet Emma was gone. I retreated to my journal and midnight googlings with a vengeance.

It's those blasted Greek and Romans again. Their astronomers looked up and found a link between the weather and the ascendency of Sirius, the Dog Star. In late summer the star rises just before dawn, burning with a cold fire—second only in brightness to the sun itself. The Dog Days were born.

Though medieval clergy weren't famed for their scientific curiosity, even they picked up on the connection. The Episcopal Book of Common Prayer from 1552 charted the "Dog Daies" from July 6th to August 17th.

On a more folksy note, somewhere along the line the Old Farmer's Almanac settled on July 3rd to August 11th. The Germans, French and Italians insisted the Dog Days run from the third week of July through the third week of August. Scandinavians grumble about the season from July to September as the "rotting months"—so-named because food spoils and turns rancid in the bake-oven temperatures.

It didn't take the rain gauge to tell my cottage garden was in trouble. Bracing myself for hellacious water bills, I took pity and wound a make-shift irrigation hose through the thirsty perennials.

The foot traffic through Groft's came looking for solutions. We handed out pamphlets telling desperate rose gardeners how to apply pesticides and fertilize, then water thoroughly enough to soak the root zone. Timing matters. If the moisture lingers on the leaves before sunset or in the cooler nights that follow, blackrot and mildew can set in. Pitchfork tines can break up the hardened soil around the bushes, but when wielded carelessly, the roots will suffer.

I didn't own up to the bottom line—that all the fuss may explain why cultivating roses has never been my forte. On his shift at the nursery, Chris Demort still loaded the cut bouquets with yellow ones whenever he got the chance.

It was a Tuesday night. I was already in bed when the doorbell rang. Sweaty even in my undies and skimpy tank-top, I threw on a bathrobe before I went to answer it. Not fast enough. The buzzer sounded again, twice, impatient now.

"I'm coming," I said.

What was it . . . *one o'clock in the morning?*

My irritation faded in a heartbeat. Standing at the door with car seat, diaper bag and Caleb in hand stood Anise. Even from the minimalist fluorescent porch light, I could see her eyes were red-rimmed and shadowed.

"What's wrong?" I said.

She shot past me into the living room without a word or so much as making eye contact. At the kitchen she came to a dead stop. Before clicking on the light, she stowed her baby's car seat carefully on the floor at her feet so that the table shaded him while he slept.

"I'll make coffee," I said.

"Tea. Cold, if you have it."

"Instant. The sun tea ran out yesterday."

While I bustled from refrigerator to table, Anise sat staring at the table top. A clattering of plates and utensils filled the uneasy silence between us. As an afterthought, I put the microwave to work on a couple of frozen muffins—*hers*.

"You were sleeping."

"Yes. No . . . in bed, but on the computer," I winced. "As usual."

"I need to know if you ever saw this . . . ?"

Anise bent down and retrieved a thick album from Caleb's diaper bag. I waited in silence while she detached one of the photographs and extended it in my direction. The faded image of a teenage girl stared out at the camera, bored from the look of it—or at least impatient that someone had demanded they capture the moment.

"Where did you find this?"

Anise hesitated. "In the cottage . . . by accident. The album was lying on one of the dressers in the guest bedroom downstairs. Every time I saw it, I kept thinking it might be safer in a drawer, away from the dust and light."

"No one would have minded that you looked," I said. "Least of all me. I think that photo is of Adam's sister."

"Adam's sister." Anise paled, then flushed. "You're sure."

"Positive."

222

"There *was* a name pencilled on the back."

I checked what I already knew. "*Leah*, that's her. I never met her, but guess she must have been seventeen or eighteen at the time it was taken. I remember Adam telling me she started college, dropped out and spent several years living in Alaska. He lost track of her after that—heard rumors she had spent some time in a commune due east of here in Wolverine before she moved out West again."

With shaking hands, Anise retrieved a second photo from Caleb's diaper bag. This one had been crumpled at some point in its history. The emulsion was scratched and missing in places. Someone had laminated it to keep the fragile image from further harm.

Except for the wear-and-tear, as the two photos lay side by side on my kitchen table, I could see immediately they were identical. The pose, the expressions on the young woman's face, the background—everything. My mouth felt stiff.

"I don't understand," I said.

"My . . . *mother* . . . !"

Her voice was barely audible. With her index finger, Anise gently tried to smooth out a ragged break in the lamination. Her expression was unreadable.

I couldn't seem to shape the words. "I thought . . . didn't you tell me your parents were—?"

"I was adopted. My parents were up front about that. So when I was ten, I started hounding them about my birth mother. They, the Gruins, finally told me everything they knew, which wasn't a lot. She was from Michigan. And there was one thing . . . the agency had given them this photograph."

Dear God. "You mean that Leah Groft, Adam's sister is—?"

"My birth mother."

For the life of me, I couldn't respond. From the album lying in front of her on the table, Anise produced yet another snapshot of the young Leah Groft. Judging by the clothes and hair, it had been taken on the same day as the first. Only this time Leah was standing alongside a tall, equally uncomfortable looking young man with close-cropped hair, in khakis and dress shirt unbuttoned at the collar. I would have recognized that face anywhere.

"Adam." There was no longer any doubt.

"He must have told you about her," Anise said. "Something,

223

anything. I need to know."

We made eye contact. In my face, Anise already had her answer.

"Adam lost touch with her years ago. He repeatedly tried to find her, a tough thing when someone wants to stay lost," I said quickly. "He certainly never ever suspected he had a niece. When the lawyer was settling his estate, a detective tried one last time."

"You mean, Leah could still be . . . ?"

"There was an article in the Seattle paper. Leah died. She was in her late forties, then, and living in the Pacific Northwest. The police say it was late, dark and she was on the median of a limited access highway—they assume walking home from work. The driver of the oncoming car was drunk."

I couldn't bring myself to share the rest. I had seen the detective's report myself. By the time of her death, Leah had been reduced to a marginal existence at one of those no-tell motels along a four-lane. The accident was a fluke, violent and without warning.

But then only one thing mattered now for this proud and wounded young woman sitting in front of me. Halting at first and my hand clutching at hers across the polished wood of the tabletop, I told her how much it meant to know something of Adam's family was still alive—living in that house he and I both loved so much.

Anise had begun to cry. The deep and aching sobs tore at her rigid shoulders. She pressed her free hand tight against her mouth to stifle the sound.

"Adam would have loved to have known you," I told her. "He would love to know how you and I met. At the *nursery*, much as he once hated the place. What are the odds of that? And he would be pleased beyond words that since that Sunday morning in the Groft's parking lot, we've become . . . friends . . . "

"*Family*," she corrected me in an anguished whisper. "My aunt."

She had given a name to the relationship more quickly than I. Technically it wasn't fact—but the truth, all the same. For the past fifteen months I had wrestled with my faith in miracles. Sitting across the table from me was living proof.

"Watching you all these months," I told her, "I was amazed how you took to cultivating seedlings in their matrix . . . gauging the changes in the watering schedule. A born gardener, I told myself."

Anise used her sleeve to take a swipe at her tears. Deliberately, she

224

slipped the album across the table, turning it so the dog-eared cover was facing my way. In the process, the strung-together binding threatened to spill the photo-heavy black pages onto the table.

"So, you've seen this before," she said.

"Only once," I said, "after Adam died. Even with most of them labeled, it was hard to put the photos into any context. Adam didn't share a great deal about his childhood. As a kid, he had loved to hang out at the nursery with Dutch . . . making things grow."

"You told me that Adam wound up in Chicago. Advertising, you said."

"Families," I shook my head. "For better or worse, Adam felt his father took the joy out of the nursery business for him. There was a time when he wanted nothing more than to get as far from those greenhouses as he possibly could. Except then his Dad grew too ill and frail to manage any longer."

"Been there, have the shirt," she said. "Don't get me wrong, Mom and Dad were great. It wasn't their fault, but turning out pastry, bread, cookies and all-occasion sheet cakes day in and day out can become way too intense. For a teenager anyway."

"As you know, the pressure at the nursery certainly is different. Nothing or at least very little happens overnight. But the stress is real all the same. Forget to ventilate, and in a matter of minutes never mind hours, the whole propagation house is gone. Over-watered or under-watered, ditto. Trust me, wilted and yellowing leaves aren't always so easy to read."

A smile tugged at the corners of her mouth. "I've killed my share of houseplants over the years."

Anise had slid her chair alongside me at the table so we could study the pages together. I carefully wiggled free a grainy black and white shot from the old-fashioned glued triangular mounts that held it fixed against the faded black page. In a sailor suit and knee high stockings, a toddler was making a show of pushing a baby buggy. The bar between his hands seemed far too high for him. Whoever took the photo caught only the top half of the face occupying the carriage. A wild halo of light hair framed the baby's intense, deep-set eyes.

"Adam," I picked out the faint lettering on the back, "age three. Leah, six months."

"My hair was like that when I was her age," Anise said. "A bird's nest."

With only black and white to go on, it was tough to draw any conclusions about color. Still, the similarity in the face shape was striking.

"From the picture, Adam seemed proud of her," I said.

"Protective."

As we turned the fragile pages, the decades sped past. Adam and his sister posed in their school uniforms. Candids caught them in an array of bathing suits and jeans. There were the obligatory skinned knees, confirmation and graduation pictures, family reunions and weddings. Eventually two young adults stared out at the camera. Only where once there had been only privilege and laughter in their smiles, a brother and sister's taut and inward-looking faces stared out at the camera.

They were Grofts. I knew well enough from Adam's descriptions of his life in Xenaphon that the expectations behind that heritage had become anything but easy. More often than not, the photos caught him standing tall—the heir apparent. Even the casual observer could tell from the strong set of his jaw that this young man wasn't going to let anyone or anything mess with him or his.

Leah looked all the world like a frightened bird left behind in the nest. Her eyes unfailingly were riveted on her shoes or half-hidden under her unruly thatch of hair. Anise reached with her index finger and tried to repair an ugly crease in one of the photos. At one point, apparently some unnamed hand had tried to rip it out of the album.

"Lost, even then," Anise said softly. "Angry, cornered . . . "

Beyond that particular page in the Groft pictorial history, photos of Leah were conspicuous by their absence. Even Adam appeared rarely—several awkward photos in mortarboard and academic gown in front of a bell tower, then a few taken with Chicago landmarks in the background. The book ended with formal shots taken at what had to be several funerals. Women, if I had to guess, judging by the choice of floral arrangements. Those latter weren't pasted into the album, just lying loose in no discernable order.

"Adam's mother and grandmother," I said softly as I scanned the group shots for his face.

Anise closed the book. But not before she turned back one last time to that final photo of Leah, the one someone had tried his or her best to expunge from the family record.

"So young," I said softly. "Hurting."

By way of response, Anise ducked her head and began to replace the album in Caleb's diaper bag. The baby stirred in his car seat.

"I better go," she said.

"No chance . . . no way, no how. You're spending the night at the homestead."

"And tomorrow? The day after that?"

"Can you still ask where you are in my life, after all this? Whatever led you here, I thank God for it. You're part of Adam's story now. Do you have an idea what that means . . . ?"

Awkward perched on those hard oak kitchen chairs, but I found myself cradling Anise like a child against my shoulder. Her fingers clung to the quilted fabric of my bathrobe. Over her shoulder, I caught a glimpse of the kitchen clock. Three in the morning. I couldn't imagine how either one of us were going to make it to work later. In the safety of his car seat, Caleb slept on.

The clock struck nine before I dragged myself out of bed. Though Caleb had stirred around six, the guest room door was still closed. I brewed up a pot of coffee and sat sipping from an oversized mug. When the phone rang I knew without checking the Caller ID that it had to be my daughter, checking in for the day.

"Something has happened," I warned Leslie up front.

And then gently as I could, I told her. There could be no doubt whatsoever about it. Anise Gruin was Adam's niece—Adam's and now mine. The matching photographs only confirmed what I already felt in my heart. We had become a family, one that had to extend to encompass my daughters Leslie and Gina as well.

There was a pause when I finished from the other end of the line. "She . . . Anise didn't know?"

"No. Absolutely not."

My daughter listened without comment as I told her about the midnight visit and the hours we spent pouring over the Groft family album. "So, what are you going to do?" she said finally.

Always the pragmatic one, my cut-to-the-chase daughter. It was no secret between us how uncomfortable I had been to assume full responsibility for the cottage and nursery since Adam's death.

"I don't know," I said. "I haven't told Anise about the conversations in the community about using the cottage as some kind of regional retreat center. And I'm glad now that I didn't. She shouldn't be made to feel obligated to buy into that or any other plan."

"Adam left that property to you, Mom."

"Based on what he, what all of us knew at the time."

"Still, what happens with that cottage should be your choice to make."

"Perhaps." My mouth felt stiff. "As for the nursery, the operation is self-sustaining, barely. I think with careful stewardship, it could provide a modest income for Anise and Caleb, certainly offer them a greater measure of independence. And I certainly have to think Adam would approve."

"Mom, you need a lawyer."

"Adam's attorney stuck with me through the whole estate settlement business. I trust him and see no reason to tamper with that."

"And Anise?"

"If she even knew we were talking about this, I truly believe she would be appalled. The money or the Groft estate is not what matters to her. Emotionally I can't even imagine what she is experiencing right now."

"And you?"

"Ask me in six months," I chuckled softly. "Right now, all I feel is a kind of strange relief. For whatever reason Adam left it to me to make sense of what he left behind. As I see it, my job has just become a whole lot simpler."

"Do you want the kids and me to come up?"

"Not necessary, but thanks for offering. I'm going to hold you to it at Thanksgiving. How's that?!"

"Have you told Gina?"

"Not yet. She's next on the list. And when she offers to fly up, I'll tell her exactly the same thing I told you."

"The choices to be made are yours, Mom. But Adam had reasons for doing what he did."

"We do the best we can with what we know at any given moment in time. Adam expended a great deal of effort to find his sister. He couldn't have suspected the search needed to include another generation. I think we both know that."

"If you need to talk this out, I'm here. I know Gina would tell you the same thing."

"Short term I am not planning to do anything." There wasn't anything more to say, except that I loved her.

When I went back upstairs to get dressed, the door to the guest room was still closed. Except then I found what I hadn't noticed before. It was a note in a familiar hand:

> Am on the morning shift at Groft's. Didn't want to wake you. Caleb is with me. Will stop by after work.

The note was signed, "Love, Anise."

I emailed George and told him I would be in later. Fishing the car keys out of my purse, I headed out for the nursery. Anise had opened the retail office, hung the Open sign and was back in the propagation house, cranking open the ventilation windows. She didn't see me coming.

"I want you to think about managing this place," I said.

Anise wheeled around. She had tucked Caleb into his front carrier—was shielding him with one hand while she operated the old-fashioned mechanism of chains and pulleys with the other. I smiled.

"I want you to think about taking a leave of absence from Marty's until ski season starts," I said. "Take over as manager at the nursery."

She turned and gave the crank one last turn. "You already have a staff."

"Artie and Viv need a rest. So do I. Our propagation house will be leaderless when summer manager Dave Fetters is back in college. With high school, Chris will be available less."

"The season is winding down. By late October, you said that we need to close the propagation house entirely."

"Can you think of a better time to take over . . . come up with a plan to clear out most of the plant stock? Artie will want to help you winterize the place. I haven't placed any of the orders for next year's bulbs or plants. Any inspiration on that score would be helpful . . . "

"Eve, I know what you're trying to do."

"That's one of us."

"You need a lawyer."

"Funny, that's exactly what my daughters said."

"I can't just let you—"

"I am only doing what I know Adam would have done."

"You can't know that. He loved you. And he chose to leave all of this to—"

"To care for . . . you're talking *own*. There's a difference. I'm supposedly retired, Anise. And I don't need the money."

229

"Neither do I."

My throat felt tight. *Proud and independent, a Groft through and through*, I found myself thinking.

"But Caleb needs a secure home," I said carefully, "along with the legacy and heritage you're trying to provide for him. And I believe the cottage and the nursery can offer you—and *him*—that future."

Her jaw clamped tight. "You're not playing fair."

"Maybe," a smile tugged at the corner of my mouth."But then this isn't Crazy Eights or Rummy. Winning doesn't mean accumulating the biggest hand."

"I could do this on my own."

"Of course you could. But I think this just might be more fun. For you and me . . . and Caleb."

And then I told her about Bea's idea for the "Roots" project, Jake's gift to fund a not-for-profit foundation and community educational center in Adam's name. Anise was way ahead of me. I didn't have a chance to finish.

"The cottage," she said. "You were planning to use the cottage for classes and other programming."

"Yes. But— "

"No 'buts'. Do you seriously think I would stand in the way of all that?"

"Okay, then. Whatever happens with the foundation, somebody needs to run it."

Anise drew in a long breath, let it out slowly. "You have an answer for everything."

"No. But I know when something feels right. And this does."

Suddenly I was seeing that Easter window at Peace through a different lens entirely. It wasn't just Adam's sister whose face I encountered in that subtly painted glass, it was Anise Gruin herself—her luminous beauty shadowed by the joys and terrible losses that living brings in its wake.

Someone once said that there are no coincidences, only opportunities. *If we have the sense to recognize those moments for what they are.* What was beginning to seem a lifetime ago, Adam had said as much—on our long midnight drive back from Little Traverse on the Fourth of July.

Without risk, he told me, *there is no love.*

I would have given the world to have him tell me again. The highway had stretched out so black and inscrutable in front of us. Only the cold glare of the headlights sliced through that life-changing night. His hands were strong and sure on the steering wheel.

My darkness was different now. Adam was gone. On any given day there seemed no lodestone toward which to direct my emptiness. Like the woman confronting the angel at the Tomb, I had no idea where to turn to recapture what I had lost.

Finally one Dog Day afternoon, I simply got in the Taurus and drove. The compass swung fitfully as I navigated my way to the interstate on-ramp. Sunlight blazed across the windshield. A hazy rainbow rose from the asphalt. Yet another summer faded into the distance behind me.

Ancient Michigami. I felt the subtle tide of Michigan's great inland sea pulling me northward. Three hundred miles long. An average of seventy-five miles wide. Nine hundred plus feet at its greatest depth. Larger than the combined states of Delaware, Maryland and Massachusetts. Lake Michigan is the sixth largest freshwater lake in the world.

I never understood why the native peoples called this beautiful place the "Lake of the Stinking Water". Except for the occasional ale-wife die-offs and the algae tides at the very head of the Bay, those mysterious blue-violet depths count among the clearest, most pristine bodies of fresh water in the world. And still the *Michigami* stuck—long after 'Lake Illinois' and 'Lake of the Puans' for a local Indian tribe were committed to the history books.

All that ceased to matter at that unpretentious sand and rock-strewn beach east of Charlevoix on Little Traverse Bay. Here I had committed Adam's ashes to the waters he loved. And here a voice inside me spoke his name as I sat bare-legged on a smooth stretch of sand.

"You can't imagine your legacy," I said.

And then I told him about Anise and her baby, about Jake and the foundation that soon would bear the Groft name. I told him about the novel and the subtle changes that I hoped would transform our story from history to truths larger than ourselves.

Light played across the water with the shifting of the clouds overhead. I could almost see Adam's face, so magical yet real was the moment. A muscle jerked along the ridge of his jaw when he was intent on something, as now. There was a hint of laughter in his eyes. When I sensed hot, stinging tears well up behind my own, they were for Jake and for myself—the ones left behind. Then as now, I had to believe my Adam was at peace.

Not so the tiny wayside pullout. It teemed with humanity for a random weekday in late August. A guy in running shorts and a Michigan State athletic top was tossing a stick into the water pursued by a very young and energetic chocolate Lab. Down the beach, a mother and two kids armed with sand buckets were apparently on the hunt for Petoskey stones at the water's edge.

Too far west, I wanted to tell them. But then sometimes it is the seeking and not the finding that matters.

Among the birches and evergreens shielding the park from the road, a man was sitting alone at a picnic table. Motionless and with gnarled worker's hands folded in front of him on the green-painted wood surface, he stared out toward the unfolding panorama of the Bay.

Strangers all. Yet in these minutes and seconds, we became bound together by our stories. Alone—yet linked by a fleeting connectedness of time and space. We do not live and love in a vacuum. An hour or a day or a year from now others will find themselves drawn to this place. And so for a while too their lives will intersect. Their lives and ours will never be the same.

I had known love and grief that passes understanding. Like the Michigan waters lapping at my feet, I too am slowly but inexorably moving on. My heart aches at the thought, but that too I know must pass.

The day is waning. A hint of fall stirs in the night breeze. Deer will soon be out on the road. My garden needs watering—a bad idea after nightfall.

In sun and shade my life in Xenaphon waits for the love and care that only I can give it. I need to get home.

Sixteen
Come, Labor On . . .

The ancients gave their gods job descriptions. I don't think that was accidental. The Roman goddess Diana—Greek Artemis—was put in charge of protecting nature and the wildwood, fertility and childbirth, women and (fragile as the link may seem), commerce. She would make a good deity for Xenaphon. I like to think that of late she has chosen to smile once again upon us.

Our bank was back in operation. Therein lies something of a miracle. CEO Mark Blandis had begun to pick up his Dad—my boss—for lunch every Friday. The genuine warmth and ease with which father and son reconnected defies any cheap platitudes about nature versus nurture. They were becoming a family of two.

Then, too, my novel continued to sell. "The word," my boss crowed after two successful signings in communities along Little Traverse, "is definitely out there." Against all odds, my work was beginning to find an audience.

Out of the blue, the print shop landed an on-demand publishing project. A local CPA whose Dad had spent WWII on a sub chaser had found his memoir in the attic. More a diary than deliberate prose, the direct and simple style made it a quick read. George put me to work editing it, a gripping tale of life on the high seas seen through the eyes of a Michigan kid barely out of high school who wound up seeing the world.

"There's a market for Second World War memorabilia," George said. "I'd guess that at least the state and local Historical Societies might be interested."

I got tapped to design the cover. The Internet was rife with enough photos of spines and cover pages from military adventure stories to get me started. Our client, the CPA, had some great old photos of his Dad with the boat. I wove bits and pieces of them into one of my favorite sepia-tinged shots from George's photo archives, waves breaking along the Michigan shoreline.

My boss had the agent role down pat. For an additional fee, he staged a signing for the CPA at the drug store, alerted the Little Traverse book stores that another local author was on the scene and sent a mass email to Michigan historical societies telling them about the book. Sales to the public, friends and relatives were enough that the CPA and his family were delighted. George's Michigan Duneside Press was off to a respectable start.

Whatever motivates someone to publish a book, it certainly isn't the money. George's fees for typography, cover design, printing, binding and a basic marketing and distribution package were reasonable. Still, the tab was more than sales of copies could realistically hope to pay.

Bottom line, a family's story and name were in print. It is tough to put a price tag on that.

And amid all the bounty, the berm and my cottage garden are blooming like they were meant to bloom—full out, the life force rushing full tilt through the cells and veins and stems to the bud. The urgency in that flowering almost borders on desperation. No matter.

"Give it all you have," a voice within me whispered. "Give it all you have."

There was a time when I first began to garden, I felt the urge to hold back such an inevitable turning of the season. Every fall I broke out old blankets or tarps against the stealth of the night air. If frost had the last word, then winter is bound to follow.

These days I find myself learning to love this unsettled time of year, to fret less and enjoy more. Gardening is the most popular hobby in the world. *Odd, though, how we choose to talk about it.*

Deeply as we may love our garden, we say we are going to 'work' not 'play' in it. At the end of the day for a lot of gardeners, the toughest thing is to cultivate the capacity to enjoy, to sit back quietly on our heels and smell the roses. Simply to let ourselves *be.*

At my invitation and in spite of her misgivings, Anise was running the nursery. That took a major paradigm shift for both of us. It occurred to me as summer slipped into fall, that the whole town was in the throes of the same uneasy transition.

With the arrival of Labor Day, families from down-state are gearing up for school and work after the lazy days of summer. Here in Xenaphon and parts north, the intense and exhausting tourist season lies behind us. Work momentarily slows, a chance for us locals to kick back. And if we are lucky and the weather holds, summer compacts for us into a few glorious weekends before the next great rush of tourism—fall's 'Color Season'—is upon us.

My garden is celebrating Labor Day in its own fashion. Weeds have long since run for cover. I am caught up on my deadheading and large patches of my garden now stand clad only in leafy green. It seems that as late August and September come along, the garden itself seems to pause for breath.

Like many gardeners, I have struggled to find some miracle-working perennial that will bridge those semi-fallow days and weeks. Varieties of sedum thrive in that strange twilight zone. Eventually mums, prairie asters, and a host of other late-bloomers will take over. But their deep-hued flowering is only a temporary respite from the monochrome late fall days to come.

In the end, there is no escaping it. Something has changed in the landscape. The hillsides have begun to clothe themselves in regal purple and goldenrod. Grasses sketch bold strokes of rust and ochre across the canvas of the fields.

Summer is over. There was a time when Labor Day signaled it was time to pack away the white shoes and bright summer hues. No more—and I'm glad for that. I'm not at all sure that I'm ready.

I try not to think of the year behind me as I write. Change has come hard on the heels of change. I'm not sure that I am ready to sort out and draw a line under the milestones—not yet, anyway.

Instead, I wake up mornings to thoughts of Caleb and Anise standing together at the bank of living room windows in the Groft cottage. Without summer's swarm of boats churning the shallow waters, the lake is still again—a burnished silvery glass polished by the slanting rays of the September sun. At least several times a week, the two of them stop by at the print shop or the homestead. Their visit is never long. It is just enough to remind me that our lives are tight-woven in a fabric of our making.

Labor Day weekend, I decided to reciprocate. Armed with a picnic basket loaded down with the fixings of a cookout, I headed down the familiar dusty road to the cottage. To a package of white bratwurst, I added hard to find but wonderful flour-dusted potato rolls and a bottle of Riesling. I arrived at the lake to a flurry of activity. Like an Eastern potentate on his throne, Chris sat ensconced on the riding mower. He was wearing his camouflage pants and a Gardners-Know-All-the-Best-Dirt tee. Headphone wires trailed from each ear as he sliced broad swaths in the still greening lawn.

Chris saw the Taurus, grinned and waved. "Yo!"

"Yo, yourself."

Anise must have heard the voices. She came out and relieved me of the heavy basket.

It struck me that sometime in the past few weeks she had begun to shed her baby weight. Tall and lithe, all she needed was a bow and quiver to pass for the Divine Huntress herself striding through the leafy glade, thoroughly at home with where she found herself.

"When did this happen?" I said. "Chris. Out there on yard patrol."

"Pretty much from day one," she shrugged. Together we unpacked the goodies I had brought on the kitchen table. "Artie's idea, actually. Chris does a great job, you know. Fast—though arbitrary sometimes about adjusting the height of the mower blades."

I laughed. "I didn't think he had it in him."

"He has his moments. A couple of weeks ago he used the mower to carve Caleb's name into the side yard, so the baby would see it from his pack-n-play. He's a wonderful baby sitter."

My eyebrow arched. "A newborn can be a lot for a teenager to handle"

"You're worried," Anise said. "Don't be. His mother wasn't much of a parent, that's for sure. But under all that smoldering angst, Chris is really a good kid. He plays a close hand, but I talked to Bea before I agreed that he could move in here. I trust her judgment. And *him*."

"So, Social Social knows . . . they're okay with this?"

"Artie and Viv were more than willing to have him stay on with them. But with all the work he's been doing around the cottage, it made more sense for him to stay here with me. I drive him into school mornings when I go to work at Groft's. Or the bus stops for him where the lake road meets the highway. Not all that far."

"A lot of running back and forth for you."

"Yes . . . no. I've been thinking about something you said once—about a lot of things actually. About the cottage, the foundation or maybe even starting a bakery," she hesitated. "You're going to think I'm presumptuous."

"Never."

"This place has six bedrooms. Even with Chris living on site, it's way too big for us. Suppose we risk a trial run to see what might fit together. Start out like a modest B&B, only we hook up with the berm and the Garden Gang to host a few immersion experiences with perennials. At Groft's we could teach the practical side of gardening and teach folks to grow as many ingredients as possible. Then I do my thing with classes in how to cook the stuff up in a pan. I've been casing out what senior travel programs charge for edu-tourism. It's a bundle, though our goal here isn't to make a profit, just stay in the black. Short-term, Jake's financial support could make up any potential shortfall and keep tuition affordable."

It was awkward, but I needed to know. "And where do you see yourself and Caleb in all of that? I don't want you to think for a minute that you're living on borrowed time out here."

Anise hesitated. "I've told Marty's I'll still work ski season but not another summer. Caleb and I don't need much. When Groft's shuts down in a month or so, I'll start peddling my baked goods any place that will take them. And if you have no objections, I'll let the realtors know we've got rooms to rent out here at the cottage. See what happens."

"A leap of faith."

She smiled. "You could call it that."

Time is compacting. I see it in the wild flowering out on the berm and right in front of my own front stoop. The year and growing season don't have long to run. *It's now or never*, the roots and stems are telling the buds of the mums and the prairie asters.

I understand—share—that urgency. When I stood for the opening hymn at Peace on Sunday, my neighbors must have sensed it, too. I heard them singing full-voice around me.

The night draws nigh. No time for rest, till glows the western sky, till the long shadows o'er our pathway lie.

To my right, I heard Matt Gaskill's strong baritone. Well into verse three of the familiar hymn, Anise joined me on my left. Her lush contralto slipped effortlessly toward the high notes. *Well done, well done.* Caleb let out a sigh of protest, then slipped back to sleep on his mother's shoulder.

A lot of gray heads always turned in the sanctuary at their entrance. Those battle-worn faces were smiling. Maybe Xenaphon was younging up.

At my suggestion Anise, Bea and I went to lunch at Marty's after coffee hour. The two had worked side by side before on the berm, but this was different. I already had shared Anise's story and parentage in confidence with my boss and Adam's attorney. It was time to widen the circle.

Bea sat listening without comment as Anise told her about the two photographs and what came after. "A Groft," she said. "I like the sound of that. Your family has been a part of this community since the Flood. We were all devastated when—"

"Groft or no Groft, I want you to know up-front that nothing has changed when it comes to your plans for a foundation or some sort of community center," Anise told her. "I will not allow Eve to deed the cottage or nursery to Caleb and me. That's non-negotiable. I just ask that we have a roof over our head. And when you get around to hiring someone to run the program, I would like to include my resume in the mix."

How much that girl sounds like Adam, I was thinking. Though she never knew him.

"I think we all know what those properties are worth." Bea was watching my face as she said it.

"Yes, we do. But then this isn't about money for me," gaze averted, Anise began toying with the sprigs of autumn leaves—too brightly colored and perfect to be anything but silk—that the wait-staff had set out on the tables. "I've never played the Power Ball or cast about for quick fixes. I am not about to start now."

"Okay," I said slowly, "now that we've collectively hit that wall, where next?"

Bea shifted in her seat. "Our plan was to use the rest of the fall and winter to put together a proposal, set a governance structure in place. Then we dot the legal P's and Q's. I'm not sure I still should chair the feasibility committee. At the very least, Anise, you belong on it."

"I can do that, for now anyway. But if there's a conflict of interest down the road, all bets are off."

The waitress brought us the bill. "This one's on me," I said.

I half expected Bea or Anise or both to put up a fuss. Instead, they leaned back in their respective chairs and let me handle it. *Diplomacy*, I fought a smile and paid the tab—scrawled 'Taxes' across the top in ink and tucked it in my wallet. From his perch in the car seat strapped to one of Marty's sturdy wood high chairs, young Caleb slept on.

A Groft. I had to agree with Bea. I liked the sound of that.

The Germans have a saying, *as green as hope*," I wrote that night in my journal.

It came to me as I arranged the crocks full of purple asters and goldenrod alongside the altar at Peace yesterday. There is something moving and beautiful in the way the colors of religious ritual and the rhythms of the garden ebb and flow alongside one another.

During most of the liturgical year—those endless numbered Sundays known as 'ordinal' or 'ordinary' time—the hangings and robes in the sanctuary at Peace are green. The color fits. Traditionally, green is considered a symbol of spring, of new life and growth. Of hope. A subtle reminder, the time for flowering has begun.

That same green prevails in the sanctuary through the summer, except for a bold splash of red in the altar hangings for Pentecost to celebrate the loving Spirit at work in the everyday. In the garden, the green now blossoms into a lavish quilt of poppy orange, hot pinks and buttercup yellows, blues as solid as that sky overhead. We salute the garden in its prime.

Autumn rains begin. With them the mood in the sanctuary and the garden becomes more reflective. In late fall, the church ushers in its New Year with the season of Advent. Vestments and hangings flower a somber purple. Out in the gardens and fields, that same regal purple stands out against the dismal skies. The holiest days of all are celebrated in white—the midnight snows of Christmas and blinding promise of an Easter sunrise.

I used to be a spring person myself. The sight of the first snowdrop can make a person positively giddy. Interesting at this season of my life, I find myself drawn more and more to fall. Cynics remind us the flaming palette of the leaves overhead is merely a sign the chlorophyl is dying. But as it does, we see unmasked new depths and richness of color we missed before—hidden under spring and summer's green-upon-green-upon-green. Sometimes beauty may come late and at a price, but it is precious all the same.

Evenings now in the homestead, fire dances in the grate. With a glass of merlot in hand, I sit and watch while I toast the season, *To whatever comes.* The future that once consumed my waking hours had ceased to grieve or terrify.

Time. Give it time, I thought. *The measure of my days is priceless.*

It seems I wasn't the only one with growing pains. Artie pulled up at the curb of the homestead one afternoon dragging a fifth wheeler so mammoth behind his diesel truck cab, that it threatened to take out the lower third of Grandma Eva's lindens.

"Really somethin', huh?" he told me. "For camping. Found if off e-bay. Viv and I are talking about really retiring—taking a trip, south and west, somewhere warm. Maybe we'd hunker down for a while and help out with that mess along the Gulf Coast. Or head out to Arizona. A while back, Viv's cousin lost his place outside of Sedona to one of those fires they kept showing on TV. His kids put out a call for family who can hammer and nail and saw."

"Wild, Artie," I said. "Doesn't sound much like retirement, though."

"I'm an on the road kind of guy," Artie shrugged. "Chris is bunking at the cottage with Caleb and Anise now. Viv's garden is about done for the season. Don't know how she's gonna like wandering around the countryside, but she says she's game to try."

I smiled. It wasn't how I pictured my friend. But then relationships realign our compass points.

"George has agreed to chair our 'Roots' committee," I said. "Plans to start meeting weekly."

Artie frowned, shook his head. "So it's moving ahead, then. Would

240

wanna be in on that. And if we're out of circulation, so to speak—"

"The library has Skype. But realistically, we certainly would want to include you via speaker phone."

"Good. We'll just drop what we're doin' and join in."

"While we're at it, there's also big news on another front," I said. And then I told him about Anise.

Artie shook his head. "That's one for the books," he said. "*A Groft*. I always thought there was something about that girl."

"Feel free to share with Viv. But for now that's as far as it goes."

"Understood." Artie unkinked his compact frame. "But folks like that girl. With her at the helm, it could be an interesting ride. We aren't getting any younger, Evie. Time to sit back a bit and let the young ones take over."

"I never thought I would hear that from you," I chuckled softly.

Artie winced. "A guy's gotta know when it's time to quit. That haulin' business was getting tougher every day. Always watchin' the clock and too much caffeine for any one man. What did Adam say once? Something about watchin' the garden grow?"

"Voltaire's *Candide*. We start out looking for life 'out there' somewhere, only to find it right back where we started. I think we all know the feeling at one point or other. The need for home, a piece of ground. A life that's rooted in home and love."

"The simple things," Artie nodded.

"Not always so simple. But, yes."

"Viv worries about that, too—being gone so long. A tribe of gypsies, was how she put it, no roots any place. I promised I would build her a grow box on the back of the camper to haul her herbs around, if that's what made her happy. Fit a hunk of clear acrylic in the top. Where we're goin', sun would be the least of our problems."

I laughed. "I will never forget that jerry-built watering system you and Adam cobbled together on the berm. With a feed trough for the reservoir, pipes snaking everywhere."

Artie flushed. "Good days," he said. "Gotta love 'em."

Good days.

Seventeen
Saints and Souls

We took down the garden in late-October. The crew got an early start. Our first breath-robbing hint of winter was in the air as a good dozen of us swarmed over the berm with weed whackers and clippers. Fearless leader Bea had tagged the plants reserved for hand-cutting. The rest disappeared in clouds of flying chaff, stalks and stems. Armed with his powerhouse of a leaf blower, Artie followed behind, coaxing the debris into rakeable piles.

And then it was done—quicker than anyone of us would have imagined. Strangely awkward with one another, we stood together as a crew for one last look over the berm. What took months of cultivation and care was stubble in the course of a single morning. Less.

"Sad," Anise said finally.

We all felt it. Only the circular mounds of roots still marked where the individual plants had been. From the off-ramp, all that would have been visible was a gash of dark earth unfurling across the grassy hillside.

"To let the frost kill everything off would be far, far worse," Bea said. "Rot sets in. Disease and mold spreads. Before you know it, you've killed the very plants you couldn't bear to level."

Anise was cradling Caleb in front of her, with her free hand shielding his face from the dust floating in the air over the hillside. "Still, it seems so final," she said.

It had never struck me quite that way before. "I liked it a lot better when my grandmother talked about 'putting the garden to bed'. Somehow it makes the process seem less brutal, more comforting in the great scheme of things."

We had cleaned up the berm just in time. A front was coming through, bringing with it a hard frost that finished off whatever perennials still hung on in the sheltered nooks and crannies. I was content to sit in front of the fireplace with my laptop and a mug of hot cider.

It's season's end—time to thin out, chop back, remove the deadwood, mulch. But when it's done, the greatest test of our gardening is yet to come. Traumatic as the take-down had been, the real measure of the garden lay in what would come after.

Winds will howl. We know ice and ground frost are going to do their worst. At winter's end, and only then, would we discover as gardeners whether our work had been in vain.

Plants have their own way of handling the bumps in their life journeys. There is a profound difference between annuals and perennials. A perennial garden assembles a community of plants whose purpose in life is not just to flower on command, but to persevere—whatever comes. As the dark of winter descends, gardeners need to feel that they have done all that they can to enable that tenacious little community to survive.

That doesn't happen by accident or in a vacuum. If we want to prevent wind damage, we trim the tallest-growing of the roses to waist height. At the very least, we stake them up. Stalks, stems and sometimes even leaves need to be left behind to nourish the root structure even under that frozen ground.

Annuals are a different breed entirely. For much of my time as a gardener, I had underestimated the contribution they make to wherever they are planted. Annuals are the risk takers. Like shooting stars they burn themselves out in the name of beauty and are gone. Longevity is not their forte. But a garden can seem barren without them.

The choices we make have consequences. As I look at the stubbled remains of my garden, I wonder if this is what 'playing God' truly feels like. We all yearn for that power at one time or another in our lives. And suddenly, here it is.

Courage, I decided, appears in very different guises.

These days I retraced my steps from the print shop to home under

243

a darkening sky and the smell of wood smoke. The last of the dried and brittle leaves from the maples were falling like November rain onto the sidewalks. Only the drab brown canopy of the oaks still rustled overhead.

The human language is full of euphemisms and images drawn from the world of gardening, not always appropriate. Like *having a green thumb,* hubris to say the least. Or *common as dirt.*

"That's a joke," I chuckled to myself. "Try buying potting soil sometime, even in bulk." *Black gold*, Adam described the stuff once. Trying to settle up the latest round of year-end bills at the nursery, I would have to say he called it just about right.

Fragile as a flower. Viv is certainly proving *that* one wrong.

I wasn't expecting a phone call from her, but when it came, I went. Viv and I hadn't seen much of each other all summer, for all the Saturdays together on the berm. More hands to volunteer on the garden crew made for lighter work, but also cost some of the closeness we enjoyed when there was just a handful of us. And of course with Anise on duty at Groft's, all of us were enjoying a well-deserved break.

"You busy?" she said.

"Same old stuff. Why?"

"Just wondering . . . "

"I can come over."

"That would be nice."

Viv was always tentative on the phone, but this was something else. I told George I was taking off for the rest of the day and headed over to her trim little bungalow. For once, her 'significant other', Artie, was nowhere in sight.

I found my friend in the kitchen, brewing tea with an uncharacteristic level of clatter. Tension had sucked the air out of the room like one of those space saver bags they keep advertising on TV.

"You came," Viv said.

"Of course."

She already had set two places at the table. Her herb bread was legendary. The mug of home-made rose-hip tea steamed sweet and fragrant in my hands.

"You look tired," I said.

Viv took several hesitant sips of her tea, face flushed and her two hands clutched tight around the curved bowl of the mug. "Artie and I had a fight last night. Not really a fight, or an argument either. I'm not sure what to call it."

"Try me."

"He bought that enormous fifth wheeler."

"Sounds like fun, girlfriend! I hear you two are going to—"

"Now he's talking about selling his house, our moving in together. We would have more money to travel, he said. And it's tough going back and forth like a couple of teenagers. Selling his house would settle things."

"Viv, that's wonderful."

"It is? I don't know . . . am not so sure. We aren't married. Artie tried it once and swore off for life."

"He loves you, Viv. Artie would walk through hellfire for you."

"Just not to the altar."

"Does that matter to you?"

Their relationship had gone from simmer to a steady rolling boil for nearly two years now. On the surface, nothing had changed. To Vivian, obviously, something had.

"I don't know. I'm being stupid, I suppose—getting worked up about a piece of paper," she said. "This isn't like it was with you and Adam. You had your daughters to worry about and what they might think. But still . . . "

"It bothers you."

Vivian stared at the table top. "I always cared too much what other people thought or didn't think. I know that now. Except all this while we've been telling Chris that your choices matter. Hard to hold the moral high ground on that one."

"I've got to believe Chris has grown a lot since then. If anyone understands by now that life isn't simple, it ought to be that young man. For what it's worth, I say, Go for it! Or not. The choice should be yours and Artie's, not the neighbors or the gang over at Peace or St. Mary's either. Look at Darla Vertina and old Elwood Klum. She's been his 'housekeeper' for years, though I don't care much for the sexist edge to it. It's a new millennium—if a guy isn't doing at least half the house-keeping, he ought to be. Rumor has it she would lose a substantial pension if she gets married again. Whatever is going on, I promise you, Viv . . . George is not going to immortalize any of this in the *Gazette*."

"I don't care what they call it. It all sounds so seedy . . . *living together, significant others, cohabiting, bed buddies, friends with privileges.* It's old fashioned of me, maybe . . . "

"But honest."

"I tell myself that," Viv shivered. "I didn't even put *life partners* on the list. And if Artie sells his house, that's what we're talking about. What if our arrangement doesn't work? This could change everything. It already has."

"So, how does Artie feel?"

"Confused . . . not about us, but about my holding back. I don't blame him one bit. The guy brought me flowers. He had this old velvet-covered jeweler's box and a diamond studded silver locket. It had been his mothers. Our pictures were inside."

My throat felt raw and tight, as if tears might conceivably follow. I was remembering the engagement ring Adam gave me—his grandmother's. "And you left things, *How*?"

"I cried. Can you imagine that. Not good. One of those drippy-nosed, hysterical disasters. Artie just sat there with this hangdog look on his face. He didn't say much, but I could tell he was hurt. I told him I loved him, but I had to think about it."

"Artie was okay with that?"

"He scrounged up a box of tissues for me and put the flowers in water. We haven't discussed it since. He still spends the night. That was a week ago."

"Fair enough. He's waiting for you."

That couldn't have been easy for Artie—totally out of character. He was the consummate take-charge guy, would cater to Viv's every whim if she let him. To her credit, she didn't.

"Not my forte, taking charge," she said. "I haven't a clue what to tell him."

"The truth. What you told me."

"He's been out at Groft's all week with Anise. Shutting valves for the season, re-caulking, going over the motors. He had quite a list."

"So, go out there. It's neutral territory. Hard to get too worked up around all that plant stock. If you decide it's a yes, you know it is going to take a while in this market for his house to sell. Either one of you or both could still change their mind."

Viv straightened gingerly in her chair. "Sciatica again," she sighed.

"Stress makes it worse."

"I know. This should have been the happiest moment of my life."

"It can be."

A whisper of a smile tugged at the corner of Viv's mouth. "I hope so."

"You'll laugh about this later. Both of you."

Prophetic words. The next time I saw them, Matt Gaskill and I were hiking downtown together for Bingo night at St. Mary's. Our monthly pilgrimage started as a joke after the Easter gathering in the Episcopal undercroft, a back-hand way of promoting cross-denominational fellowship. I decided there were worse ways to get out of the house.

Artie was helping run the caller's table. When he saw us, he gestured for us to come over and say, Hi. Alongside him keeping track of the numbers, Vivian blushed a fiery red.

"Hung up the For Sale signs on my place yesterday," he said. "Though I'm not exactly moving—not far anyway . . . "

He left it to Matt and me to fill in the blanks. One look at Viv's glowing face told me that move had taken them both a lot farther than he thought. I felt nothing but happiness for them.

"So, a hot date, you two?" Artie said.

My mouth felt stiff. Whatever the rest of Xenaphon thought about our innocent little habit, I would have thought our friends knew better. *Make a note to skip next month*, I told myself. *Maybe even two.*

"Just a delegation from the Episcopalians," I forced a smile. "Show some support for the parish and Father Brannen. My boss picked up a rumor that the foundation at St. Mary's has developed some ominous cracks."

"It's gonna take an awful lot of Bingo cards for us to deal with that one," Artie hinted.

Matt just laughed. "Twenty-five bucks worth," he said. "My limit."

"Speak for yourself," I said. "I stop at fifteen."

Mercifully, Artie had moved on. As for me, I spent the rest of the evening walking circles around Matt Gaskill. If the whole awkward incident or my behavior afterward bothered him, he gave no sign.

Bingo night at St. Mary's had one lasting impact. It got me to rethinking my official status. I had been hedging about the use of 'widow'

to describe myself publicly. But that is exactly what I had to do. The difference is that mentally I inserted Adam's name and face instead of my ex-husband in how I defined that word.

Widow. I had been loved. That reality no one or nothing could take away from me. All these months, Adam's engagement ring had stayed on my left hand. I now took to wearing the wedding ring we never used on my right. The two of us never had the piece of paper either, Adam and I. My friend Viv had made gigantic personal strides to learn to live with that ambiguity. So can I.

What regrets still linger for me have nothing to do with the loving vows we never had a chance to say publicly and out loud. They are the quiet private moments we have missed—the ones that require no spoken language at all.

My year's journey through the calendar, the maze of red and black letter days that shape our lives, has taken me from the sacred to the profane and back again. It has taught me more than I dreamed possible.

I was no longer a woman alone. I had become a woman alive.

Time shapes us. Time heals us. Time brings with it suffering and joy. Time is the currency of our lives, more precious than silver or gold. We cannot store or hoard it. Time is meant to be spent—open-handed and cups spilling over. Hanging on will not stop the fearful rush of time's passage. We either live our days or we die.

The waning of the day and the wisdom that comes with it are not all roses and sunshine. The autumn brings with it the Dead of the Dead, Halloween, All Saints, All Souls. In the end, we celebrate all of it with Thanksgiving.

I had to believe it wasn't entirely coincidental for those particular holidays to come together in the calendar. Hard as we try to bury the ghosts and demons that lurk in the recesses of our lives and memories, they tend to rise up when we least expect them. They frighten and haunt our dreams and waking. Like little children, we flee the shadows, afraid of the dark. We name the bad and celebrate the good.

Studies show that popular culture finds the demonic more credible than the Divine. We try to trivialize and laugh away the nightmares, clothing ourselves in the

248

things we most envy or fear. When that fails, we flee toward the sacred, our hopes like wisps of incense rising to Heaven. Torn between despair and hope, our lives go on. I, for one, don't regret a precious moment allotted to us.

The Friday after Halloween, I decided to stop after work to change the altar flowers at Peace. The purples and hot pinks of the field asters were bloomed out now, even in the most sheltered of garden niches. In their place I decided to put together a cornucopia of autumn's bounty. By the time I was done, gourds and pumpkins spilled out of a stoneware crock turned on its side in front of the altar. In and among the arrangement, I was in the process of fitting dried milkweed pods and thistles in a pair of woven straw baskets.

The church office was closed. Foot traffic in the tiny sanctuary on a random Friday afternoon was nonexistent. Which is why I was surprised to hear voices coming from the undercroft. Matter-of-fact and almost unintelligible at first, they gradually become more heated. And neither participant in that dispute had reason to suspect they would be overheard, least of all by me.

"All I'm asking," a voice said, "is that you look at what you're doing from my perspective."

"We're friends, the beginning and end of it. Friends."

"Together every weekend. Sitting in the same bench on Sunday. You know how that looks, what it means in a town like this."

"You're overreacting. Friends choose to sit together—or *not*. They garden together. So does half the town."

"How does *she* feel?"

"We never talk about it, why would we? I enjoy her company, would hope the reverse is true."

Stunned and confused, I stopped dead still, every nerve ending alert. There was no longer any doubt about it. Those voices belonged to Matt Gaskill and his son. And the subject of their muffled altercation couldn't, but almost certainly had to be *me*. The silence was unbearable.

"Maybe you honestly believe that. But I maintain that—"

"I never lied to you. Tough as the choices were in that last terrible year, you *know* how much I loved your mother. I have no intention of ever having a serious relationship, much less marrying again. And none of that has changed since moving here. I have no reason to feel *her* situation is

249

any different. The Groft family casts one heck of a big shadow in this town. Flattering you should think so, but I am *not* her type."

Her, as in *me*. I shouldn't be hearing this.

The milkweed stalks in my hand slipped to the floor. Light-headed, I planted my two hands hard against the front edge of the altar. The crisp linen cloth began to crumple under my hands.

"I only know how it looks," I heard Ben mutter.

"What are you saying?"

When no answer was forthcoming, a steely edge crept into Matt's tone. "Because my personal life is not up for negotiation, if that's what you're suggesting. These people have taken me into their world. I am grateful for that. Call it a fresh start or anything you want. If you can't handle that, I'm sorry, but—"

"Small towns aren't Minneapolis, Dad."

"I know that."

"People are starting to trust me here."

"*Meaning* . . . ?"

"Half that garden crew are my parishioners."

"Some are. Some aren't. And what I do or do not do outside of these four walls has absolutely nothing to do with you. If you're making it your business, then you . . . are . . . *way off base*!"

"You're my father."

"And you're the vicar here. After hours, we're family. You're my son—and I'm proud of that, believe me. As for the rest, what happens in Vegas . . . *finish the sentence*. I have a life and you have yours. I respect that and trust you will do the same!"

Outside a car alarm began sounding, muffled but persistent. I half willed it to stop, half relieved that it drowned out the terrible pounding behind my temples.

"You're naive if you . . . let's just say, we don't see eye to eye on this one," I thought I heard Ben say. The senior Gaskill's response was too muted to decipher.

I counted to ten. The basement exit door slammed shut, quickly, twice in a row. It was metal. The flashing had been sticking for some time now. Feeling suddenly bereft, I let myself down on the chancel steps, arms wrapped around my knees and head bowed—waiting for the room to stop spinning.

Slowly my breathing began to steady. Outside the car alarm was wailing louder than ever.

"I'm sorry you had to hear that."

I looked up—shocked—to see I was not alone. His face lost in the shadow of the arched side entrance to the sanctuary, Matt Gaskill stood motionless. Watching me.

"You heard," he said.

Silence. Though one look at my face already gave him his answer.

"We didn't know you were . . . should have never . . . ," his voice hardened. "That was uncalled for."

Something in his words, his voice, reminded me of my own—once, a long time ago. It was in the car with my youngest daughter after I told her I loved Adam. And whatever she thought or felt about all the heartache between her father and me, it had nothing at all to do with where I found myself.

"No need to apologize," I said.

"Beyond embarrassing."

"True."

"I would ask, what now? But then I have absolutely no intention of walking circles around you," he hesitated. "Unless that's what you want, of course."

"You're a decent man," subconsciously I found myself grasping at words from another time not all that long ago, words other than my own. It was how Anise described him to me when they first met. "And I want you to know that I . . . appreciate our friendship very much."

A soft rumble of laughter broke the tension stretched to breaking between us. "I'll take that as a compliment, Ms. Brennerman."

"And your son?"

"Our good vicar has got some growing up to do."

"Don't we all."

Outside the car alarm gave one last broken sequence of gasps and stopped. Feeling as self-conscious as a teenager, I got to my feet and awkwardly began to close the distance between us.

"Unfortunately, our children don't come with instruction manuals."

"Or something," Matt winced.

I extended my hand and he took it. His grasp was warm, steady.

"Friends then," I said.

"Friends."

"For the record," I said as he slowly relinquished my hand, "would you have chosen to share this conversation with me . . . that is, if I hadn't already heard most of it?"

A flicker of a frown tightened between his brows. "I would like to think so. Yes."

"I appreciate that."

"Don't worry about my son. He'll get over it. And he certainly would be mortified to know we talked."

"Understood."

"I'm not apologizing for him, but you should know that as a kid he and I had a lot of issues. I'm not sure why . . . fixing blame on one side or the other sure doesn't make any sense. He and his mother were always very close, if you discount their occasional flare-ups over all things 'garden' and 'gardening'. She was always his biggest fan. Cross-country runner, captain of the tennis team, Big Man On Campus. The road to this whole priest-thing was not the easiest for him or the rest of us."

"People seem to feel he's a wonderful fit for Peace."

"Big time out of line on this one—"

"But then you're his father. That can't be the easiest thing in the world either."

"Damn awkward at times, that's for sure. Maybe I should think about giving Father Brannen's shop down the road at St. Mary's a try."

"Not on my account."

His eyebrow arched. "Our pew then . . . third from the back, on the left."

"I remember something like that showing up in Oscar Wilde, only wasn't he talking about palm trees?"

Too late I realized I was remembering a punch line from the playwright's comedy, *The Ideal Husband.* Consider Matt Gaskill's background, it was time to stop randomly quoting fiction unless I was very sure of my source.

"Anyway," I added quickly, "I guess once someone stakes a claim on a seat, best they stick with it."

He smiled, gave a curt nod. "Makes sense."

"I suppose . . . I guess it may also make sense, just this once, to take separate exits . . . ?"

Jaw tight, he broke eye contact. "Thought I'd hang out here for a while."

"It was good to see you."

Somehow I mustered the will to head for the nearest exit. The sanctuary aisle stretched out ahead of me, row after empty row. As I put my shoulder to the heavy narthex door, I couldn't help looking back at the chancel from where I had come. Matt had settled down on one of the benches. Shoulders tight, his upturned face sought the tall window of Christ at the lakeside over the altar. The artist had embedded thin-sliced Petoskey stones into the pebble-strewn beach.

My anchor point lay elsewhere. To Matt Gaskill's right on the sanctuary wall, rendered in luminous fragments of glass, sat the grief-stricken Mary amid a bank of lilies. Behind her in the shadows stood the angel and the empty tomb. And across from that monument to hope, Eve and her Adam still moved effortlessly through the garden in the cool of the day, serene and vulnerable. Never guessing what lay ahead of them.

I had sat in that self-same spot with Dutch after Adam's death. Or close enough to it, anyway. Dutch told me he had chosen that spot as his source of hope when he needed it most in the years after the death of Adam's grandmother. The page in one of the well-worn pew Bibles had fallen open as if by itself in my hands, to the Gospel of John.

I will not leave you comfortless, the words had etched themselves on my heart. *I will come to you.*

My boss, George, told me once that the Midrash, an evolving collection of sacred interpretive writings in the Jewish tradition, shares many stories about grief and loss. Among them, there are those which say it is no accident that the ancient texts speak of God's presence written 'upon' our hearts. That way when our hearts break wide open in times of deepest sorrow, it means Divine love can freely flow in. Instead of our hearts and lives shattering into a thousand sharp and brittle pieces, our souls receive the healing they need to bud and flower again.

We are never as alone as we think. I didn't have to look far to find others around me in need of that message.

Eighteen
Doxologies

For the sunlight in the sky,
For the trees that grow so high,
For the love and friends we share,
Lord, we thank you everywhere.

From over the decades, the doggerel church camp prayer of my childhood played itself out in my head. We sang it together, packed tight on narrow wood benches. In front of us on the long banquet tables covered with sheets of off-white butcher paper lay settings of scarred silverware, thick stoneware plates and sweating metal pitchers. Our heads were bowed. Under the table, our scuffling feet took badly aimed potshots at one another.

Truly astounding, I thought, *what one remembers!* It was the Tuesday before Thanksgiving. I was headed out to the farm stand north of Groft's. An end-of-season sale was in progress. Impeccable timing.

Our local grocery had just begun to run ads for the T-Day feast when I got the official word. My son-in-law Dan found a job. Grandson Justin in Arizona didn't get the flu. And so rounding out my "grateful" list for the season, the whole bunch of us would be assembling in Xenaphon for Thanksgiving after all—daughters, spouses and kids alike. We had not been together in one place since Adam's memorial service two years earlier.

For the first time, Anise and Caleb would join us. Family, all.

The notice was short, but the distractions few as I got ready for the visit. Book signings had slowed to a trickle. The greenhouses at Groft's had closed for the season. When I got a call from a local artist-crafter who wanted to rent the retail area at the nursery for two weekends to sell Thanksgiving centerpieces, I happily could pass the buck to the new manager, Anise.

A week later when the Lion's club called, I did likewise. Their plan was to set up a small Christmas tree operation in the Groft's parking lot—intercept locals and cottagers on their way north for the Holidays. A gas station had let the Lions run their stand in the past. New management nixed the arrangement.

"Don't know what to tell the Lions. We're talking a whole month here," I automatically began to fret when I asked Anise to return their call. "The Almanacs are predicting a huge dump of the white stuff in early December. Artie's truck and plow aren't big enough to keep the lot clear."

"Give me an hour or two," Anise said. "I'll get back to you."

She discovered that a cousin of a cousin of one of Artie's euchre cronies had bought a surplus county plow several years back. The monster of a vehicle was ancient and rusted out, supposedly rattled like a tank navigating a mine field. Artie volunteered to drive it.

"You can't kill these old machines," he chuckled. "Feel like that guy in Mad Max. All I need is a leather vest and . . . did he wear sun glasses? I forget."

I had expected Artie and Viv to be headed south by now. But then snow and sub-zero wind chills seemed to bring out my Teamster friend's neighborly instincts.

"A die-hard fan of TV shows about ice road truckers," Viv told me. "Much as he says his old bones could stand some sun about now, face it . . . he's in his element decked out in that shaggy hat with ear muffs and red lumberjack coat, plowing out all the elderly housebound within a six-block radius!"

Problem solved. Anise gave the Lions the thumbs-up. Groft's was open yet again with no help whatsoever from me.

There was plenty to do with a home and hearth to decorate for the season. I blitzed a weekend make-over on the interior. The last of the porch furniture had to be hauled inside. In the process, I noticed the homestead's wrought iron fence and crimson branches of the variegated leaf dogwood weren't enough to mask the sad remains of my cottage garden. At the farm stand, I rescued a bushel of gourds and squash to display at the base of the porch steps. It was simple enough to tie two tall bundles of corn shocks against the center porch pillars. I hung a vine wreath on the front door.

Emma called Wednesday on the road with her mom's cell phone. I told her to watch for the pumpkins on my porch.

"Awesome. But you're gonna need a pilgrim, too," she said. "We made hats in school. I'm bringing mine."

The disappointed look on her cousin Justin's face came to mind. I could still do something about it. Weeks ago the dollar store had overstocked those black cardstock top hats with the belt buckles in front. A quick pit run scared up enough head gear for the entire crew. Fussing with the holiday bird would keep until tomorrow, but Grandma Eva's recipe for cranberry relish was a major production. By the time I finished grinding the berries, oranges and lemons, daughter Leslie and her family were pulling up in front of the homestead.

The hugs were rapid-fire, intense. My greeting, part tears and all heartfelt gratitude. "Happy Thanksgiving!"

"Happy Turkey Day, Grama!"

Emma came bounding back into my arms for seconds on the hugs. Her white felt Pilgrim bonnet cocked rakishly over one eye like a sixteenth century buccaneer.

"Down . . . me down," her brother Harry was having none of it. His bright red cartoon super-hero shirt scrunched up under his armpits exposing a goodly share of his tummy, he already had squirmed his way free of his mother's grasp. He made straight for the dried clumps of sedum flanking my front walk.

"I hear congratulations are in order," I told my athletically handsome son-in-law as I scooped up my youngest grandchild. It took some doing to pry free the clod of dirt clutched in his chubby fist.

"A long time coming, but yeah, I'm back on a payroll," Dan shrugged. "Les was getting ready to run off with—"

"The mailman," she snapped. "It wasn't funny the first time you said it."

The shared laughter sounded awkward. "Well, I was thrilled to hear the news," I said. "Leslie said you're going to be working for—"

"The school district," Dan shrugged. "Not the bucks I was making in the private sector, but maybe more stability."

"Well, good for you!" I said. "They say most searches these days attract a couple hundred applicants."

"Try seven hundred eighty-five," Dan said. "I still can't believe my luck."

"Skill, I'm sure," I said. "They're lucky to get you."

By now the whole Canfield gang including the luggage stood assembled in my living room. Looking tired and distracted in his cords and black henley shirt, Dan picked up two of the heavier cases and started up the stairs.

"Just aim me," he said, forcing a smile. Those weeks and months out of work had begun to take their toll. His always taut athlete's frame had begun to take on a hint of a spare tire around the middle.

"Master bedroom," I called out to his retreating back.

My daughter stood transfixed mid-point between living and dining room. "Mom, I can't believe it!" Leslie breathed. "When on earth did you repaint the place? You never told me . . . "

Meaning, I suspected, that my daughter wasn't sure she liked the change. To celebrate my new-found freedom with the closure of the greenhouses, I had raided the hardware for paint, just in time for their annual Fall Color sale. On the mixed-but-unsold shelf, I struck the Mother Lode. A frenetic weekend of painting later, my dining room was now avocado and the living room a satin pewter. Stylized deco coral, yellow and pale mustard flowers bloomed against the black ground and lush greens of the wide wallpaper borders.

"Full price but worth every penny," I said. "A treat to myself before it starts to snow. With only two seasons around here—snowplows and road work—I wanted to bring my garden indoors."

"Amazing patterns. Not quite like the chintz on the chairs," Leslie frowned. "But close, I suppose."

"Close enough. You'll get used to it," I told her.

While Leslie and her Dan settled in upstairs, I distracted Harry and Emma. We sat on the living room rug and stacked wobbly towers with my childhood Lincoln logs. A huge grin on his face, Harry waited his chance to knock them over. To groans and peals of laughter, the game began again.

"An exercise in futility," my daughter sighed as she eased herself down next to me on the thick faux Persian area rug.

I laughed. "Life. Harry and Emma just don't know it yet."

257

"Dan wasn't teasing, you know. The last month or so has been insane at our house—always so near and yet so far in the final round. I just hope the job will get things back on an even keel."

Something in her tone got my attention. "That bad . . . ?!"

Leslie grimaced. "I may have thrown out the D___ word a time or two in the heat of anger."

"But still . . . Les?"

"I know."

We both had forgotten. In the silence, I sensed Emma watching us. "How about you take your brother out to the kitchen for some crackers?" I said. "You know where to find them. They're in that cupboard—"

"Next to the stove," Emma sighed.

I felt a momentary stab of remorse even suggesting it. The look on my granddaughter's face as she horsed her brother to his feet spoke volumes. *You're just trying to get rid of us*, it said, *and I don't like it one bit.*

"Mom, don't worry," my daughter said when we were alone. "I always blamed you for sticking it out all those years with Dad. The women, the booze . . . all of it. I know Dan is a good man. None of this—losing his job and the depression afterward—was his fault. I know all that. So, how do you get beyond it? We've been seeing a counselor. But sometimes I just don't know."

My throat felt tight watching her blink back the tears. "I don't have to tell you, I'm no expert. I only know as long as you're both still breathing, even going through the motions, anything is possible."

"You're talking about Adam."

It hadn't started out that way. "Two years, Les. I still miss him so much it hurts."

"You rarely talk about it any more. I just assumed you were beginning to make your peace with what happened."

"What's there to say? How do you bring yourself to unload on friends who have lost spouses of forty or more years or even try to stack up your grief alongside theirs? We're all at that age now. I can only say that I'm past the anger—on good days, anyway. But acceptance comes a lot harder."

"I can't even imagine."

"You and your Dan have had . . . what? Ten years together now. Maybe I was a coward or wrong to stick with your Dad all those years. I don't know. I only know that under the surface of a relationship, even as bad as ours was, the roots can get pretty tangled. Tough, if not impossible to separate."

"It isn't like that. Dan would never, ever intentionally do anything to hurt me or Emma or Harry. He would sooner cut off a limb."

"You'll handle it," I told my daughter as I struggled to my feet.

From the kitchen, we heard the sound of something shattering, too heavy for glass. The loud wails that followed could only be coming from my grandson.

Leslie had already sprinted half-way to the kitchen. Turns out, Emma had fished a plate out of the cupboard for the snacks. Her brother thought it was still a game and swept the thick stoneware on to the floor. Razor-sharp shards had flown everywhere. Otherwise, no harm done.

The mother-daughter moment had passed. Whatever the past terrible months behind them had done, I couldn't bring myself to believe the damage to my daughter and Dan's marriage had been beyond repair. My heart bled for them both.

We didn't have a chance to revisit the topic. It wasn't long after that daughter Gina and the men in her life, husband Will and son Justin, pulled up in their rental. I smiled at their choice of a ride. The airport in Traverse City must have been out of sensible family cars. I suspect Gina had talked the place into that tank of an SUV.

Emma and Harry were all over their cousin in a flash. An awkward traffic jam ensued before my daughters and I finessed a group-hug.

"Should one of us be keeping an eye on those guys?" Leslie wondered out loud as the three kids disappeared inside my front door.

Gina laughed. "Mom told me she invested in outlet protectors. Not to worry."

Was this the tight-wound youngest daughter who my lithe, geek-squad candidate of a son-in-law had wooed in college? Will flashed an atta-girl grin in his sister-in-law Leslie's direction.

"Trust me, OCD is curable, Les," he said in a conspiratorial whisper. "A vodka or two and you'll be just fine!"

"That coming from a skinhead . . . a fine one to talk," Gina teased. What had once been her husband's mop of curly black hair was now a serious buzz cut, visibly thinning around the edges.

Leslie studied the results. "Supposed to be cool, is that it?"

"*Cool-er*, anyway," Will shrugged. "It was over a hundred in Tucson last week!"

By now Leslie's Dan had joined us, a hand wrapped around a genuine pigskin football he had found in the basement. From the patina of dust, I guessed the thing had to go back at least a generation.

"What say we unload the SUV, then toss this thing around a while?" Dan said.

"Finding open space is not an easy business around the homestead these days," I told them. "There's an empty lot a couple houses west of here."

"You're on!" Will said as he scooped up Harry in one hand. Justin squirmed in protest in the other. "The bags'll keep."

"Tradi-tion, tra-di-tion," Dan bellowed in an off-key baritone as he dropped back to pass on the centerline of my street. "T-Day and football, boys. Gotta be done"

Shaking their heads, my daughters plotted our attack on the turkey and trimmings for tomorrow. The odd ones out, Emma and I prowled the garden, front and back, with an eye to weeds and the weather. Her pilgrim bonnet hung around her neck from its already well-worn ribbons.

"Is our new garden going to make it through the winter, Grama?" she said.

"We did all we could," I told her. "Remember the Pilgrims took their chances, too. They almost starved to death the first year. And then the next summer's crop failed, too."

Emma nodded solemnly. "Our teacher said a hund-rid who came died because people were so hungry. The Native Ameri-kins brought them food."

"When you garden, you learn fast not to be so hard on yourself," I said.

"We took care of the big W's you taught me. Weed and water. And we fed everything and put down *mu-ch*."

"Mul-l-lch," I said. "Yes, we did. Though sometimes even the rules don't help. You can do everything right and stuff still happens."

Wide-eyed, Emma stared up at me. We weren't just talking about the perennials any more.

"I'm scared," she said.

"I know."

"Mom says I'm being silly."

"She doesn't really mean that."

"She's worried, too. I heard her talking to Daddy."

"It's hard for kids to understand grownup talk sometimes. Have you talked to your mom about it?"

Emma shook her head, No. We were standing in the middle of what had been the day-lily corner of the flower bed. My granddaughter scuffed the toes of her sneakers against the stubble.

"I think maybe you should talk to your mom," I said. "It would make you feel better."

"Mommy has been so sad." I hadn't heard her call Leslie that in a long time.

"She loves you, Emma. Your dad does, too. That you can always count on."

And so we gave thanks. In the middle of life with all its uncertainties, we had each other. While Gina and Leslie had met Anise on Mother's Day, my two son-in-laws had not. With Caleb in arms on Thursday morning, Anise watched the guys and all their alpha energy at play.

The look on her face said it all. Someday her Caleb, too, would be a part of this. I had to believe that somewhere, somehow Adam knew, was smiling.

We feasted and shared. And while the community service at Peace wasn't on the agenda, love flowered all around. At Leslie's suggestion, we scoured the cupboard for canned goods in the course of our preparations. While the turkey was cooking, she and Gina drove the kids over to the church to drop off the largesse in the food pantry basket in the narthex.

"Spotted a friend of yours," Gina said upon their return. "Name of Gaskill. He sends his, Hello."

"Matt. His son is— "

"Actually it was Father Ben we ran into." Leslie's eyebrow arched. "He said his dad was in the kitchen, up to his elbows in stuffing for the community Thanksgiving dinner. We met them both at that Mother's Day banquet last spring."

"You did. I remember."

"Your priest said his dad is moving to Xenaphon permanently."

"I heard that, too."

A half-smile twisted at my daughter's mouth. "Xenaphon. Population, what is it now?"

"I've honestly lost track," I said. "Since Dr. Jaidev and Mark Blandis, though he's on-again-off-again. And we have to count Caleb."

And just that quickly the weekend was over. The population of my world diminished by seven, nine if I counted Caleb and Anise.

"Can't stay over," Anise said Sunday night as she left for the cottage. "I've got a sales rep coming in first thing tomorrow morning. The company carries a line of instant potting frames for home gardeners who want to start their own. Figured I might as well check it out."

"Sounds promising."

"I thought so."

"*So. . .*"

"What say we get together for lunch on Wednesday?" Anise said. The ache of empty arms is impossible to conceal.

I knew what she was trying to do with her invitation, and just that quick, I accepted. We were light-years beyond worrying over what was and was not family any longer—Anise, my daughters and I. The empty spaces in our lives are meant to be filled to overflowing.

"For the love and friends we share . . . ," my heart sang as I drifted off to sleep under Grama Eva's garden of a coverlet that night. "We thank you."

I woke Monday morning to dust-devils of snow skittering across the front yard. My first thought was, *a good thing that my girls and their families had headed back home and to work before whatever was brewing out there hit us.* The bedroom floor felt icy underfoot.

Grandma Eva's homestead might be empty, but no one said my life had to be. A week before my family's visit, Artie had helped me pick out a gently-used Scion to replace the Taurus whose retirement was so long overdue. I knew that if I called beforehand, Jake would refuse my visit. Instead, I got in the car and drove, headed south to Chicago. Thanksgiving was not quite over.

As I rounded the southwest corner of Michigan, the flakes were heavier and had begun to stick. Lawns were salt-and-peppered with white. Forecasters on the car radio warned we could be in for the first major snow of the season.

It took me a few tries with the GPS to find Jake's condo apartment. The elevator to the tenth floor opened on a luxury suite with hospice on the scene. A hospital bed had been set up in the solarium so that Jake could watch the skyline and the sullen waters of Lake Michigan stretching off toward the horizon. Hooks on a mobile hospital drip tree held multiple clear liquids and tubes, including what I guessed had to be pain killers. At any rate, Jake seemed fixated on the monochrome landscape, hadn't seen me coming.

"Good powder coming down out there," I said.

Startled, he turned my way. A half-smile twisted across his features, gone as quickly as it began.

"You pegged me just about right," he said. "Downhill and cross-country. A hot-dogger of the first order, though you would never guess it now."

"I know you told me not to come. But I just had to tell you again how much your very generous gift has accomplished."

And then I told him about Anise and Caleb. "She has agreed to manage Groft's in the off-season," I told him. "Is house-sitting at the cottage. I also broached the possibility of my deeding over both properties in her name."

"And?"

"She refused. Would agree to manage whatever emerges, perhaps. But ownership, as she sees it, is out of the question."

"Same place Adam was coming from for much of his life." A wave of pain washed over Jake's drawn features. "And the foundation . . . ?"

"My boss is chairing a committee to explore our options. Adam's lawyer is on board."

Jake nodded. "Good, then."

"Good."

I sat at his bedside as the clouds began to thicken over Lake Michigan. The wind rattled against the glass of the solarium. "You're going to have a rough drive back," Jake said finally.

"I'll be fine."

"I'm not sorry you came," he said.

We wouldn't see one another again. He didn't have to say it. I stood looking down at the hospital bed. Jake's pale features gave no further clue to what he was thinking.

In my search for words, I found his hands instead. Without fanfare,

I cradled them awkwardly in mine.

"Adam loved you, Jake. I love you," I said. "And I wanted, needed to tell you that. Not in some email. But here . . . now. It was important for you to know about Anise and that you're changing lives in our little corner of the world."

It cost him an effort. The pain killers seemed to be wearing off. But Jake smiled. "You didn't have to."

"Yes," I said. "Yes, I did."

When I got back to the car, I sat quietly for what seemed like a long time, staring out the windshield at the steel and concrete of the parking garage. Jake was right, it was too late to make the trek back to Xenaphon tonight. As if drawn by an invisible homing beacon, I found myself outside the small hotel near the lakefront where Adam and I had spent several days getting ready for the wedding. The wedding that was never to be.

I hadn't asked for the same room. The desk clerk assigned it to me anyway. Fortunately, I didn't discover that fact until I was standing, key in hand, in the hallway outside the heavy walnut-paneled door. Throat tight, I half thought about going back to the front desk and demanding the clerk change it. Instead I worked the key in the lock until the door swung open to my touch.

The filmy drapes were open and light flooded the room. Through the cluster of buildings, I could see the steel gray of the water. Snowflakes swirled against the windows in a silent dance and for a split-second, I was transported to another gray winter afternoon living now only in my memory. Adam's hands were warm against my shoulders as the pale-gold lights of evening came on around us.

I don't know how long I stood at that window, transfixed. But when I roused myself to go down to the desk to see about dinner, it was dark. The skyline blazed with neon. On the short walk to the neighborhood restaurant where Adam and I had eaten together our last night in Chicago, the wind was cutting and harsh. When I settled in for the night, climbed into the heavily quilted bed, I slept more soundly than I had in years.

Next morning, the journey north was not quite as bad as Jake had predicted. The salt trucks were out in force, shaking the roadway as they braved the rising storm. Whenever I saw the amber lights sweeping the landscape, I clutched the wheel and hung on for dear life. I hit the outskirts of Xenaphon by one o'clock.

Exhausted and my eyes wide open from the strain of driving, I sat in front of the fire for a while nursing a brandy-laced tea. It occurred to me that I had missed the column deadline for the first time in months. Without anything in mind, I retrieved my laptop and let the keystrokes carry me wherever they would.

.

Poets speak of the dead earth of winter. Nothing could be farther from the truth. But we forget to prepare for that fallow time at our peril.

As Xenaphon slipped into hibernation mode over the past weeks and days, seasoned gardeners listened for cues that their plants were doing the same. Annuals here are at the mercy of the first hard frost. There's no preventing it, short of taking the plants indoors.

But perennials rely for survival on their own built-in time clocks. Changes in temperatures and length of days will warn them when and how to protect themselves. If we rush or tamper too much with the process—cut back the plants too early or prune too late—we risk encouraging new growth late in the season. Potentially fatal.

Through a subtle "hardening" process, plant roots on their own become accustomed to the brutal conditions to come. That shutting-down of a perennial for the winter seems to be akin to a quiet going to sleep. Under that hardening earth, life still goes on.

To predict how hardy the roots of a plant will be in the winter ground is at best an art not a science. The short answer? It all depends.

Disease or insect-prone perennials like hollyhock, columbine, day lilies, delphinium and irises need aggressive prune-backs to maximize their chances over winter. In the case of many woody-stemmed plants like mums, it is best if we leave the plant structures alone, so the new growth can absorb nutrients in the spring. The "dead" growth can always be cut back after sprouting begins.

When possible, a good gardener leaves behind some seed heads. Birds and woodland creatures need support, too, in the dreary days ahead. As the snow piles up and the wind blows the flakes into standing drifts, the garden is still the refuge it is meant to be.

While I wrote, I kept seeing Jake Dorokoski's hollowed face as he looked out at the falling snow. My heart ached—even as I gave thanks for Adam's friend, now mine. Thanks for the power of friendship. For the enduring promise of love.

265

How fragile we are, for all our tenacious love of life. In Jake's eyes, I had seen the courage and dignity of which humankind is capable. I would never forget it.

Jake's greatest gift to me was not that he had endowed a memorial in Adam's name. It was not the hope that his legacy might enrich the lives of a place and people we all deeply loved. His greatest gift to me was far, far more personal.

Death had robbed me once before of someone I loved. Only this time, I had known the healing miracle of being able to say goodbye.

Nineteen
Silent Night

December. The date needed no annotation. I refused to mark its passing within the numbered space on the calendar assigned to it. I cannot even bring myself to name it in my heart. Adam died on that gray December afternoon two years ago. And for all the passage of time—730 days, 17,520 hours and over a million minutes later—the empty black-bordered square could not hope to contain what was in my heart.

My family's visit over Thanksgiving had borne unanticipated fruit. For the first time since Adam was gone, I felt as if Death did not have the last word. The morning came. I had a good cry. And then, I roused myself to begin a new day as best I could.

The intended Christmas gift to myself—a gigantic splurge and weeks of hunting on e-bay—was the six volume set of David Attenborough's "Private Life of Plants". A classic with gardeners everywhere, the series was first broadcast on the BBC in 1995. Drawing on examples from around the world, the videos are a lyrical journey though the life cycle of plants, from birth to death and beyond.

Most of the available copies are British-standard videos, unplayable on American machines. Used ones showed up piecemeal and only occasionally in the complete six-volume sets. I agonized over quality and quantity and finally grabbed a complete set, expensive but from a reliable online vendor. I hadn't spent that much time picking out my slightly-used-but-new-to-me car. Like me, that vehicle came equipped with a story. I liked that.

Just so, the video set's arrival had the aura of spring itself arriving on my doorstep. Before I squirreled it away under the tree, I even wrapped the darn thing in a green foil paper dotted with surreal-looking poinsettias, the most abused and maltreated of plants of all time. I shook my head at the irony of it.

But then some things ought not to be postponed and this was one of them. Ripping open the holiday wrapping, I slid the first cassette into my ancient tape player.

Thus began a solitary marathon, frame after incredible time-lapse frame as the life-span of plants and the garden unfolded before me. I paused only to light a fire in the grate between episodes two and three. Between five and six, I opened a can of chicken soup and ate the contents cold out of the can. When the final episode ended, I eased the cassette back into its case and rewrapped the entire collection.

In passing, I glanced out a front window of the homestead to find myself thrust abruptly into an alien landscape. Snow must have been falling for hours. A thick, wet accumulation of white had blotted out even the globe of the porch light. By its almost non-existent glow, I could barely pick out the last vestiges of my cottage garden, wind-tattered heads of the sedum standing alone above the mounting drifts.

Winter had begun to do its worst. *In vain*, I found myself thinking, after that eloquent testament to the enduring mystery of life I had just witnessed.

If only in the fertile soil of my imagination, my garden and its precious stories stirred and teemed about me in the December night. As a gardener and a writer, my callings had become forever inseparable—to take the ashes of my days, work them into the earth and enrich the life that follows.

I had learned a great deal since my *Time in a Garden*, both the writing and living of it. Some things are too powerful to die. Whether I intended them or not, soon new page after new page would begin to fill my laptop screen. More tales of a fictional Eden and the undying love of man for woman would glow through the lens of two fragile glass panels, set into the walls of a quiet rural sanctuary. A young woman's eyes, wiser than their years and framed by an open car window, would draw me silently again into their secrets. A Teamster and a lover of herbs would struggle to redefine love as they found it.

This was Xenaphon as we knew and lived it. Fathers and sons, a mother and her daughters, a man at the end of his road and a boy at the beginning. Generations old and new would thrust their hands into the earth and emerge grasping at truth and beauty in all their complexity. Their stories were a sacred trust.

But for now, tired in body and soul, I passed on supper and headed straight to bed. The wind shook the eaves and pelted against the shingles, and still I slept. Mine was a peace-filled, dreamless sleep.

At first light, I got up and lit a fire in the grate. The blizzard had continued through the night. If the icy crust got any thicker on the trees, the lines would begin to go down. A quick phone call to the Groft cottage confirmed my fears had their basis in fact.

"Snowed in out there?" I wondered.

"Three-foot drifts and rising," Anise said. "Thanks for asking."

I could hear the worry in her voice. "You know that Artie would be glad to drive out and get you with the plow," I said.

"Give it an hour before we panic."

A half-hour later she was calling from her cell. "We lost power. Wind gusts are topping fifty miles an hour."

"Artie is already on high alert. Pull together some stuff for yourself and the baby. He'll be on his way the minute I phone him."

I needn't have bothered. Viv said within minutes of my original call, Artie was out the door with the truck and plow, headed north toward the lake. I paced and took in far too much liquid caffeine until I saw the headlights pull safely into the homestead driveway. With the door threatening to wrench itself free behind me, I waited on the porch until I saw the huddled shapes appear at the base of the steps.

Anise had brought Chris Demort with her. While she and the baby laid claim to the guest room, he bunked on the sofa bed in my office. School was cancelled for that day and the next. Chris professed nothing but enthusiasm for that turn of events. He was fooling no one. Some months back he had let slip that he had talked to the counselor about enrolling in the branch campus of the community college after graduation.

"Plants," he scowled. "Who woulda thought the darn things could grow on a guy like that?"

Laughter was becoming a daily routine again. After several mornings scrambling for the upstairs bathroom, Chris took to hiding out in the half-bath downstairs.

"Way too much women's stuff," he muttered.

But then privately I would catch him looking at Anise cuddling Caleb with a mixture of awe and envy. And though his probation would soon enough be over, his ties to our garden gang were now anything but. He was already clamoring for me to set a date for planting the peat pots out at Groft's.

At this point, I hadn't even put up the Christmas lights on the sturdy blue spruce outside the nursery office. Thank goodness, Chris and Artie took it upon themselves to do the job first weekend in December. Meanwhile, I dragged out my artificial spruce at the homestead and decked it out with the least breakable ornaments I could find in the attic.

"You're a gardener," Anise said when she saw the results. "So why the plastic fantastic?"

"Allergic to pine."

"Sad. But then I'm a fine one to talk. Artificial or not, at least you *have* a tree. I haven't even dared to put one up yet—am getting so blasted tired of saying, No and Don't and . . . *stop* . . . !"

Anise made a lunge for Caleb just as he teetered dangerously close to the tree. It took some stealth and skill for her to maneuver between the clutter of chairs and end tables displaced by my holiday decorating, but she managed before he tried to pull himself up with the help of either branches or trunk. Caleb let out a lusty howl and started squirming.

"No way, Big Guy!" his mother said. "That's enough Rambo for one afternoon."

I laughed. "I forgot how fast aspiring toddlers can move, given half a chance."

"You have no idea."

Xenaphon's calendar had begun to burgeon with celebrations of a pending birth. Father Ben had set his sights on a community-wide living Nativity. A recruitment ad ran in the bulletin beginning early November. That was the last I heard of the project until he showed up on our doorstep.

"Is Anise home?" he said. "Or back at the cottage? I saw her car."

"Here. But just overnight."

I stood aside to let him into the living room. Anise had just rewound the mechanism on Caleb's baby swing, so her back was turned.

The music box was playing an unrecognizable sing-song tune, that sounded suspiciously like "Rain, Rain, Go Away".

"M-m-m," her son squealed with each arc of the pendulum.

"Is that a 'M-m-mom' or 'm-more'," I laughed.

Anise shrugged. "Who knows."

"Maybe I should be proposing a speaking part," Ben said.

Anise looked up, startled. "I didn't know we had company."

"Not exactly company. I was going to ask a big favor."

"How big?"

"The pageant." A smile twitched at the corner of Ben's mouth. "I was thinking maybe you would agree to let Caleb play the baby Jesus."

"You're kidding. He would never sit still that long. And pity the poor Mary who gets stuck with *that. . .*"

Ben's smile widened. "You up for the role?"

"The Blessed Virgin. That's different, considering. And Joseph?"

"Right now, that's me."

Anise flushed. So did Ben Gaskill.

"You've thought about what Xenaphon will be making of that," she said.

"A lot, yes. I thought about it a lot—folks'll get used to it."

"In that case? Let's do it."

Even halfway across the room, I heard the good vicar exhale sharply. The man doesn't know it yet, I told myself, but he is half-way to falling in love with Anise Gruin. Not the only guy in town to nurse an oversize crush, but on some level the least expected. I was remembering that unfortunate conversation between Ben and his father in the undercroft.

Love isn't convenient, I would have told him if I could. Love has precious little to do with common sense. It is the wind that shakes the branches and scatters the buds of the maples. Love's spring comes, with or without our consent.

"Good then," Ben Gaskill nodded.

And so bathrobes and *mardi gras* crowns emerged from musty cardboard boxes. The Angel Gabriel, a very uncomfortable-looking Chris Demort, sported well-worn sneakers under his elegant white satin costume. I suspected it had been cut from the voluminous skirt of an old wedding gown. Two under-aged shepherds, visiting grandkids of parishioners, rode tentative herd on my neighbor's aged sheepdog—the only livestock in the production. A local farmer had offered up a couple of live sheep, but the director went with stuffed instead. The head of the altar guild was in a tizzy over what the real McCoy might do to the already marginal carpeting in the sanctuary.

Anise as Mary had every male in the audience holding their breath. Her cobalt blue velvet robe had come from a school play decades ago and I was told on good authority that no one else had been able to fit into it for years. Over the simple but stunning gown, someone had draped a veil made from a pair of heavy lace curtains, sheer enough to reveal discreet flashes of her fiery red hair.

By the time the pageant was over, young Caleb as the Holy Child had one major and two lesser meltdowns. So much for cheerily naive Christmas songs about a Baby Jesus who never cried!

The pageant ending more than made up for the rockier moments. For the final tableaux, the sanctuary was pitch-dark, except for the bank of candles at either side of the altar. Transfixed in shafts of golden light, the Virgin's upturned face glowed like the gilded illustrations in a medieval Book of Hours. No feeling soul who witnessed Joseph hovering shyly over his beautiful bride-to-be could have argued with the casting.

All is calm, we sang. *All is bright.*

Out of respect for George, our honorary Jewish parishioner without a synagogue, we added a menorah to the sanctuary decor. My boss' son Mark came back from a business trip to Pittsburgh in time and the two, father and son, sat front and center through the ragged Nativity as if it were the most natural thing in the world. A surprise twist on what seemed to be becoming a Blandis tradition, Mark brought the pageant's leading lady flowers—if I had to guess, all the way from the Pittsburgh airport. High end, snow white roses like that most definitely were *not* in any florist's inventory within fifty miles of tiny Xenaphon.

In those days there went out a decree from Caesar Augustus. I even caught up with my Romans again, just when I least expected them *or* their Julian Calendar.

A lot of googling had run its course for me since the groundhog sent me on my nocturnal chases into the mysteries of time beyond my knowing. I learned to my amazement, that after most of the world gave up on the ancient Roman attempts to set time right, the Berber on Mount Athos in North Africa *still* to this day claim the Julian calendar as their own.

We human beings are only as large as our dreams. That doesn't originate with me, but it is the central theme of the amazing poem, "Abt Vogler", by the English writer Robert Browning. In verse, Browning tells the story of an eighteenth-century musician, an Abbott, famous for his incredible skill at improvising on the pipe organ. In that very moment Abt Vogler finishes extemporizing, he shares how it felt to create that soaring structure of notes and silence, rising up like a magnificent palace around him.

The minute the musician's hands left that keyboard, all the beauty vanished, like the sound itself—forever beyond recall, a mere echo in the memory of the hearer. And yet, as the Abbott says as he mourns his lost music, "All we have willed or hoped or dreamed of good shall exist . . . when eternity affirms the conception of an hour."

Louis Comfort Tiffany, perhaps the greatest artist in glass of his or any time, built the same vision into his stained glass windows. As he began mounting the shards and shapes into their lead channels, the first pane he set was always deliberately flawed.

Nothing lasts, the gesture said. Perfection is for Heaven.

We are all the children of the garden. We lay out our plots and dig in the beds, cultivate and water and nurture. But then like the proverbial lilies of the field, the whole business of growing is more or less out of our hands. It is up to patience and time, love and laughter—maybe even a minor miracle or two—to do the rest.

Jake died yesterday. I had checked my email at dawn and again at noon of Christmas Eve Day. Sometime during that fleeting span of hours, another piece of my life with Adam Groft slipped into memory. The heart attack put an end to Jake's suffering. It would have been wrong, wicked even, to wish otherwise.

There was to be no memorial service. Still, I could not let the moment pass. I picked up the phone and called Father Gaskill.

"I would appreciate it if you would add Jake Dorokoski's name to the prayer list," I said. "The prayers for the dead."

"A friend?"

"And benefactor." I told the priest about Jake's friendship with Adam and his gift to the foundation that was being established in Adam's memory.

"I had heard there might be something in the works," Father Gaskill said.

"That legacy will outlive us all."

I picked up on a subtle hesitation from the other end of the connection, hesitation all the same. "And Anise . . . Ms. Gruin . . . will that impact her situation?"

"She has agreed to administer the program," I smiled. "I had offered to deed the property at Groft's and the cottage to her. She refused. And I can understand her decision—that it makes more sense than her owning everything outright. Taxes and maintenance could be killers."

"If you folks ever need help out there, let me know. Peace would certainly publicize any and all activities."

If the man's interest in Anise Gruin was casual, he wouldn't have felt compelled to dodge and weave on the subject. I wondered if he knew himself. It was going to be an interesting New Year.

Little whirlwinds of flakes had begun to filter down once again from the steel of the sky. I suspected there was more to follow. Just when I had resigned myself several weeks ago to a solitary, snowbound Christmas Eve, Anise invited me out to the cottage for a long weekend.

"We've even got a tree," she said. "It's a live one that Chris is going to plant when the weather permits. Caleb is wild about it. Call the invite a desperate appeal for help chasing him around the living room, but I won't take no for an answer."

I drew in a breath, let it out again. *Two of a kind*, I thought. Stuck somewhere between our need for independence and our loneliness. Working on it, though.

"I would love to," I said.

"Good. I thought maybe we could all drive together to the Christmas Eve service at Peace. I wanted Caleb to hear the music and see the lights and candles. After that disaster of a pageant—"

"*Wonderful.* The pageant was wonderful. But of course, it makes sense to drive to the service together. I'm looking forward to it."

Just that easy, I had a place to go. But then it wasn't just about company. This was Adam's family, mine too, and we loved each other.

Their presents were already wrapped and sitting under my tree. Way too many toys for young Caleb. I knew that as soon as I began collecting them at the summer sidewalk sales that Anise would protest. If I was going to incur her righteous indignation, I might as well go all the way. On a whim, I googled several travel sites and came up with a shockingly low post-holiday fare for flights to Arizona. Young Caleb could travel for free.

I stuck the ticket voucher in a manilla envelope and concealed the unimpressive looking gift in a larger box I resurrected from my cardboard recycling heap out in the garage. Childish that little touch, but it had to be done. By now I had run out of wrapping paper. Newspaper would have to do. On top I taped an elaborate rainbow cascade of curls that finished off the last of the ribbed paper ribbon.

Anise saved that ostentatious package for last. I watched her face carefully as she disposed of the wrapping and peered inside. Envelope in hand, she made eye contact.

"Open it," I said.

She opened the envelope and skim-read the contents. Reread it, more slowly this time. "What is . . . ? I don't understand."

"Your parents. They're going to be waiting to see that new grandson. I picked early February, but you can change the dates if you want. A week seemed like a reasonable amount of—"

"You shouldn't have done this."

"A bargain and a half. And once the greenhouse opens, you won't be going anywhere any time soon."

Without a sound Anise had started to cry. A film of tears glistened along her lower lashes. They trailed in rivulets down her cheeks.

"What do I tell them?" she said in a broken whisper.

"As much or little as you choose when it comes to Adam and his sister. And Caleb. Caleb's really what they are going to want to know about. Are you safe and settling down. Do you have help if and when you—"

You have no idea what this means to me," Anise said.

One look at her face, her eyes brimming with tears told me all I needed to know. "I'll drive you to the airport when the time comes."

When I came back to the homestead, I was baffled to find an

275

unexpected gift of my own waiting for me on the front porch. The elegant paper and ribbon appeared a far cry from the pitiful wrap-job I had managed for Anise. Thousands of millefleurs dots of red, yellow, green and white were strewn across a dark green ground. A cascade of paper grosgrain ribbons curled over the shiny surface. There was a card attached.

> Came across this online. Great reviews. Thought you might enjoy it—even find a column in it somewhere. Merry Christmas, Matt

I laid the note on the coffee table along with the unopened package.

Thoughtful. A friendly gesture, nothing more, I told myself.

Still, I couldn't bring myself to open the gift. Was I misreading the man? From the get-go, I sensed Matt Gaskill was still grieving for his wife. Even in that angry conversation with his son in the undercroft, an exchange to which I should never have been privy, he made it plain that he considered himself my friend. I had no reason whatsoever to expect otherwise.

At times it seemed that our friendship took on a borderline flirtatious edge. But under the circumstances, I considered it no different from my teasing relationship with my boss. Both men were safe. For very different reasons, but safe.

I nuked a mug of leftover coffee and sipped away at it on the sofa. "Get over yourself," I told myself.

Carefully I slid the ribbon from the package, slipped my fingertips under the tape. The book was about art and gardening, a thoughtful study of paintings and their possible influences on garden design. Matt Gaskill was right. The book looked fascinating.

I clicked on my cell, and by force of habit, punched in the number of the rectory by mistake. "Matt," I said. "I caught you."

"And you found it," he chuckled. "Good."

"The book looks amazing."

"I'm glad you like it."

I drew in a long, deep breath. "I've been waiting for the holiday rush to be over. But I owe you one of my traditional German dinners. Way too much starch and protein, but fun," I said. "A bit like carrying coals to Newcastle considering your own chef-ly skills."

"That wasn't my intent when—"

"I insist."

"Alright then. Name the date."

I hesitated. Friday seemed too much like a date night. "Next Thursday. Noon, the Germans have their big meal of the day for lunch."

"Fine. I'll be there."

He came decked out in business casual, a subdued gray striped button-down collar shirt and black cords. His house gift was an excellent Mosel Piesporter. No way in heck could he have found that one locally.

"German." He extended the bottle in my direction. "I assumed a white would be safest."

"Sauerbraten with knoedel and red cabbage. But I prefer whites to reds regardless. Anise whipped me up a *Sachertorte* for Christmas. I froze the leftovers, thawed them out for our dessert."

"I noticed no mention of blood sausage on the menu."

"You're kidding, right? Even with all my Germanic corpuscles leaping up and down, *Blutwurst* is going just a tad *too* far!"

"Whew!" he laughed. "On the subject, the Greeks also have some interesting notions of how to define 'edible'. Some of my wife's relatives were fond of whipping up Pig's Head Mould and baked tripe. I stayed as far away from the buffet as possible."

I smiled. "I remember you telling me she gardened. Do Greeks have a distinct garden tradition? You got me to wondering."

"Ancient, ancient, ancient and Laia never let me forget it. Gardens and gardeners leave poor records, though, especially since the Greek city states were constantly under siege. But I read somewhere that the Minoans appear to have gardened. Archaeologists say they apparently tried to reshape the landscape without destroying the impression of nature in the raw."

"Sounds like the English. I had no idea."

"No one is sure, of course," he shrugged. "Archaeologists haven't found a lot of evidence, just walled pits that might have contained enclosed gardens. Greek literature is full of images of sacred groves and rose gardens and early as the eighth century BC, the poet Homer described gardens full of flowering fruit trees."

I googled it later. Came up with the quote. *And the yield of all these trees will never flag or die, neither in winter nor in summer, a harvest all year round.*

"Tough, I imagine, to recreate in Minneapolis."

Matt chuckled. "Laia went for the practical. She had quite an impressive kitchen garden, mostly Greek herbs. Eggplant, of course. The pergola out back of the house was covered with grape vines—awful wine, but great jam and stuffed vine leaves. And she loved roses. I guess all of that fits."

"Sounds like Vivian's back yard," I said. "I have a lot of slips from her herb garden growing outside my kitchen."

"No roses?"

"Viv has tried a few. Though I've never been too fond of roses myself. Way too thorny for my taste, plus too much work. I've always gone in for benign and undramatic stuff like daisies and coneflowers."

"Well, I must say, I've enjoyed working on the berm," he said. "Those Saturdays even seemed to be humanizing my usually reclusive son. From where I sit, gardeners are good folk—generous, no nonsense. What you see is what you get. I like that."

"Well, you are about to get an introduction to the Brennerman version of German cuisine, if I don't burn it."

Matt took one look at the table and let out a low whistle. "You sure set a heck of a table," he said.

Sauerbraten was an occasion that called for the fine china and crystal. I hadn't polished Grandmother's heavy rose and ivy pattern silver in ages. By the time I finished the two place settings, I remembered why. All the while I pressed the earth-tone linen napkins, I kept feeling vaguely guilty that maybe I was sending out the wrong signals.

"Tradition," I said. "Sauerbraten in the homestead is always a state occasion."

"I'm honored."

"You haven't tasted it yet. I usually tell guests *afterward* that I marinate the beef for five days in a crock on the kitchen counter. The health department would probably lock me up."

"I trust you."

"Thanks . . . I think."

I laid claim to the chair closest to the kitchen. Matt settled in across the table. Grateful for the alone-time, I shuttled back and forth with lidded serving dishes and a platter for the meat while he uncorked the wine.

We toasted to the New Year. "With any luck," Matt said, "I'll finally close on that house I've been looking at. A contractor could have built the thing from scratch in the time it's taken for the bank to get the deal done. . ."

"You're working with Mark Blandis?"

Matt nodded. "Nice guy. But he's got his work cut out for him. After everything that's happened, I suppose caution makes sense. Can't fault him for that."

We ate and talked and laughed, and then the man was gone. As I shut the door behind him, I caught my reflection in the front hall mirror. *Who was this woman?* I recalled the angel's question—Whom are you seeking?—and felt a momentary stab of guilt. Face flushed and eyes glittering with contentment, I could have been a young woman seeing off a beau, not a widow caught behind a dark veil of loneliness.

But this wasn't my Adam, it was a veritable stranger. And whatever I felt in Matt Gaskill's presence, it was not romantic love.

The growing awareness was there to read in my eyes. I had caught a glimpse in that unforgiving glass of a woman someone's love had created—confident in her own womanhood, and yes, even flirtatious, aware of her power. This, too, was the legacy of Adam's love. I vowed to make it a point to get to know her. For that woman was me.

Whatever my fears, sometime between the knoedel and the strudel, the lunch with Matt Gaskill helped me articulate what I felt about my life and my place in it. *Words*, I wrote, in my journal.

> *Woman. Mother. Widow*—someone who was and is loved. Someone who loves in return. All true and yet those words do not define me, any more than other words in my emotional vocabulary like 'gardener' or 'writer'. My life is a work in progress. It is tough to put labels on that.
>
> I have gotten off the ash heap. I no longer flinch when Genesis, Eden or Adam and Eve come up in public contexts. If pushed to defend my ongoing presence in a pew on Sunday morning, sharing the great feasts and ordinary moments with my neighbors, I would admit that after all the anger, I am declaring a tentative truce with all things religious. To explain what and how I believe, I need only to look to the seemingly dormant cottage garden in my own front yard.

Philosophers say it is the quiet hunger for the spiritual—the quest to understand—which makes us human. Personally, I still find as many questions as answers. What does it all mean? Is there something out there, a deeper reality, to which our lives at their fullest can connect? Faith, it seems, is the journey, not a destination.

I find comfort knowing I am in good company in my search. All I have to do is to watch my boss George's angst as he shares the essence of his Jewish heritage with his son. Our good vicar, Ben Gaskill, wrestles not just with finding his own peace, but with accepting his father's path through that self-same labyrinth. Together and separately, my friends and I seek to redefine the meaning of true *neighborliness*. I watch my daughters trying to make sense of their childhood faiths as one difficult price of adult living in these troubled times.

An odd stab at ecumenism? Perhaps. But then as Alfred Lord Tennyson once wrote, "There lives more faith in honest doubt, than in half the creeds." Whatever else my late-life foray into organized religion was accomplishing, I have never felt freer to question *and* to hope—commit both to the written page, without fear of being misunderstood or judged. By myself most of all.

And so like the sepia world of an old family album, my fall garden slips into memory. Winter's monochrome sets in, not with the first of the snows but with the smallest, most delicate of icy crystals that glisten on the morning grass.

In the midnight quiet of the homestead—with past, present and future all around me—I no longer prayed for solutions or even peace. I gave thanks for the simple possibility of new beginnings.

We Flower Children of the Sixties can find fall and winter a problematic time. Ours was the generation that thought thirty was over-the-hill. Forty meant encroaching senility. Anything or anyone beyond that no longer even qualified as organ donors. But then as the saying goes, where you stand depends on where you sit.

Right now seventy seems downright young. Ninety-year-olds are skydiving. And I'm told there are so many candidates for the hundred-plus birthday club on one popular morning TV show, that the host has had to resort to a lottery when reading the names.

That expression Golden Years finally has begun to make sense to me. Like Anise single-mindedly refusing the Groft empire and all that goes with it, I wouldn't trade this time I have been gifted for anything.

Twenty
Resolutions

Epiphany lies ahead. The Wise Men are on their way. On New Year's Eve, I resolved to read the quote-for-the-day that came up on my grandson Justin's resin trellis sitting on my kitchen counter. I was into my third year using the thing now and counting—had become a great deal less fastidious about how or if to scramble the cards.

> *What lies behind us and what lies before us are small matters compared to what lies within us.* Ralph Waldo Emerson

As usual, old R. W. hit my mood square on the head.

I always thought that as a holiday, New Year's Eve was pretty contrived—a clock strikes and we expect to be instantly happy. Confetti rains down and noisemakers sound. In any case, I didn't wait for the traditional ball drop to send me off to bed. Midnight the fitful sound of fireworks in the distance woke me. Muttering under my breath, I wandered to the bedroom window to check it out.

Road crews hadn't repaired the streetlight down the block so I could see the stars glittering crystal bright through the lindens out front of the homestead. I lay awake for a while in the darkness, listening to the steady rise and fall of my pulse.

Resolved . . . to live. Simple as resolutions go, but enough. There's an old Irish saying, that God created time and we humans invented haste. For all my awareness of time passing, I determined to savor more and rush less, to enjoy the winter rather than yearn perpetually for spring.

That, too, would come in due time. Meanwhile the New Year dawned clear and cold. A light dusting of snow glittered on the sidewalk in front of the homestead. On a whim I whipped up a batch of the traditional German New Year's casserole, *Dibbekuchen.* I hadn't made it in years—grated potatoes baked in a crock lined with bacon slices, heavy on the onions and fresh-ground pepper.

With a good hour to kill as it baked, I lit a three-logger in the fireplace. I poured myself some eggnog and for once, I didn't look at the scale or the calories on the back of the carton. For good measure, I tipped in a hefty quantity of rum. Anise's fruitcake was resting untouched on the counter in its red foil wrapping. I opened it, cut myself a generous slice.

There were worse ways to usher in a New Year. Ensconced in the wing chair, surrounded by the good things of life, I watched the flames dancing in the grate.

"Happy New Year!" I said.

The room to which I raised my glass was anything but empty. Faces in the frames over the mantle smiled out at me, new ones among the old—all very much alive to me.

The warbling of the doorbell took me off guard. When I stood to answer it, I nearly lost my balance. Over my jeans and scruffy sweater, I wrapped myself in the snuggi-blanket with sleeves that Emma had given me for Christmas. Forward movement was awkward as I tried to disentangle myself. The doorbell rang again, more insistent now.

Ridiculous answering it in that get-up. I must look like one of those bizarre two-sided medieval sculptures that depict youth and life on one side, age and decay on the other. *Memento mori,* my college art history instructor told us. *Remember your mortality.*

Still chuckling to myself, I opened the door. Even with his back turned, I recognized Matt Gaskill stamping the snow off his feet on the mat. As of its own volition, the door swung open enough to let him into the front hall.

"A nice surprise," I said.

"Happy New Year."

"You, too."

"We missed you at the morning service."

"Caught me playing hooky," I laughed. "Keeping warm. Enjoying be-jillion calorie fruitcake, eggnog before 10 in the morning—all of it incredibly decadent."

"Sounds great."

"With or without?" I offered.

"*With*. What the heck, it's New Year's. Is that bacon I smell coming from the kitchen?"

I told him about the Dibbekuchen. While he settled down into the matching wing chair, I shed the snuggi-blanket and padded out to the kitchen to round up eggnog and fruitcake.

Matt lifted his glass in salute. "To the New Year!"

"To the New Year," I said as I refilled my glass.

"And a good growing season. My first seed catalog showed up yesterday at the rectory. Bea must have gotten us all on some list."

"Speaking of growing, made your Resolutions yet?"

"As a matter of fact, Yes," he said. "I put a down-payment on that house on Mound Street."

"Good for you."

"And I'm planning on ripping those awful woody yews out from in front of the parsonage. Artie's going to loan me a chain and his winch. Anything I come up with by way of replacement has to be an improvement."

I laughed. "Your son's take on that project?"

"The move or the yews?"

"Both . . . either."

Matt shrugged. "Selling the house in Minneapolis was the real blow. Ben grew up there. His memories of his childhood, his mother are all bound up in that place. And mine, too, when it comes down to it. By comparison, a couple of bushes are small potatoes. Until the deal on the Mound Street house comes through, I've decided to give the kid a break and get out of town. Some obscenely cheap post-Holiday fares showed up on the Internet. I decided to grab a flight to Tampa, spend some time with my daughter and her family."

"Soon?"

"Next week. I figured there's no time like the present."

"How about snagging me an air plant down there? For my terrarium."

Matt grinned. "A reasonable request."

284

"Though I warn you, the last one Viv and Artie brought back for me last winter was dead within a month."

"Nothing ventured."

"True."

"Ben and I been getting along so well lately, it seemed prudent not to push my luck. He's still having a lot of trouble figuring out where love stands on his check-list. But he's trying . . . actually skied the road out to the cottage to see Anise yesterday. Wound up with an interesting case of windburn."

I scrounged for some politically correct answer, like *It'll be quiet around here with you gone* or *We'll all miss you.* Instead, I found myself blurting out the truth.

"Well, I'll miss you," I said.

Matt smiled. "I was hoping you might. It's why God invented cell phones and e-mail."

I didn't immediately respond. But we got beyond the awkward silence—spent the whole afternoon talking. Nothing earth-shaking. Just about kids, the weather and what might or might not materialize about the Reclaim Our Roots project out at the cottage. Anise had already started work on a website. Meanwhile, I broke out the Dibbekuchen and Matt and I took turns trouncing each other at gin rummy. When he left around eight, I watched him pause and turn at the curb to wave.

A decent man, I found myself thinking. It always came back to that. I could think of many worse ways to begin a New Year.

Matt's exodus started some kind of unsettling trend. It seems a major chunk of Xenaphon was suddenly on the move. Five of my neighbors had flown or driven to places south for the winter. Artie and Vivian had moved on from the Gulf Coast to helping one of his family rebuild their forest-fire-ravaged home near Sedona. George flew to London for a long weekend and wound up stranded in Heathrow for two more days.

I even surprised myself by winging down to Tucson for two weeks to see Gina. Then I changed my flight and stopped off for another week north of the Windy City with Leslie and her family on the way home. Self-defeating after escaping to the low eighties in the Southwest, I ended my pilgrimage with wind chills of 20 below.

Somehow the year had come full circle. Back home in Xenaphon from my wanderings, I slipped back into the sanctuary at Peace in time for Groundhog Day. Only this time Job and his ash heap were gone from the lectionary cycle. On another note entirely, the readings for the day talked about prophetic voices and what is required of us as caring human beings.

I spent the evening watching a repeat of that classic film, "Groundhog Day". I had forgotten how much I loved that movie. In a world where there are no do-overs, the prospect of working at life a day at a time until we get it right can be tempting. But personally, I'm grateful that we never step twice into the same stream—liberating, if we appreciate the gift for what it is.

Some things, of course, never change. February skies were still gray as often as they were sun-washed. But as I poured through my gardening catalogs, I sensed my heart opening to the possibilities. I have begun to learn to love again—differently, but love it is.   And the opportunities to show it were all around me.

My boss gifted me for the New Year with a framed photo of the Garden windows in the sanctuary. I had shared with him once the story of how Adam Groft's grandmother had come to create them, how much they meant to me. Adam and Eve tending the Garden. A wistful Mary and her angel seated in the garden in front of the empty tomb. The way George stitched the images together, it is difficult to tell where one story begins and the other ends.

"Breath-taking," I told him. I hung it on the wall alongside the door in the master bedroom, one of the last things I saw at night and the first I saw each and every morning.

They say that in the Qur'an, history begins not with evolving galaxies and massive geologic formations, but with the creation of human beings. Allah shaped and molded them from clay—placed them in a Garden. Eve is never mentioned by name, but in Islamic tradition, she is called Hawwa. I like the idea that she sprang not from Adam's rib, but mysteriously from the same simple earth as her partner and love.

Independent. Her own woman. I liked that. We

286

daughters of Eve are a resilient lot. I had to believe that whatever life sent her way, our spiritual mother found the courage to pick up her hoe or rake and begin again.

I still had a lot of sifting and winnowing ahead if I am to reclaim fully my time in the garden. But I greeted the sunrise determined to remember Adam and me as we were—happy, even blessed.

His enduring presence lives on all around me. I hear his voice in the laughter coming from his beautiful home along a now barely passable access road to a frozen lake. His smile lives on in the loving glances between a young woman and her baby . . . Caleb, the bold. It lives on their stories that have become inextricably linked with my own.

Caleb is growing. Whenever I'm in charge of rocking him, I find myself humming that sing-song children's nursery rhyme, "Farmer in the Dell." Anise says she hopes that digging in the dirt might one day slow down her rough and tumble young man. At six months, the baby already appears on the verge of walking.

"Who knows," I laughed. "Adam was a track star in high school. Maybe it's in the gene pool."

The prospects of digging in the dirt any time soon are not too favorable for any of us. The groundhog saw his shadow—bringing with him goodness knows how many more weeks of snow showers and wind chills in the teens or worse. By daytime, the dried flower-heads of the sedum and the sturdy stands of grasses in my front yard lose their thick glaze of ice. But in the hours after midnight, my heightened senses can pick up the brittle-hard stems of the bridal wreath rasping against the aluminum siding next door.

These cold winter nights, I find myself dreaming of gardens, I write in my weekly column:

Carl Jung, prophet of the subconscious, has a lot to say on the subject. The impulse to dream is involuntary, but it can be a mirror of our health and well being, emotionally and spiritually.

Dreams of the garden sometime foreshadow a time of profound creativity. They can signal professional and personal growth.

In the daylight of his own garden, Jung was drawn to flowers that resemble a mandala. The word comes from the sanskrit for circle. Within a circle we are whole and sheltered. In that fairy round, we belong to one another and God.

The living art and language of flowers has become the currency of my life. I am learning what makes my experiment in cottage gardening my own. Hollyhocks signify both ambition and productivity. Daisies raise their heads in innocence. Gratitude and humility tinge the deep blue of the Bell Flower.

Poppies commemorate what I have lost and violets, the faithfulness of those memories. Faces of absent friends bloom in the zinnias. Iris transports the souls of women to the underworld. Mine is not yet among them.

In the land of the living, Coreopsis bids me be of good cheer. The vivid crimson veining on a wild geranium petal tells me that true friendship endures, runs deep. Pray for me, the Verbena pleads. The twining vines of the clematis promise nothing but love radiating from the children and grandchildren of my extended family.

Every new season speaks to my heart. In springtime, the hepatica gives me confidence. The deep-hearted clusters of the late summer Phlox remind me how privileged I am to share the lives of others. Fall grasses teach the art of patience.

As a gardener, I also know how important it is to rake up the dead leaves with the season's changing. A garden, mine among them, cannot afford to tolerate those emblems of sadness and despair.

The column's ending eludes me. But then with careful editing, I still have thirty-plus words to figure it out.

The year, the calendar, the Almanac have made their rounds—more in seconds and minutes and hours and days than Adam Groft and I ever were privileged to share. And yet . . . ah, and yet in that precious span, my life had changed forever.

So whatever Punxatawney Phil or Essex Ed or their fellow prophets of the growing season come up with, I'm ready for them. At the risk of rushing the season, I brought some forsythia indoors this morning and tucked the stems in one of my Grandmother Eva's pickle crocks. I'm prepared to wait and see what comes of it.

Two-year appointment book in hand, I skimmed last year's entries. I was looking for tax deductions. By comparison, I am working with a blank slate for the year ahead. But then Bea already has set a tentative date for the spring garden clean-up. She and I are planning a jaunt downstate with Anise to a regional garden show in March. The when and how of what happens at Groft's no longer falls entirely on my shoulders. And for that I'm grateful. The Reclaim our Roots project is beginning to take shape. Plan is to file incorporation papers by spring.

Meanwhile under its crusted snow-cover, my cottage garden slumbers on. Every time the wind drives a shot-gun blast of ice pellets against the windows, I suspect maybe I should have considered mulching a bit more aggressively, after all.

"Much-ing," my granddaughter Emma called it. *"Much-ing."*

I'm not obsessing about it. My granddaughter's right. There's already so very much enriching my life for the new year that lies ahead. Everything considered, I have to believe that out there in the wintery darkness, that garden of mine is growing just fine.

Mary A. Agria

Author of the best-selling
TIME IN A GARDEN

Eve's story, like her garden, keeps on growing. Ever since novelist Mary Agria's *Time in a Garden* hit best-seller lists all over northern Michigan in summer 2006, readers have counted the population of tiny Xenaphon among their circle of friends. This sequel, the second in the EDEN SERIES, answers the question "What's next?" When life hands us the best and worst it has to offer, we need to respond.

Raised in Wisconsin, Ms. Agria earned her B.A. and M.A. from the University of Wisconsin in Madison. For forty years, she has cultivated a deep appreciation of Little Traverse life—a region that is now year-round home to two of her four daughters. The other two daughters live in the Phoenix area. In between her Michigan summers and winters in New York, she and her husband John, a professional photographer and retired university president, travel extensively from coast to coast and internationally.

After retiring from a successful career as a technical writer and researcher in the field of community development, Ms. Agria turned to fiction to express the "greater truths" that only a good story can tell. She has worked as a college chaplain and as a Minister of Music in Protestant and Roman Catholic congregations. Her syndicated column on work force ethics ran for 22 years; excerpts were published as a book by Wm. C. Brown. The *Rural Congregational Handbook* (Abingdon Press) she co-authored has been used by seminaries around the country for ten years. Her novels also include *Vox Humana*: *The Human Voice*, *In Transit* and *Community of Scholars* (awarded 5 stars by Midwest Book Review as "highly recommended"). Her characters are older Americans and their families, struggling to make their peace with their changing lives and the changing face of rural communities.

COMING. . .**From the Tender Stem**

Book Club Questions:
Garden of Eve

1) With which character or characters in the novel can you most identify? And why? Eve herself, her daughters or granddaughter Emma; Anise, Artie and Viv, George and Mark Blandis, Bea, Jake, Matt and Ben Gaskill or Chris Demort.

2) Grief changes everything, Eve writes as the novel begins. Discuss what contributes to her ability to move beyond the ash heap on which she finds herself to discover new reasons for living.

3) More than plants grow in Eve's garden. Discuss the plot of the novel and its title. How does the image of the garden reflect Eve's personal journey?

4) We are all broken people at one time or another in our lives. How do the characters in the novel use their vulnerability to help themselves and one another grow?

5) Which of the novel's character(s) most reflect where you find yourself at this stage of your life journey? And why?

6) How do the sense of time and the changing seasons impact the characters in the novel? Why do you think human beings find the notion of "time" spiritually so important?

7) How have an awareness of passing time and the rhythm of life in the garden played a role in defining your own sense of what life is all about?

8) Gardening is the number one avocation or "hobby" in the world. Discuss how gardening impacts the lives of the characters in the novel.

9) How do the characters' experiences help explain the importance of gardening as a way of "grounding" human beings in our urban world?

10) As a mother, Eve Brennerman finds an ongoing challenge in the relationship between herself and her two daughters. How does Anise change that dynamic?

11) Discuss how the growing relationships in the novel redefine what it means to be "family". Anise, Eve and her daughters; George and Matt and their sons; Viv, Artie and the young Chris Demort; Eve and her granddaughter, Emma; even young Caleb.

12) Why is intergenerational gardening so important? Compare how the novel's character are drawn to gardening with your own experiences.

13) Define community as you experience it? as it exists in Xenaphon?

14) How does 'time in a garden" shape your personal search for meaning?

15) If you had to predict where the characters in the novel would be on their life paths a year from now, where would they be?

GARDEN OF EVE

PORCH OF THE HOMESTEAD

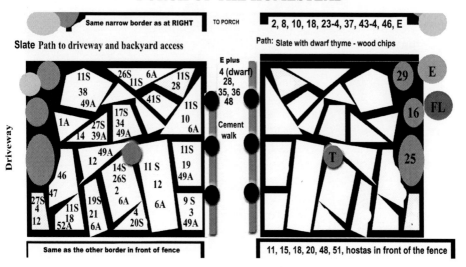

Same narrow border as at RIGHT | TO PORCH | 2, 8, 10, 18, 23-4, 37, 43-4, 46, E

Slate Path to driveway and backyard access

Path: Slate with dwarf thyme - wood chips

Driveway

E plus
4 (dwarf)
28,
35, 36
48

Cement
walk

Same as the other border in front of fence | 11, 15, 18, 20, 48, 51, hostas in front of the fence

PUBLIC SIDEWALK IN FRONT OF THE GARDEN

The front yard is separated from the public sidewalk by two sections of vintage wrought iron fence. In front of it, Eve planted two narrow borders of perennials and annuals. The two main sections of the garden behind the fence are designed as mirror images. Plants are chosen to bloom through the four seasons, with clumps of darker flowers surrounding large clumps of lighter varieties (*see Shade Intensity scheme at RIGHT*):

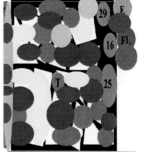

Range of shades, from dark to light.

> **S**= Spring
> No letter code = Summer
> **A**= Autumn

Bushes act as frames at the garden edges and at the porch ends (*large gray ovals*). **Winter Plan:** Red-twig Dogwood and evergreens (**E**) add color. Dwarf evergreens along the central walkway (*small unnumbered black ovals*) are trimmed to low "button" shapes. **Spring:** Forsythia, Bridal Wreath and Lilac are in flower. **Summer:** topiary hydrangeas (**T**) mid-garden give a Victorian feel. **Fall:** Flamebush (**FL**) adds brilliant fall shades to the plan.

> **Not shown:** Ferns, wildflowers and low "woodsy" perennials fill the area between the public sidewalk and curb (marked with **W's** on the plant lists that follow), under the shade of Greatgrama Eva's lindens.

Garden Plan & Plant Lexicon

In choosing perennials for her garden, Eve drew from floral lexicons, combined with her favorite traditional prairie plants. *Plant lexicons* or dictionaries of the emotional meaning of plants were wildly popular in Victorian times. Favorite prairie plants (eg. Coneflowers) are listed by season but not numbered below.

For a color version of Eve's Garden plan, visit www.maryagria.com

SPRING

7 Cinquefoil - *Beloved child*
9 Columbine - *Anxiousness*
11 Daffodils - *Unrequited love,*
14 Delphinium - *Big-hearted*
15 Fern - *Magic, Fascination*
16 Forsythia - *Anticipation*
17 Foxglove - *Stateliness, youth*
22 Hepatica - *Confidence-* **W**
25 Hydrangea - *Thanks*
26 Iris - *Faith, wisdom*
27 Larkspur - *An open heart*
29 Lilac - *Beauty, pride*
38 Peonies -*Marriage, compassion*
41 Poppy - *Eternal sleep, creativity*
42 Snowdrop-*Hope/Consolation-***W**
48 Violet - *Faithfulness* - **W**

SUMMER - also coneflower, brown-eyed Susan, Obedient Plant

2 Bachelor Buttons - *Single blessedness*
3 Bluebell - *Humility, grief*
4 Dianthus/Carnation/
  Sweet William - rose lexicon
8 Clematis - *Love for a child*
10 Coreopsis - *Always cheerful*
12 Daisy - *Innocence*
18 Wild Geranium-*True friendship*
19 Globe Amaranth-*Unfading love*
20 Grasses - *Submission*
21 Hearts Ease-Johnny Jump Up -
  In my thoughts
23 Hollyhock - *Fruitfulness*
24 Money Plants - *Sincerity*
28 Lavender - *Love, devotion*
30 Liverwort - *Confidence-***W**
31 Love in a Mist (Annual)
32 Love Lies Bleeding (Annual)
33 Milk Vetch - *Melts the heart-***W**
34 Mullein - *Good nature*
35 Pansy - *Merriment*
36 Parsley - *Useful knowledge*
37 Passion Flower - *Faith, fervor*
39 Phlox - *Souls united*
43 Mint *(warmth)* near porch
44 Sunflower - *Pride*
46 Verbena - *Pray for me*
47 Veronica/Speedwell - *Fidelity*
51 Woodbine/Honeysuckle-
  Fraternal love (on fence)

LATE SUMMER/FALL - includes Autumn Joy Sedum

1 Asters *(Fidelty)*;
6 Mums *(Long life)*
49 Yarrow *(cure for heartache)*
52 Zinnia *(Remembrance)*

At Home
in Eve's Xenaphon

Dibbekuchen - A traditional German New Year's dish popular in the Rhineland. It often is served with applesauce, sour cream. Soften 2 hard rolls in milk. Finely chop 1 onion, parsley. Grate 4 med. raw potatoes, spice with salt, pinch of nutmeg, coarse-ground pepper. Add 2 well-beaten eggs. Optional: add grated apples, small bacon pieces. Mix ingredients well. Line casserole with bacon slices; lay several over the top. Bake in 220-230 degree oven 1.5 to 2 hrs. Serves 4.

Doxology - song of thanksgiving in the Jewish and Christian traditions, from the Greek "praise" + "word".

Easter Gardens - a Protestant-Catholic Holy Week custom in which the Faithful recreate the Garden of Gethsame and/or the Garden of the Empty Tomb. The Tradition stems from an earlier practice of venerating the True Cross. *Venantius Honorius Clementianus Fortunatus* - (ca 530 AD) author of the Ode to the Cross quoted in this novel was a Roman Catholic Bishop of Portiers, best known for his "Sing, O tongue, of the glorious struggle". The hymn inspired St Thomas Aquinas to write the beloved *Pange Lingua Gloriosi.* Eleven books of Fortunatus' Latin poetry survive.

Gregorian Calendar - official 'civic' calendar in use throughout most of the world today (introduced by Pope Gregory XIII, 1582) replaced the less accurate Julian Calendar. Adoption was delayed during the Reformation.

Lectionary (Lectionary Cycle) - The official schedule of readings used in the Christian tradition. Most Protestant and Catholic churches are on a 3-year cycle, labeled as Lectionary A, B or C. The biblical reading (Old Testament, Psalm, New Testament and Gospel lessons) remain fairly constant for a given Sunday in each of those yearly cycles. The three cycles of readings cover most of the Old and New Testaments.

Liturgical Calendar - divides the Christian Church Year into seasons, starting with Advent (4 weeks pre-Christmas); Christmas; Epiphany (Three Kings); Ordinary or "ordinal" time when Sundays are numbered not named (post-Christmas is 'One'); Ash Wednesday; Lent (7 weeks); Holy Week (Palm Sunday to Easter) and Pentecost. The Year ends with Christ the King Sunday, before a new Lectionary Cycle begins.

Salsify Soup - 2 c. salsify, 3 c. water, 2 c. cream (half-and-half), 3 T butter, salt, coarse ground pepper, pinch of nutmeg. Clean and peel the salsify roots, cut in ½ in. slices. Cook the roots (do not boil) in the water for around 20 minutes. Root should be soft but not mushy. Add cream, butter (and flour) to thicken; spices. Serves 4. Usually served with an oyster cracker garnish.

Other Mary Agria novels

TIME in a Garden

...the 2006 best-seller set in northern Michigan's resort country. The unforgettable story of Eve Brennerman and Adam Groft and their crew of community gardeners celebrates perennial gardening, family and the enduring power of human love.

"A compelling read. Adam and Eve in the garden . . ." Five-Star judge's review, 2007 *Writer's Digest Self-Published Book Awards*, Literary Fiction.

VOX HUMANA: The Human Voice

The intriguing worlds of pipe organs and weaving come together in this poignant story of love and forgiveness. When Philadelphia counselor Char Howard is force-retired, she returns home to western Pennsylvania and a community of strangers.

"a reflective portrayal of the ascent of goodness, reconciliation and love," *AGO Magazine*, 2007

IN TRANSIT

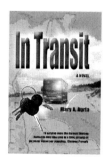

Lib Aventura, a former travel agent, is widowed only three years after she and her husband sell their East Lansing home and go on the road as full-time RVers. When she finds the courage to return to the UP and reclaim her abandoned motorhome, she discovers that her journey is only beginning. **". . .wisdom, the kind that only a lifetime of experience can give. Like Lib. . .may we never grow too old to live."** *Dan's Hamptons*, 2008

COMMUNITY OF SCHOLARS

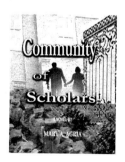

An accusation of sexual harassment shakes a tiny Pennsylvania campus to its very core and a distinguished professor learns to rethink what it means to be an "academic community". **"Five stars, highly recommended. . .a riveting thriller of academe."** *Midwest Book Review, 2009*

For sample chapters of her novels, visit maryagria.com